TRANSFERENCE

D1417224

TRANSFERENCE

B.T. KEATON

Copyright © 2019 by Brandon T. Keaton. All rights reserved.

ISBN: 978-1-64570-150-7
eBook ISBN: 978-0-473-48035-6

This book is a work of fiction. Any references to historical events, real people, or real places are used fictitiously. Other names, characters, places, and events are products of the author's imagination, and any resemblance to actual events or places or persons, living or dead, is entirely coincidental.

No part of this publication may be reproduced, stored in a retrieval system, or transmitted in any form or by any means, electronic, mechanical, photocopying, recording, or otherwise, without the express written permission of the author. If you desire said permission, please reach out to the publisher or author directly.

Cover art design and formatting by Damonza.com
Ingleside Avenue Press logo by Talal Ali Basham

10 9 8 7 6 5 4 3 2 1

First Edition

www.brandonkeaton.com
www.inglesideavenuepress.com

INGLESIDE
AVENUE PRESS

For my beloved Mama and Daddy.
You are both profoundly missed.

Until we meet again…

ACKNOWLEDGMENTS

To my editors Pat LoBrutto & Bodie Dykstra—
thank you for your assistance, guidance,
and overall general brilliance.

To fellow authors Robert J. Sawyer, J.J. Marsh & Mandi Lynn—
thank you for your insight, your humor,
and inspiring me to revive this
nearly decade-old book from the dead.

To my brother Trenton and my sister Megan—
thanks for always being there.

To Renée—
thanks for your willingness to listen
and your infinite patience.

To my dear family and friends scattered across the globe—
you have each had your own part to play in my life
and thus in the very making of this story.
I love you all.

And lastly, to you,
the beautiful soul holding this book—
from the bottom of my heart, I thank you for your support.

CHAPTER 1

BARRABAS

YOU MAY HAVE heard of me. I guess it depends on whether or not you frequent moral or immoral social circles. I am the one they call Barrabas.

My habitually reckless, albeit inventive, feats earned me quite a bit of renown. Consequently, I can't count how many times I've been told I was the most infamous thief to grace the good Earth since Jesse James. I always preferred to think of myself as more akin to Robin of Locksley, though I never had a band of merry men. Let's put it this way: if the *Mona Lisa* had survived the wars, I could've absconded with the damn thing and been back at home asleep before the painted lady herself was even aware of the deed.

But no matter. I was raised never to boast, so I'll spare you any more of the pissing contest. Now, if I am indeed this Barrabas of legend, as they say, then there's a rather large kink in my little tale. You see, *his* story came to an end. The *real* Barrabas Madzimure died more than thirty years ago.

Currently I find myself treading an all too familiar place—the gray area that lies right between unconsciousness and vigilance. You might find yourself straddling that line after you've been drugged or beaten senseless by someone or something demanding your full cooperation. For my most recent refusal to play ball, I was cold-cocked right into next week. I expected as much.

What I *didn't* expect to find when I opened my eyes mere minutes ago is that I'd be blindfolded and bound fast to a smooth metal chair. But to be fair, I've been put here because I deserve to be here. I'll admit that without hesitation, however, if they really knew me at all, the use of force against me might've been slightly less abrasive. In defense of my captors, though, my actions of late have been rather caustic. As a result, I killed a man today.

Admitting that to myself sends a slight wave of nausea up from the pit of my gut and into my throat. I've killed before, but I am *not* a murderer, at least not by nature. In the past, there has been more than one occasion where I found myself in a him-or-me type of situation, so that doesn't count in my book. And it's not so much that I mind dying at this point, either, but I'll be damned if I'm going to let another man take my life from me. The point is, I don't enjoy killing, and I never have.

But life is hard on any man here. I've been sitting here long enough now that I'm beginning to wonder if I might die from the boredom. Or maybe I've not been here long at all. It's hard to tell since my head, along with the room, is still spinning like a good yarn.

Regardless, this is the first time I've been outside the mine in years. I know that because the air in my nose isn't completely filled with the rancid stench of stinkspar and gypsum. Part of me can't help but feel a small bit of gratitude for that.

I smile involuntarily at my last thought, and then out of nowhere a shiver runs down my spine. I get the feeling that I'm not alone in the room. It's then that a very obnoxious and rather nasally voice calls out to me.

"State your name, murderer."

It's definitely a man, but I don't recognize the voice. I think the creep's been watching me. I purpose not to answer him.

A few seconds later, someone to my right takes in a quick breath through their mucus-filled nose just before something the size of my own head plows into my midsection.

"Your *name*, prisoner."

After a momentary fit of gasping and gagging, I chuckle a bit at the warm, tin-like taste of blood in my mouth. Then, turning my head, I look toward the hired muscle who must've hit me and grin just as wide as I can. I can't help thinking that I may actually lose a kidney over that last blow, though I do my damnedest to hide the projections of pain throwing themselves across my abdomen.

"I'll ask it only once more," the man says. "*What* is your name?"

"Barrabas," I say with a rasp in my throat.

The man says nothing in reply, but within the cool room, his shallow, shuddering breaths reverberate around me.

"And... your surname?" the man asks.

"Madzimure."

I could swear the Torquemada in front of me stops breathing for a split second. Fingers snap, and there's a quick movement behind me, followed by a shuffle of feet. Then the greasy shroud stinking of petroleum and shielding my eyes is suddenly snatched free. The overhead lights blind me for a few seconds, and when my pupils constrict, I'm surprised to find myself in such a confined space.

The windowless room is gray, and the walls are shiny and slick— almost like the blubber of a dolphin. Well, now hold on. Is that memory even real for me? I can't be certain that I've ever seen a *real* dolphin.

"Madzimure, you say?" the man asks quizzically.

I am certain I've never laid eyes on this slender man in front of me before today. His hair is dark brown, almost black, and from the looks of it, it seems to be held in place by a sort of glossing agent. Hair product is an extreme rarity here. And by extreme, I mean it's nonexistent. He's sporting a scrawny mustache, too—the kind a teenage boy might be proud of. It's just as equally coifed and well-maintained as his hair. All that and to boot he's wearing the nicest damn coat I've seen since coming into exile.

"You are undoubtedly aware that you have less than a standard week remaining until your execution?" he asks, sighing and without so much as a glance my way.

"And just who the hell are you?" I ask, clearing my throat. "And what are the charges?"

The slender man ignores my questions, studying what looks like a digital pad or ledger of some sort lying on the brushed steel table set between the two of us. He taps on the screen briskly, his nostrils flaring.

"I'll be damned," I say, almost laughing. "You're left-handed? You belong in here with us."

The brainless muscle still standing behind me smacks me across the back of the head with an open palm.

"It says here that you abetted in the murder of one Leroy Baxter, not but nineteen hours ago," the slender man says, biting the inside of his cheek. "Baxter was prison warden number zero five dash six."

The display on the slender man's ledger is nearly translucent, like a thin sheet of quartz crystal. I lean forward slightly and can plainly see an inverted thumbnail of old Leroy himself displayed on the left side of the screen. The moving text and numerical data underneath the photo, which seems to be holding my jailor's complete and total attention, is illegible from my vantage point.

"Mmm… am I *correct* in my information, prisoner? Or do you wish to still deny the deed?" the slender man asks.

"For the record, I bore Warden Baxter no ill will. But the man had it coming," I say.

The slender man continues to stare at the ledger, his eyes flittering left and right and never stopping once to look upon me. He frowns for half a second, as if debating whether or not there's any truth to my previous claim.

"So, you do not deny it then?" he asks.

"I didn't say that."

The slender man continues to glide his index finger across the ledger with a quiet precision.

"Mr. Baxter had been transferred multiple times. He was valuable to the Church. When you took his life, you not only killed him here, but you terminated his host at home. This constitutes a double-murder charge in the eyes of the law."

"The law?" I ask. "There's no law here, string bean. Never was."

My scoff prompts the slender man to scratch the side of his cheek.

"It sounds as though this is funny to you," he says, shaking his head slightly.

"Look, if Baxter is an agent of the law, then *the law* was raping one of the women. She was too weak to stop him, so *I* did. Nothing funny

4

about that. If that's earned me death, then why not toss me down one of the shafts and be done with it?"

"Because those who destroy company property always visit with one such as me before meeting their scheduled demise. It's policy. You understand, I'm sure," he says, feigning a smile at the last. "And who were you originally, prisoner? Prior to your transference?"

Now we've come to it.

I pause to reflect on the question for what feels like an eternity. Almost instantly I actually feel the pores on my forehead open, and the sweat begins to bead faster than I can think. The slender man continues to tap hastily on his ledger, all while managing to still avoid any eye contact with me. I get that old feeling—a fluttering in my chest—the same one you get when you're staring down the barrel of a gun.

"The *name*, prisoner," the slender man says impatiently. "Or your brain will be on the wall in less than five seconds," he adds while pointing toward the wall to his left. "Four."

The muscle-head behind me edges closer.

"Three."

I open my mouth to finally answer the question, and my voice cracks almost pubescently.

"Kilraven… Thaniel Kilraven."

The slender man's tongue pauses behind his lips from where it had been gliding across the top row of his teeth. Then he finally looks at me from over the top of his thick black-rimmed spectacles. The hard swallow in his throat is audible, and he half-laughs as his eyes narrow simultaneously.

"Kilraven? As in Kilraven the Cursed? That's impossible," he says, smoothing one of the lapels on his coat before looking up at the sentry behind me.

I've seen the look on his face before. He's not buying it. But I'm not blind enough yet to miss the fact that he's still curious, and the more I keep him talking, the less likely I am to get bludgeoned again.

"Thaniel Kilraven is dead," he says. "Everyone on Earth knows that," he adds, barely keeping himself from smiling.

"If you say so. And we're not on Earth, shithead," I say, mustering a sort of lazy smirk in return for the slender man's disbelief.

The sentry grunts, and I feel the air behind me move. In my peripheral, the sentry's arm rises to strike. I hold my breath, expecting it to be knocked out of me a second later, but the slender man puts his hand up with the palm forward and clears his throat. The sentry grumbles through his nose and relaxes.

"Clearly, the rod was spared with you," he says, shifting in his seat and adjusting his glasses.

I note that the slender man's fingers are long and smooth, and the tops of his hands are strangely pale. The avoidance of any sort of manual labor your whole life will do that to a man, I guess. That means wherever they sent his ass from, he's most likely a glorified pencil pusher.

"Now, there have been a handful of other prisoners in the past who made this very claim," he says, shaking his head, "and always I have been disappointed at the last. Granted, the combination of transference and the trip to this planet can addle the mind of some. Turns the temporal lobes into a concoction akin to cheese stew."

The slender man pauses and looks at me sidelong, then leans across the table, his face now a mere meter from my own.

"But *you*… hmm. Well, you might actually believe what you're saying," he says with a whisper.

For the briefest moment, the muscles in my lower extremities spasm, and I nearly piss myself.

Meanwhile, my mind does a one-eighty, teasing me to the brink of humiliation, and the part of me that's eternally a child pretends I'm in a motion picture. The constrictor knot binding my hands, which I could never possibly undo, mysteriously falls free to the ground. Getting up from my chair, I strike the slender man square in the larynx. His eyes bulge as he falls back, and his fingers desperately clutch at the base of his throat while he's raucously vying for breath. Naturally, the guard behind me pauses for much too long, and it's all I need to strangle him with the restraints he undoubtedly fashioned for me.

Then the fantasy vanishes quicker than a wisp of smoke.

"Prisoner?!" the slender man shouts as he raps me almost comically across the mouth with his cold and clammy palm. "Answer me!" he squeals. "Do you believe you are Kilraven?!"

I say nothing and he simply squints, his forehead now a mass of wrinkles. As he studies my face, I see a small flame of delight spark up like a newly struck match in the center of his eyes, but it fades just as fast as it ignited.

The slender man sighs and relaxes in the seat, and his face is once again masked by an unreadable countenance. He glances up at the sentry behind me and nods curtly before excusing himself.

"Do try not to go anywhere, prisoner."

It's astounding how quickly and almost imperceptibly the slender man leaves the room, leaving behind only a scented trail. It's a strange odor. Like camphor oil or... something slightly floral. I turn my head to the right as far as I can in an attempt to get a look at the sentry behind me.

"Just you and me now, cannon fodder."

The meathead decides that it's time to reassert his clout by seizing the back of my neck with an icy, gloved hand.

"Shit, you're a mollydooker, *too*? I didn't realize the Church was employing so many *lefties* these days. Are you even human?"

"Don't you say another friggin' word to me, criminal!" he says gruffly.

"So, he speaks with words, after all," I add.

The guard squeezes the back of my neck so hard I momentarily become his personal stress-relieving device. But I knew he might do something like that, so I close my eyes and focus on his grip. I count six fingers.

He must have been made fun of in school for that. Probably a low-level service goon back on Earth, and this was his meal ticket. I don't blame him, really. His voice, though... It isn't one that I recognize, either, so he's likely not one of the wardens. And with those six digits he would've had a nickname floating around this place that I'd have heard by now.

After a few torturous minutes of silence, the slender man returns, and the weighty hand still gripping the nape of my neck loosens. Taking up his seat once more, the slender man gazes at me curiously with one eyebrow raised, and the two of us set about waging a silent war. His gray eyes are the first to look away.

"As a representative of the Church, I have been charged with the task of, shall we say, speaking to you *ad nauseam*," he says.

"I don't know a thing," I reply, wagging my head from side to side and trying to roll my shoulders as best a man can when he's constricted from head to toe. "And I've got nothing else to say to you, Doc."

I call him that because he reminds me of a man I saw in a film once in my youth.

Out of nowhere, the force of a freighter lands square at the base of my skull. As I'm blinded by the red flecks of light dancing through my eyes, I hear the slender man clearing his throat before sighing heavily.

"*Tsk tsk tsk.* You most definitely know something, or you would not be here at all, prisoner."

The red lights fade, and then I thank the sentry for reminding me of who and what I am. Then the six-fingered ham fist hits me again. Harder this time, too.

When the screeching in my ears subsides and I regain my sight, I get a sense that a few minutes have passed because the air in the room has changed considerably. Through a haze of red dots I see the slender man still across from me, but now he's looking quite a bit more relaxed than before. He's sitting cross-legged and smiling in that sort of way someone might should they take pleasure in another person's struggle. Like watching an animal in a trap.

"I've dismissed my guard," the slender man says. "You'll be talking only to me from here on in. That is, unless you continue to be verbally unpleasant."

The slender man reaches across the table in my direction, placing a device about the size of a sim-chip in the center of the table. I quickly recognize the familiar rainbow-colored, fruit-shaped logo, which oddly no longer has a chunk missing from it.

"This is merely a customary precaution. For quality-assurance purposes, of course," he says.

"Haven't seen one of those in a long time. Helluva lot smaller than they used to be."

The slender man licks his thumb, then affixes it to the corner of the ledger. There's a quick popping sound, and the slender man winces. His hand recoils, and he studies the tip of his thumb along with the dot of crimson forming at the end of it. The ledger pings several times with an approving tone.

"Indeed. *Much* has changed," he says, licking his lips. "I would bet you wouldn't recognize your home, let alone anyone or anything else you once knew. That of course is based on the ridiculous premise that you could or would somehow manage to find your way back to Earth."

"Stranger things have happened. Maybe, uh… maybe I'll take that wager, Doc."

The slender man pauses for a moment and shakes his head in dismay.

"Well, you know your history, clearly. If I'm your *Doc*, then that means you must be *my* John Ringo. And you know what happened to Mr. Ringo in the end, don't you?" he asks cruelly, glaring at me with an icy rancor.

"You tell me, Doc."

"The man had a bullet put through his head. And there was not *one* soul there to mourn him. Now, if you want to continue this game of name-calling, I have no hesitation in inviting the watchman back inside so that he can have words with you," he says, smiling to himself. "I can already tell Haden doesn't like you."

"What do you want me to call you then, Doc?"

"Say it again, prisoner," he says, no longer smiling, "and I'll have the sentry remove your tongue in such a manner that the two so-called physicians at this facility won't even bother trying to repair or replace it!"

"Well, man-with-no-name, then you'd have a damn hard time getting me to talk, wouldn't you?"

The slender man laughs in a lilting and feminine sort of way and slaps one hand on the table.

"Very good!" he says, clasping his hands together. "Yes, well then… if you feel inclined to address me directly, and cannot resist the urge to do so, then call me Corvus."

The slender man stares squarely at me, removes his glasses, and places them quietly on the table.

"You've got some expensive-looking implanted gray eyes there, Corvus," I say slyly. "You must be from one of the free city-states in the East."

Corvus places his forearms on the table and leans toward me slowly. His previous demeanor, which was ambiguous at best, is now transformed as though he were a dog foaming at the mouth.

9

"Enough!" he snaps. "I know that life here turns more than half of you into half-wits, so pay close attention, please. I am *not* here to be civil with you. I am not your friend. I have spoken at length with the chief operator. They're ready to tear you apart for what you did to Warden Baxter. I'm the only thing standing between you and them. The chief and the remaining wardens have unanimously agreed that I can end your life at any time if your desire is simply to waste mine!"

Interesting. At least now I know how to push one of the bastard's buttons.

Corvus leans back in his chair and stares into the ledger, the light from it reflecting in his beady little eyes. And what he says next I am altogether unprepared for.

"After you're dead and the gooey clumps of your reprehensible face have been scooped up off of the floor, the Church will ship the Kilraven family here. They will no doubt suffer the same fate as you."

My heart quickens. My stomach and entrails gnash. I feel the warm sting of tears longing to be loosed, and it takes all the strength I have left to keep them at bay. Lucky for me the bastard misses the welling flood. All these long years I've received no news of my family, and until this moment, I believed them long since dead.

"Even now, the family of Kilraven the Cursed still lives," Corvus says while looking at his fingernails. "If you could call it *living*, really. The poor souls have been transferred so many times it's... well... one might even call it an atrocity. But you didn't hear that from me."

Corvus is looking down toward the floor now, relishing his authority with the kind of gratification that must come only to those who have a complete lack of pity. He'd fit right in with Verdauga's men on the east side of the mine—some of the most tried and true bastards are among that lot. So, what do I do?

I have no choice; I have to play the game. But I'm gonna play it *my* way. Caution will be my ally now.

And with that thought, I turn my face toward the door behind me.

"You're offering nothing for sale that I'm interested in, pal," I say.

"The Council has kept their original bodies still intact," Corvus says, licking his lips and ignoring my last comment. "And if memory serves, they were all being well-tended to in the Halls of Waiting, under the

Church's supervision. If you are who you *claim* to be, you could hold the means to their potential freedom. They are, of course, innocents in all of these matters."

Corvus glances up at me slowly, searching for something—some sign of sympathy in my face, perhaps. Rather than attempting to further mask my emotions, I mentally damn myself instead, least of all for the fact that the apple-like lump sitting stubbornly at the back of my throat takes more than a moment to settle. Corvus reaches out for his eyeglasses, puts them back on smoothly, and looks at the ledger.

"We are well aware of your cohorts in the mines as well. Point of fact, I have a rather informative dossier on each of them right here," he says, adjusting his frames down to the brim of his nose.

"We're all cohorts here."

"The old man, Iyov… a homosexual degenerate. Here's one… Mel Sinosian, also known as *Magpie*… a fornicator *and* adulterer. Mmm, let's see now… another called Tarsil. Queer theorist and musician. Yes, we know him *quite* well," he says, glaring at me over the top of his glasses, grinning like a bushel basket full of possum heads. "Shall I go on?"

"That's a nice sack of tricks you've got there, company man. But you're a little misguided if you think anyone in this place means shit to me."

"Is that so?" he asks, raising one eyebrow.

"That's right, *Santy* Claus."

Corvus folds his arms in his lap, one of his eyebrows still cocked toward the ceiling. He *knows* that was a lie.

"You are a dead man. Do you understand? Regardless of what transpires here, you are dead already. You get to live a few more days, gifted with the foreknowledge that you yet have time to make peace with your maker, if you trust in one. And, for your cooperation, we'll leave your friends *and* the Kilraven brood out of this. That is all I can offer you," he says, shrugging nonchalantly.

Within the sterile room, the weight of his words pounds on the walls and then back against my eardrums. For the first time in decades I feel something rising in the pit of my stomach, something that I thought had almost departed from me: fear.

In my mind's eye, I'm instantly transported back to the moment I last held my wife. I looked in her eyes and they were full of terror, and it was such a fright that I had never seen before, nor have I seen it since. And I did nothing. I could do nothing. If this buffoon across from me *is* telling me the truth, and she is still alive, then I must know. For her sake I cannot sit idly, and not least of all for my friends.

"If you want some kind of assurance, *thief*, I can promise you that everything you say and do in this room after today will be fed back to the Church," he says while tapping on the sim-chip in the middle of the table. "I'm sure you have learned by now that they honor their agreements, and I will not make you this offer again," he adds with a reveling smile.

The bastard's right.

"We have access to more than you could fathom," he says. "Now, with that having been said, there are some vital components still *missing* from the Kilraven file. And if you *are* him, then there are things only *he* could possibly know, which we may come to in due course."

"So, how do you suggest we play this out?" I ask.

"Well then!" he nearly shouts, laughing to himself. "In mere minutes you've proven that cooperation, unlike chivalry, is not yet dead! Even if it *has* been coerced. You must be a romantic at heart."

I watch as the son of a bitch actually takes pride in his gloating. He licks the front of his perfect teeth as he laughs through his nose. I stare back at him blankly, refusing in what pride I have left to give him even the smallest satisfaction.

When Corvus finally gets the better of himself and his mirth, he adjusts his glasses carefully. Then, taking his eyes off me, he puts the frames back on the table right next to the ledger again.

Hmm. He's very *precise* in his movements.

"Oh, goodness me!" Corvus says. "Well my *suggestion* is that when we resume first thing tomorrow morning, you start from the beginning. You will leave nothing out. I want your entire life, as you recall it. Yes?"

"I'll tell you what, why don't we just get this over with now?" I ask.

"You do not set the pace, prisoner. Besides, I have half a dozen more prisoners to see today, and some of them have *far* less time left than you do," he says. "And frankly, you smell so bad it's making my eyes hurt. Didn't your mother teach you how to bathe properly?"

Every instinct I have tells me not to oblige the scrawny worm. I should just open my mouth and say the words *Go fuck yourself, Doc.*

And I nearly do. But right before that baser urge reaches my lips, Corvus interrupts me.

"You cannot save yourself, whoever you are—or *think* you are. But you do have this one chance to implement some final merit with your no doubt *pathetic* existence. Every single thing you've done, right or wrong, has led to this. I suggest you think of them and not yourself. Or has time in the mines been so cruel that you've completely forgotten how to be a good little lad?" he asks, sneering at me.

I can't tell if his ploy is a trick or not. First the asshole wouldn't even look me in the eyes, and now he's damn near pleading with me.

You're not a fool, Kilraven. Don't be fooled. These company types are always looking out for one thing: their bank accounts.

And so I do exactly what Corvus tells me to do. I think of *them*, and the choice I must and will make becomes pretty obvious. In fact, I realize I made the choice minutes ago. It's the same thing anyone else with half a heart would do in my situation.

"Dying sooner rather than later is very low on my priority list," I reply in the dullest tone I can muster.

"Excellent. We will proceed first thing tomorrow morning. Good day to you," he says, appearing plainly pleased.

Corvus taps on the ledger softly, and within moments my favorite sentry comes back in and pulls the shroud down over my eyes once more. As I'm dragged out of the room, the smooth but squeaky movement of the chair tells me it has wheels on it. But just before I'm shuttled through the doorway, I hear Corvus's raised voice attempting to pour salt into an already open wound.

"You have six days left to live, prisoner."

CHAPTER 2

THE SLENDER MAN

THE CHIEF OF the mine has recently seen fit to quite vehemently suggest that I confine myself to my quarters when I am not interrogating the prisoners. He even had the nerve to post a guard outside my door to bring me that which I might need during lockdown hours. When I asked the chief if he also expected his guard to accompany me to the bathroom, he told me it would be in my best interest just to *piss in the sink*.

Needless to say, I do not find this viewpoint suitable under most circumstances. Excreting in the same place that I wash my hands and my face is a reprehensible thought, though I doubt of course that my employers will feel the same way I do about the matter.

It is at times like these that I cannot believe what I left behind in Neo York. I imagine the wondrous lights of the old Bowery, the smell of the culinary decadence of Restaurant Row, and the view from my penthouse apartment at the *Gehry en Spruce*. And though at one time all these things could practically be counted as the very desires of my heart, I gave them up easily, almost instinctively.

But what I received in return for my obedience to the Church was an assignment in a damned quarry pit millions of light-years away from

Earth. Despite decades of men who have come and built careers and even established lives here, this planet is still miles away from being civilized. As far as I am aware, indigenous life of any kind has yet to be found here. It's certainly devoid of any worthwhile earthly luxuries.

Take my very room, for instance; it is hardly bigger than a child's nursery. The only amenities include a vanity with a basin that's rusting, a reading light that flickers if I don't tap it every thirty seconds, and a stack of vintage spring mattresses tossed into the corner. I find the lamp to be the most curious object, as the open-mouth breathers I've encountered here are many things, but being *learned* readers is surely last among them.

The experience thus far is like living in the days immediately following the Great Wars. Material possessions lost most of their intrinsic value, but even the least of us found it hard to forget how to appreciate the simple pleasures of little things like hand towels or pillows. There isn't even a place to put my shoes. To call this place utterly primitive would be an understatement.

The chief operator here, a hairless primate of the highest order named Rullerig, is a disgrace to his title in addition to being of a most disagreeable sort. Then again, he does tend to leave me to my own devices, and that is usually the most stable kind of relationship to have with someone you do not know well. Consequently, however, I don't trust him one iota.

These deep-space types tend to have an agenda all their own... one which often does not comply with company regulations. They feel that because they are outside the boundaries of the Earth, this means the law is flexible, and in some circumstances, they believe they *are* the only law.

I find this train of thought absolutely puzzling. The Council tells us the law itself by definition must be absolute and never flexible. It no longer serves its purpose if it's allowed to bend, let alone be broken. If either were to happen, the only thing left would be what this place has plenty of already—chaos. The prisoner I met earlier today said it himself:

There is no law here.

Perhaps there's more than a grain of truth in his words. I once heard an old phrase that swiftly springs to mind:

Even the archfiend himself knows sacred writ by heart.

If that assertion is true, it can only mean criminals are capable of not

only reciting doctrine, but also subscribing to it to suit them when necessary. Well, perhaps that's only true in part. Being a criminal at the core of
one's being is not akin to being a Calvinist; some things are inherent and
can never be reformed. I learned that particularly the hard way.

Over ten years of studying transference trials still unhinges me—
females being transferred into male bodies and vice versa. The men always
maintained a strong sense of inherent strength, typical of the average
staunch masculine aggressive. The women sustained a very distinct passive-
ness, and though emphatic in their desire to revert back to female form,
the same adjustment which men found difficult to accept and ultimately
fought back against became only a sort of sad restlessness in the females.
It pained me to watch at times, and it—

"No, Corvus. Regain the mastery. Possess your soul, you fool!"

My sudden verbal outburst causes me to develop an instant annoyance
with the fact that I've allowed myself to become so chafed by my own
thoughts. It is not befitting someone of my stature to be as such, and the
current situation might be far worse. After all, I could be lodging in the
mine itself—a place so hot and dry that it's nearly impossible to breathe
or think clearly. It is most definitely the more wretched place of the two,
so I must remind myself to be content with this bottle of a room they've
seen fit to shove me into.

Possess your soul, you fool.

I can blame half of my tetchy manner on the fact that I was transferred
right before I left Earth. A fresh body is always mentally frustrating. I liken
it to breaking in a pair of shoes.

You look in the mirror and see yourself, but your mind races, whirl-
ing like the wheels of a vehicle on automatic pilot. One minute, the brain
feels like water going down a drain hole, and the next it's a barren lake
of calm, slowly filling up with water or, rather in this case, old memories
long forgotten. It can drive one to absolute madness. I was fortunate to
be able to avoid the usual adjustment period that comes with the process
by remaining in total stasis all the way here.

The rest of my disfavor I place on my superiors at the Tribunal, who
have given me no extra authority for this mission. This is more than likely
due in part to the actuality that the prisoners have not rioted in years, nor

has any escape been attempted in almost five. The precious ore shipments sent to Earth continue to arrive on schedule and by the mother lode.

In short, I cannot as of yet warrant any kind of supplemental action against Rullerig. The mine serves its purpose, and a blind eye is turned toward the lack of adherence to the established codes of conduct. The treatment of the women here, for example, is most distasteful. And for all the good it likely will *not* do, I make a mental note to address that matter in my next few reports.

Still, I take some mild comfort in knowing that one can rely on the men in charge here to behave in a predictable manner. Just about the only other thing I can rely on these days is my COM tablet. Speaking of which, I must now use it to give my daily report on the latest findings. The Council will want to all know about this *Barrabas* character.

And yet, I hesitate. Should I tell my master anything regarding the prisoner just yet? Perhaps it is something he need not know about for the time being. Maybe I should uncover more about this man before I jump to so great a conclusion, and no doubt my lord will appreciate the effort after the fact, viewing it in the least as a desire on my part to not waste his time.

Still, my heart misgives me in this. It is highly possible that this Barrabas is no one… just some poor lost wight who's working at an attempt to keep me preoccupied. Another vagabond, or a traitor at best. The mine is full of them—thieves, rapists, homosexuals, and deplorable denouncers of the Prophet. Nevertheless, there are undoubtedly still among them those few who are sent here unduly, and perhaps they—

My COM disturbs my thoughts and announces its presence with a boisterous *ping*. Before I open the communication channel, I give the twisting in my stomach a brief moment to settle. I have always had a weak constitution, and one never gets used to the food here, I think. Then, to my chagrin, I recall that I've not actually eaten dinner this afternoon. The lower abdominal cramping must be phantom pain—yet another aggravating and unexpected side effect of my last transference.

"Your Eminence, I am ready," I say confidently when the tablet prompts me that my master is receiving a signal.

I find myself staring, which I have always deemed impolite, and looking around the room as I calmly await a reply. I wonder for a moment whether or not any men have died in here. After that thought passes through my synapses, I realize how bizarre it is to even ponder it. Men and women terminate in the mines quite often, and no one thinks twice when the wardens toss them into the furnaces without ceremony. The great pity is that their originals back on Earth fail in the process—and yet another bloodline is gone from the world.

No, it is not a pity. It is the *way*.

But why do these thoughts plague me now? Why should I care? Did I ever care before today? I nearly have to shake myself to fend off my double-mindedness.

"*Corvus, we hear you. You may proceed with your communiqué,*" says a voice from my COM tablet.

"Yes, sir. I'm ready to make a full report of my latest dealings in the mine, including the forthcoming scheduled execution of a very peculiar transferee I spoke with no less than seven hours ago."

"*We are waiting.*"

I cannot place the voice speaking to me, though I am certain I have heard it in the past.

"We?" I ask.

I do not get a reply. It is not protocol for me to be questioned by anyone other than His Eminence. I raise my head high and remember my bearing. It is perhaps a good thing *they* cannot see me in my boldness.

"To whom am I speaking?" I ask assertively.

I am met again with nothing but dead air.

"I… I generally make any audible reports directly to His Grace, especially ones of such significance. If he is transferring at the moment, then I must insist on—"

"*Corvus, this is Lord Alpha. His Lordship is busy with other errands and tasks that are more imperative at the moment than your findings. I will relay whatever feedback you have to him directly at a later time. I suggest you get on with your report quickly, as I have duties that even you cannot comprehend.*"

An audible groaning starts in my diaphragm, and in the nick of time I successfully fend it off before it reaches my throat. It would likely earn me more than stripes were it to be heard. Lord Alpha is the sort of man one would actually wish to be left alone with… if, let's say, one were trapped in a lion's den. Brutal when necessary, ruthless at times, and seemingly without fear. He is as notorious as his fame has made him—a distinction he earned due to his nigh-grotesque enjoyment of eviscerating those found guilty of treason. I never saw anything of the sort with my own eyes, of course, as I've kept my distance from him for obvious reasons.

Patience, Corvus. Deep breaths. Just *breathe*.

"Yes, of course. Please excuse me, Lord Alpha, and accept my sincerest apologies for the insolence," I say, failing to remember until the last that Lord Alpha is utterly immune to flattery.

"Where was I, Lord Alpha?" I ask, hardly concealing my nervousness.

"Your dealings with the mines, Councilor."

Despite instituting my breathing technique, I break into a sweat as though Alpha himself were in this very room. I quickly retrieve a small towel from the vanity and use it to wipe my brow.

"Thank you, my lord. Yes, the chief of the mine has been more than difficult, and to put it bluntly, my accommodations here are still seriously lacking. At minimum, my duties alone warrant that I have unlimited access to all the files and areas that the chief himself would—"

"Corvus, do you have anything of relevance to report?" Lord Alpha asks.

"Forgive me, but how is this not of relevance?" I ask, forgetting my place.

"Your living quarters, which are temporary, might I remind you, have little to do with the task at hand. And you sound dangerously close to questioning me, the operation of the mine, and His Lordship's purposes. None of these fall amongst your obligations, let alone your authority. One such as yourself, who is being paid quite handsomely, should recognize his place in the great plan."

"Yes, Lord Alpha, you are right."

"Very well, then. Now, what is this supposed significant business of the transferees?"

"I have… umm… spoken with over two dozen of the workers this week alone. Six of them were never transferred, and consequently are not housed on Earth. They are originals. All six have opted not to stay their execution. Three of those six gave me reason to believe that any forthcoming attempt of insurrection amongst the miners has been quelled, and all of them cursed the name of the Prophet and of the—"

"*Corvus?*" he asks, sighing heavily afterward. "*You are wearying. The prisoners are going nowhere. A supposed mutiny is of absolutely no real concern, and once again, must I remind you that His Grace will hear this report? I don't wish to have him upset by barbaric slurs flung by queers and shirtlifters who have chosen banishment by their own hand. As of right now you are merely wasting my valuable time.*"

Now this is extremely odd. I pause to ponder for a moment the brusque treatment I am receiving from the other end of the COM. Never before have I been spoken to quite so callously, not even from Lord Alpha. In the few chance meetings we have had, he was always reserved and spoke very little. Why would His Grace choose such a man to be his chief of security?

Then I realize in the moment of the asking that I've answered my own question: Alpha would just as soon pull your head from your shoulders as look at you. Looking back, I can see that Alpha never trusted me from the very beginning. And for that he had good reason. I am not a soldier. Much of that lifestyle prescribes to the indoctrination of the Church and dictates that you be loyal to one man—a chief commander, as it were. I've always found that train of thought to be rather difficult to swallow, and I would say so if only I were able to speak freely and honestly on the subject.

"*Now, I ask you once more, Corvus, do you have anything relevant to relay?*"

At the present moment, my gut instincts warn me to be cautious, for I have had a new thought now and am made to wonder if my superiors are beginning to feel that I have outworn my usefulness. My role within the Church ranks, though unique and vital, comes only from maintaining a budget surplus.

"I believe so, my lord," I add. "During my interrogations, I have found one prisoner due for execution very shortly. One who is claiming to be Barrabas Madzimure."

I get no immediate response. Even now I suspect orders and commands are being given. Information is being repeated, sent, and retrieved across the Network, and gloved fists are pounding angrily on nearby surfaces.

"*Are you certain, Corvus?*" Lord Alpha finally asks slowly and skeptically.

"He said so himself. I think he believes that he is Kilraven," I say. "And if he is who he says he is, then he would know things… important things that must not be brought to light. The discovery on Fornax, for instance. And if he were to prove his existence as Kilraven, that would further prove his word right in the matter."

There is another lengthy pause, and I am absolutely certain that I hear Alpha speaking to someone else. For all the things he does well, Lord Alpha is not famous for being adept at using technology—unless you count a gun as such. He probably doesn't even know there is a mute function on his COM.

"My lord? Are you still there?"

"*Corvus, can you describe this man's appearance?*"

"He is filthy, my lord. Dark and curling hair, dark eyes. And his beard is disgustingly unkempt. There are identical scars on both arms that run from the top of the wrist to the middle of the forearm."

"*And what of the hidden mark, Corvus?*"

"What do you mean? What hidden mark?"

Indiscernible chattering commences yet again, followed by a ten-second stint of low static. Lord Alpha must be referring to the mark of the Prophet. He gives it to those he deems his most trusted servants or his most detested enemies. It's a tattoo of sorts. A symbol of faith when it's branded right side up, or an eternal reminder of your failure when marked upon the flesh upside down.

"I've no wish to see this particular man stripped bare, my lord. But if necessary, I can have him searched immediately."

"*No, Corvus. No. At least not yet. Tell me, though, you have not given this prisoner any information that would cause him to suspect our ongoing search for him? Am I incorrect?*" he asks, his voice rising.

I have to lie.

"I have told him nothing, my lord. Merely that he must and will give an account of his life before his death."

There's another long interlude, and Alpha leaves me yet again in suspense. Other than the sound of my breath, I wait in silence while my frowned-upon curiosity gains the better of me. At this point in my career all I have is a little bit of credit in the bank. Truth be told, it's *a lot* of credit. But I find that when I pit curiosity against credit, as is the case here, curiosity wins more often than not.

I've been working for the Tribunal so long that on occasion I *must* err, and when I do so, I tend to dismiss the fact that I have a full understanding of how and why it operates in the manner that it does. It is at times, for lack of a better designation, unlawful.

I despise the fact that the Church is hypocritical in some ways, and it is in these culpable areas that are so ardently kept from the public at large. However, there are those amongst us who believe being overtly zealous in other methods balances out the former. I disagree, even though I would lose my soul in a nanosecond if I spoke such things aloud in an open forum.

"Corvus, for what reason has this so-called Barrabas willingly agreed to oblige you in this request?"

I must tread extra carefully now. I do not wish for the Council to contemplate replacing me or, worse, send someone else here to assist in my investigations. I've seen it happen before, and that I cannot tolerate. While the Church's motives would also no doubt drive them, and remain at one with my own, they would also equally be at odds with the purpose of my work.

"We have threatened his friends, my lord, and some others that he pretends not to care about here in the mine."

I mute the COM tablet momentarily and take a drink of water from the glass at my bedside.

"We are not sure that this will be enough, Corvus," Alpha says shrewdly.

"The prisoner in question puts on a facade of being a rough and tough character, my lord. Most men who face the block behave in a similar manner, and I'm convinced that he will fold when placed on the table for all to see. The years in the mine may not have bowed his spirit, but if I have learned anything so far about those who—"

"Corvus, listen very carefully. You must break him. You must find out what he remembers and how he remembers it."

"Do not fear: we can administer the standard narcosynthetics, and Barrabas will talk. He simply will have no choice in the matter, my lord."

"Yes, but when he does speak, the sequence of events must be precise. If he

mentions the planet Fornax, and that which transpired there, then he must be broken. And if you are found lacking, you will be broken in his place. Do you understand what I am telling you?" Lord Alpha says.

"I do, but I doubt he is truly Kilraven, my lord. Surely he was reduced to nothing when His Grace took on the great task of sub—"

"Corvus, you are in no position at this time to lecture us on the merits of doubt!"

"No of course not, my lord."

"Need we remind you why you were chosen for these assignments? Must we send another squadron with the next shipment of inmates?" he asks.

"No, Lord Alpha... you need not remind me."

Alpha is right about me. He's right about why they chose me. I moved up within the ranks of the Church rather quickly, I must say, and it was much easier than I ever thought it would be.

No job worth doing is ever easy, my father often said. But I do not confuse my own use of the word to mean a lack of hardship. I have given up everything for this, and in more ways than one, you might say, the Church owns me the same way it owns this place. I am its property.

"How much time is left until Barrabas is to be executed?"

"Less than six days now, my lord."

"Mmm... clearly it's not possible to send backup if it is required. You may need to report your findings to Chief Rullerig. You will have to do the rest by yourself, alone, for the time being. I should say our faith in you is now going to be put to the test, Corvus."

"My lord, my purpose here is clear, and I have not questioned my faith in that purpose."

"If this prisoner is Kilraven, know that he was sent to the mine for a specific reason, as were you, Corvus. Can you give us assurance that you will not fail us in this burden now set before you?"

"I will... do my absolute best, my lord," I say.

"Your best is not what I asked for."

"My lord, I have taken an oath, and I have not sworn lightly. I will find the truth, I will get it from this man, and I will do so in whatever way I deem is necessary," I add assuredly.

The voices on the other end of the COM whisper, like children telling secrets in a chapel.

"*We are relieved to hear this, Corvus. Now, moving forward, we are going to expect that you will provide reports on this matter every twelve hours. No exceptions.*"

"Do you mean to say that I should provide you these in addition to my normal standard-day reports, my lord?"

"*Yes, Councilor. Every twelve hours. I trust that this will be suitable to your schedule and not inconvenience you in any way?*" he asks mockingly.

"No. Of course not, my lord. I live to serve the Church and His Grace."

The echo of footsteps begins retreating into the background of the COM's white noise.

"*Excellent, Corvus. But… there is just one more thing before you go,*" he says at the last, pausing for a moment as if he's about to give a long-prepared speech. "*I would hate to have to send a legion of my finest men on the next boat as an escort for your replacement. If I have to do so, what I offer you now is the distinct pleasure of the assurance in knowing that you will not be coming home. Do I make myself clear in this, or do I need to explain it in more literal terms?*"

"Yes… Yes, my lord, you are clear. Thank you."

"*Faith unshaken, Corvus.*"

"Faith unshaken, Lord Alph—"

The transmission ends abruptly in a barrage of static. I feel so light-headed it's as if I had not taken a single breath during the entire conversation.

"Damn him."

This is not going to be as routine a task as I had hoped it would be, and it is clear now I cannot take lightly the things that must be done from here on out. Many of my colleagues would not have come here for any amount of money. But this reaffirms what I already knew—that unlike them I had a purpose, and what I could achieve here would gain me more in the end than mere company perks.

My pride swells slightly and I smile to myself at the thought that perhaps I wasn't the only one sweating during my report. I gave Lord Alpha good reason to be suspicious of this so-called Barrabas, and in return he all but confirmed this is the one they are seeking.

I cannot help but smile again with the notion that things are now going to proceed exactly as I had hoped, and if my fortune holds, maybe I stand to gain even more than just a promotion out of this little power play.

CHAPTER 3

A MINER'S LIFE

AS I SLOWLY regain consciousness, it dawns quickly on me that the reason I can hardly see is because my eyes are almost completely swollen shut. A crushing weight bears down on my neck, and my temples feel like someone's driving a red-hot poker into each of them. I guess Corvus gave the order, and I got the six-fingered-sentry special to go—a beating about the head and shoulders.

My throat's so parched it feels like I've swallowed burweed, and the pungent acrid smell of ore means one thing: I must be back in my cell-block. The ore dust gives off a strange, distinct odor. What's even more bizarre is that I've never really gotten used to it.

The only way I can think to describe it is a sort of weird combo of melted copper and burnt flesh. It's fatal if you manage to ingest it in its raw form. Many of the prisoners figure that one out within their first few days here. Sometimes it starts with a fit of gasping, as if all the oxygen had been stolen away from their lungs. On other occasions, they just faint and stop breathing. Others just keel over from time to time for no apparent reason whatsoever. It's like watching someone have an aneurysm. The phrase *"drop dead"* comes to mind because, well, that's exactly what happens to them.

It's all pretty damn weird when you consider this planet's atmosphere is nearly identical in every way to that of Earth. Besides, when any of us do die it's not something the wardens particularly care about—we're expendable and easily replaceable, after all. Our two resident doctors, if you can even call them that, are the only ones that might know why the men die, and they ain't talking.

No one really presses the issue anyway, since a visit to either Doctor Hecht or his assistant usually means you're going to be tortured before being put down like a rabid animal. With a cold and calculating clinical precision, I might add.

I suck in the air and cough so hard I see little white binary stars behind my eyelids. What intrigues me most about the events of the last day is that I've never even heard of this *Corvus* fellow until now. If he's been here as long as I have, I should've heard his name at some point. My cellmate would know.

I roll over toward his general direction and find that someone is standing near my cot. The silhouette of the figure is hard to make out, but I know it isn't Iyov.

"You smell like one of Verdauga's altar boys, so you either wanna fuck me, or fight me. Which is it?"

"Time to get up, you manky mott!" the figure growls, kicking me in the ribs.

"Manky?" I ask as I try to get up off the floor. "Tell me again, when's the last time you washed your ass, Ubasti?"

Ubasti snorts and kicks me harder this time.

"Keep that mouth up 'Rabas, and I'll make the rest of yer dapper face match them bug eyes!" he says, laughing.

"Dapper's a big word for you, Warden."

I shouldn't have said that. My sense of hearing alone tells me what's going to happen next. With a flick of his wrist, Ubasti extends the flanged plasma mace he typically carries in his right hand, then shoves it directly into my excruciatingly sore ribs.

"Get up now or I'll have ya flayed and then toss yer arse into the latrine lines!" he bellows without any hint of playfulness left in his tone.

I quickly get up and on my feet. Having feces embedded into an open laceration is not the way I want to spend my day. I can worry about my eyes later.

"How long was I out, Warden?"

"Not long enough to miss the second half of the day shift, prin-cess," he says.

"Oh damn, I missed lunch?" I ask.

"You won't be gettin' no provisions until lockdown! And I don't care that ya got less than a week left. I'm workin' yer fuckin' ass to the very last!" Ubasti says, laughing and swinging his plasma mace in circles.

After I'm led away from my cell, Ubasti stays unusually silent the rest of our march toward the center of the mine. It's quite out of character for him, especially when a lifer like me is sporting brand-new battle scars.

We leave the prison block and neither of us utters a word. An almost eerie, strange quiet goes with us as we walk. All I can hear is the heaviness of his breath behind me and the crackle and hum of the now-ignited plasma mace he's holding at his side. I was told once—by someone I only met once—that the wardens have an energy core somewhere in the mine, where each of the maces has to be charged every twenty-six hours. It's a master docking station where all the maces are kept in one, centralized and secure location. No one alive's ever seen it, of course.

In just a few quick movements the weapon could be mine, you know. Pivot ninety degrees right with the right foot, coming to a left front stance. Ubasti would lunge for my arm at that point, but I'd have fully turned by then, giving him a horizontal strike to the temple. Follow that up with a prong to his groin and an overhead smash just in case he's not already on his knees. Lastly, make sure you give a short thrust to the face for good measure. Then I'd grab the mace, if he hasn't dropped it by now, and render the final blow to the top of the skull. The maces are messy, though. You might as well fling a vat of oat porridge onto the floor.

Besides, I'm not offing anybody today.

Even in this place, you can't kill a man unless you know you're square with him. I guess that's because all of us here share one thing in common: we're *outcasts*. We refused to become slaves to the will of a governing body that no longer has the consent of the people. Those who are in power on Earth rule because of what they now offer through transference. No one here but me, and maybe a few dozen others, knows quite how it works. You get physical life unending, free from the trappings of illness and pain, if you want it. In return for this so-called gift, the Church gets your body.

And that's the rub. You then become its property—a walking billboard serving the franchise. Problem with that is, some folks back home just want to follow the natural order of things. They want to live out their fated seventy or eighty years and be on their way to the great beyond. Maybe that seems like such an old-fashioned notion now.

As for the outcasts, to the best of my knowledge there are three classes of us. Those in the first class have either made themselves enemies of the Council or they're just plain old hardened criminals. Theft, murder, and exercising free speech are still the easiest ways to get a one-way ticket here. They send all the homosexuals here, too. They're identified even earlier now from the stories I've heard.

Then there is the second class—those like me—the poorest of souls who were transferred in the earliest trials. They might not even know who they really are anymore, and that's why *this* thief chooses to retain some honor. Sparing a man takes more strength than taking his life from him, and if I have to be the one to take it, I need to know I don't owe that man a debt. But in saying that, for all I know some of them might be people I once knew in the great city—a friend of a friend or maybe just someone who showed me a brief kindness once.

And then, of course, there's me. Me, myself, and I. A class all my own.

I suspect everyone who was part of my crew was also sent here with me decades ago. Long dead, killed simply for being witnesses to the unexpected. We saw the first transference happen right on our ship. The only mistake we made after that was trusting in our superiors on Earth when we relayed the findings back to them. They were nothing more than company yes-men, and the Church wanted everyone on the planet to think *it* created transference—that transference came to it from divine inspiration, or from heaven… or some god, maybe.

I still remember the day I woke up after I returned home. My eyes were swollen shut, just the same as they are right now, and one by one my fellow crew members and I were transferred into the bodies of death-row criminals. They chose Barrabas for me, the most well-known of them. I awoke never again in this life as Thaniel Kilraven, nor did I ever see my original body again.

The next thing I knew I was swimming in and out of consciousness. Days went by, maybe even weeks or months. The next time I woke I was staring at the light of a different colored sun. I didn't recognize my own hands, let alone the faces of anyone around me. My crew was lost to me. And even on the off chance that any of them were alive today, I wouldn't know who they were anyhow.

The fact remains that I've not met a single man or woman in the mines who claimed to know Thaniel Kilraven. The face of every person here is not his or her real face, and the face I'm forced to look upon when it's reflected back is not the one my mother and father gave to me.

Or maybe… Maybe it is my true face. Maybe I am Barrabas, after all? Maybe I am a thief and a murderer.

No, Kilraven. It cannot be. Possess your mind. Possess your soul, you damned fool.

It's the confusion again. It comes and goes. Some days are much worse than others. The trouble that comes along with being transferred to a body not your own is much like the onset of dementia, I'd wager. Your thoughts betray you. One might think that with time the effect would diminish, but in fact it's just the opposite.

"Quit laggin', eyeballs!" Ubasti shouts, and drives his fist into my shoulder blade. "Getcha feet movin'!"

"You know, I can't quite see where I'm going, Warden."

"Forward," he says. "And if you're about to fall into one of the pits, I'll be sure to warn you after th'fact!" he adds with a dry laugh.

Ubasti the Warden. Now *he* is something else altogether. He's only been here five years or so, and that amount of time means you're still green. You get zero respect. That's probably a better way to put it.

It wasn't long after Ubasti arrived that he needed to prove his worth to the wardens, and it just so happened that at the same time there was a particular prisoner who'd taken a disliking to me. Everyone called the man Rutterkin. He was bald as a coot, except for a stripe of red curls that ran right down the middle of his gigantic head. I had heard that he claimed to be from just outside Old Leeds in the European Isles. One thing this place has taught me is that you should always make a point to remember where a man says he's from. Sometimes it can tell you all you need to know about him.

Anyway, I had never actually met or even spoken to Rutterkin, only seen him from afar. I can only now surmise that he didn't like the cut of my jib, or maybe he just didn't like the look of me. One day I was working at one of the aquifers, and to my bewilderment then and now, Rutterkin managed to get behind me. After he pinned me up against the wall he nearly took off one of my ears with a pneumatic saw. But before he could do that, and before I knew it, he was laid out flat on the ground. Ubasti had come up behind him as quiet as a thief in the night and snapped Rutterkin's neck like a switch.

Afterward, Ubasti just nodded at me, then spat a few times and walked away without a word while dragging Rutterkin's body away by his foot. That was the one and *only* time Ubasti showed any sort of a redeeming quality and acted like a human being. And, well, for that alone I still owe him one.

"Oi! Wake up, pretty eyes!" Ubasti barks.

We stop at the bridge that leads to block 91, just a short distance from my own. Ubasti puts the butt of his mace against the middle of my back and tells me not to move a goddamn inch. Then his greasy hand slaps down on the entry pad attached to the security key post responsible for opening the block door. A few seconds later, after his palm print is scanned to confirm his identity, the computer asks Ubasti the name of the prisoner to be extracted. He responds by prompting me to manually key in the number instead.

"Zero, five, three, dash, nine, one," he grunts.

I recognize that number as soon as I finish keying it in. It seems fate has decided to be good to me today in some respect. The block doors lumber open with a blast of steam and oxygen, and what do my bright eyes see but my friend Tarsil shuffling his feet to what can only be a tune inside his head. He crosses the iron-wrought bridge that spans the distance between the egresses of the block and then joins me and Ubasti at the main haulage entry.

"Oh hell, not *him*!" I say, groaning.

Ubasti ignores the remark. It's best that you pretend you're not attached to anyone here. Rivals in other cellblocks—and especially the staff—can and will use that sort of thing against you. If you haven't got the intestinal fortitude for doing someone else's dirty work, then I highly suggest practicing the masquerade.

Ubasti takes his place behind the two of us, and Tarsil winks at me just before we're both cattle-prodded forward. Tarsil has been here for well over ten years now. He came from Triangle City, a place I once resided in for a brief time when I was young, so we immediately had that to talk about. His last few years on Earth are somewhat of a mystery even to himself. That's no surprise, though. He does seem to remember being part of a queer gang in Harlem, and he talks a lot about recurring dreams he has—most of them revolving around him being the son trapped in the body of his own father.

He's got the kind of smile that somehow manages to light up an already bright room. Naturally, he ignores the female population working in the kitchens and the mess hall, though they still fawn over his blond hair and green eyes. Despite Tarsil's pretty face, he doesn't take much shit from anyone if it comes down to it—the wardens least of all. And he does it all with a gentle mocking at the risk of getting his nearly perfect teeth knocked in.

From what I know about his life back home, he never joined the Academy or the Peace Force on account of his sexual identity. Most of the people in Triangle City were pariahs—either because of genetically related health problems or birth defects like myopia, herniation, or a cleft palate. Tarsil has none of these, of course, but the place of his origin was also certainly already a strike against his record. To his credit, the blond bastard must've learned to shoot somewhere because he's damn good with a weapon. Or at least so he claims anyway.

Supposedly the story goes that he was sent to Neo York to make restitution for his crime. A letter Tarsil sent to a male admirer with whom he had courted in secret was evidently uncovered, and the insinuation of the words therein was enough to damn him. He ended up taking out eight guards of the Peace Force when the time came for his transference trial. I mean, he knew the punishment since he denied the trial, so he figured, why not take as many with him as he could? You've got to admire guts like that.

"The two of you soppers are gonna be workin' with Magpie for the rest of the afternoon!" Ubasti growls.

"Oh *man*, Cunningham? I can't stand that hag!" Tarsil says.

Ubasti doesn't hesitate, and out of the corner of my eye I catch the wheeling of his mace just as it whacks Tarsil a solid one upside the back of the head.

"Zip it, straw head!" Ubasti snarls. "Now since the other two crushers got caught in the haulageway after lockdown last night, she needs the extra hands," he adds, following the statement up with a phlegmy, gurgling sort of laugh.

It's no laughing matter, either. After lockdown, the ore-liquefaction process starts, and if you breathe any of it or get it on you, you're as good as dead. That's why they process it here, prior to sending it to Earth. It's a nasty, painful way for a man or woman to die. The stuff makes plutonium or uranium poisoning look like kitten play.

But the Church needs it. It needs it for transference. After I became the Church's spacegoat, little less than a decade had passed before I was hearing stories that transference had become compulsory when one came of legal age back on Earth. If you were to refuse your offer from the Church, the outcome was simple—you were marked as a criminal, or branded a traitor, and sent here to mine the prize—*eridanium*.

That's what they call it now. Eridanium. Like it's a new element or some holy artifact or something. As a matter of fact, I've heard some of the slightly more brainy wardens refer to it as "venerated violet" on account of its unusual dark-purple color. I'm sure that sanctimonious term comes from the Prophet of the Great City. Sounds like something he'd say.

The ore itself, though? Nothing more than a product really—one that allows the men who run the Church back on Earth to control the souls of men. In this way, the deceivers protect their own investment by forcing those who refuse transference to mine the very stuff they need to make thralls of those who don't oppose them. It's a sickening meditation and one that never leaves my waking thoughts.

Ubasti snorts like a hog and stops us before opening the door to the milling area.

"Here we are, limp wrist sissies," Ubasti says, spitting on my boot.

I've got to hand it to him, even for a big dumb animal like Ubasti, he sure knows how to assault one verbally just as well as he does physically.

As we're prodded inside the mill, I turn around full stop to face Ubasti after we cross the threshold. He doesn't bat an eye.

"I'm not a crusher, Warden," I say. "Besides, I'm supposed to be discussing my ticket off of this rock with a company man. A company man that even *you* don't want to piss off. Also, I think you owe me an apology for getting your spittle on my shiny boots."

Ubasti looks down, clearly noting my boots are not shiny. He half-smiles and takes one step toward me. The tip of his oily nose actually collides with my own.

"Nobody gets off this rock alive. Not while I'm here, o' prince of thievin'," he says, the hot stink of his breath nearly blinding me again.

"Alright, fine. What about my boots then?" I ask, wagging my foot as the heel digs into the dirt.

Ubasti grumbles and turns his head slowly to the right as if to pop his neck, then he headbutts me. In the instant my ass hits the ground, he's already over me, pointing the tip of the plasma mace a few inches from my forehead.

"I'll be back at twenty-two hundred hours for lockdown! And I *better* see some results out of you ladies by then!" he shouts.

Ubasti spits a brown wad of mucus onto my other boot and laughs before taking his leave. The locks of the mill door clang forcefully behind Ubasti after he exits, and I'm pretty sure I still hear him laughing. I look up at the huge ventilator turbine some forty-odd feet above our heads, and through the intake I can see a sliver of daylight. It's the first time I've seen heaven in weeks. Then Tarsil ruins it all by opening his mouth.

"You have an unusual knack for getting hit in the face," he says, looking sullen but snickering at the same time.

I forget I'm in pain for a moment and laugh along with him as he extends a hand to help me to my feet.

"It's been, what, a month or two since I saw you?" I ask, coming to my feet again and dusting myself off.

"Nothin's changed in the old T-block, bud. We got us a dozen newbies or so. Mostly scared kids who ain't never been kissed, but that's about all there is to say really," he says.

"That bad, huh?" I ask.

"Yep. Someone musta mentioned I was from Triangle, too, 'cause a few of the young'ins in particular have taken to nippin' at my heels," he says, rolling his eyes playfully and smiling that smile of his.

"Can't trust those Triangle City folks one damn bit," I say.

Tarsil just laughs again and pats me on the back.

"How's Old Man Shadow doing?" he asks.

"Haven't seen Iyov today actually, but I'm certain he'll have a superb opinion to offer on the fine state of my face," I add.

"I heard the old man was up to something… after they took you off to see the Church clown this morning," Tarsil says.

"Who told you about that?"

"C'mon, you know how news travels here," Tarsil says, winking at me. "And everyone sure as shit knows what you did to Leroy Baxter. Just today I overheard some of the wardens say Verdauga and the eastside fellows were keepin' close tabs on Iyov *and* you."

"Well that's not unheard of. Verdauga's always got someone following him," I say.

"Yeah well, when I heard 'em drop *your* name, I made a point to clean out my ears," Tarsil says with a smile as he shoves his index finger into his right ear.

"Didn't even know you had ears behind all that hair," I say.

Tarsil laughs. Then suddenly we're interrupted by another familiar giggle coming from the machinery behind us.

"Jeez, are you two gonna kiss already or what?" the voice asks.

Tarsil and I both turn around and see Cunningham leering at us from behind the giant crusher. She removes her ore-caked goggles, puts her hands on her hips, and grins at us. The dullness and the dirt of the room are swept away by the glory of her.

"To what do I owe the honor of this *rare* duo?" she asks.

"I'm not quite sure, Miss Magpie," adds Tarsil.

He practically leaps to her side with both arms extended, working his charm with that infernal smile of his.

"Lookin' good as ever," Tarsil says, getting so close to her that I think he may just try to steal a kiss.

"You too, blondie," Cunningham says with a wink, then pushes Tarsil away with both hands.

Cunningham takes one look at me and manages to both smile and frown simultaneously. Talk about devastation. The effect I have on women is astounding.

"Dammit, Barrabas, what have you done this time?" she asks.

"What? *This*?" I ask, pointing to my face. "Ah, just a small disagreement Ubasti and I had over today's menu. That's all."

"Har har," she says, rolling her eyes.

Then she throws one arm around me, patting me on the back and sending silver dust into the air around us. Her mop of curly brown hair brushes against my face, and it's the loveliest thing I've smelled in ages.

It's in this moment that I recall what Corvus called her earlier—Mel Sinosian. There's no other Mel here that I know of, and she's never revealed her surname to any of us. It has to be her. She's just yet another… another of many… another poor soul who doesn't know who she really is. Or it's the transference confusion that's got her, too.

Cunningham's embrace ends too quickly, and I look on her with newfound pity as her smile nearly knocks me dead.

"Somethin' wrong, darlin'?" she asks.

I hate to lie to her.

"Nothin's wrong, Magpie. Just nice to see a real woman for a change," I say with a nod toward Tarsil.

"Tell that to your face," she says.

"Everyone's a comedian today, huh?" I ask.

Cunningham's story is all too common. She says she was diagnosed with arthritis early on, and her parents' wish for her was to take the transference trial as soon as possible. A new body would've fixed all her ailments. To her father's great surprise, she defied both her parents in this prior to turning eighteen. She was essentially forced to leave home and later became a pickpocket or some other kind of street thief for a time. Just before she was brought here, she had turned to selling her body in order to keep a roof over her head. Fornication got her a one-way ticket to Eridania, so flash forward and here she is, working alone in the crusher.

To her credit, the male wardens in her block have taken a liking to her because not only does she do what she's told, but she can kick ass with the best of them. I once saw her break the jaw of an overly amorous gent with a single right hook. I don't think the poor bastard ever even so much as looked at her again.

"You boys haven't been to the gyratorium in ages. I was just about to get things cracking, since I kinda took a nap after grub and got behind on my quota," she says, wrinkling her nose.

"Sounds grand," Tarsil says.

"Comminution is the name of the game, boyos, and we—"

Cunningham stops the crusher in mid-warmup.

"Oh *shit*! I almost forgot!" she says, covering her mouth with her hand. "Did you guys hear about Luan and Garza?"

"Yeah," Tarsil says. "We heard."

"Ubasti told us they didn't make it out before lockdown. A damn shame," I say.

"I know, right? I had another one last week, fresh off the boat, and he dropped dead after just two days. Two days!" Cunningham says.

Tarsil grimaces and whispers solemnly, "May their souls find their way."

Cunningham and I nod in agreement, and at that moment another voice from somewhere else in the colliery repeats the phrase.

"May their souls find their way."

The three of us freeze. I stop breathing, and Cunningham puts her index finger over her lips.

"Shh!"

No one moves a muscle.

"Dee-Dee, you bitch, is that you?!" Cunningham whispers.

In one nearly silent and swift movement she bends down to grab a mining hammer close to the base of the crusher.

"Answer me, you shithouse!" she says.

Cunningham turns her head nearly one-hundred and eighty degrees and scans the room. I look up toward the crusher, and that's when I see it. Cunningham points to the same exact thing—an aged brown hand reaching up from inside the bowl of the machine. Then another hand grips the opposite side. A second later there's a head covered in hair as white as snow emerging from the hollow.

"Iyov, you blimmin' crackpot!" Cunningham says, dropping the hammer.

"Give me a *hand*, you fools!" Iyov adds with a single, dry chuckle.

Tarsil and Cunningham each grab hold of Iyov and set to pulling him from the machine.

"You could've been crushed, old man!" Tarsil says.

"What'n the hell were you doing in there?!" Cunningham shouts, beating the ore dust from Iyov's clothing as he gets to his feet.

"Waiting, of course," Iyov says plainly.

Iyov breathes in deeply, holds his breath for a moment, and then exhales a long sigh of relief.

"*Phew*! Well then. If I'd continued to stay in there any longer, I might have fallen asleep!" Iyov says, clasping his hands together and looking at each of us in turn.

He pauses and looks at me almost skeptically, not finding anything to say about the state of my face. Good old Iyov. The day after I arrived at the mine, he greeted me with a smile and open arms. *All men here are brothers at heart. Remember that*, he said. That sounds crazy to some.

In truth, I was and am still amazed by his clarity. I soon learned he'd been slaving in the pit and that he was here even before me. How that is possible even I don't know, and neither does he, for it seems he has forgotten almost all of his past. As I said, transference has a tendency to tamper with one's faculties and, like the universe, it is no respecter of persons.

Iyov spends what time he has to spare by preaching what he calls gospel truth to those with open ears and open minds. We were banished from our home because we *bear verity,* he says. A good majority of the miners heed his words, but less than half of them actually walk the walk. The other majority follow another, one who is just as charismatic as Iyov… a dangerous man called Verdauga. He sees himself as the unofficial head of the mine. Something unknown to me but significantly tragic apparently happened between the two of them, and Verdauga is always eager to gainsay Iyov at every turn.

All that business aside, Iyov is still held in reverence by everyone since he toils selflessly without complaint in the galley. I still don't understand how someone of his age and stature manages the travail of *that* labor.

"Shall we begin?" Iyov asks.

"Begin? Begin what, old man?" Tarsil asks.

"What are you on about, Iyov?" Cunningham squeals, sounding a bit more than slightly confused.

"Well, who else could've arranged for the four of us to be in the same place at the same time?" adds Iyov, his left eyebrow raised toward heaven like the tip of a pyramid.

"Ubasti?" Tarsil asks unsurely.

Iyov cocks his head in Tarsil's direction and ruckles his lips, pretending to be mildly insulted.

"Would someone just tell me what'n the blazes is going on?" Cunningham retorts, putting her hands on her hips.

Iyov looks about the room with caution in a silent effort to confirm it's only the four of us in here. He then motions for us to all come together as one.

"Come in, come in," he whispers.

In unison our arms interlink, forming a huddle, just like in the scrums of the Old World Games.

"Oof, you guys *really* stink," Cunningham whispers as we all draw closer to one another.

Each of us looks upon the other and in turn back toward Iyov, and then the old man finally whispers two words, slowly and dryly.

"Kill. Raven."

CHAPTER 4

MEMORIES

IT WOULD SEEM that someone other than Corvus suspects who I really am. Yesterday's events confirmed it. While I was in the crusher with Tarsil and Cunningham, Iyov told us about a rumor that's spreading like a brush fire throughout the mine.

Kilraven is here, and the Church wants him back.

That's what Iyov said to us. In fact, he said it three times. And then I knew: that's why I hadn't heard of Corvus before. That's why the slick-faced bastard is here. He was sent on a specific mission to seek me out. He was sent here because of what I know.

At the risk of sounding dramatic, my head's a veritable book containing memories that might unite a people against the established regime on Earth. The truth behind transference is all in my head. And the one man who now controls it plays a game with peril by sending this polished prick to find me.

Everyone in the mines knows the story of Kilraven and the Great Lie. They all tell it differently, exaggerating the details so ridiculously that the tale becomes almost unrecognizable. For a time, I even told my *own* version, for fear of being identified, filling it with embellished half-truths.

While in the telling, I actually became fond of watching the look in the eyes of the young men especially, growing so dumbstruck by the tale that their chins might as well have been touching the dirt under their feet. But the accurate version is still as fresh in my mind as the day it happened, though, perhaps, the details have lessened in certitude as the years have passed.

After I returned to Earth to bring back the alien technology we discovered on the planet called Fornax, my crew and I found ourselves on trial for treason. It was hard for me to even accept what was going on around me. Imagine yourself smack dab in the center of a nightmare that you couldn't wake from... a nightmare that turns out to be reality.

The charges laid against us were a carefully orchestrated pack of lies devised by the Church to make everyone on Earth believe we tried to steal the technology they claimed they had created and keep it for ourselves. Everyone on Earth took the prophets and the Church at their word. After all, they owned the lion's share of the media, and we were traitors of the worst kind once we'd been supposedly caught red-handed for all to see.

The trial itself was a farce. No evidence was held or shown to the public, as was law at the time. My memory of it is now so sketchy that I have every reason to believe I was drugged during the entire process, so as to not be able to properly defend myself. It was as if I was watching everything happen around me, fully coherent in mind yet without the ability to open my mouth.

When the gavel went down, they'd painted a grand picture of how my crew and I detested the people on Earth and coveted their technology—hence the reason for our expedition to Fornax in the first place. They added a cherry on top, saying perhaps it was our intention to create a utopian settlement where those we alone deemed fit would have this newfound gift.

The prophets spoke harshest against me in particular. *Thaniel Kilraven authored the plot to keep the technology hidden*, they said. *To keep it amongst themselves,* they said. To this day I still don't know why I was singled out, and it no longer mattered, really.

Once the Church's plan came to fruition, it now had a nearly infinite revenue stream. Control over the majority of the populace was a byproduct of the technology, and the name of Kilraven became accursed. Everyone with an asshole and an opinion in the mines grew to cringe at the sound of it.

And so, it became a sort of unspoken rule of thumb to never mention my name, if only for fear of being an associate of the one responsible for our exile. In time, everyone forgot why they were sent to Eridania in the first place, and many solely blamed my family's name for their misery.

But not Iyov.

He was always different from the rest in one respect—at every turn he would deride the mocking of my true name, reminding those who spoke against it that they too were equally as guilty of some heresy or sin or trespass in the eyes of the law. Over time, either by some strange fortune, or Iyov's words, the name of Kilraven inadvertently began to take a different shape and became more of a mascot or a chant against the wardens. I've watched it happen slowly—the reputation of the name taking precedence over the man—especially during the last three years, as there's been an influx of a sexually rebellious generation of young people looking for something with gravitas to rally behind.

In the crusher yestereve, Iyov had a glint in his eyes the entire time he spoke about all that he knew—rubbing his hands together with a level of excitement I've never quite seen from him before. Whether the old man suspects it's me or not, I don't yet know. Last night in those moments with Cunningham and Tarsil present, I didn't have the heart to tell any of them the truth. The words were right on the tip of my tongue, but I couldn't pry them out with a jimmy bar if you paid me.

Regardless, I can't be sure if Iyov would believe me or not, so I've kept my true name hidden from everyone—and for so long now that even I myself have cursed the name of Kilraven openly in front of others. And before I even attempt to open my mouth, now I must find out how things are going to play out with Corvus. Hope of that result and fear coincide. An inherent part of a man's fear is given life and breath when he arrives at that moment in time when he knows he's come full circle on the path he purposely took to avoid his fate. Or maybe it's just the long years and transference twisting my cerebrum. Either way, I should not trust in hopes.

After I finished working yesterday, Ubasti clambered into my cellblock just prior to lockdown and said he was there to personally escort me nearer to the chief's quarters. For the first time in my life on this planet, I got to sleep in a cell entirely my own. The floors were like a sheet of ice. I wasn't allowed to bring any of my personal effects, but hey, it beats vying for a cot in a room full of two dozen others until you finally settle for resting your head on the warm dirt.

As of this moment I'm black-bagged and bound again in the clutches of Corvus. Sharing the interrogation room with this company slime is not how I'd like to spend my remaining days, but I'd be a fool to think this couldn't somehow work to my benefit. And I'd be more foolish to think that Corvus has anything other than big plans for me, undoubtedly to his own benefit.

Maybe he has no plans. Maybe this is all happening for no other reason than to give me a false hope.

No.

The fear of Barrabas in me is playing a mind game with the hope of Kilraven. I know full well that Corvus has plans. All of them do.

Possess your soul, Kilraven, you *damn* fool.

A hand grabs me by the top of the head, removes the shroud, and pulls out some of my hair with it. I grit my teeth to keep from wincing. The revelatory light of the small room fades a bit, revealing Corvus seated across from me with the shroud still in his hand. To my surprise he actually puts the black cloth close to his face, sniffs it several times, then throws it onto the floor.

"You smell much better today, Barrabas," he says pretentiously. "And a good thing, too, since we'll be here for an hour or more before I send you back to work. As I suggested last time we met, you should start from the beginning," he adds, placing a small device on the table in front of me. "This is the account of prisoner six one nine, dash nine two. Whenever you are ready, Barrabas."

I close my eyes and breathe in deeply. I'd be lying if I didn't admit Corvus smells rather pleasant. I struggle to gain a clear focus on how exactly all of this began for me. I can't decide if I even *want* to tell him… but I almost do want to. I'm almost compelled to. It's as though my mouth would move of its own accord, losing in a battle of wits against my will.

How did I get here? How did a life that started so ordinarily land my ass in the biggest prison this side of the Seyfert galaxies? Sometimes I'm not quite certain I can remember. But my childhood... that I *do* remember.

And then, behind my eyes, a white flag waves on a subject that's always been close to my heart: the longing I had to know my father.

"Tick tock, tick tock, get on with it!" Corvus bellows, brusquely breaking the silence. "Must I spell it out? Start with the year you were born, the where, the when, how, *et cetera*," he adds.

I begin to speak with a boldness that seemingly comes out of nowhere, and any fear I had leaves me. The sensation can only be described as feeling like someone else begins to talk through me.

"I was born via the normal embryo-cell culturization process in the year 2045, after my parents Natalia and Jonn waited for the standard four-year pre-birth period to expire. Alongside a Council-approved union, my parents coming of age meant that I was going to be yet another epitome of the CFD's perfected handiwork."

Corvus shifts slightly in his seat before interjecting. "Record?" he asks, and his ledger makes a singular tone. "The prisoner refers to the early *cloning and fetal design* franchise, now owned by Advanced Cell Technology and the—"

"So, the CFD's gone bupkus? Have I been gone that long, or is your little doohickey there incorrect?" I ask.

"The bio division of the Council now governs fifty-one percent of the technology. For fairness and justness for all. And let's clear this up once more... *I'm* the one who will be asking the questions here," he says, his voice rising at the last.

"The questions were more rhetorical really," I say, shrugging off his bark.

So, the bastard hates being questioned. Most people in a position of unmerited command do.

It reminds me of the one and only time I challenged my parents' authority when it came to my speech patterns at home. Because Mother was a teacher, she refused to allow me to speak in her presence using contractions. Many hours standing with my nose in the corner were to be had over that peculiarity of hers.

"Now then," Corvus adds, "were you made aware of any *special* enhancements that your family might've selected for you prior to your birth?"

"No idea about that," I say, and Corvus scowls at the ledger. "Look, I just always counted myself lucky that my parents chose to allot me the standard ten fingers and ten toes, okay?"

"So, you were imprinted without so much as a slice of knowledge of the world prior to your own existence?" Corvus asks.

"Not that I was ever aware of. They wanted me to stay in public school and be socialized with other people naturally. From my earliest days in academia, we were taught what we needed to know about the wars, if that's what you're referring to."

"Let the record show the prisoner is referring to the twenty-first century. You were instructed that this was the ultimate social and moral low point of human history, I take it?" Corvus asks.

"Yes. I'd heard stories about men that killed one another for material goods and that that sort of unfortunate business was typical news of the day."

"And were you taught these lessons at home also?" he asks, raising his eyebrows.

"Some of them."

"And what about your father? Did you learn of his supposed demise whilst in study, or did someone within your family inform you?"

"When I was old enough, Mother explained that before I was birthed, father had tried to stop a group of bigots."

"From what exactly?"

"From burning down a polyclinic of some kind. He was shot in the back multiple times. The resulting injury was a ruptured cerebral vein… and he bled out right onto the pavement."

"Do you recall if his brain was removed for cloning?" Corvus asks.

"They didn't even try, not after seeing the size of the wound. Transference was still years away. As far as I know, my father's sacrifice went unreported."

"And this bothered you?" he asks.

"Hell yes it did!" I say. "And it still does. He deserved better than that."

"Most people find it easy to adapt to loss now. The genetic predisposition to grief has been nearly eradicated via cloning. Why do you think you feel the way that you do?" Corvus asks.

"I don't know. But, I... I yearned to know him. I've never understood it. The longing just sort of, well, *gnawed* at me, I guess."

"So, in your mind, you've worked him up into some sort of hero then?" he asks, hardly hiding his scorn.

"I was told he was a great man, and so was his father before him. They both fought in the wars. What little else I know about him came by way of passing comments or some random remark uttered by a distant relative who might as well have been a complete stranger to me."

"Mmm. Very well. Were you told anything else of relevance in regards to your father?" Corvus asks.

"Well, Mother rarely spoke of him. All that she ever told me you now know in a broad sense."

"What about your forbearers?" he asks.

"I knew my grandfather fairly well, on my mother's side. He loved to teach, and I was thirsty for all he had to say, especially what he knew of the Old World, the forbidden doctrines, all things prewar. Everything he said I pretty much counted as canon."

"Are you claiming that your supposed grandfather taught you about prohibited documents?"

"Yes. The Magna Carta, the Constitution, the Emancipation Proclamation, all of them."

Corvus holds up an open palm and stares at his ledger.

"Make a special note of that, please," he says, and the ledger beeps.

"Now, tell me about your early childhood," he says, bidding me to continue with a glib wave of his hand.

"I was raised in the great city that took my father's life. Maybe that's why out of all the city-states, and I've been to them all, that... well... Neo York seemed to me the most unremarkable," I say.

"Nonsense. The city is the much-lauded pride of the Earth," Corvus says, as if repeating a line that was spoon-fed to him.

"You *would* say that," I retort, clearing my throat and waiting for Corvus to take the bait. He doesn't.

"Go on," he says.

"At any rate, I've not been to the great city since the late sixties. Back then they were calling it a *utopian metropolis*, but it was overrun more by profiteers than it was by prophets. Posters in the shop windows said it was a new haven for the destitute. Anyway, the years I called it home weren't entirely unkind to me."

"In which part of the city did you reside?" he asks.

"We lived in quadrant four. That afforded me the luxury of wandering the streets at will, provided I was home before zero-hour curfew. My cousin and I had a knack for staying out of trouble. Well, let's say I was good at escaping it. I always felt guilty for it, though, mainly when my mother would randomly embrace me."

"So, physical contact with your supposed mother was common?" he asks.

"Of course. She was my mother. She would always call us her songbirds," I say.

"Birds only a mother could love, obviously, by the looks of you now," Corvus says with a tense glare.

"She loved birds. You must not fly so soon, she would say. Little songbird you have to grow your feathers first," I say, smiling to myself.

When I look up at Corvus, the look of abject disgust on his face tells me I've said far too much. It takes all my mental energy, straining, to change the topic.

"After a while I… well, I began to suspect Mother knew what I was up to. But looking back, I'm fairly certain she was oblivious to the trips my schoolmates and I regularly took in search of prohibited materials."

"Boys are known to be notoriously difficult at that age," Corvus says with a sort of frown. "And were your recreant guardians still alive, they might just find your past exploits laughable. But perhaps not so much humor in the position you currently find yourself in."

"As if you could ever possibly be able to understand a parent's thought," I say.

"You are absolutely correct, prisoner. But it is my duty to understand why people do and say the things that they do. For instance, what did you do with these prohibited items you spoke of?" the scumbag asks, smiling.

47

"Well, you're the expert, Corvus. You tell me," I say.

"I would wager a few hundred credits that you traded them for even more contraband," he says.

"Well… never let it be said that you're simply a bookworm desk jockey. And you're right: we *did* trade them, to other kids who were too afraid to venture outside of their quadrants to gain what we had."

"And what were the types of contraband, for the record?" Corvus asks.

"Mainly music and movies. Graphic books. Novels. Console-based games. Twentieth-century stuff was the best. Mother would have disabled my brain stem herself if I had ever been escorted to the front door by a peace officer carrying any of it. But I knew better. The peace officers had more important tasks to attend to in those days. They were busy with the nurbs and thieves and all the homosex—"

"Stop," Corvus says and taps his ledger twice. "The prisoner is referring to the dangerous faction that was the *nonurbanite* population. Now, please, continue."

"I myself would later help the Peace Force suppress the nurbs, and I had a… well, I guess because I—"

I hesitate to finish the sentence. What happened to the nurbs, for my part, was something I never forgave myself for. Though some might blame such mistakes on youth, duty overcame conscience at that time in my life… and I simply could not make a choice that defied the former, and I damn myself for it.

"Because what? Because you hated them?" he asks.

"No. In those days, the nurbs had little reason to surface. They were self-sustaining in almost every respect. They didn't need anything from above."

"But?"

"Yes, their hatred toward the culture above them grew day by day. That's when they became more militant."

"Acting on or discussing their bygone creeds within the city limits is still a punishable offense," Corvus says authoritatively.

"No surprise there. The only reason they never truly succeeded was because of the concrete sidewalks that separated us and them. Not to mention they were outgunned," I add, trying to hide my remorse.

"Was this at all about vengeance for you, prisoner?" he asks.

"Maybe. I suppose I might've held them responsible for what happened to my father, in some small way," I say.

It's then that Corvus stops me by raising his hand. He taps his fingers on his ledger slowly and slicks back his hair. The only thing I can gather so far, based on his slightly exasperated expression, is that everything I've said is nothing new under the known suns to him.

"Mmm. I want to hear more about where you grew up. What your home was like. And the rest of the Kilraven family," he says.

"Well, I lived in Neo York in the early years. Up in Jericho Tower. For a time, my family was relatively privileged. My father's death provided us a substantial amount of credits, and we—"

"City and travel points, you mean?" he asks.

"Sure. Enough for half a dozen families. We never felt want for things like food, drink, or livery. Mother obliged me in almost all things that were within reason, and she didn't keep a damn thing for herself. Well, all save one."

"And what was that?"

"A piano. A decommissioned Steinway that was the centerpiece of our home."

"Ah, yes. A music aficionado. Did she ever play it?" he asks.

"I just said it was decommissioned. But yes, she would sit at it from time to time. I had to imagine what it might have once sounded like. I still remember rubbing my fingers over the original date stamp."

"Do you recall where your mother acquired it?" he asks.

"She claimed that it once belonged to a twentieth-century actor or… a comedian, maybe. I don't remember now. I never knew anyone else who owned one, and I haven't seen one since."

"Did your mother own or ever show you any other decommissioned materials?" he asks.

Lie, dammit. You *have* to lie.

"Not that I'm… aware of."

"What about documents? Travel licenses?" he asks, placing his elbows on the edge of the table and looking intently at me.

"Travel wasn't a problem for us since we owned a city-blazer. The license was valid for employment, academia, and leisure purposes," I say.

"A city-blazer?" he asks, rubbing his index finger and thumb across his mustache.

"Yeah… this was prior to Lockheed emerging from the vehicle format races as the *de facto* standard. I must've been around seven years old when all the econo city-class vehicles were replaced with the new inter-atmospheric blazers. It crushed me to watch the old model destroyed by the city's nuke regulators for no longer being fission-efficient. That might've also been the last time I cried."

I nearly laugh out loud at my last comment. But Corvus doesn't laugh or smile. He just narrows his eyes a bit, stands up abruptly, and tells me he'll be right back.

"Time for a piss break?" I ask.

"Shut up. And don't move," Corvus says curtly before opening the door.

"Honestly, where do you think I'm going? I'm practically part of the chair's molecular structure," I retort just as the door closes.

My stomach rumbles. I close my eyes and wonder if I'll be served my ration anytime soon.

How can you think of food at a time like this?

When Corvus returns minutes later, he sets a glass half-filled with what looks like brown liquor down on the table next to his ledger. Now I know for a fact that there's no alcohol anywhere here. The chief operator of the mine doesn't even have a secret stash.

"Back to business," he says after taking a small sip. His right eye twinges a little bit, and when he exhales, I can smell what I think is vanilla and charcoal.

"Let's see," he says, coughing and daintily covering his lips with his index finger. "So by this time in your life, had you given any thought to your future occupation?"

"The *future* is right now."

Corvus looks at me curiously and takes another sip from his libation.

"What does that mean?" he asks.

"It's an odd phrase, right? Far less confusing to me now than when I initially heard it spoken by a man with one eye."

"Was this someone you knew well, prisoner?"

"No," I say, feeling the tiniest amount of pity that Corvus has no idea what I'm talking about. "I heard it in the first motion picture I ever saw."

"Surely you are jesting?" Corvus asks slowly.

"C'mon. Everyone remembers their first movie."

"What year would this have been?" he asks.

"In 2052 or thereabouts. The copy was obtained illegally, of course, by my cousin Orin during our formative years prior to joining the Academy."

"And where did he get these movies?" he asks.

"He would never tell me. And when I persisted in knowing he'd say, *Alchemy, you nimrod!*"

"Keep going," Corvus says, taking another sip of his drink.

"Orin and I would ditch classes together. He would splice together digital footage of whatever he'd downloaded or ripped to try and make a complete clip. He was obsessed with them. He said every movie has a beginning, a middle, and an end. Without the beginning, it's nothing. And he'd stay up all night searching for scripts and missing dialogue, even to the point of making foreign subtitles for the damn things."

"Would it surprise you then to know he was eventually arrested and imprisoned for grand thievery?"

"Are you sure it was him?"

"*Ah,*" Corvus says, his forehead creased as he studies the ledger. "I see here now that he was executed over ten years ago."

"Where? How? How did he die?"

"It says here he was mercifully flung from the precipice of the Great Tower after he ridiculed the Prophet on the city's free LiFi connection," Corvus says, squinting his eyes at the ledger. "Understandable," he adds with a nod.

"May his soul find his way, then. He was always… the stealthy one. I suppose that's how he managed to keep his collection such a supreme secret."

"His collection?"

"Of movies. He couldn't have had more than a few dozen or so. And none of them were ever wholly complete. We never even knew the titles of most of them. More often than not they were just images, without audio, or vice versa."

"You were aware that obtaining unapproved films was and is worthy of immediate arrest?" he asks.

"We were kids. We didn't care. We just wanted to watch them. Years later my grandpa taught me how the making of motion pictures was once commonplace but had been prohibited by the Supreme Council long before I was born. Before the wars even."

"So, your supposed grandfather encouraged illicit activities as well?" he asks.

"Yes and no. With movies, no, he didn't. He said he'd tear my ass up good if he ever caught me with any. Anyway, like I said, we didn't really care. Behind closed doors we were brave kids, and we marveled at the rumor of them amongst our peers."

"Did these heinous materials have any effect on your future decisions?" he asks.

"I suppose not. By the time I was eight, I was almost ready to make a selection based on my academic results anyway."

"But you didn't?" he asks.

"Well, not long afterward, Mother decided city life had grown much too debauched. Much too immoral, and she—"

"Indeed? And what is it you remember most about her?" he asks.

"I guess... I remember feelings now more than anything else. How she smelled. How she laughed... not that she did laugh much anyway, but when she did, it made me laugh, too. All this time later I just have to think about it and I'm... Well, I guess a part of me feels back at home. Wherever that is."

I realize then that I've said too much about her once again. *You idiot.*

Corvus looks bewildered—unsettled even—at my revelation of motherly attachment. It wasn't common in those days to display affection, especially publicly. I decide to test him further in the hopes of pressing another one of his buttons.

"A cold, hard company cock like yourself probably couldn't understand a thing like that," I say.

It works.

The skinny mongrel turns off the recording device and grins viciously from ear to ear.

"My job on this planet pays me well, and my tenets reward me with the thought that I will long outlive you, Barrabas," he says, smirking. "But if you think for a second that I will put up with any further insubordination, then you've underestimated me greatly."

Corvus's amusement ends the moment the door behind me is thrust open. The weighted clattering of the sentry's footsteps insinuates he's come to send me back to the land of Nod. Corvus bids him to wait a moment, and in one slick movement the snake is out of his chair, admiring a pair of black gloves I never even noticed him fit.

"Do not forget, there are other souls precious to you which are at stake," he says. "And many more than just your own," he adds, now standing over me. "A *cock*, was it, you said?"

Then, faster than a bolt of lightning, he punches me square in the face. As my head reels back, the resulting crack, followed by a spreading spasm of pain, tells me my nose is most definitely broken. The sentry grabs me by my hair, and right before I black out, I feel Corvus's breath on my cheek.

"Take solace in the fact that thirty years of hell is soon coming to an end for you," he says. "You have five days left," he adds with a cruel hiss.

CHAPTER 5

I, KILRAVEN

I'M FLOATING. NO, I'm not floating… I'm *swimming*.

I can't see a thing. I feel my arms and legs moving against a powerful and crushing current of freezing, briny foam. My entire body aches and every one of my muscles strains to keep me above the water.

Then I open my eyes. I'm in my cell, already up on my feet and trying to stand up. When my shuddering legs give way, a strong and firm hand catches me.

"Easy, son. *Easy*," he says.

I recognize the voice immediately. It's Iyov. His right name, of course, is something else entirely. He's never asked mine, and oddly enough, I've done him the same courtesy. In this place, we learned long ago that we are who they say we are, and our names are not our names. The fingerprints you leave behind are no more an indicator of who you truly are than the gray matter inside your skull.

"They gave you one hell of a beating, kiddo," he says as I struggle to keep my feet flat underneath me. "I said *easy*, you stubborn mule!" he adds, supporting me as best as he can.

"You'd have better luck trying to get a wet noodle to walk, Iyov."

"Tell me about it, son. I'd thought this time we'd seen the last of you," he says, helping me recline into a seated position against the cell wall.

"How long was I out?"

"A little more than a day," he says as I feel the old man putting my boots back on my feet. "Set your feet out straight already!"

"Surprised the wardens let me sleep that long."

Corvus must have had something to do with that. I've no doubt that he'll be wanting me to sweat what time I have left in this farcical game of his. My one chance here is that he may not yet realize his own liability in the game we're playing.

"What are you doing here?" I ask, my vision slowly coming back to me.

"Ubasti dropped you off outside the *mise en place* and left you drooling in the dirt. He told me to clean you up because that man from the Church took offense to your aroma," Iyov says, grinning precociously.

"Did he?"

"Not that any of it matters, boy… You'll be dead soon anyway," he adds with a sly wink.

"Yuck it up, *old* man."

"What in all the hells do they want with you, son? I've not seen them treat any one of us quite this brazenly in many a year now," he adds.

"It's yet another long story… and part of it you need to hear, though you may not believe me," I add.

Iyov begins to hum. He pretends to ignore me and begins re-tying the laces on one of my boots.

"Well, after what you did to Warden Baxter… hmm… I suppose they think this broken nose of yours is a just reward for the time being?" he asks finishing the knot.

"That's the third break in ten years."

"Do you want me to fix it?" he asks, reaching for my nose.

"For God's sakes, leave it, old man!"

Iyov laughs thunderously. It sounds the way I'd imagine an ancient wizard or Old Saint Nick might. I cover my mouth and cough up a mist that feels warm on my hand.

"Iyov, listen. There's something I need to tell you. It's important. For your ears alone… at least… until the time is right."

Iyov's countenance changes, and a grim-faced concern settles over his wrinkled visage. After tugging at his short gray beard a few times, he nods for me to continue.

"Go on then," he says.

"Have you… Have you ever heard of what became of the *real* Kilraven?"

"Of course not!" he says, waving his hand at me. "And if I had, I'm not so cracked yet that I'd repeat the tale. Certainly not now, with everything that's going on at the present time."

"Tell me what you remember."

"I suppose everyone knows the rumor of the great betrayal. To think that Kilraven could still be here among us is folly to speak of. And folly to hope for. You know *that*," he says almost mockingly.

"So, that's the only reason you've never spoken of this with me?" I ask.

"Indeed," he says with a suspicious prudency behind his tone. "Besides, what has that got to do with you, Barrabas?" he asks, his eyes slowly widening.

"The Church man told me something. Something about Kilraven's family."

"You know, company men will say anything to get what they want."

"But what if he's right and they're still alive? I can save them. I could *save* them!"

Iyov stops breathing for what feels like an eon. He goes so quiet you could hear cirrus clouds scraping together. After glancing at the floor several times and then back at me, he covers his mouth with his hand.

"It cannot be!" he gasps, barely above a whisper, his eyes hectic as they search across the landscape of my face.

"It's me, Iyov. I *am* Kilr—"

"Shush! Shush now!" Iyov says, raising his hand in front of my mouth while frantically looking around the cell. "The walls in this damned place yet have ears! And you should not be telling me this right now!" he mutters quickly, wagging both hands from side to side in protest.

He quickly jumps to his feet and scuffles to the front of the cellblock, leering out of the small window in the center of the iron doorway.

"Ubasti must be on another break. That bastard," he says, coming back and kneeling quickly beside me. "Do you believe them, Barrabas? Do you *believe* what they say about the Kilravens?" he asks, wiping the blood from my mouth with the sleeve of his dusty cloak.

"Deep down? I do, though I can't be sure why. I thought I was the only one left."

"Did he mention their *names* at all?" Iyov asks with a look near to terror on his face.

"No. He only called them Kilraven's family."

"Hmm… and *you*… Are you certain you are not really Barrabas? Are you *certain*?" he asks, the hope behind his question now quite plain.

"Well, if I'm not, it's like you said… I'm a dead man anyway."

Iyov grabs my shoulder, gripping it firmly and scanning my eyes with the power of discernment in his own. He's searching for the truth. I pray he sees it somewhere.

"I know who I am, Iyov," I say, placing my hand on his shoulder in return.

"You're absolutely *sure*?"

"What? You don't believe me?"

A breath or two later, the light in Iyov's eyes grows from the size of a pinpoint to that of a roaring fire. Tears well up in their corners, and his lip quivers as he grabs my forearm. His hands start to tremble as he speaks.

"The very fact that you so emphatically deny being Barrabas means only one thing," he says.

"What's that?"

"That you are *not* him," Iyov replies with his eyes ever-widening.

"Then who would I be?"

Iyov pauses for a moment, sighs, and then turns away. His eyebrows shift from side to side, creasing in the middle. Less than five seconds later he gives me the most restrained look of astonishment I've ever seen.

"Of course. Of *course*! You would be the most famous of criminals amongst us!" he whispers.

"I'm surprised no one else has put it all together before now, old friend."

"Curse me for being so damned blind!" he says.

"Don't be so hard on yourself, Iyov. I never had any reason for making it evident until today."

"And it was a lie, wasn't it?" he asks. "The argument they so skillfully wove against you, and all those aboard those ships?"

I can only nod slowly and take just a small bit of pleasure from the relief I feel in finally having told my friend the truth.

"And they sent you here… to languish in the knowledge that they tarnished your name and took all that was yours to serve their own evil purposes," he says.

"Well, when you put it like that, it's all becoming clearer to me by the minute."

"Then this is it! The time has come!" Iyov says, clenching both his fists together and pulling them to his chest. "All these many years I have waited for this moment. You were very wise to keep it a secret… but you must go forward now with great caution, my friend."

"You're the only one who knows, Iyov… and maybe Corvus, too."

"No, no, no. It's even more grave than that. I didn't tell you yesterday that the wardens also know that Kilraven is amongst us! The Church wants him back, they said," he adds, rubbing his hands together and sighing heavily.

"Will you help me?"

"You're going to need much more than my help. The man to your left might turn you in for an extra meal," Iyov says, rising to his feet and pacing the length of the cell, "and the man to your right may surrender you for sport. Need I mention that incident with Rutterkin?"

"Don't remind me."

"I thought so. This is quite a predicament. Yes indeed," he says, pouting his lips. "I dare add if you reveal what they want *too* soon, then not only will you lose your soul, but they will slaughter your kin without thinking twice."

"I know, Iyov… I know. But I don't believe there's any walking away from this now. It's gone too far. Either I die, or they die. Tell me, what would you do?"

Iyov bends down and leans in close to me. Then, gripping my forearm within his own, just like in the films of my youth when the gladiators of old would greet one another, he simply smiles.

"I was always settled on this. Now there's nothing for it," he says with a wink.

He lets go of my arm and starts pacing the floor once again.

"I've seen that look. What're you thinking, old man?" I ask, incapable of restraining a smile.

"We're going to need more time. The few days you have left aren't enough if I'm to see the way ahead more clearly. I'll be in the submain entry working full-stop for the rest of the day, though I might be able to make my way to the gyratorium and have Cunningham get the girls onboard."

"Onboard with what?"

"Why, a *mutiny* of course, dear boy."

"Are you nuts?!" I ask, and the old man only chews on his lower lip. "What'll that achieve other than the deaths of everyone here, Iyov? It's not as if any of us can actually get out of here."

"Perhaps. Perhaps not. Why do you think the Church sent that man here? *Hmm*? You are his prize. If we play things out carefully, there may just be a way for one to return," Iyov says, still pacing the floor.

"Waitaminute, do you know something you aren't telling me?"

"Logic alone leads me from one conclusion to the next, my friend. Firstly, the other miners won't think long on whether or not to stand behind Kilraven the Cursed. Second, there are those who will choose not to stand at all, though they might be few. After all, you were sent here with the rest of us, so Kilraven can't be half as bad as everyone thinks you—"

Iyov quickly turns and faces the door, as if something unseen has startled him. He's always had a bit of a sixth sense.

"Get up, boy!" he says.

Then, coming quickly, Iyov stops short in front of me. He grabs me by the arm with both hands, and with some hidden strength, he wrenches me boldly to my feet.

"They're coming for you. Let them see you standing," he says as the cell door opens.

Once more I'm knocked upside the head a few times, then blindfolded and led by an eight-wheeled lorry to the other side of the mining colony.

I spend all my waking energy focusing on the various turns we make to get to our destination. Two times to the right and then straight ahead for several minutes the rest of the way until we come to a full stop. By my best guess, we're roughly about ten klicks away from the cellblocks. It also doesn't smell as bad here, and that means we're closer to the landing platforms that run parallel to the Kasmodian Desert than we are to the mines themselves.

I'm once again fettered tightly to the seat, this time by no less than two sentries. Before leaving me alone, one of them tests my bonds, and his breath stinks of cooking spices. I make a point to tell him so, and he slaps the back of my head so hard that I have to bite down several times afterward to make sure all my teeth are still in place. Then one of them sticks something into the side of my neck. I can only guess at what the bastards keep injecting me with. I can't fault them for being thorough.

Prior to meeting Corvus, I'd have said the worst of all this was having to get used to being restrained. There's just no real need for it here. Most of the miners keep in line out of fear because even if you made it as far as the platforms you'd find no docked ships. Fresh inmates arrive monthly, but those transports never stay more than two days, tops. Getting back to Earth with a fresh batch of ore is the *numero uno* priority. Even if you managed to hijack one of the transports, you have two or three dozen peace guards to take out, not to mention you'd need to know how to pilot the ship *and* get back to Earth without being shot down on arrival.

The sun here also poses a slight problem. It's blue and shaped almost like an egg. They call it the *Achernar*, or the demon star. It gives us an intense light for eighteen hours of a standard twenty-four-hour clock. Imagine being in the hottest desert you can think of with no water, no coverings, and no sustenance of any kind. Add that all up and it equals one thing—escape on foot is absolutely impossible.

Every six months or so, though, you'll catch wind of how one of the inmates managed to sidestep the wardens. The story is usually re-spread by those who've been here less than a year since they're the ones who tend to cling blindly to some hope. No one who gets out and stays gone for more than a few hours ever returns. Not one.

A door opens behind me right on schedule and I hear the clack of high-quality soles upon the stone floor. I wonder if they were made by an Englishman.

"Comfortable?" a familiar voice asks.

When my hood is removed, I quickly ascertain that I'm back in the same room as yesterday. I know because the table in front of me has the same zig-zag markings scratched into the lower right leg. Could be a mark from the manufacturer. It almost looks like a trident.

Corvus tosses the blindfold onto the table next to a half-empty plastic cup and takes his seat directly across from me once more. The room already reeks of some smooth-smelling type of liquor.

Seems the long-necked ostrich has got a drinking problem.

"Barrabas, Barrabas, Barrabas!" he announces in that mocking way someone might greet you in front of others, pretending to know you better than they actually do. "Judging by your state, you look as though you had a night of hard rest. We have a lot of ground to cover today, and time is of the essence. We left off discussing your harlot mother and her desire to remove you and your siblings from the great city. Please, continue from there," he adds, folding his hands and awaiting my reaction to the shame he just laid at the feet of my saint of a mother.

The thought occurs to me that when this whole affair culminates, I'll do my damnedest to dispatch him, whether it's necessary or not. I won't even enjoy it, but I'll kill him slowly, too. By hand if I have to. Or maybe we'll face one another down like a gunfight in the street, something akin to the old western American duels.

But before I'm able to plan that little scenario out any further in my head, I cough up more blood. Since I've nowhere to put it, I spit it out on the unsoiled table separating me from the Church degenerate.

"*Oh*. It looks as though you'll be needing a doctor," Corvus says.

Not the doctors. They're *insane*.

"I'm fine."

"Are you sure?" Corvus asks, wiping the blood up with the hood that was previously over my head.

My insides slowly begin to sink into a quagmire of fear. Do something, Kilraven. Say *something*. Tell him what he wants to hear. Don't let him see your *fear*.

"I was awoken suddenly in the middle of the night. Mother stood over me and covered my lips with her finger and said we must leave with all speed. *Hurry, child,* she kept repeating. I got dressed as quick as I could, and I took nothing I cared about. I didn't know at the time that leaving a city-state without Council consent could result in severe disciplinary action."

"So, you are saying she had no documentation which would allow for any of you to leave your home at that time?" Corvus asks, jotting a mark of some sort with his finger on the surface of the ledger.

"I'm not totally certain of that."

"You just said you took nothing. No identity chips? Not even a pass card?" he asks.

"Mother might've had something like that."

"Mmm. And your two sisters, you have made no mention of them yet. Were they also involved in these events?" he asks.

"Yes."

"Well, go on," he says.

"We went south. The trip is hazy in my mind, but I recall catching a liberty boat out of the city. Mother bade us not to speak until we'd crossed the Long Island Memorial Sea. Meg'n broke the silence first. She was always a bit of a wiggler. She asked Mother whether we'd ever return."

"And did you?" he asks.

"Mother said the city was no longer a place for ones such as us. She must've had some kind of… foresight, maybe."

"Meaning?" he asks.

"Meaning we left none too soon, because within a few weeks the peace officers had a permanent presence in the city. Every single entrance, in and out, was heavily monitored. From then on, coming and going became another matter entirely. I didn't give it a second thought at the time, but… now I have an inkling as to who they were looking for."

"And who would that be?" he asks.

"Me."

"You? This is not quite clear. Had you committed any solitary criminal acts that would warrant your detainment?" he asks.

"No. I mean to say they were looking for Madzimure."

"Ahh, yes, I see! His criminal activity and blatant disregard for the rules of peace made you a vile sort of celebrity, didn't they?" he says.

"Everyone talked about *me*. How I defied anyone—and everything. Evidently, I had just stolen something precious from the Council headquarters in Tokyo. Somehow or another I'd survived this great leap from the tower, and there was gossip that I might be coming to Neo York."

"And did you?" he asks.

"Eventually. From what I heard after the fact anyway."

I could swear that Corvus nearly smiles, but this time it doesn't surprise me. Intrigue has ever been synonymous with my infamous second name.

"Alright, enough. We have little time for deviation, and the Madzimurian is *well* documented. What happened after Kilraven left Neo York?" he asks.

"Well, after some border jumping in the outskirts of the Old Madrid Zone, Mother set our roots down in Triangle City."

"Triangle City? Where was this?"

"Yeah, it's where the Mississippi River came together like a noose. The city was nearly surrounded by water on all sides."

"Had you been there before?" he asks.

"No. But I remember studying the great earthquakes that leveled what mountains there were in that area during the wars. If there was ever any semblance of law and order, by the time we arrived it'd pretty much dissolved. Men and women carried unregistered weaponry openly. Talk about having berkelium balls. It was a first-class joint."

"What types of weapons did they have?" Corvus asks.

"Simple ones. Sonic pistols, blasters. Didn't use clips, though. You know, the models where the plasmic pellets had to be inserted one at a time into the chamber?"

"Mmm," Corvus says, nodding and tugging at his earlobe.

"In many ways, it was a much more dangerous city than Neo York. But well, my sisters adored the hysteria of it all. Around this time, they too began studying the forbidden principles of freedom and the—"

Corvus clears his throat and his eyebrows rise. "Describe your sisters for me please."

"They were… um… beautiful. A mystery, the two of them. Despite being twins, they were both models of perfect health."

"You mean their inherent genetic flaws should have made it otherwise?" Corvus asks.

"If that's how you wanna look at it. I thought it was a kind of magic. They finished one another's sentences. Damnedest thing I ever saw. One would hurt when the other hurt. I really thought some of their more peculiar behaviors must've been due to something unseen. Something they shared maybe… like they were part of the same soul or something."

Corvus leaps from his seat and slams his fist on the table.

"That is *heresy*! Record, make note that the prisoner's last comment should be later stricken!"

The ledger beeps furiously as Corvus slowly sits down again, reclining back into his seat and watching me with a furrowed brow. I notice then that he begins rubbing the golden symbol of the Prophet pinned to the peaked lapel of his jacket.

Now I know what really gets your goat, you son of a bitch.

"Let's continue discussing your sisters… and without any more blasphemous nonsense, if you would," he says.

"Well, in my mind they were fascinating. Not least of all because they were one of the last set of twins born naturally and conceived via physical intimacy."

"You mean fornication?!" he asks, nearly coughing.

"They say those were the good old days."

"When was the last time that you saw either of them?" he asks.

"After less than a year in Triangle, my memory of Goldie and Red stops at that time… and I was left with just a sense of—"

"Wait. What exactly do the colors signify?" he asks.

"Mara was golden. Meg'n was red. You know, as in the color of their hair?"

"Right, of course. As you say, then. Yes, those details have not been recorded," he says, tapping on the ledger. "So, your sisters deserted you then?" he asks, smiling with a cocky pleasure.

"No. I was going to say my memory of them came to an abrupt end because they left Earth."

"Were they authorized to do so?" he asks.

"If you remember your lessons by rote, you'll recall the wars weren't ended by force of arms but because the Japanese discovered how to travel faster than light. All nations were united in celebration. One cause, one people. All that shit. There was no class system for that particular draft, and anyone and everyone that wanted to go was shipping off. Fuck knows we had enough ships left from the old wars."

"And how old were you then?" he asks.

"Eight or nine."

"This was the last time you saw your mother and sisters then?" he asks.

"Meg'n and Mara, yes. They never came back."

Corvus studies his ledger like a man who's frightfully bored, as if he already has intimate knowledge of these events.

Of course he knows, you idiot. It's right there in front of his face.

"Ah yes, the infamous disappearance of the *Bermuda* frigate. It was the thirteenth ship to depart, correct? Ironic, wouldn't you say?" he asks, the question dripping with sarcasm.

"Yes, it was odd. My mother decided to join up with SIM and she set about looking for the lost ship herself. I had turned a corner with my—"

"Record, what is SIM?" Corvus interrupts.

The ledger beeps twice and, to my surprise, replies audibly. "Space Interferometry Mission. Disbanded in the year 2010, rearmed again in the year 2039."

Wouldja look at that. The damn thing speaks.

"Record, what was its significance?" Corvus asks.

Corvus begins swilling his drink and exhales so heavily afterward that I catch not-so-subtle hints of the drink's finish on the air. It's almost leathery to the nose.

"SIM's discovery of the bending of matter to move objects from one point to another via fusion-based energy was groundbreaking in its simplicity. If the desired destination was known and subsequently charted through declination and/or by right ascension, non-linear but segmented fluctuation dispersal was then made possible…"

Corvus finishes the drink and looks about the room as if looking for someone to serve him another one.

"… and thus, a nucleo-core-powered means of transport was the next logical step in the evolution of flight craft—"

Corvus stops the recording with a clumsy tap of his finger and delivers a false apology for interrupting me.

"I never could quite wrap my head around that myself. I was always more of a soldier," I add.

I lie in order to reassure him. His apparent lack of basic flight knowledge makes it clear to me—Corvus never studied intergalactic travel.

"And I a facilitator," he says. "Let's get on with it already. Now, back to your mother. She then left you behind, correct?"

"Yes. She said she'd never forgive herself if Meg'n and Mara were lost and if she didn't at least try to find them. I mean, the scary thing was that no one really knew what'n the hell was out there."

"And that was the last you saw of her?" he asks.

"She assured me I'd be kept safe in her absence. Right before she boarded the transport, she kissed me on the forehead, and I waved goodbye to her. When she was just out of view, a man I'd never met took me by the hand."

"And who was this man?" he asks.

"My grandpa. I spent the next nine years living with him."

"The prisoner refers to the traitor named Nathaniel C. Manning," Corvus says.

"He was no *traitor*. He left the service of war when it was still voluntary. And no one ever called him Nathaniel."

"Why is that?" Corvus asks.

"How do you even know his name? He never joined the Registry, not even when it was compulsory."

Corvus smiles and peruses the screen of the ledger for a moment. "The file we have on him is also relatively incomplete. What else do you know about this Jake Manning?"

The prick knows his *real* name.

"What do you want to know?" I ask, going against my instinct and better judgment.

"Where he was born, his documented personal traits, *et cetera*," he says.

"He was born sometime in the late 1970s, somewhere in the state of Tennessee. Or what used to be Tennessee."

"Within the former United States?" he asks.

"Yes. He fought in the wars, too, briefly. He seemed… grief-stricken through all the years I knew him."

"And it was this turncoat that prompted you to enter the Academy?" he asks.

"I certainly wouldn't have learned the skills I needed to gain entry without him."

"Such as?" he asks, raising his eyebrows.

"How to load and fire a weapon. How to throw a knife."

"And when was it you last saw him?"

"When I graduated the Academy—2066."

"Hmm, yes," Corvus adds, rubbing his chin as the light from the ledger illuminates his pale face. "Describe that encounter, prisoner."

"We didn't part on the best of terms. I was full of indignation after graduating, and I got even angrier when I caught him imbibing alcohol in the middle of—"

"Alcohol? Where did he get it? Did he make it?" he asks.

"I don't know. He'd never done it before, and I had never before seen him act so strange. Naturally, I wanted to know what was wrong, but he just went into a nutty tirade about a man named Simpson. Someone he must have known decades earlier."

"Simpson who?" Corvus asks.

"I don't know. He just called him Simpson. Evidently this guy sold his soul for an inexpensive bit of… pastry or something. Grandpa laughed and laughed about it."

"Pagan *lunacy*!" Corvus retorts, the contempt in his voice cutting through the air like a hot blade.

"Maybe so," I say. "When grandpa finally stopped laughing, he just looked at me as if he was waiting for something. He'd been crying, too. The tears had run down into the lines of his face. He… umm… He just stood up, walked away, and said, *At least Simpson got something for it. God left us the future.*"

"What did he mean by that? Did he call God by any other name?" he asks.

"He never said another word, and I never said goodbye. I'm glad he didn't live to see the part I was going to play in man's glorious future."

Corvus sneers at me, and I feel the sudden and overwhelming urge not to indulge him any longer.

"You know, Corvus, maybe I'm not Kilraven, after all. Everything I've said, you know, this knowledge could've easily been implanted during transference. You just might have the wrong guy… again," I say, smiling in the most annoying way possible.

Corvus turns off the recorder and taps the ledger twice. The door behind me opens with a subtle click, and two sentries enter and take their places behind me—one to the left and one to the right. The movements Corvus made with his fingers and the sound alone leads me to believe that the door and the sentries respond to whatever he's last keyed into the ledger.

I've got to get my hands on that ledger.

"Three days," he says, holding up three fingers.

"You're running out of *time*, Barrabas," he says, waving his hand to dismiss me. "Get him out of here," he adds just as something sharp and hot pierces the skin below my jawline.

CHAPTER 6

JUST WHAT THE DOCTORS ORDERED

"HOLD HIM, WOULD you?!"

I'm shocked back into sobriety by a searing pain in my left and right forearm. I try to recoil, but I'm held down firmly by something. Whatever the hell it is, it won't let me go, and I can't break free from it.

Blinding lights overhead shield the identities of the dark figures standing over me. There're two of them. The demons. Each one takes turns driving something sharp into my inner thigh. Blood spurts. Flesh is seared. They're branding me.

I howl in resistance, but my cry is inept, and I am physically powerless. I gasp for relief and everything shrinks. The darkness closes in around me like the narrowing of pupils, and I feel as if I'm sinking into a thick sea of pitch black.

I suck in a quick breath through my nose, and suddenly I'm no longer drowning but standing upon a pillar of rock, looking out upon a great expanse. Behind me there's a mounting wave. I don't see it, but I can hear its roar, and the damp air is heavy with the smell and salty spray of seawater.

Out of nowhere my wife appears in front of me. She's reaching out toward me with her arms outstretched, her fingers straining as they grasp for mine. Then I hear a *voice*. It's a strange voice, almost inhuman, calling out from the depths raging behind me.

"Barrabas! Can you hear me, Barrabas?"

I turn toward the voice and I see no wave, only a tiny light at the end of an immense living darkness.

"I can't… I can't hear anything," I reply.

"You answered the question, which means you most certainly can hear," the voice says.

"I… I can talk again?"

"Yes. Congratulations," the voice says.

"The ephedrine and steroid cocktail, would you?" the voice asks, and I feel a burning sensation in the side of my neck.

I turn back toward my wife, and she shrinks away from me as though she were a mist being collected into a bottle.

"Now hand me those dressing forceps, if you would," the voice says.

"Your work is *unrivaled*, Doctor. This is quite an achievement!" says a weaselly voice in response.

Something slaps me across the face, hard.

"Now, wake *up*!" the voice orders.

I open my eyes and find myself strapped to a gurney.

Oh, dammit all. It's Doctor Hecht and that son of a bitch assistant of his, Rathbone. Hecht grins from ear to ear and removes a pair of bloodied gloves, the rubber snapping dryly as it pulls away from the ends of his fingertips.

"Rathbone? Would you be so inclined as to sort out the patient's nose, please?"

"Yes, Doctor!" Rathbone exclaims, leaping toward me and placing the palm of one hand over my forehead and grabbing my nose with the other.

Before I can get a word in edgewise, Rathbone pulls my nose hard to the right with a feral but scientific *yank*. There's a crunching that's not only audible, but it causes an involuntary shudder throughout my entire body. The pain's so intense that I instinctively cry out, but there's nothing to hear, only an impotent squeak at the back of my throat.

"I'm surprised the bridge held," asserts Dr. Hecht, leering over me with analytical joy.

"You... You bastards! Broke my nose?!"

"Of course we didn't, you imbecile. It was already broken. We *corrected* it," Dr. Hecht proclaims.

Rathbone giggles at the doctor's comment and rotates the gurney forward, setting me and it into an upright position. To my left, Dr. Hecht sifts through several stacked drawers that make up a large stainless-steel cabinet on wheels.

"Hmm. We seem to be *out*," he says, slamming shut the bottom drawer.

"Rathbone, do me a favor, would you?"

"Yes, Doctor?"

"Be a dear and retrieve a new supply of sodium thiopental from Chief Rullerig," Dr. Hecht says, placing both hands on his hips. "We don't want our patient being anything less than *garrulous* for his next interrogation."

"Yes, Doctor, right away!" Rathbone exclaims like a giddy schoolboy before he exits the room.

Dr. Hecht draws his face close to my own and mutters something indecipherable before retrieving a brand-new pair of unsoiled gloves.

"I regret I had to wake you so, but you seemed to be in a dream from which you didn't wish to wake, perhaps," he says, putting on the gloves.

Then Hecht mumbles to himself while intently studying my injuries for a minute or so.

"Damn these eyes!" he exclaims, stepping back over toward the surgical cabinet. "My vision just isn't what it used to be. Even for all its majesty, transference can't fix the immaculate wonder that is our eyes," he says, retrieving a magnification glass from a metal tray on the top of the cabinet.

When he returns, he holds the glass up to my face and carefully examines my chin, throat, and ears.

"Funny, isn't it?" he asks. "We can fix the housing of the soul, but not its windows. Unless of course someone with perfect visual acuity is willing to switch with you... hmm... and I am old school. I much prefer to stay with my *own* body, don't you?"

I fake a cough and set my sobering mind to the task of formulating a way of getting out of here before these two turn me into one of their permanent lab rats.

"Mmm. Yes. You've taken several *brutish* beatings of late. But it's procedure that we restore you to maximum health prior to your execution," he says, smiling.

Then, to my complete amazement, the doctor loosens the bonds holding my right wrist firmly to the gurney.

"And I think we can fix these skinned knuckles rather easily," he says, turning my hand over several times, examining it gently. "I must apologize for the extravasation of your arm," he adds, pressing his thumbs into various areas of my forearm. "My impetuous colleague tends to be a little *zealous* with these sorts of extracurricular procedures, and Mr. Brenner required blood and tissue samples for his reportings."

"Brenner?" I ask, pretending as though I'm still waking.

"Does this hurt?" the doctor asks, pressing his index finger into my forearm more firmly.

Without thinking, I overact the part, wincing in return for the most minute discomfort.

"Yes. Mmm. Well, we don't want tissue necrosis now, do we?" he asks, turning back toward the gleaming stash of sharp surgical tools on top of the drawer. "We'll just have to use the femoral arteries."

"Why... Why are you doing this?" I ask.

"The wardens and Mr. Brenner have tasked me with making sure that men like you appreciate every single *nuance* of discomfort in the days and hours leading up to your last moments with us."

Hecht puts down the magnifying glass on the drawer and then returns with a large pair of scissors and begins cutting away at my pants just above the knee.

"I've always found it ironic that those such as you choose to fight. You refused the Church's offer back on Earth, and yet, here you are, *working* for the Church," he says, removing my pants leg and rolling it up nearly to my crotch. "None of you seem to grasp that your resistance is utterly infantile. The entire purpose of what we are—"

The doctor stops mid-sentence, pausing for a moment to go down on one knee and examine the mark on my inner right thigh.

"Well, well, what have we here?" he asks, pinching his chin and reaching once again for the magnifying glass. "Isn't that odd? Now *why* on Eridania would you have the symbol of the Prophet on your adductor longus? And why—why is it upside down?" he asks, standing up straight.

Dr. Hecht's eyes meet mine, and half a second goes by. His look switches from one of mild confusion to sudden clarity. I've no idea why he loosened the restraint on my arm. Some reservoir of strength kicks in, and I grab him by the throat so hard he drops the magnification glass and nearly bites off the tip of his tongue.

"You know what I did to Warden Baxter, don't you?"

Hecht nods. Then, gasping for breath, he begs in short, raspy syllables for me not to kill him. While he clutches at my wrist, I ask myself why I'm doing this.

I have to know. I have to know what happened to my wife.

"Untie my left hand or I'll crush your windpipe right now."

Hecht fumbles and shakes so fiercely that the buckle of the restraint clangs noisily against the side of the metal gurney as he loosens it. When my left hand becomes free, Rathbone walks back into the room and drops a large supply of syringes, his open mouth chattering in disbelief.

I grab Hecht's right arm and spin him around so quick that I damn near break it. I manage to put him in a chokehold before Rathbone can do anything other than blink.

"You! You let him go!" Rathbone exclaims.

"I'll kill him if you don't get over here and untie my feet," I say.

"You wouldn't *dare!*" Rathbone shrieks, the sweat on his brow glistening.

I squeeze Hecht harder at the back of his neck, and the sides and top of his nearly bald head turn a bright shade of purple. Then he pisses himself.

I pissed myself once before, too. My cousin woke me in the night by placing the cold barrel of a pistol against my left eyeball as I slept. I didn't even realize I'd urinated until he was laughing and pointing at the wet spot around me. And he never let me forget it.

"He'll be suffocating next, Rathbone. Better get a move on."

Dr. Hecht manages to gurgle and sputter out Rathbone's name as his gloved hands feebly claw at my forearms. Rathbone quickly obliges his superior and sets to unbuckling the belts holding my legs to the gurney. I glance around the room, hoping for another weapon besides trying to hang on to seventy-five kilos of mad doctor.

To my right I notice two rather large black canisters standing in the corner—one labeled *sevoflurane* and the other *nitrous oxide*. Set conveniently in between the two is a three-foot-long heavy-duty pipe wrench, gleaming red, like the sword in the anvil.

Rathbone frees my legs and then steps back a few paces, his hands raised as if I were holding him at gunpoint.

"Now let the doctor go!" he says, his voice quivering.

"Throw me those keys hanging off your belt first," I say, nodding in Rathbone's direction.

He does as I ask without resistance and slides the ring of keys across the smooth floor toward my feet.

"Does he have any keys?" I ask, shaking Dr. Hecht, his arms dangling and flopping from side to side.

"The doctor entrusts them to *me* and only me! Now let him *go!*" Rathbone says.

I squeeze Hecht for a few seconds more, and he goes as limp as a wet dishrag. Then I fling his body into Rathbone's open arms, and stooping, I grab the keys in one swift motion. As I quickly make a move for the pipe wrench sitting near the gas containers, I see Rathbone cradling Dr. Hecht out of the corner of my eye.

"By the Prophet, you've *killed* him!" he cries.

"Check his pulse, idiot. I thought you were a doctor," I say, hefting the wrench from the ground.

"There's a guard right outside the main entry, waiting for us to bring you out! You'll *never* get away with this!" Rathbone screams through his tears.

"Wrong again, bonehead."

Raising the wrench above my head, I use its leverage to break off the withdrawal valve from the top of each canister. Odorless gas starts filling the room, and I make for the doorway with the wrench and Rathbone's keys in tow.

"What are you *doing?!*" Rathbone shouts, pulling a white handkerchief out of his coat pocket and covering Hecht's mouth with it instead of his own.

"Jumpin' jack flash, Rathbone," I say as I step out of the room and slam the door shut behind me.

The look on Rathbone's face at the last is one of complete bemusement. I heard it in a song once. I don't even know why I said it—it was just the first thing that came to mind.

Rathbone watches with mouth agape as I lock him inside the ward, and the last thing I see through the ballistic glass window is Dr. Hecht sitting up and coughing violently. I figure they'll live. There's not enough in those small canisters to kill them. And it'll be a half a day or more before anyone finds them since the only people that get sent to this area of the medical wing are death-rowers.

I walk the fifteen-meter-long section of the main medical ward toward the doorway leading back to the mine. There are five or six other miners joining me in here, also strapped to gurneys. I contemplate setting them free. In my hesitation, I see a sentry waiting for me through the plate glass window of the entry door, just as Rathbone said.

I approach the door without drawing a breath and clamp the hook jaw of the pipe wrench closed before tightening the nut. I hate to play baseball with this guy's noggin, but sometimes you have to do what you have to do. After crouching against the door for a moment, I rise slowly to get a look out the small window in the center. The only thing I see is the back of the sentry's head. I put my back to the wall, and the door to my left, and then tap on the glass. The sentry reacts and does exactly what he's supposed to.

The door opens, and as soon as he steps inside, I thrust the pipe wrench forward and tag him directly on the temple. He crashes to the ground like a ton of bricks. For a split second I feel badly for hitting him so damn hard. Then I get over it and search him for anything useful. He doesn't even have a plasma mace on him, the fool. Then I see it—his left hand. His *gloved* left hand to be exact.

"My favorite six-fingered sentry."

I finish searching Mister Six Fingers, and rolling him over, I find a fun-gun strapped between his shoulder blades.

Nobody in his right mind would keep a gun holstered there, let alone draw that way. Then again, this fellow probably isn't used to having his back to anyone. Even more bizarre is the fact that I've never seen a gun in the mines before. Some of the women working the kitchens have supposedly seen the wardens hoarding them, but that's never been officially confirmed since anyone who claims to have seen a gun has mysteriously died afterward.

A few meters in front of me there's a woman I vaguely recognize, strapped into a restraint chair. I didn't even notice her before. Her eyes are watching every move I make, and she's drooling into her lap. I tell myself that I can't help her.

Think of your wife, idiot, and keep moving.

Above the woman's head I see a clock on the wall and note the time. At this very moment, everyone'll be locked into their respective areas, hard at work while the wardens inspect our cellblocks for contraband. I look back at the woman and the thought occurs to me that she might also be someone's wife.

If you leave her here, you'll always wonder.

I move closer, and she starts to shake in the chair, making more noise than a bag chock-full of tin cans. On the mobile operating table next to her sits a tray with dozens of razor-sharp surgical tools. I grab the largest scalpel off the tray and place it in her hand. That's more than enough for her to get free with. She calms instantly and looks up at me sad but thankful, her smile full of missing teeth. Then she lets go of the scalpel and it clatters as it strikes the floor. She groans and convulses a few times before lapsing back into a lethargic state. I tell her that I'm sorry.

There's only one thing left for me to do—head for the gyratorium and hope that Iyov is there. My hand goes to the Six-Fingered Man's weapon. It's been a while since I held a gun of any kind, but I remember to check the gun's charge level on the butt of the handle.

Damn.

Only two shots left at the most. And if I run into Ubasti, I'm gonna need both of them. Back at the main entry door I take a preemptive look out the window. I don't see a single soul, but it's a long way—the crusher is a little less than half a klick from here.

Man up, Kilraven. There's no other course now.

With a deep breath I stuff the fun-gun into my waistband. Then I'm out the door, running as fast as a man can when bare-footed and carrying a cast-iron wrench weighing twenty pounds.

I can't let any of the miners lay hands on me, especially not Verdauga's men. I have an instinct rising in the pit of my stomach, a feeling, really, and one that I've had all along telling me Verdauga's the one behind the spreading report of my identity. He is a dangerous man—more or less the opposite of Iyov, if I had to put it simply. They are rivals of a sort. So Verdauga is also my enemy, if only by association.

This design was not of Verdauga's making, though. The event that drove a wedge between him and Iyov is still a tall tale, even to me, and what came after it was just the natural order of things, I guess. I've lost many a companion here over this nasty business, and Verdauga's surly myriad are already dangerous enough, least of all because they have chosen their side so staunchly.

For the last twenty-odd years, the mines have basically been split into two factions. There are those who believe Iyov is in the right, desiring to maintain peace against our captors and spread the truth in love to disavow the deeds of the Church back on Earth. Then there are those who side with Verdauga—and he is a man who seemingly only wants to rule this place as his own and set up a new sort of... *society*. It never ceases to surprise me that when men are left to their own devices, in captivity, they seek to set up a dictatorship rather than find freedom in the ways that still remain open to them.

The whole bloody mess reminds me of this graphic book I read once when I was very young. My cousin had secured it for me from Chemical Alley in the great city. That area was famous for its relics from the 1980s, all behind the counter, of course, and never openly for sale. Anyway, the book had a sort of circus freak type of rogue who dressed as a clown. He was a real jokester of the oddest sort, and his arch-nemesis was even weirder— a guy that dressed up as a bat. They hated each other—and needed one another. It was the strangest dichotomy, but I reckon you could describe Verdauga and Iyov's relationship exactly like that—a twisted brand of an off-kilter love. It needs hate by definition, doesn't it?

I stop in the active workings just outside my own cellblock. The sounds of hammers and tumbling rocks tell me the miners are hard at work in the shafts below, and the rising steam is a perfect cloak for my presence. If the clock on the wall in the medical ward was correct, there should be a handful of wardens inside right about now, inspecting our cells.

Stepping smoothly over the bridge to the block door, my eye catches the blinking of the security pad. The display, a flashing green ring of light with a green checkmark at its center, indicates the entire block is secured. Leaning against the door, I release the safety on the fun-gun, slide back the skeletonized hammer, and wait for it to charge. It vibrates in my hand slightly and the inner workings whirl like a top when it's ready to go.

I check the rear once more, looking through the wafting pillars of steam for signs of anyone following me. Turning back toward, the cell door, I approach with caution and slide the cover plate open as slowly as possible. Inside, and to my complete chagrin, I count more than a dozen wardens—nearly one-fourth of the total of them from my block. They're taking turns looking through my belongings, which can only mean one thing—they *know*.

Damn you, Corvus.

I don't waste another second. I'm back over the small bridge toward the security pad and hefting the wrench over my head before I even know if this is going to work. The wrench comes down, and the force of the strike rips the security pad clean off its steel post. It falls silently down into the mineshaft below.

Heads up, boys.

No sooner do I get back to the cell door to see how our wardens are faring than the internal block alarm goes off.

Damn. Should've known that would happen.

But it still buys me time. No one'll hear it unless they're right outside the block, and all the other wardens are either sleeping or making rounds in the kitchen right now.

Precious seconds tick by. I nearly make it the rest of the way to the crusher without incident. I hide behind some barricading near one of the bleeder entries about seven meters away from the door, and two wardens walking the beat cruise right past me. It dawns on me that I'll never get inside without some form of ID from one of them. The two wardens, one male and one female, part like a narrow sea, and I can't *believe* my luck. It's Ubasti.

I wait a minute or so for the woman to clear my line of sight and watch as Ubasti stands there cracking his neck. I silently emerge from my hiding place and the trusty wrench—which I decide in the moment to name *Excalibur*—slows me down so that I have to pace the final five meters to Ubasti.

I tap the butt of the fun-gun against my tailbone to charge it, but when I pull back the hammer, Ubasti hears it and turns around, growling and drooling like a wild animal. He cracks me good in the left shoulder with one of his watermelon-sized meat-hooks, and I both drop to my knees and lose my grip on the pipe wrench.

"Well looky what the kitty cat dragged up for us today! How in the bleedin' hell did your ass get out and about?" he asks, pounding his right fist into the palm of his left hand.

Then Ubasti picks up *Excalibur* and flings it over my head so that it's well out of reach. A wise decision on his part. It rattles as it knocks into the rock wall somewhere behind me.

"You aren't worthy... Aren't... supposed to be able to lift that," I say, still catching my breath.

"What you on about, dearie? Where's your pants gone to, eh? You get *bum*-rushed again?"

I look up and Ubasti's licking his teeth with the end of his tongue, the tip of it split down the center just like that of a snake. Then he spits a wad of brownish-violet phlegm into the dirt next to me.

"You missed my foot, for once," I say, rising up to one knee.

"Always a funny one," Ubasti responds, laughing and cracking his knuckles.

Before I can stand, he punches me in the chest full-on, and I find myself once again bowing in front of him, struggling to breathe. Ubasti removes the plasma mace at his hip and ignites it. The purple light illuminates his oily, soiled face as he raises it above his head to bring it down on mine.

It's moments like the next one that feel as though Father Time himself has chosen to intervene, and everything stops. I sense the fun-gun wedged between the top of my buttocks and my waistband, and I draw without err and ram the tip of the gun directly into Ubasti's rib cage. The look on his face makes the events of today and whatever is due to come entirely worth it. The giant drops his mace and sets to flopping around in the dirt like a fish out of water.

I go back for *Excalibur*, thanking the six-fingered man under my breath for his unintentional contribution to my cause. Coming back to Ubasti, I lay the pipe wrench on his chest, then drag him by his feet toward the gyratorium door.

When I reach the security panel, I place his brawny wet hand on the entry pad, and the mill's lock clacks noisily. The door plods open, and as I pull the still-twitching warden's body, inside I see Cunningham, Tarsil, and Iyov watching me—frozen in utter amazement.

"One warden down. Two hundred and fifty more to go. Give or take a few."

CHAPTER 7

CORVUS

THE WARDENS HAVE relocated me to better quarters on campus, in a manner of speaking. I am not far from the chief's own lodging, which I have visited once. I found it curiously decadent for a man whose elementary nature I have come to understand quite well. By elementary I mean just that—his responses are often that of a minor, and thus he's quite predictable in a certain sense.

This new room, however, is also somewhat abysmal—though slightly less dank—still dark and gray. It would be little more than an oversized cubicle of deafening silence were it not for the low hum of the white-hot generator by the entryway. It's an archaic way in which to power a cabin, really, but I have to make do.

At least *this* room has a dressing table, and a surprisingly charming one at that. It's made from some kind of bird's eye maple, or perhaps walnut, neither of which I have seen in what feels like a lifetime. The chief must have had it brought here. How the man afforded it is beyond me; it must be a relic of the prewar era. A rather costly *antique*, as some would say.

Looking at the ornate handiwork of the piece and admiring the crafts-manship that went into carving the legwork alone, it reminds me that even the men of the Old World were once capable of creating beauty. There's a tingle in my fingertips as they respond to the stimulating coolness of the genuine brass handles, and I cannot ignore the fact that I miss the Earth.

I close my eyes and pretend that I can smell ozone or the fragrance that only hangs in the air after a heavy spring rain. Homesickness is something of a companion of mine and something I have had to get quite used to over the last few years especially. Ultimately, I have turned this flaw into one of my strong suits, though—if I were incapable of fending off my emotions about such things, I do not suppose I would be where I am today.

The moment of rumination passes when I sit up and put my bare feet on the warm, polished floor. After I straggle out of the new cot, which I fashioned from some heavy-duty insulation blankets, I rub my face and temples for a minute or so to alleviate the sluggishness from my catnap. I have been justifiably on guard of late, and as a consequence I have not been sleeping well at all during the night. My thoughts concerning this would-be Kilraven have kept me deeply troubled.

Nevertheless, I do believe I know just the cure for what ails me on this fine day—a good shave. Before I left Earth, I managed to acquire a new shaving kit with a German-made straight razor. They're hard to come by these days. Anything German-made has an automatic exorbitant price tag attached, unfortunately. However, as with most things, you get what you pay for. And I have been aching to use it.

I drag my feet for more than a bit as I step toward the dressing table, and I take my time filling the shiny chrome washbasin with hot water. This planet has one thing going for it at least—an abundance of fresh water on account of its solid ice core. The unusual amount of naturally occurring isotropic aquifers in the mines alone is astounding. The life-giving water alone makes it seem as though the planet were fated for an operation such as this, and not least of all for human civilization.

Taking a look in the mirror, I ask myself for the hundredth time whether or not one ever gets used to the gravity on this dreadful orb. It has caused dark circles to form under my eyes, and though they look downright shocking, I am still loath to admit it. Then I recall that I have some tea bags stashed in my medicine case, which I can use later to remedy the twofold problem.

I enjoy a brief moment of secret pleasure in knowing they were pilfered from the chief's own stock. The very moment that I reach for my shaving brush, the room gets nominally brighter. My COM tablet goes through the usual series of repetitive pings and beeps in its demand for my attention. Then I hear it.

"*Corvus? Make yourself known.*"

The timing is impeccable, to be quite frank. Talking to *him* makes me nervous, and a shave always calms me down. The perfect combination for a moment such as this. If there's anything he abhors, being unassertive and unprepared at the same time are at the top of the list.

"I am here," I respond confidently.

"*You are late, and His Lordship requests another progress report, Corvus.*"

"Of course he does. Just one more moment," I say, grabbing my soap brush.

It seems that lady luck herself is shining down upon me today. *He* is only listening once again, though this does trouble me. It's quite an odd thing for him to do.

He hasn't spoken to me since I started interrogating Barrabas, and his silence worries me, for it often says more than his words do. This time it's not Lord Alpha speaking. Perhaps he's been dismissed. Good riddance either way.

I quickly play advisor and tell myself to relax, and I set to doing so by working up a nice lather in the soap bowl. The bowl I have at home is an enchanting porcelain variety, but this particular one I brought for just this occasion. It's special to me not least of all because it's made from rimu, a wood that can no longer be found growing on Earth, but because it was a gift from a great man I once knew.

I look at the bowl now and think it's a pity that such a mighty tree now exists only in this form—and such a small reminder of home. I suppose one gains pockets of strength from such things when facing times of duress.

"*With haste, please,*" says the voice.

"Yes, my apologies for the delay. I am ready for a full statement, my liege."

"Are all things proceeding with due caution and discreetness then?" the voice asks of me.

"Everything is as it should be. The two prisoners I interrogated earlier this week, the same who blasphemed His Grace, were taken over twenty kilometers out and executed via live burial in a place the wardens referred to as the Kasmodian Desert. Chief Rullerig himself saw fit to see that particular brutality right through to the end."

The billowing steam from the warm water fogs up the mirror, and I wipe it away with my hand. I brush the side of my face with my palm. The coarse hair of the face should be softened up before one puts a blade to it. I nearly laugh, recalling how it took me several painful shaves to figure that little trick out.

"The Kasmodian Desert is Chief Rullerig's priority, not yours, Corvus. Additionally, your assessment of the aforementioned execution reeks of disapproval. His Lordship asks that you clarify your wording so that the report may reflect a more accurate depiction of the event," the voice says.

I must choose my next words carefully. I cannot linger. To hesitate any further might ruin me.

"Yes, that would indeed be favorable, my lord. The execution was... a *venerable* ending for two men who were lawbreakers their entire lives. Their final moments, however slow and drawn out they might've been, were *befitting* for men who would dare speak their minds against the Church, and its lord, with words of such heinous and hateful slander," I add.

"We hear you, Corvus. Excellent work. The record will reflect only your correction. Now then, we must move on to the more important matter of the prisoner claiming to be Kilraven," says the voice.

"Yes... ahh... Barrabas has given me little else than what is already known. This has happened before. The purge of the mine, enacted by my predecessor over ten years ago, produced two other Kilravens, if my memory of the report on this matter is correct," I say.

Looking again at the mirror, I spot a gray hair protruding directly from where my hairline meets the top of my forehead. My insides quaver for the briefest moment, and then I'm angered and surprised that I had not noticed it before. It's several inches long, which clearly means it's been there for quite some time.

"That was then, and this is now, Corvus. His Lordship is only concerned with the happenings of today," says the voice.

"Uh, yes, well… the prisoner's details in our meetings, especially the one earlier this morning, have been quite extensive. But we… We seem to have the bulk of that on file already."

"Have you been recording your interrogations per protocol as His Lordship has requested of you?"

"Yes, of course. All of this data should be scanning back to the Church. I have also sent blood and tissue for analysis. Has His Grace not seen them yet?" I ask.

Studying my own visage, I imagine that I'd give a professional barber a run for his credits as I carefully apply the coconut-scented lather to the sides of my face, chin, and neck. I stop at the mustache. My mustache is, well… Quite frankly, it's my one small vanity. I can afford it.

Honestly, I could never even grow one before this time in my life, and I like to give it more particular care and attention when I'm finished with the rest of my face. I wonder, do other men feel the same swelling pride when it comes to the bristles of their own labium superius oris?

"Corvus, His Eminence informed me that the earlier request was a precautionary measure. His desire was to keep this particular matter more discreet than the standard interrogations… and so the footage has not been seen by anyone, as of yet," the voice says.

"Oh?" I ask, unable to conceal my curiosity. "Well… yes of course, my lord. In that case, I must say at this juncture I am fairly certain Barrabas is not who he claims to be. His thoughts and recollections are, so far, ones of textbook memory. The wardens have nearly beaten him beyond recognition and he has been able to only minimally resist the thiopental injections. Were he really Kilraven, I think he would have given up in the face of these measures."

I pick up the ebony-handled razor and begin shaving my neck. What a superbly edifying and lost art this is. No one ever takes the time to *enjoy* it anymore. I vaguely remember watching my father do it when I was young, though he never taught me how. I seem to recall he had a rather high level of disdain for the task.

"His Lordship hears you."

I finish shaving one side of my neck and wipe it clean with a fresh washcloth.

"*His Excellency iterates that he did not ask for your opinion and that it is neither warranted nor necessary,*" the voice says.

"My apologies," I add swiftly.

I dip the razor into the chrome basin and watch as the shavings' excess float up and onto the surface of the frothy water. *It's very important to keep your blade clean*, I can hear my father saying.

"*However, His Lordship would like to hear your thoughts on another matter. He asks whether or not you believe that you are still fit for the task or whether a replacement is necessary?*" the voice asks.

In that very instant the thought crosses my mind that perhaps Lord Alpha is already on his way here. That perhaps this is a trick question and that maybe this is why I am not speaking to Alpha now.

Then I'm seemingly struck by some hidden force I cannot explain, or perhaps merely taken aback, because I immediately let go of the razor. It clangs boisterously as it hits the bottom of the washbasin, and I fumble for a moment in an effort to retrieve it. I do not wish to lose sight of my goal, or theirs, and the last thing I need is for His Lordship to think I'm not giving him my full attention.

"That will not be necessary. I—"

I nearly maintain certainty, and then I swallow so hard I have no doubt that it is audible on the other end of the COM.

"*Are you sure of yourself in this, Corvus?*"

"With all due respect," I say, "I am more than capable of handling this matter, my lord. And need I add that my record of service to the Council has been spotless?"

The voice on the other side does not reply. I pause for the length of a heartbeat and the pounding in my sternum urges me to save this situation right now.

"If perchance this prisoner does become more suspect, and if I believe the man is any danger to our operations, your faith in my abilities is the last thing you need question, my lord."

"*His Grace hears you,*" says the voice.

I plunge my hand into the murky water of the basin to collect the razor.

"His Eminence concurs and wishes you faith unshaken."

"I… I thank you, my lord. Faith unshaken to you also," I say humbly, realizing my hand is still submerged in the warm water.

"Please be ready to report again with little to zero notice within the next six to twelve hours."

"That soon? Well… yes, yes of course."

My tablet pings once, and the bluish light from the screen grows gradually faint. I'm alone again, with only the generator hum and the gaze of my horizontally reversed doppelganger looking back at me.

"Damn!"

I found the razor.

I pull my hand from the water, and the lacerated tip of my middle finger begins to gush. I grab a nearby washcloth and wrap it tightly around the wound. I curse myself again for being careless as I watch a creeping blot of crimson tarnish the rather lovely white of the towel.

The blood evokes another time in my life full of skinned knees, broken lips, and milk teeth hanging on for dear life. As I begin to ponder these things, my mind moves toward that which may come to light in my next round of questioning with Barrabas.

"Brenner!"

"It's Corvus," I reply, turning my glance toward the shrieking voice coming from the external COM near my door.

"Brenner?!" the voice shouts again.

"Can I get absolutely no peace by night or day?" I ask aloud.

Without any haste whatsoever, I walk over to the door and press my thumb to the reply nodule. The display appears at the touch of my finger, revealing the chief operator bouncing up and down on his heels just outside the door.

Ugh. What a chore this one is. And a *bore*.

"Yes?" I ask.

"It's Rullerig."

"I can see that. What do you want?" I ask, adding an ever so slight dose of contempt.

"We needa talk, chum," he says.

"Not now, Rullerig. Come back later this afternoon, after my interrogations, if you please."

"Listen here, you lil' *peon*. I'm the rooster in this here henhouse, eh?
Now open this goddamn door, or I'll open it for you!" Rullerig shouts,
causing the communicator to howl with feedback.

I buzz Rullerig in, and he snarls like a wild boar as he crosses the
threshold. The only thing I can imagine that could be harder than dealing
with this fellow would be attempting to teach the pig to sing.

"In case you forgot, this here is my operation Mista Brenner!" he
barks, jabbing me repeatedly in the shoulder with his middle finger.

"It's Corvus. And please, do *not* touch me again. You're sweating."

"Eh? What's that?" Rullerig teases, wiping his forehead and blocking
my path.

"The *name*, Rullerig. My name is Corvus."

If I had my way, I would prefer to always be at least a few feet away
from this disgusting lout, so I walk around the chief and retake my stance
at the dressing table in order to resume my shave.

"My surname is Brenner. Mister Brenner was my father," I add.
"Now, if you don't mind, Rullerig, I was in the middle of a shave prior to
your intrusion."

"Oh, well that's just so thrilling to hear, Brenner, that my balls
are tinglin'!"

In the mirror, I note that Rullerig is smiling, reveling in what he thinks
passes for wit.

"Something I can help you with, Rullerig?"

"Matter of fact, yeah. Somethin' *is* goin' on. One of my wardens
mentioned bringin' Barrabas to the medical ward for his mendin'. Then
he was supposed to take his bearded ass and a backfiller named Tarsil
to the crushin' room. I did this, you know, just in case you were to
come a'knockin' and needin' to chat with him later in the day, as you've
been doin'—"

"And *why* does this information bring you to my quarters now?" I ask.

"Because it's good for morale, which is why I would never put the two
of them troublemakers together. Least of all in the crushin' room!" he says.

"Rullerig, please don't take this as insolence, but I have a sneaking suspicion that this planet is going to lapse into a new ice age before you get to the point," I say, finally finishing my shave.

"Alright, *Buttons*, here it is: we can track everyone here at any time throughout ninety-nine percent o' this entire facility. One of the rooms that *ain't* in that one percent, chum, is the crusher," Rullerig says.

"And you're telling me you put Barrabas into *that* room?" I ask, looking at Rullerig behind me in the mirror.

"He was *supposed* to be there," he says.

"And you felt it wise to just *now* bring this to my attention?!" I shout, turning to face Rullerig.

"Well, s'hardly ever an issue! But the atmospheric conditions mess with our tracin' system, since the crushin' room is so near the surface an' all. I usually put the womenfolk in there so the boys can have a bit of fun with 'em. But I hadn't had anyone in the trackin' room for a few days since you executed the last one for stealin' rations... and seein' as how you been gettin' cozy with Barrabas and all, I just figured—"

I retreat into my imagination at this point and play out the most splendid, yet sordid, of daydreams. I'm sitting on top of Rullerig, strangling him with my bare hands. He's squealing like a stuck swine, begging me for mercy. I call him *Rullerpig*, and he beseeches me to spare his pitiful existence. I don't let go until his eyeballs burst from his skull.

Then, sadly, I snap back to reality.

"You had one of the fucking *prisoners* running the damned tracking room for the entire mine?!" I shout, shoving Rullerig out of my way and grabbing my shoes and coat.

"Well, not anymore! I put one of them female wardens in there... Works out jus' fine, but that ain't the half of it. I passed the medical ward and I found your man missin'!"

"What do you mean *missing*?" I ask.

"Goneburger! And the fella you brought with them six fingers is out for the count, too!"

"Barrabas is *missing*?!" I ask.

"Well, not exactly. So, I look inside, and I sees your sentry sprawled out an' spread-eagle on the floor. I had to unlock the door to get in, and I find your security tail's plum out of it. Sportin' a giant lump on his head.

And then I hear a bangin' at the back and find the docs was locked up, too! One of them doctors was laughin' so much I could barely understand him! I made out the important stuff... Barrabas got loose!" Rullerig says, scratching his head.

"I told you to keep your eyes on him, damn you! Don't you have procedures for eventualities like this?!" I holler, slipping into my favorite pair of shoes.

"Well, we do and we don't. No one's tried anything like this in over half a decade. Ever since *you* showed up it's been nuthin' but trouble around here!"

"The Church and His Lordship are going to hear about this, Rullerig!" I shout while pointing a finger fiercely at him.

Rullerig almost gasps and put his hands up in front of me in a plea for clemency. "Nah, nah, nah, Corvus! You gotta help me contain this!"

"I will do nothing of the sort. My assignment here does not include aiding you in your job, Chief."

"Oh, okay. I see. So, you wanna play it *solo*, eh?"

"Where is Barrabas now?"

"He has to be in the mine somewheres. We can't track him, though, and the warden who usually watches him has gone off as well... Ubasti, I think he is," he says.

"You moron! Don't you get it? You just said yourself that the crusher is the *one* place you cannot monitor! I think it's clear where Barrabas has gone," I shout, buttoning my shirt cuffs.

Rullerig stands there blathering on for another thirty seconds, making some kind of an attempt to give validity to the senselessness behind his actions. I can't even make out the words because my heartbeat is thumping in my ears so loudly that nothing else in the room is getting through.

When I finish dressing, I adjust my tie as I step directly in front of him. I catch the tail end of whatever it was that he was trying to express using that limited vocabulary of his, which I've no doubt hasn't improved since he was an infant. He's staring at me with a look of such profound stupidity that I nearly strike him across the face with the back of my hand out of pure spite.

"Rullerig, the situation at hand has suddenly become quite clear to me. What's happened is that the lackadaisical attention you give to even the most *minimal* tasks in your job description has prevailed here. Have you ever heard the story of John the Forerunner?"

"John the *who*? What's that got to do with anythin'?" he asks.

"He too brought news of great importance, and they served his fucking head on a platter."

"Wha—? Now wait just a sec, chum! Are you *threatening* me, you lil' shit?!" Rullerig says, his voice elevating.

"It's not a threat. You and I both know I'd be doing you a favor if I just killed you right now," I say, gritting my teeth and pointing my still-bloody finger in Rullerig's fat face. "You had better *pray* that I uncover the truth of all this and that His Lordship does not need to learn of your severe oversight," I add, pinning the symbol of our prophet onto my jacket so that Rullerig has little choice but to take notice.

I half expect Rullerig to knuckle-dust me after that outburst, but he only stands there, frozen, with his mouth ajar. I would laugh if I thought it wouldn't make him think I was actually joking about what I've just said. As I burn a hole directly through his forehead with my stare, every bit of pink that's in his jowls retreats to the floor.

"I can't trust you to do this yourself, Rullerig, so I'm going to accompany you. I expect you to take Barrabas without incident and get him into the interrogation room within the next half hour, or I swear by the Prophet, it will be the last mistake you ever make, *chum*!"

CHAPTER 8

CELLMATE SCHEMES

UBASTI'S SWEATY, STINKING, elephantine frame convulses in a plasma mace–induced seizure at my feet.

"What were you thinking?!" Cunningham asks with eyes wide, staring at me with an intense sort of shock. "And what'n the hell happened to your pants?"

"Long story, Magpie," I reply.

Iyov searches the pockets of Ubasti's vest and trousers, his dust-caked fingers groping for anything of value.

"Ubasti, you magnificent idioso!" Iyov proclaims, removing a small plastic bottle of toothpicks from the warden's side pocket. "Put a few of these in the right man's hands and he could kill you with them."

Some of the wardens have become lazy and accustomed to the ease of the job since, after all, there's no getting off this planet. But this thought concerning the wardens plays to my position in the Church's game. If Corvus wants me, he's got me right where he wanted me.

"I can get some composite rope if needs be, 'cause that isn't gonna hold him very long," Cunningham says, wiping her hands on the front of her pants.

Tarsil and Iyov each grab one of Ubasti's wrists and drag him over to the crusher. Tarsil hastily removes his boots while Cunningham binds the warden's sweaty hands to the side of the crusher's gearbox using his own bootlaces. She ties a knot that would put any of my own to shame.

Cunningham turns and stares me down with the same disapproving look on her face that my wife once gave oh so well. I frown at the uncertainty of the memory, and though the gesture is not meant for Cunningham, she believes it's aimed at her. So, I let her let me have it.

"Well goddammit, Barrabas, say *something*! Are you trying to get us all killed or what?!" she says, pushing me in the shoulder.

"C'mon, darlin', *easy* on the man," Tarsil says, trying to placate her.

"Don't gimme that!" she shouts. "Shit's bad enough with everyone on edge! Verdauga's men are doin' all they can to find this guy that the Church wants so damn bad, and the—"

Cunningham stops mid-sentence, looking almost astonished, and turns her gaze to Iyov. She *knows*.

There's the slightest clearing of his throat, and Iyov affirms her inclination with a subtle nod.

"You're kidding me?!" she asks, looking back at me suspiciously. "I *knew* there was somethin'."

"Knew what?" Tarsil asks obliviously.

"I always knew," she says, her brow furrowed. "I'll be damned to the depths if you don't always have some kinda shit cloud hanging over you."

A dubious sort of amazement fills her face before she speaks again.

"Who *are* you?" she asks slowly and gravely.

"Something tells me you already know the answer," I say.

"Who?!" she says, shoving me in the chest with both hands.

"An innocent man," I reply quietly.

"Ha! Just like the rest of us!" Tarsil says, laughing so heartily it echoes and bounces around us like a wall of sound.

Cunningham takes a deep breath and looks up toward the sky peeking through the turbine ventilator above our heads. The corner of her cheek bulges and she rolls her tongue around inside her mouth before finally looking back at me. When our eyes meet, there's a slight and slow nodding—the smallest gesture of trust. I close my eyes and roll up what's left of my pant leg to reveal the Prophet's mark on my inner thigh.

"By the elements!" she says, almost inaudibly, her right hand trembling in front of her mouth. "It's you?"

"Yes," I say. "I am Kilraven."

Tarsil nearly chokes on his own tongue and takes a few steps back, putting his hands on his knees and leaning forward with his back against the rock wall.

"Well, holy fuck me sideways!" he says, coughing amidst a hysterical but nearly silent fit of laughter.

Cunningham slowly paces toward me, her eyes aflame with a dangerous sort of ambiguity.

"You are a selfish, no-good son of a bitch, you know that?" she says, stopping two feet in front of me with her hands propped on her hips. Then, looking at my leg for a half-second, she throws her arms around my waist and squeezes me tightly.

"I can't believe it. Kilraven the Cursed, right here in our company all this time!" she whispers. Then, looking up at me slowly, she says, "You know what this means, don't you? You're our ticket off this rock! You're our ticket back *home!*"

"That's a lie. I'm nobody's ticket anywhere."

"Iyov says the story is a lie," she says, her hazel eyes flitting from left to right, groping the features of my face.

"Yes. And if you believe Iyov, then believe me now," I say, looking at her and then to Tarsil. "The Church wants to control the entire world. They deceived everyone… made them think they discovered transference. A holy power, given to them by divine right. They killed my crew members, took my wife from me, and sent me here so that I could rot… with zero hope of ever telling anyone on Earth what we really saw and what we found."

"I don't get it. Why? Why would they go to all that trouble? Why wouldn't the Prophet just kill you?" Tarsil asks.

"I've asked myself that for thirty fuckin' years. The Prophet made a merciful mistake when he left me alive. Maybe the only mercy he ever had in him. But now, I'm his one loose end, and he seeks to tie it up," I say.

"Put it in layman's terms for the blondes in the room," Cunningham says, nodding toward Tarsil.

"Because I'm the only one left to tell the *real* story, I'd imagine."

"It can't just be that simple," she says. "There's gotta be something *more* you're not telling us."

"Clearly, it isn't simple," Iyov says. "But the only choice now set before our friend is this—to get back to Earth and to find out what *more* there is to tell."

From the look on her face, I expect Cunningham to punch me in the jaw with one of her famous right hooks at any second. But what she does next is something that surprises me altogether.

Holding up three fingers, she spits in the dirt and tells me she can have her entire cellblock ready to fight in *tres minutos*. Then the curly-haired goddess pulls Ubasti's mace from my belt. Turning, she holds the handle of it out for Tarsil to accept.

"Are you in, you green-eyed pansy?" she asks. "'Cause you're pretty good in a fight from what I remember."

"A fight? With what? Pots and pans?" Tarsil asks, gazing at Iyov. "C'mon, old man. Tell 'em this is ridiculous!"

"Ridiculous is wakin' up every damn day knowing you'll spend the rest of your life here. Knowing that you'll never see the yellow sun again. Hell, even shitbox there believes in what he fights for, so why shouldn't we?" she says, tears in her eyes and pointing at Ubasti.

Life here is harder on the women. Damn hard. Every couple of months when the Church sends us another morose mob of new arrivals to add to the population, they bolster the food supply as well. The "sustenance pack-ages"—as they call them when they arrive by hundreds of crateloads—are pretty grim. Well, unless you count the pickings the wardens get to enjoy.

The dross is divided up and rationed by the women put to work in the cookery. They are left responsible, and held thus, for the exact amount of food that everyone gets. You can imagine how some of the miners treat the women because of this, forgetting the fact that the provisions are not actually supplied by them.

There are roughly eight or nine women for every one hundred men, I wager. Most of the women are still kept on Earth by the Church for good reason—some more obvious than others. But the main one is that it makes selling their product easier by having a smiling female face behind the counter.

Now I was never sexist, but I look at it this way—the average man that goes into a shop, he's almost always there to buy something. There's no browsing or perusing the stock—he knows what he's there for, and he's likely going to buy it. The bonus is just having someone nice to look at it while he does it, because it makes the affirming process of buying more pleasurable. Evidently in this the Church agrees with me because the flip-side of that is also true—women *tend* to trust women. So, I suppose it works both ways, really. Unless you're like Tarsil, and you're a man that likes men, then my whole theory is shot to hell.

From all the reports I've heard, the Church keeps the women who deny their first transference trial as employees for a minimum of five years. They serve the Church for that time in various occupations before being re-offered two choices: transference or coming to the mines. By then most of them have children because the standard pre-birth waiting period is over, and if they don't, it's the fear of indentured servitude that's enough to force their hand. The rest, as they say, is history.

"We're gonna need more than the one mace you've got there," Tarsil says, turning to Cunningham. "Have your gals managed to smuggle anything lately?" he asks with a gentle mocking in his tone.

"I think Clayton and Yockney have been stashin' back a little nest egg of plasma maces not far from the loading pocket," Cunningham says. "You know, over on the north end? They could only have four or five of them, at most. Pretty sure they don't even glow anymore."

Cunningham bites the corner of her lip and glances around at the rest of us.

"But if they do, we could uhh… We could maybe take out all the wardens within three or four blocks," she says, frowning with uncertainty, knowing that it's not enough.

"I'd rather take out a few of the willing with my own mace," Tarsil adds, grabbing his crotch.

Tarsil winks at me, and his lewd comment is followed accordingly by a round of silence from the lot of us. When I can't fight smiling any longer, Cunningham does what I should have and punches him firmly in the shoulder.

"Ugh, you are *such* a man!" she says.

"Save your strength," Iyov quietly interjects.

The old man begins pacing the floor with his hands raised, and I could swear I see the slightest look of amusement on his face.

"Save all of it," he adds, eyeing each of us in turn.

The moment is all too brief, and he's soon wringing his hands together, bringing the seriousness of the situation back into focus. Other than to make sure he's not carrying a shiv, I don't make a habit of studying another man's hands too often, but I comb across Iyov's mitts for the first time in a long time. They resemble something *tired...* something worn, like leather, stretched over the bone.

I think about how perhaps there was a day long ago when they weren't like that. I wonder if maybe he had a family, though he says he can't remember that now. Maybe his hands held his children or his lover. Or maybe he was an artist or an orator. Maybe he was no one at all.

"What do you think, Barrabas?" Iyov asks, turning to me.

"About?" I ask.

"The *guns*, my friend," he says.

"Hmm. I just don't know," I reply, shaking my head. "We can't really trust in hearsay now. But I too heard once that there are guns here, on the other side of the conveyors, the east pocket, opposite from the chief's quarters where the—"

"You mean the *fault* zone? Are you fuckin' kidding?" Tarsil says while scratching his jaw in disbelief.

"Yeah, I know. Getting across that and back wouldn't be a problem for *one* person. But you couldn't carry more than two or three guns without being noticed, if you were to even get one, and that'd slow you down big time," I add.

"And what if the guns don't even work?" Tarsil asks. "When's the last time any of you remember someone getting blasted? I sure as hell don't!"

The look in his eyes is full of genuine fear and doubt. No one responds. There's not even a wisecrack from Tarsil.

I study my league of companions, one by one, and I can almost see their thoughts. I watch them succumb to the seeming hopelessness of the situation. The dismay in the room becomes palpable, like an insidious entity, whispering both skepticism and false hope in our ears. And because of it we laugh sadistically at ourselves on the inside.

Suddenly, Ubasti groans and snores in his unconscious state, startling us and gaining our now undivided attention.

"Oh no you don't!" Tarsil says, sparking the plasma mace and tapping Ubasti on the wrist with it.

The warden flops about for a few seconds and recommences drooling on himself.

"Look, Corvus is going to come for me at some point," I say. "And I'm gonna be forced into telling him everything else that he wants to know. The only reason I've said what I have already is because they've threatened your lives. The longer I keep him occupied, the more time you'll have to make a move."

"Yeah, but you've still got, what, two days left? There's *time*," Tarsil adds.

"Not after what I did to him," I say, pointing at Ubasti. "And the mad doctors."

"Oh shit! Not the deranged duo?" Tarsil asks.

"Yep. Both of them."

"What happened? Did they cut into you?" Tarsil replies, his voice wavering.

"They tried to get me to talk… in their own way," I say, tugging at what's left of my tattered pant leg. "Still, I left them alive. They're locked in the medical ward, and I sealed a dozen or more wardens in my cellblock, too."

"He's right. Docs'll just pump him full of truth juice or something," Cunningham says, nodding at me and kicking the dirt.

"Truth juice?" Tarsil asks.

"It's some sorta reagent, you know, like a serum they shoot you with to get you to say what they want. They do it to the kitchen girls all the time. Probably been using it on you already, Barrabas," she says.

"They have. I just didn't realize it at first," I add.

"Dammit," Tarsil says.

"And why the hell does this Corvus guy have it in for you?" Cunningham asks.

"He wants me dead, for his own financial gain, maybe. He won't stop until he gets exactly what he wants, but I haven't given it to him… not yet. It's clear now that he's come here specifically for me, and I don't believe he plans on leaving *without* me. Whether he wants to take me back alive is the only thing that remains to be seen."

"So, all those damn stories are true, then?" Tarsil asks, taking slow steps toward me and sizing my entire frame up and down. "The Prophet betrayed the man, sent him here, and all for what?" he asks, turning to Iyov.

"The whole tale is a really long one to tell," I say. "But yes, he sent me here, and I've never fully understood the reason for it. I've told you all everything I know."

Cunningham scratches the top of her head and looks at Iyov with a sigh. She's waiting for a sign. Some kind of direction. Anything.

"There is a traitor here in the mine," I add. "I know because Corvus named each of you. Your *real* names. Only the Prophet's ilk would take note of whom I've become close to. Only a spy would have access to that kind of information. Whoever it is, they're working directly for him."

"And why in seven hells would the Prophet do that?" Tarsil asks.

"So that he can pull your plug back on Earth, maybe? You'd all die, which is no skin off his back. But I'd be left here, alone. Maybe he thinks I'd finally come forward then in an effort to face him, having nothing else left to lose," I say.

"That's some heavy shit," Tarsil says, nodding his head toward the floor and shuffling his feet. "You know what I think? I've got an inkling to say, uh, don'tcha think all that warrants a heavy response?"

Then Tarsil moves so quickly that all of us jump back a step. "Pow, pow, pow!" he shouts, grinning and holding each hand pointed toward me as if he's aiming two pistols. "Well, ya'll wanna see the end of this shitshow or not? We need firepower, Magpie!" he says, spinning around to face her. "And, darlin', I need to feel a real gun in my hand one more time before I kick the cluck bucket."

"Who said anything about *dyin'*?" Cunningham asks.

"We should not dawdle any longer," Iyov says quietly.

"Alright… you're all men," Cunningham says, "which means you couldn't formulate a working plan to save all our skins even if it sat right on your faces. So, if we are gonna go for the guns, I think Sam could do it. She's the smallest of us. Not but five feet tall, if that. She can jump like a bullfrog and climb like a ring-tailed lemur."

"But can she leave her post without getting noticed? And do you *trust* her?" I ask.

"She's a runner in the kitchens. If she's not doing that, she's cleaning out the johnny lines. Wardens don't really keep tabs on anyone when they're covered in shit," Cunningham says.

Working the latrines is not an easy job, although I suppose breathing the stink of human waste all day isn't any more taxing than sucking in the ore dust. I shudder at the thought.

I've never understood the wardens' thought process behind this. I suppose it's a privacy issue, which they feel they can afford for the women, as if we're back on Earth still trying to maintain some civility and discretion. Still, this could work to our advantage.

"Oh, you know what?" Tarsil asks. "The wardens hardly ever check the women's shitters, right, darlin'? We could all rendezvous there!"

"Yeah, but there's a problem with that," I say. "Anything and anyone that goes in that room can be tracked. The girls would have to bring whatever they can scrounge back here to the crusher."

"And even if they did, where would the gals put the stuff?" Tarsil adds, probing the room with his arms akimbo.

"Blondie's got more than a good point," Cunningham says. "We can't very well have everyone attemptin' to make some kind of final stand in here."

"And I didn't wanna be the one to bring it up, but isn't anyone gonna mention the big pink elephant in the room?" Tarsil asks, his eyes widening.

"What's that?" I ask.

"If this whole thing is gonna go off rightly, you're gonna need Verdauga on your side. No *doubt* about that," Tarsil adds matter-of-factly.

"Nobody can ever say you're as dumb as you look, blondie," Cunningham says with a wink.

"Hmm. Yes. That's it, my friends," Iyov says, followed by a heavy sigh.

I had almost *forgotten* the old man was in the room.

"Tarsil is right. We can accomplish nothing of value by an impetus of arms," he adds.

"But all our asses will be one foot in the grave right from the start if we don't have any weapons!" Cunningham says.

"We are *all* dead here, Magpie. Yes, that much is certain," Iyov says plainly. "We've been dead since we crossed the parapet, my dear. But how and *when* we die is not yet certain," he adds, placing a hand on Cunningham's forearm.

"They're gonna kill Barrabas and they're gonna come for us, one by one," Tarsil says. "And stars willing, if any of us do still have loved ones left at home, they're gonna go after them before pullin' the plug on us. So, what'n the hell are we gonna do right now? What are *we* gonna do about it first?"

"That's right, boy. We strike first. Hold yourselves ever at the ready!" Iyov says shrewdly. "Because I don't know the moment when this stone will be set to rolling. It could be a day or even within this self-same hour!"

"Hey, now. Don't do anything *stupid*, old man!" Tarsil retorts, glancing at me with concern.

"I must speak with Verdauga, and I will do so urgently," Iyov says.

"Iyov... you *can't*. He'll kill you!" Cunningham says.

"Maybe. But he will *listen* to me first, especially if I put myself at his clemency. It may come down to fate now that I must lay down my life so soon in all of this," Iyov says, as if he's speaking to only himself. Then he points a finger at each of us in turn. "And I can almost guarantee that death is likely the outcome for all of us, whether in success or in failure."

"So, the odds are stacked against us. What hope have we got, even if we win?" Cunningham asks Iyov, then turns toward me.

"It's not for yourselves," Iyov says.

"And if Verdauga offs you and it's just the three of us? What success can we possibly have then, old man?" Tarsil asks.

"Success is to not waver, even in the moment you face your death," Iyov says quietly. "And when you die, you die knowing that a change may come from your sacrifice," he says, turning toward me, his voice rising. "For another, who may or may not put an end to this madness for us all."

Tarsil exhales deeply and looks at me, and then, turning his eye back upon Iyov, he shakes his head from side to side. He laughs, leaning up against the wall and folding his arms. "That doesn't sound like much of a plan. Maybe I'll just say a prayer or two and watch ya'll from the sidelines," he adds, continuing to laugh.

"Tarsil, if there's one thing I've learned in all my years of knocking on heaven's door, it's that all things are as they are meant to be. That includes *your* involvement here," Iyov says, followed by a coy smile.

Tarsil looks at me sidelong.

"So, what would Kilraven do?" he asks, raising his eyebrows.

"Look… I think it goes without saying, but I don't want any of you to come to harm over me. This isn't your war. But the old man is right. Either we die today, or we die tomorrow. If it's all the same to you, then *join* me. If we fight together, at least we have the smallest of chances. If we roll over now, we may fall forever."

"And on that note, I think I've lingered long enough," Iyov says. "But I will do what I must, and swiftly. Melissa, gather what weapons you can. Barrabas, I suggest you stay *here* until I return. I don't want to throw you into Verdauga's den just yet," he adds, climbing quickly to the top of the crusher.

"And what if you don't make it back?!" Tarsil asks, worriedly rubbing his forehead.

"What we do from here on out may very well govern the events of the future for all parties concerned. And remember what I said: hold yourselves at the ready!" Iyov whispers, and slipping silently into the shaft beneath the crusher, he disappears.

"Well, fuck! We haven't had this much excitement since they served pumpkin soup during the solstice!" Tarsil says, balling his hand into a fist and punching the inside of his palm.

Cunningham stands near the crusher, pursing her lips and watching Iyov as he descends farther into the darkness.

"I know he's a tricky old bastard, but is what we're doing worth the risk?" she asks.

Tarsil says nothing in reply and simply hangs his head.

"I believe in one thing. The Prophet wants me back on Earth, alive maybe. And if that holds true, and even if he kills me when I get there, my going back could still shake everything we know right to its very core."

Cunningham stands motionless, still watching me with uncertainty. I can only muster a nod to console her any further.

"The Prophet... you knew him? He really betrayed you?" she asks quietly.

"He betrayed everyone, Cunningham. And if he wants me, I can't stop him in that. The Prophet always gets what he wants. But I swear to you on my *life*, and my family name, that if I can find a way back, then I will try to find a way back for us all."

"Then let's get a fuckin' move-on already!" Tarsil says, handing the plasma mace back to Cunningham.

"And we do *exactly* what Iyov said," Cunningham says. "Ubasti's gonna come to any second now, and he ain't gonna be easy to restrain. I say one of you break a rock over his head now."

Cunningham climbs up into the operator chair and starts up the crushing machine with a few kicks on the gearbox pedal. After putting her goggles back on, she tries to light Ubasti's plasma mace and finds the charge has only a few cells left.

"Not much zap left on this," she says as the mace flickers faintly. "Ubasti's a third-place winner if I ever did see one. Can't even keep his mace lit up," she adds, tossing the mace toward Tarsil.

Tarsil laughs and picks up the mace, holding it with a baseball batter's stance. "I reckon I can still whack a few heads with it," he says, swinging the mace near Ubasti's head.

"Alright, boys, I got the crusher on auto. I think Barrabas and I should get word to the girls together," Cunningham says, nodding in my direction. "If we cross any of the wardens, I don't know if I can take them without you," she says, shaking her head from side to side.

"Okay, let's go then. We'll make for the kitchens. Tarsil, you stay here and watch Ubasti."

"Hey, the old man told you to stay *right* here, goddammit!"

"Look, Tarsil, we can't do this without Cunningham's girls. We'll come back with whatever we can, within the hour if we—"

I'm interrupted by a deep clang, then a heavy clicking of the mill lock as it's opened from the outside.

"Looks like we're fucked before we even had time to undress," Tarsil whispers.

The door opens behind us so fast that the three of us hardly have enough time to form a line against the crusher. Standing in the opening is Corvus, flanked by Rullerig and four of his hand-picked wardens. Looking much less pleased is the six-fingered sentry, standing at the back of the lot. All seven of them are each grasping firmly his own plasma mace, already ignited.

"You ladies got somethin' you wanna say to us?" Rullerig asks, stepping alone into the room and standing a few feet in front of me.

Tarsil gets between Rullerig and me and twists the handle on Ubasti's plasma mace. In another cruel twist, the mace only spits and sputters, its power extinguished.

"Damn that Ubasti," Tarsil says, tapping the tip of the mace against his boot. "Well, Chief, to answer yer question... we were... ahh... you know, just discussing the very best way to get our *rocks* off, weren't we?" he asks, pointing back to the crusher.

"Oh, this one got a smart mouth, huh, boys?" Rullerig says, looking back at Corvus and the sentries.

There's a flash of purple light as Rullerig's mace connects with Tarsil's chest. The concussive force knocks him backward. He collides with me, taking us both to the ground.

When I look up, one of Rullerig's sentries yanks an unconscious Tarsil from off of me and flings him aside. As I reach for my friend, I see two of the wardens subduing Cunningham by smashing her face against the side of the crusher.

Then someone steps on my arm at the elbow, pinning me to the ground. Rullerig holds his plasma mace directly in front of my nose, and out of the corner of my eye I see that it's Corvus who's actually standing on my arm.

"We have more to discuss, prisoner. Do we not?" he asks.

CHAPTER 9

REDISCOVERY

"I MUST SAY, you really had me going, *thief...*" Corvus says, breathing heavily.

The slick slimeball paces the floor in front of me, all the while nursing an injury on his hand. But he never takes his eyes off of me.

In the previous twenty minutes I've been kicked, maced, and given the distinct pleasure of watching my friends suffer at the hands of Rullerig and his favorite lackeys. They also didn't fail to stick me with two separate injections during my sojourn to the interrogation room. Along the way, Corvus hardly spoke. But he did make a point to tell me that the mad doctors would be most pleased to see me again later.

"Fucked me without a prophylactic again, didn't you, Corvus?"

"*You,*" he says, sighing. "You seem intent on making things harder for yourself and those that you would call your friends. Have you always been like this, prisoner? Forgetful of the fact that you are not your own? You are the sole *property* of this company!" he growls, standing next to me and driving his index finger into the table in front of us.

I hold myself solely responsible for what's happened. What was I thinking? Did I really believe that I was going to walk out of here? How could I believe the Prophet had any intention of paving the way for me? My thoughts go to Cunningham and Tarsil and what Ubasti might be doing to them in retaliation. I wonder if Iyov managed to get to Verdauga?

"Are you listening to me, Barrabas?!" Corvus shouts, slapping me across the face with an empty glove, his steely eyes burning a hole in my head.

"Yes," I say, "I'm listening. And I'll finish the story. Whatever you wanna hear. I don't want my friends to bear any injury because of me."

"Oh yes, you *will* tell me what I want to know, like it or not! There's enough serum in you to make even Old Scratch repent of his rebellion!"

Corvus sits down and turns on his ledger once more. "Get out!" he snaps, dismissing the sentries from the room.

When the door closes, Corvus crosses his legs, then leans back, staring at me with such an intensity that his closed lips purse repeatedly as his tongue wets the teeth behind them.

"You have little more than two days until this whole charade ends, and you've given me *nothing* of value. The chief, the wardens, and nearly every staff member here is ready to take you apart, piece by piece. I'm the only one standing in their way," Corvus says, placing his black gloves on the table.

"And what is it that you want for this grace?" I ask.

"I want to know the details surrounding your grandfather and the last time you saw him," he says, pounding his fist into the table, "and I want to know about *what* happened to you at the Academy. I want to know *how* you supposedly discovered transference on Fornax. And I want the *exact* details regarding your extrication here to Eridania," he adds, adjusting the Prophet's symbol affixed firmly to his jacket.

I study Corvus's hands as he twiddles the enameled pin between thumb and index finger—his face uncaring and callous. His pores are glistening strangely under the lights. He blinks repeatedly before clearing his throat and nervously smoothing his jacket, then rotating the Prophet's pin to an upright position last of all.

Now this is a *first*. The son of a bitch is actually *sweating*.

"Do not forget your friends, Barrabas," he adds. "I have no control over what Rullerig may do, and you will not get another chance with me, either. After this you will not see me again, though I may or may not participate as a spectator among those who'll witness you breathing your last," he says slowly, watching me with a strange look in his eyes.

The Church man just called checkmate. The great worm has me backed into a corner.

I want to scream as loud as I can and leap forward and drive my thumbs into his eye sockets. I want to stand before the creator of the universe and ask him to undo all of this unholy mess. I want to see the end of this godforsaken place… even the whole planet. For that level of intervention, I would gladly lose my life.

"Tick tock, tick tock. You are losing precious minutes, prisoner!"

I take a deep breath and feel the forceful euphoria of the truth serum Cunningham warned me about coursing through my veins. And I give in… I give in to Corvus, warmly, for what I hope is the final time.

"The time I spent at the Academy was the best time of my life. A friend introduced me to the girl who would later become my wife. She'd been third officer on one of the missions to Fornax—searching for the *Bermuda*. They had returned unsuccessful. When I found out that she had been on that flight, I purposed to get to know her and we… Well, we just connected instantly. I told her about my sisters. How they were lost. I'm sure for a time she only felt pity for me because, honestly, she was way out of my league."

"What was her name?" Corvus asks.

"Elisabeth Enjora."

"And you fell in love with her, yes?" he asks.

"Yes. I even loved her name. It reminded me of all the heroines I dreamed of, the ones in the books I read in my youth. Were it not for her, I wouldn't have ended up on the *Grimalkin*."

"And why is that?"

"My test scores were rubbish. I was always better with my hands. Real-world applications."

"But you mentioned in our last meeting that anyone could leave on the expeditions to Fornax. Are you certain your recollection is accurate?" he asks.

"Yes, anyone could go, provided they passed the mental and physical exams. But by the time the first ships were returning with their findings, the Council suddenly shifted their policies without warning. Only the Academy's seminary graduates were allowed the opportunity to travel outside the atmosphere."

"And how did you know this?"

"I had a friend named Jovian. He… He was the one who fed me information."

"Jovian was on the ship with you, then?" he asks.

"No, he was in the Academy before me."

"What was his station?" he asks.

"I think he was a chaplain then… maybe fifteen or twenty years older than me. I never really knew his exact age."

"So, you befriended him?"

"Not exactly. The reports coming back from the expeditions, among other news he'd heard, had frightened him."

"Why do you think he told you these things?" he asks.

"We had a lot in common. And I looked up to him. We were colleagues of a sort, I suppose," I say.

"You said he was a chaplain. On what ship?" he asks.

"He was on the *Grimalkin* during one of the earlier missions. I think he'd grown afraid of what they had seen out there, and when he returned home, he left the Academy altogether to join the Council."

"When was this?"

"Up until he had taken his vows," I say with a tightening in my throat I can't shake.

"You said he fed you information, prisoner. What *kind* of information?"

"He was uneasy about the growing power of the other Council members."

"So, he was not a prophet, was he?" he asks, raising one brow.

"I don't even know what that means. He was ordained, maybe… and he was close to one of the more respected dignitaries of the time."

"Did he give you a *name*?" he asks.

"No. But he did tell me at the rate things were going, the Council's fear in the face of uncertainty would give them over to holy influence. The Council would then be nothing more than powerless puppets and the voice of the people rendered insignificant. His words, not mine. I wanted no part in that, so I wasn't reticent about leaving Earth."

"And what else did he tell you?" Corvus asks, combing his mustache with his index finger.

"He said one of his brethren was excommunicated, and the very same man was killed under unlikely circumstances not long afterward. He said this man took part in a secret meeting, wherein some of the Council members discussed a discovery made by the crew of the *Bermuda*."

"The missing ship, you mean? And what were their findings?" he asks.

"An undiscovered planet. Not far from Fornax. It had an atmosphere a lot like Earth. They hadn't seen it before because it was hidden on the other side of a large asteroid belt."

"Keep going," he says, taking a deep breath and placing his hands firmly on the edge of his tablet.

"Jovian said there was unusual technology there, which the *Bermuda* had found after they landed. They wanted to bring it back to Earth."

"They found no life forms?" he asks.

"There were remnants of another civilization, but they hadn't found anything living yet. And I thought… I thought that maybe my sisters were there, so… I had my Academy tutor put in a good word for me. He was well respected, and he also—"

"Who was this person?"

"William Winborne."

"Record, is he documented?" Corvus asks, and the ledger beeps compliantly. He studies the ledger for a few moments, still playing with his mustache. "Yes, William Wilson Winborne has an extensive file. But… his name is unfamiliar to me at this—"

"Winborne was the best man at our marriage service," I say, purposely interrupting him.

Be careful, Kilraven.

I don't want Corvus knowing anything more about Winborne than necessary. He always wanted to move away from Neo York, farther west maybe, and nearer to the Great Dry Lakes. When we last spoke, he was beaming from ear to ear. He said he'd received correspondence from a family member living near Lake Mendota—and that he had every intention of seeking them out and leaving behind a life of service. He was a good friend, and even though we lost touch not long after that, my hope for him is that he's somewhere out there, having escaped from this hell.

"Ah, yes, your nuptials are fairly well documented. So, was it around this time that you left for Fornax?" Corvus asks.

"No. Winborne's letter wasn't enough to get me on the next boat," I say. "So, Elisabeth said we ought to get married, and that would ensure we'd stay together, since she was on the crew. The *Grimalkin* was set to leave in less than a week, so it worked out perfectly. We were married right on the ship, and Jovian stood by in witness. I had begged him after the ceremony to reenlist and come with us. But he wouldn't leave... and I didn't see him again, not until I returned from Fornax years later."

"That's very *moving*, I'm sure. What year was this, prisoner?"

"I came back in 2071."

Corvus taps on the ledger twice, glaring intently at the screen. "Are you sure about that year?"

"I think so... I was once sure. Maybe my mind is playing tricks on me."

"When did you get to Fornax?" he asks, following the question by chewing on the inside of his cheek.

"In 2069, I think."

"And what did you find there?"

"They were right," I say, surprised at the trembling in my own voice. "The *Bermuda* had found a people... a culture of some kind."

"They *had*?" Corvus asks, the light in his eyes growing.

"Well, there was no one there. There were no graves, no bodies, no... nothing. It was like waking up after an apocalypse and finding that you're the last man on Earth."

"Did you locate the *Bermuda* at that time?" Corvus asks.

"No. We never found it, though we knew they had been there. The closer we got to Fornax, we were able to more accurately pinpoint the origin of their last communication. When we landed on the planet, the source of the signal led us to a small city... almost like a fort. We found weapons in a multichambered synagogue at the center of the city, and we assumed they belonged to the *Bermuda* crew... until we looked more closely. The technology we found inside was so advanced. It was just as Jovian had told me."

"So, you brought your findings back to Earth?"

"Not immediately. The captain of the *Grimalkin* relayed our findings to the Council, and they conferred with the Church, and presumably Jovian, for several days. We were left hanging about, but we had no idea why."

"Prisoner, who served as the captain onboard?" he asks.

"Captain Burnham. Timothy, I believe."

"Yes. Hmm… it would seem Burnham was lost to us," Corvus says with a glance toward his ledger. "And did you find anything else on Fornax?"

"We did. While the Council deliberated, we passed the time studying the alien machinery and the tools we found. We noticed a pattern. Everything we found that was made by craft was powered by the same strange mineral. We couldn't identify it."

"Is that when the holy accident occurred?!" Corvus says, his voice rising to a controlled elation.

"Yes."

"Tell me!" he says in an anxious and almost greedy whisper.

"Some of the crew discovered these large capsules… pods of some kind, one linked to another. The tower in which they were found was lined with a strange metal. So were the pods, both inside and out. They were connected by a cord, like twins… and it had a gas or a liquid flowing through it. At first glance, it looked like advanced cryogenics or something. Analysts on the *Grimalkin* said it was from the same mineral that was in the lining of the pods and in the tower."

"And what did you do with the pods?"

"We did what anyone else would do: we followed orders. We loaded them onto the ship… and then… we got inside them."

"The first transference trials!" Corvus gasps, his excitement reaching a fevered pitch.

"Yes. Two young corporals. They were foolish. They defied direct orders from Captain Burnham and got inside the pods during the night. Once they closed, we couldn't get them open. We couldn't even hear the boys inside. And we didn't know if they were even trying to get out or not.

The process had started by then. All the workings of the machine were inside, and we—"

"Did you try to stop it?" Corvus asks.

"Of course. We later discovered the pods were designed that way purposely so that the process couldn't be interrupted. We almost blasted the connectors that linked them!" I say, laughing to myself.

"And? Why didn't you?"

"Well, we didn't wanna kill them."

"So, the pods succeeded in transferring them?" he asks.

"We didn't know what it was yet. Everything went dark, like a void. There was a massive energy surge, unlike anything I'd ever seen. The pods somehow drew from the energy of the *Grimalkin* itself, which we only figured out later because the nucleo-cores were depleted by over thirty percent. That was *huge*."

"And the two corporals?" he asks.

"Mishal's pod opened first, and he seemed fine… as if nothing happened. He asked us what had happened. Then he started looking at his hands and he went into a fit… laughing… crazy-like. We thought he was mad. He said *he* was Keeran. I can still recall the fear I felt in the moment I looked into his eyes."

"And Keeran?" Corvus asks.

"Same thing. He came out minutes later and took one look at Mishal and screamed at the top of his lungs… then he fell over, convulsing in a fit of shock."

"Did they die?"

"No. They were taken back to the medical deck, and after a few hours they finally settled down. Captain Burnham had them sedated pretty heavily, and naturally, we separated them. Burnham put me in charge of keeping Mishal in his room. Hours later when he woke up, the captain and the chief medical officer onboard questioned him again. Then they did the same with Keeran. Each one of them kept insisting that he was the other."

"Had the Council replied as of yet?" Corvus asks.

"No, and I broke post to tell the captain that Mishal was incapacitated for the time being. So, he sent another message to the Council, telling them about the pods we had found. He told them about Mishal and Keeran, too. The Council then ordered him to bring the ship home immediately with everything that we could fit onboard."

"So, you left? Just like that?" Corvus asks.

"Not exactly. As that transmission was going out, the same energy surge we had seen before happened again. We all guessed what it was. Mishal and Keeran had gotten back inside the pods."

"What did you do, prisoner?" he asks.

"We could only wait for them to open again… and they did. Mishal and Keeran both came out and they seemed totally normal. They were hugging one another like… children opening gifts or something. The medical team examined them both and found nothing wrong. They were themselves again."

"So that was all? The first transference trial was completed? Did the Council know of this before you left Fornax?" Corvus asks.

"The engine cores were so depleted we weren't sure if we'd make it home. The engineers ran diagnostics and said we'd arrive just shy of Earth. The Council told us that they'd have every available ship waiting for our return."

"So, you returned as heroes then?" Corvus asks, one eyebrow raised.

"I think you know what we returned to."

"I want to hear you *say* it," Corvus says, his piercing eyes cutting through me as if I were a cube of butter.

"We were taken by the *Saint George* when we returned. There must've been a dozen other frigates there ready to blow us to kingdom come if we hadn't surrendered. They took us captive, separated us, and questioned us each in turn, alone. There was a secret trial that I can hardly recall. After that, I never saw my wife again," I say.

"So then you were all brought back to Earth?" Corvus asks.

"I don't know. I definitely was… at least, for a time."

"And then you were sent away? Without explanation?"

"We had no idea that before we ever left Earth the lost ship had already made a discovery on this very planet or that the mineral found with the pods on Fornax was also here on Eridania—and in abundance. It was the lost *Bermuda*. They were the key. The key to finding everything," I say.

"And we know that all this was relayed back to the Council before you found what you did on Fornax, don't we? Because the Council were one step ahead of you, weren't they?" Corvus adds mockingly.

"Yes, they knew about the ore... that it was here via the *Bermuda*. They knew it was linked to Fornax once we found the pods and sent the data back. They knew the ore was the master key behind making the machines work. The Council used us, Corvus, and they're using you now."

Corvus shifts smoothly in his seat, folds his arms, and uncrosses his legs. "What makes you think I'm being used by anyone? I am my *own* being, and I make my own choices. I always have. No man steers my fate."

I laugh at him. It's the hardest I've laughed in a long time. The look on his face is a mix of both bewilderment and anger, and it makes all the time I've spent in his loathsome presence well worth it.

"I don't see what is so funny, Barrabas. You've given me exactly what I needed—the final piece of the puzzle, hidden deep inside your pathetic skull," he says.

"How do you reckon that, then?" I ask, still laughing.

"Because everyone who knew that the *Bermuda* had discovered the ore here on Eridania first is either dead, detained, or transferred into a permanent state of delirium. Everyone who knew precisely what happened on Fornax was executed by firing squad. Everyone but *you*," he says with the smile of a devil.

"And you, it seems," I retort, staring into his dark eyes.

"The Council will be expecting you to return with me shortly," he says, "and I swear to you now, you are going to be made to suffer like *no* man has suffered before," he adds, putting his gloves back on.

Alarms begin to blare. At that very instant, the door to the interrogation room opens, and from behind me I hear a familiar voice snarl.

"Time's up, *chum*!" he says.

It's Rullerig.

CHAPTER 10

ENEMY MINE

I AM THE sort of man who rarely, if ever, complains. I learned long ago that it gets one nowhere fast, though whether it's a trait carried over from my previous life is a mystery to me. So, to put it quite simply, I will just say life here has been rather difficult for me.

I have been in this mine since its inception. I suppose if circumstances were markedly different, I might be proud that I had a hand in its making. The men here often refer to me as the Mage.

Others call me Old Man Shadow, after an incident in which I managed to remain unseen while a warden attempted to deny my entire cellblock their daily water ration. Stepping from the darkness behind the warden, I rapped him across the back of the head with a jagged block of erdanium the size of a durian. Naturally, I fled the scene before any other wardens bore witness. The warden in question never again trifled with my cellmates, though he often glanced at me strangely, as if there was a shadow covering the memory of the event in his mind. None of the men in my cell went thirsty that week due to my furtiveness, and thus the name has followed me around like a domesticated animal.

Anyway, the titles themselves are more than a bit juvenile, I know, but there's something rather tender about them that I'm quite fond of. Hearing them spoken aloud prompts me to think on my forgotten youth when Iyov wasn't my name. Try as I might, I cannot remember what my real name is, of course. I owe that to transference.

And strange as though it may seem, I *do* remember before I came here that I was part of a convoy that set forth from Earth on a great expedition. At the time, I was working for credits, and I had a growing family I needed to support. I cannot now recall their faces, and even using all my strength, their very names are a blurry haze to me.

I think, perhaps, I must have done something illegal in my previous body. Accordingly, I am troubled by a seemingly deep-rooted doctrine that clearly was imprinted upon me—that I was not to take a wife or to father any children. Over the burdening years my heart and mind torture me daily for this, and I've damned my own name verbally even more often than that. It's the strangest feeling… knowing that you know something, but not to possess the means to pull it out from under the rug buried in a far corner at the back of your mind. It's as if a long net of misty white clouds hangs over the very memory of all those who I knew or ever loved.

My regret is further extended to the fact that I do remember the *feeling*. Revenants of that feeling not only scolded me for leaving Earth and my loved ones behind, if that's who they were, but also because it utterly broke my heart and theirs. But I had a streak in me that needed satiating. Most young men going through middle age do. I found part of what I was seeking in adventure and even more satisfaction in the possibility of *revelation*. Little did I know that what we would find in the depths of space was no more than a wolf dressed as the proverbial lamb.

On Earth, I like to think maybe I was a man of faith… but I cannot of course be sure of the possibility of *that* anymore, either. I've been in this body for so long I doubt nearly all things that my mind would conceive prior to my arrival, only making exception, naturally, for that which comes to me in the present. Was I ever even on Earth? Was I called Iyov there? Maybe I've been here all my life.

But no… *no*.

My mind clears once again and I think of Barrabas, my friend, and I remember who *he* was. I did not know him in the old days. But I know him now, and that is more than enough.

During my tenure in this consecrated colliery, the evocation of my aforementioned faith has awoken me many times in the night. There are moments in which the dreams are so real that, when I wake, I forget where I am entirely. And other times the darkness is so full of anxiety for me that I am told I call out names in my sleep, names upon waking that I do not recognize or do not stir the strings in my heart. I even repeat the name of the Prophet, and I ask him questions… ones that I do not wish to repeat.

If what I have heard is true, then the Prophet will have Barrabas hung on a pole for all to see. I have purposed in my heart to help the holy man see it through. I do not wish Barrabas dead, of course, but rather for his return to Earth in the vain but not certain hope that providence might aid him in setting things right.

But the lanky fellow… he vexes me. The man from the Church. He could be the hitch in that plan. I deem he will not return to Earth without the Prophet's treasure. My truest and only real hope is that Barrabas somehow can find a way back, and then and only then could it potentially put the final nail in the coffin of this cruel place. And I will do what I must in order to make sure no other man comes here.

I step across the gangway leading to the gathering conveyor and through the eastern haulageway. Verdauga and his crew will undoubtedly be near the shafts that lead to the transfer points. You see, they are responsible for much of the heavy lifting that goes on here in the mines. I had a hand in that play by currying favor with the wardens when I discovered the first of the cold-water aquifers. It's not far from where the chief operator's headquarters is now. Water is plentiful here, but it is still a precious necessity, and one that the wardens do not wish to share with—

"Who goes there?!" a voice booms from the darkness, interrupting my meditations.

"It is I, Iyov."

"Who? Iyov? What's *your* crusty ass doin' here?" retorts the rather uncouth voice from quite some distance behind me.

"I recognize your call, Daraemon. Have you forgotten mine?" I ask, placing my hands up in the air.

"That's right. Keep 'em up, old man. Didja think you could just waltz through here as ya please? Boss says you weren't ever suh'posed to come this way," he says, catching up to me.

"I've come to speak with him. It's important," I say as Daraemon steps in front of me, wielding a plasma mace.

"Where did you get that, Daraemon?"

"We've got our ways, and you got yours, Mage," he says, wiggling his face at me and igniting the mace.

"I thought it was customary or, rather, just good manners to greet an envoy who shows you no threat whatsoever with less impudence?" I ask.

"Wha—what's that even mean?" Daraemon says.

"Don't worry about it, son. Will you take me to Verdauga, or will I be forced to disarm you and drag you behind me the rest of the way?"

I rub my hands through my hair slowly, and Daraemon thinks about my offer for far longer than he should. I laugh at him, though I should know better. Then, as I lower my hands as a sign of surrender, the boy jumps back as though he were a frightened cat.

"Don't you move!" he shouts.

"Daraemon, if I don't move we'll be forced to stand here, and I can't very well talk to Verdauga from here, can I?"

"Alright, alright, stop confusin' me! Just *shut* your mouth already! You stay in front of me with your hands behind your head, and I'll take you to him," he says.

I do as Daraemon asks, and as he circles around me, the pinkish glow of the mace feels warm against my skin. While Daraemon shuffles behind me I hear the mace power down, and he digs the end of it into the center of my back.

We walk onward in silence, and I see dozens of Verdauga's men lining the haulageway. Some of them are beam-building, and some are pillar-robbing. None of them resting. It's a model of efficiency, really. They all stop what they're doing briefly to watch me and my escort, and I cannot help but imagine why they haven't begun throwing rocks at me.

During my last visit here, I was jeered at, like an entertainer who's just lost control over the crowd. Verbally mocked, bloodied, and bruised so badly that my eardrums ruptured. That was many years ago now and I've yet to return until this moment. Maybe they've forgotten me.

"Go on! Get back to it!" Daraemon shouts at the workers. "If the wardens come through here and ain't happy, then Verdauga won't be happy, neither!"

Then it all becomes clear to me—the rumor of Kilraven has reached them. They are *afraid*.

And as well they should be, for Verdauga has no qualms about taking a man's life, especially not one so desired by the Church. The men that come up for execution will not even dare to cross him, though they have only days to live. I'd say that level of fear outrivals just about anything I've seen in the past, even beyond the level of respect the chief operator ought to command. But Rullerig has grown fat. Slothful. He would rather stuff his face and do whatever it is that he does all day than bother getting involved in our petty class war.

In this moment, I should be worried for myself. But a cool tranquility I've not felt for quite some time settles over me. It's likely that Verdauga will have me stoned after I've said what I plan to. I've been dreading it for years, and the words are sticking in my throat even now.

But I must put aside that fear for a greater good. I must put aside all fear in this moment, for deep down I know how to get through to Verdauga. His weakness, if you can call it one, is that he will not abandon those that look up to him. He is a leader through and through, though the years have diminished his stature. Much like me, he is now more or less a shadow of what he once was.

Daraemon leads me across a narrow bridge over a row of shortwalls. Below us, the clinking and tinking of hammers working the rock echoes along the cavernous facade. One gets a sense of drudgery here. In some ways it's a mirror of a kind of feudal system. Verdauga has men in place that serve him, and those men in turn have men underneath them, men that are charged with the lesser tasks of daily activity. Any man who does not do as he's told usually finds himself falling down one of the mine shafts. Some of them, it is said, have no bottom. My stomach jumps up and greets my Adam's apple at the thought. Very shortly I may be finding out firsthand whether those tales are true.

I look up ahead, and at the end of the bridge before me is the competent rock. It is a place deep in the mine that is capable of actually supporting its own aperture without any further structure. It's a marvel to behold, really. The ceiling within forms a kind of pointed dome, and thus there is no fear of having it fall on you—that is, as long as the entire mine doesn't collapse due to some greater external force. This particular area has also been hailed as a place of providence or a sort of symbol of power due to its natural formations, which resemble what I can only describe as a throne room. And this can only mean that Verdauga is there.

"C'mon then," Daraemon says, prodding me into the opening.

Coming inside, I see the room is filled with a soft reddish light from a cache of veiled lanterns bolted into the rock overhead. The odor of ore is not wholly missing but has gone curiously light, though the air is still and stale. There are half a dozen men in the room who have their hands upon hilts of handmade weapons slung at their sides. All eyes are upon me dubiously, and the only thing I hear is the sound of my own feet crunching into the dirt.

My eyes set themselves forward, and I see Verdauga himself is seated on a smooth, flat rock that almost resembles a bit of slickenside. His seat, which stands roughly a meter above the floor, is formed also from the natural rock but has been fashioned to resemble a great chair.

"Well, well!" Verdauga bellows. "If it isn't the minister of the mine and the righter of wrongs, Old Man Shadow himself!" He laughs, and his men laugh with him.

"Hello, Verdauga. It's been a long time," I add, half-bowing.

"I almost didn't recognize you..." Verdauga says, wiping his mouth with a spotted bandana tied around his neck that appears to be covered in blood. "If not for that silvery mane of yours."

"Have you fallen ill?" I ask.

Verdauga ignores my question and gestures to the man immediately to his right. "Shall I have one of my men shave it for you?" he asks, clearing his throat.

From behind me his men laugh again and I hear the edges of knives coming together.

"No, don't sharpen your blades, boys! This merry-andrew can get a hack job with the dullest shank you can find!" Verdauga howls.

The men cackle at me once again.

"You're right. The years have not been kind to me, have they, friend?" I ask, praying in my vanity that he doesn't remove the one physical sign of wisdom I have remaining.

"Friend? *Friend*?!" Verdauga shouts, clambering up from his seat for a brief moment. "We have not spoken in years, and even before that we did not call one another friend, *friend*!"

"I see you have a makeshift throne, of sorts. Is there a valid reason you have put yourself up on so high a pedestal, Verdauga?"

"The rock's less friable here," Verdauga says, no longer laughing. "Comfortable enough to sit on, and as you can see, it's about the only place fit for a king. Am I right, boys?"

His followers laugh generously and, funnily enough, in unison.

"You are *no* king, Verdauga. If there was ever royal blood in your veins, I think fate would have led you down quite a different road," I say.

"And you! What are *you*, Iyov?!" Verdauga shouts down at me, while purple spittle runs from the sides of his mouth. "You're no man of the cloth!"

"Perhaps not. But our fate has come upon us, and serving a purpose greater than myself, I come bearing this terrible purpose to you," I say.

Verdauga narrows his eyes, and rubbing the sides of his face, he then brings his hands together, interlocking the fingers slowly.

"Well then, let's hear it, yes?" Verdauga asks mockingly. "And after we've all heard your bullshit, you can tell us what gave you the *nerve* to think I wouldn't rid myself of your presence entirely simply for coming here."

"If I'm not mistaken, there are events that have been set in motion which cannot be stopped. And if there is a faithful god, it will be the undoing of this place," I say.

"A faithful *god*?" Verdauga repeats, licking his lips.

"Yes, Verdauga. *If.*"

"Well… what say you to Iyov's words of wisdom, eh?" Verdauga asks, surveying the room and his men. "Anyone?"

No one replies, and Verdauga grips the rock resting underneath his hands.

"If, you say, eh?" he asks, followed by a single short chortle. "It seems brother Iyov here is shaken in his beliefs! What say we test him further, boys?" he asks, clapping his hands, and everyone in the room howls on command like a pack of rabid hyenas.

"Do what you want to me, Verdauga. I meant it when I told you this is bigger than what has happened here. And it's greater than what's passed between us. Your pride *and* mine will be brought to naught either way," I say.

"Your pride? So, you stand there knowing full well that you may not walk out of here alive?" Verdauga asks.

"Yes, I am prepared for that."

"Really? And why should I allow you martyrdom?" he asks, one eyebrow raised and half-grinning.

"Because whether you kill me or not, even *you* do not want to see another soul sent to this place." I swallow hard, and the sound of my beating heart is like rolling drums in my ears. "You... don't want to see another father lose his son."

Several of the men behind me gasp.

"How *dare* you speak of him!" Verdauga shouts angrily, stepping down from his throne. He marches forward and strikes me with the back of his hand so forcefully that I nearly lose my balance. Daraemon shoves the mace into my back again, preventing me from losing my footing.

"Get *back*!" Verdauga roars. Then, Verdauga leering closely over me, I close my eyes and feel his exhaling breath on my face. "You *fool*! What happened to him was entirely your doing! And I hold you and you alone responsible!"

"That may be," I say, wiping my broken lip, "and it may be that I am deserving of your hate forever. But the men of this mine need you. And their children, too."

Verdauga ascends his rock throne again, then sits down slowly, pulling the folds of his cloak around his considerably large frame.

"The men will follow you, Verdauga. They will not follow me. What is about to happen will require a leader, both before and afterward. A strategist. Someone with an intellect greater than most," I say, and Verdauga licks his lips and eyes me suspiciously.

For a split second, I can almost see the gears of Verdauga's mind turning. I hope that my plea will crush through the stone around his heart. A hard man he may be, but he is not a dolt.

There was a time not long after I arrived that he would walk and talk with me, though his opinions on most things were, more often than not, at odds with my own. Something switched in him, though, even before the loss of his son, and I saw it in his eyes. If the eyes are indeed the windows to the soul, as I have heard, then the windows to his became empty and shut up.

"Go on," Verdauga says gravely.

"There is a man here called Corvus. Have you heard of him?"

"Are you *thick*?" Verdauga asks, leaning forward in his seat. "He's not unknown to me. Do you think the Church rules this mine?"

"Don't they?"

"Rullerig believes *he* rules it. None of them realize that you cannot govern from afar, old man."

I say nothing, and Verdauga looks up at the ceiling and begins shaking his hands satirically. "Oh yes! Tell us! Tell us if the mighty man of the unknown god has something of real value to add!"

I cannot help but smile inside. If I were God, I would smile in this moment. If all things redound and serve God's purpose, then it stands to reason that praise misguided is still praise nonetheless.

"Corvus has come seeking one man. A man whose identity is now highly treasured. The Prophet wants him returned to Earth."

Verdauga laughs, and the blustering echo carries about the room for several seconds before fading without dignity.

"That's not possible," he says. "The Church has *never* sent anyone back. You know, Iyov, I'm starting to wonder a little. It seems the love of your work has caused your mind to brittle like a bag of hard candy."

Everyone laughs.

"They laugh," Verdauga says, looking at his men. "They don't even know what candy is. But let me entertain this notion of yours for just another minute," he adds, smirking. "Why would they want him returned?"

"To kill him, of course," I reply plainly.

"Clearly. And how does this man's death serve me, or you? Or any of us, shadow man?" Verdauga asks, laughing at me again. "Or what was it they called you? The Mage? I tell you what, why don't you *conjure* up a reason why I shouldn't kill you now?"

A symphony of unsheathed blades takes flight behind me.

"Because, Verdauga, if the Church and Corvus do not succeed, there is a very slim hope that all of us may one day return home."

There's the briefest stillness, and Verdauga bursts into laughter. "You *are* a fool! Have you have lost your ever-loving mind, Iyov?!"

"Verdauga, when have you known me to be untruthful? When have I ever been anything but honest with you? Did I not tell you that I held your son's hand over the abyss?"

"Stop!" Verdauga orders, barely above a whisper.

"Did I not tell you with all honesty that I just wasn't strong enough to hold him?"

"Fuck you! Fuck you for that!"

"Did I not tell you that he called me by your name before I let go of his hand?"

"Damn you, Iyov! Damn you to *hell!*"

Verdauga flails and howls. He curses. The blood rushes to his face as he rises again from his seat. His proud fists pound into me as though I were putty. Deep down, I know his fury upon me is warranted, so I take it without defense.

After what feels like only a moment, my head goes light. My vision blurs, then darkens. Just as I think I'm going to lose consciousness, someone pulls me up and onto my feet, and I see three of Verdauga's men are dragging him away from me.

"Unhand me! *Unhand* me! Never lay hands on your captain! *Never!*" Verdauga shouts.

"But, boss, he says maybe we can go home?!" Daraemon asks.

"Pull your head out of your ass, boy! He's cracked! A goner! Lost his mind! He doesn't even *remember* who he was back on Earth!" Verdauga shouts.

"Stop! Stop this now!" I cry out, falling to my knees as the men release Verdauga. "And you are right. I do not remember," I add, "but this is not about me. This is about you... because *you* remember! You remember that you were a mighty captain over men. You remember, don't you?"

"No more games, you silver-haired bastard! Come out and say it! What is it that you want?!" Verdauga asks, his lip quivering.

At the back of my tongue I feel one of my molars has been knocked loose. I spit the tooth out at Verdauga's feet.

"I want the aid of the mightiest man in the mine. What do you want, Verdauga? Do you wish to see me go down on bended knee in front of you? Because I do it now. Is it your desire to see me trounced in front of everyone here? Because you have done that. And I will *not* leave, either until you've killed me or you've agreed to help me help you."

"Help *you* help *me*?" he asks, one brow raised.

"How else can I make this plain to you?"

Verdauga takes several deep heavy breaths and resumes his place in his seat. He covers his mouth with his folded hands, and then his eyes lock with my own for a great length.

"Get out. All of you. Get out right now!" Verdauga shouts, his hands shaking.

His men obey him swiftly. Taking another deep breath, Verdauga closes his eyes and slowly draws a sable-handled push dagger from the sash around his waist, then sets it upon his knees. Half a minute or more passes while he repeatedly wipes his mouth and chin with the violet-stained neckerchief.

"If I don't kill you now, *they* will kill you. Probably both of us, after what you've just said," Verdauga says, scratching the underside of his chin with the small blade from his lap.

"Then what is it you propose that we should do?" I ask.

Verdauga sighs, then clears his throat. Things have come to the balance of a hair. The tension in the room is thicker than a jug of the finest Irish stout. It's like watching someone play that game where one puts their hand on a table, and spreading their fingers out as far as possible, they use a blade to stab rapidly between them. You close your eyes because you fully expect blood to flow. I expect that blood to be my own any second now.

"What I do now, Iyov, I do for myself. If you come near me, I will cut you from balls to brainpan. Do you hear me?"

Before I can utter a word, Verdauga drives the dagger slowly into the side of his lower right abdomen, snapping off the handle as the blade penetrates through his red robe. I heed his words no longer, and rush forward as the handle of the knife clangs across the hewn stone of Verdauga's seat and onto the floor.

"What have you done?!" I ask, picking up the handle as Verdauga goes to his knees.

"It doesn't hurt. Not really."

"What did you do?!"

"Look here, old man. S'hardly even bleeding."

"The girls can mend it! We can fix you!" I say, reaching forward to staunch the wound.

"You leave it be, goddamn you!" he snarls, the dryness of the room unable to hide the budding tears in his eyes.

"Verdauga, I needed your help!"

"And you shall have it. At least, for however long I have left. This is my gift to you. You've *bested* me... see?"

"I did not come here to best you!"

"I've hated myself, Iyov... for not being able to *truly* hate you," he says through his tears, "and hating you all the more for being right. I've always known you were. I was great once... wasn't I? But I'm nothing. Less than nothing now... and all the things that I've loved are gone... gone away, forever."

"No. Your son is always with you in heart. And you still have friends," I say.

Verdauga shuffles forward, still on his knees, gripping the edge of my cloak. He looks up at me and I see his tears have run river-like pathways through the filth embedded in his face.

"I was jealous. I was always so jealous of you," he says.

"Whatever for?" I ask, placing my right hand on his shoulder and kneeling in front of him.

"My son... He... he loved you. He worshipped you! As if you were his father... and you... You let him go!" he says, sobbing uncontrollably.

"I loved him, too. He was a good friend. And maybe... Maybe he reminded me of the son I may have had once... a good son. And he was a *good* son, Verdauga. He loved you more than anything. I told you, the last thing he said was not my name, but yours."

Verdauga reaches for me. In the pits of hell, we embrace one another. The years that have come between us seem to melt into the pages of this perverse history. I had my reasons for coming here, mostly out of compassion and some of them self-serving... but even still, I thought I was going to my death. Maybe now the moment comes when the tides begin to turn in our favor.

"The weight of this damned place lies like a steaming shit pile on all our shoulders," Verdauga says, rising to his feet and bringing me up in arms with him. "And I am tired, Iyov. I'm *tired* of this bondage. I am tired of a life without any purpose. So, what is it? What is left? What does your so-called deity leave us?"

"He leaves us the moment. Though your knife has now robbed me of even more precious time. We have *got* to give Barrabas a chance to get back to Earth!" I say, gripping Verdauga's forearms.

"Barrabas? *He* is the one they want?!" he asks, sounding more than surprised.

"Yes."

"So, Barrabas is Kilraven the Cursed?" he asks, his face full of amazement.

"I believe so. And so does he. If the Church is not allowed to have him, they will come here. In fact, they may be sending others here this very moment. But if we can get him out, and get him out alive, then there is a hope!"

"What is this hope? There's no hope left here anymore, except in death, maybe," Verdauga says, his voice echoing in the painful stillness of the room.

"I don't know what else to say, Verdauga. But I do not see death as hopeless."

"Well… you were right in one thing, Iyov. You have never lied to me before," he says, and we smile at one another for the first time in nearly a decade.

"What say you now, then?"

"I think it's time we got down to some fucking business, Iyov."

Verdauga claps his hands sharply together, twice, and the echo of it darts across the walls. His men goosestep back to their posts without a word. Seconds later I once again feel Daraemon's hand on my shoulder and the cool tip of the plasma mace probing my lower spine.

"Alright, boys, listen up. Listen good," Verdauga says, rubbing his chin and eyeing me with a keen light of interest in his face. "The crazy old man's got us a plan."

CHAPTER 11

COSTLY REVELATIONS

TO SAY THAT things for me just got a bit more interesting would be the understatement of the year. My two enemies are facing one another. Rullerig stands at arm's length away from Corvus, rapping an unignited plasma mace inside the palm of his overly red hand. Corvus, meanwhile, has his arms folded, tapping his right shoe on the floor nervously in repetition.

"You shoulda been a dancer, you soggy *quim!*" Rullerig bellows, gritting his teeth and motioning his mace toward Corvus's rhythmical feet.

The beat level of his footwork pulls me out of the moment. The sound of it taking precedence over all else, like the second hand ticking away on the face of a vintage timepiece.

In the blink of an eye, I recall my entire childhood at home, and amidst the lounge where the piano sat, against the wall and above the instrument, there hung a schoolhouse pendulum clock that never worked. Smiling, my sweet sisters would sing to me of the sound it once made. "*Tickety tickety tock, that's the sound of a rusty old wooden clock.*"

As I'm yanked from my dream and back into the present, my eyes are already fixated on the table in front of me. Then I see that Corvus's digicorder isn't there. It *hasn't* been there. The entire conversation we just had wasn't even being recorded.

"So, you wanna tell me why you been runnin' your own game, *chummy?*" Rullerig asks Corvus, poking him in the shoulder with his index finger.

"This is none of your concern, Rullerig," Corvus says, backing against the wall directly in front of me and eyeing each of the sentries flanking me. "This man is property of the Church. As a representative of it, I am authorized to do whatever I—"

"Shut yer *fuckin'* trap!" Rullerig says, shoving the handle of the mace into Corvus's stomach.

Corvus bends forward, then goes down on one knee. He looks up at me with bloodshot eyes, heaving dryly at first, then nearly gagging as he tries to catch his breath.

"I had me a feelin' you were up to somethin'!" Rullerig bellows, pulling Corvus back up on his feet again by the lapel of his jacket.

"What are you talking about?! I'm doing my job, you petulant *clown!*" Corvus cries.

"Well, if that's so, how come I just received me a transmission from your superiors? Hmm?" Rullerig asks, wagging his head from side to side. "How come they ain't heard a goddamn word from you in the last twenty-four hours? Answer *that* one, Corvus!"

Rullerig begins pacing the floor in front of Corvus. I turn, glancing over my shoulder, and the two helmeted sentries behind me simultaneously come together at the shoulder in an effort to block the doorway.

"Didja really think you were the only bloody one with company goals to meet?" Rullerig asks. "I have to make a report or two myself 'bout the shit we're digging up in the desert, ya know. So, since you ain't been in contact with 'em the way you oughts to be, tell me, Corvus, what in stinkin' hell is goin' on here?"

"I don't know *what* you're talking about," Corvus snaps sharply.

"I knew there was somethin' *off* about you, Brenner."

"Rullerig, the only thing *off* here are your powers of deduction," Corvus says.

"I don't think so, chum. I didn't like the smell of you when you was sent here. Like a dirty maid's coozer!" Rullerig snarls, sniffing the air around Corvus.

Corvus nearly shivers from head to toe as Rullerig waves the mace a few times and takes another step closer toward him. Then, shrugging his shoulders, Corvus adjusts his jacket and smiles almost flippantly.

"Rullerig, I'm going to make you a deal here. But it's only since your station in the mine has obviously made you paranoid and lessened your mental faculties. Before you had the brilliant notion to interrupt me, I was just on my way to tell the Council that *this* man is the one they want," Corvus says, pointing at me. "And I'm bringing him back with me. I can give you a piece of that action. But I must make my report immediately," he adds with a nervousness now apparent behind his voice.

"No, no, no, mister fancy man. No one's goin' *anywhere*, least of all your man Barrabas here! You're gonna wait right here with the prisoner until I sort out what's really goin' on!" Rullerig barks, pointing in my direction with his mace.

I open my mouth to interject, but Rullerig's massive body is spun around with his broad chest facing me. The mace is no longer in his hands. There's a purple blur, a flash of energy, and a crackle of sound.

I blink one too many times, and when I see the mace is fully ignited, it's being firmly held directly in front of Rullerig's neck... by none other than Corvus. The slippery snake.

"Alright, gentlemen, let's not *lose* our heads here. Or rather I should say, let's not lose Rullerig's head?" Corvus asks.

"Goddamn you!" Rullerig says, spitting through his teeth.

"Put your guns on the floor." Corvus says coolly. "Hurry, please."

"Do it, ya daft fannies!" Rullerig growls.

The sentries comply and back up slowly toward the doorway.

"I don't think so. You two come back over here," Corvus says, beckoning both sentries as he circles the table and takes up a position directly behind me with Rullerig. The two sentries stop when their backs hit the wall directly in front of us.

"You ain't gettin' away with this!" Rullerig shouts.

"Set him free," Corvus says, releasing Rullerig and kicking my chair away from the table.

"I ain't doin' no such thing!" Rullerig says, crossing his arms.

The chair that is my rolling prison comes to a stop against the wall. The two sentries are moving nervously to my right. Rullerig's back is to me and I see his hands balled up in defiance.

"Do it, you *pig*," Corvus orders.

Rullerig refuses, his jowls wobbling as he shakes his head.

Corvus takes a deep breath in through his nose and hesitates for only a microsecond before kicking Rullerig in the kneecap. Then he raises the mace above his head to strike.

"No, no! Don't!" Rullerig shouts, putting his hands up as he goes down on one knee.

Then, in one swift arc, Corvus brings the mace down, lashing the top of Rullerig's head. The chief falls with his back against the wall toward my left, his eyes widening from the blow. A wet gurgling begins in the back of his throat. He looks at me one last time, and whatever light was in his eyes leaves as he slumps prostrate against the floor.

"You two, unbind Barrabas. *Now!*" Corvus shouts.

The sentries free me from the chair without hesitation. Then Corvus urges them back against the wall once more with the mace. But before Corvus can stop me, I move with almost astonishing ease and pick up both guns from the floor. In record time, I've got one aimed at Corvus and the other at the sentries. I forgot how good a real pistol felt in my hand. As I cock the firing pins, my hands prove that some things can't be forgotten—it's like second nature.

"One right between your eyes, Corvus," I say, "and the other on these two pinheads. So, what's it gonna be, asshole?"

"Kilraven, you don't want to do that!"

"*Oh?* So I *am* Kilraven now?"

"*Listen* to me!" Corvus says, his right hand raised and the left still holding the plasma mace. "You can take your chances with me or with these two. Your choice. But you can't kill all three of us," he adds, the mace trembling in his hand.

He's right. The only workable scenario in such close quarters is to take down two of them and hope the third runs or freezes in fear.

I turn at breakneck speed, changing my aim, and fire two bullets at the sentries. They fall to the ground with a clatter—the black armor of their helmets melting where the gun blasts found their mark. Before I can turn and get Corvus back in my sights, the snake practically skewers me to the cell wall, his bony elbow digging hard into my throat.

"I can crush your larynx right now, Kilraven."

My thumb pulls back the hammer on the blaster in my right hand, and I stick the still-smoking barrel directly in front of where Corvus's nuts ought to be. But at the click of the hammer, the purple light from Corvus's mace appears in the corner of my eye.

"What now, pencil dick?"

"Listen to me, damn you!" he shouts. "I *knew* you were Kilraven from the start! You described the events on Fornax perfectly, but I needed to be sure! Don't you get it?"

"I'd be more worried about your little acorns if I were you, Corvus."

"You *cretin*! We want the same thing!"

"And what's that?"

"I want what you want," he says, easing his grip on me. "Freedom from tyranny. Comeuppance for those who would mask the truth. So, will you listen to me now, or am I going to have to wallop you, too? You saw what I did to Rullerig. And I liked him little less than I like you."

"Looks like we're at a standstill here," I say, wagging the gun toward Corvus's crotch.

"Enough!" Corvus says, sighing heavily and taking his elbow from my throat.

After he steps back a few paces, I raise both guns and cock the other pin on my left. I've got him square in the center of his chest. He's as good as dead.

My fingers hesitate when I see him backing away from me even farther. He lowers the mace and powers it off. The purple light fades, and it's just the two of us, alone again in this damn room.

"I can get you out of here," he says calmly.

"Is that so? Why the *fuck* would I trust you?"

"Because I haven't killed you yet, you *fool*," he says. "And I've had more than one chance to do it. Now… are you going to put those guns down?"

"No, I'm not," I say, my fingers tightening on both triggers.

"You might look like a fool, Kilraven, but you are not one. We need to be gone, and right now!"

"Who'n the *fuck* are you?!"

"You're going to have to trust me, Thaniel. We must go!" he exclaims, pointing to the two dead sentries. "Get their clearance cards!"

I remove the cards from the sentries' utility belts and see two names I recognize—Boddiford and Rhys. Now I don't feel quite so guilty. They were both pricks.

"And how do you plan on getting across the causeway with me in tow?" I ask. "This place'll be like Dodge City as soon as the wardens spot us."

"Dodge *what*?"

"Never mind."

"We're not going across the causeway," Corvus says, pointing to our left. "The platforms are near. We need only get to the ship."

"Fuck you. I'm not leaving my friends! When the wardens find Rullerig, there's gonna be hell to pay!"

"Kilraven, this is your only chance! If you go back to the mines, you may not get another one. I *will* leave here, with *or* without you!" he squeals.

I call his bluff and place the barrels of both guns on his forehead.

"Everything that's happened here is because of you and those like you, Corvus," I say, driving him back against the wall with the barrels still on his head. "I'm not playing games with you anymore. You are not leaving, and I'm not leaving yet, either. And if you won't help me, your brain will be... What was it you said? When we met?"

I scratch the side of my head with the barrel of one of the guns and Corvus swallows noisily.

"Oh, now I remember. You said my brain'll be on the wall in less than five seconds."

"Listen to me, you stupid overgrown *child*, I cannot risk the—"

Corvus stops at the sound of me cocking both firing pins.

"Five... four."

"Alright, alright! But this is suicide!" Corvus squeals, his hands shaking at his sides.

"Didn't you know, Corvus? We're all dead here," I say with a quick smile as I lower the guns. "Now let's go."

Outside, we find the empty sentry Marauder, a dust-covered eight-wheeled behemoth. I use one of the bastard's clearance cards to start the engines. Corvus takes the seat beside me, and I stick the barrel of one pistol directly into his stomach and tell him not to move. He doesn't utter a word.

As we ride across the causeway between the platforms and the mines, I feel a strange sense of freedom at last, despite the fact that Corvus is so near. Were I to die, even ten seconds from now, it would almost make everything that's happened today completely worth it. The heat of the blue sun gives me strength. The Eridanian crosswinds in my hair refresh my spirit. And the air is almost sweet.

"You can't even smell the ore out here. It's almost like being home, isn't it?"

Corvus says nothing but leans forward suddenly and points toward my left across the sandy distance. "My ship's there!" he shouts, motioning frantically toward the tiniest golden rocket of a vessel that I've ever seen.

"Sit *back*, dammit!" I order, digging the barrel of the gun into his rib cage. "Now I *know* you're nuts, Corvus. That soup can can't possibly hold more than one person!"

Corvus glares at me with a look of shock, the wind finally loosing the agent that has held his hair so firmly in place. The strands of his fringe flap like a banner caught in the wind, and I catch the scent of his cologne… a soapy and flowery musk.

"The ship can hold two," he says, "and there are cryo-tubes for the journey."

"For cryin' out loud, look how small the engines are! They wouldn't have enough steam to get us back in less than a year's time! We'd be sleeping for ages," I say.

"Wrong. It has enough nucleo-cores to get to Earth and back a few times. The ship is *special*. It's much faster than you might think."

"Well I hope you're right."

"Looks can be deceiving, Kilraven. I would have thought that lesson would be clear to you at this point," he says, staring perturbingly into my eyes.

Then the snake smiles in a way that I've not seen prior to now and twirls his mustache slightly between his index finger and thumb.

I slow the Marauder down as we reach the end of the causeway approaching the mine entry, and then I see a row of purple light. The closer we get, I realize that something has gone horribly wrong. All the wardens have formed a line at the gate with their maces ignited, blocking the prisoners rushing from the active workings. The mob looks like an army of confused bees—some of them are running, some of them are fighting one other, and I don't see anyone that I recognize.

As I jump from the Marauder, Corvus doesn't budge an inch.

"Get your ass out of there, and let's go!"

"No," he says, staring blankly ahead. "I will wait here for you. You must be delivered intact."

"Corvus, I will put a hole in your head, so help me! Now get your *bony* ass moving!" I yell, pulling him from the seat by the neck.

To my surprise, Corvus doesn't resist.

We both make a run for the overdeveloped melee before us. The first to see us is my favorite warden, Ubasti.

Damn. I'd hate to have to kill him now since I still owe him one. Must be karma.

Ubasti breaks into a sprint to meet our path. I aim the pistol in my right hand in his direction, and he stops in his tracks. For a moment, I'm stupid enough to believe he's going to just let me pass without incident.

"Madzimure!" Ubasti shouts, pointing at me. "We got us a score to settle! So whatcha gonna do with that thing, fella?!"

"I'll plug you first, Ubasti. Then as many wardens as I can before we take this place for ourselves!"

"Go ahead, then!" he says, laughing. "G'wan! See what happens!"

"Kill him. Or he will kill you," Corvus says quietly.

Ubasti just keeps laughing through gritted teeth, calling up from the seemingly infinite supply of mucus at the back of his throat. Then out of nowhere, Corvus has his hand on top of the gun and is lowering my arm.

"Wait! He's right!" Corvus says. "The dust and vapor from the ore is just like methane. If you fire and miss, the whole place will become an inferno."

"Bullshit."

"Not bullshit," Corvus replies. "Besides, I don't ever remember reading whether you were a good shot or not," he adds with a slight wince.

Instinct prompts me, and I raise my right arm again and put the barrel on Corvus's chest, forcing him to back up a few paces. Then I draw the gun from my left and take aim at Ubasti's not-so-hard-to-miss pumpkin-sized head. He doesn't have to know I'm not left-handed.

"'Bout time you *sacked* up, pussyfoot!" Ubasti snorts.

"We're far enough from the bug dust that I can still pop you, Ubasti! Now, step aside!" I say, giving the bastard one more chance.

"Listen here, you bearded *runt*. You ain't gettin' outta here alive! Neither are any of the other sods in there that don't crawl back into their cages!" Ubasti roars, still walking toward me.

"Dammit, don't do make me do this, Ubasti!"

"*Shoot* him," Corvus says quietly.

The warden keeps moving forward. And I *should* shoot him, but I do the exact opposite. I drop the guns.

"I knew it! Knew you was nothin' but a chicken-shit scaredy-cat! You gonna just surrender now?" Ubasti asks.

"Nope. I'll just beat the living shit outta you, Ubasti."

Ubasti grins from ear to ear with a mouthful of brown teeth, then reaches into his back pocket and pulls out a plasma gun I never even saw.

"*Oh* shit."

"I told you to kill him!" Corvus shrieks.

"Hey, how 'bout we settle this the old-fashioned way, Ubasti?" I ask, putting my dukes up.

"Already settled," Ubasti says.

I hear the cocking of the firing pin, and Ubasti takes aim. Some force that feels like a steam locomotive smashes into me from the right. A shot rings out loud and clear. Cymbals clash. There's an orchestra of percussion playing in my ears.

I'm on the ground, looking at the sky. I reach for my chest. It doesn't even hurt.

Shouldn't I be cold?

I touch my stomach. There's no wound.

Am I dead?

I look at my hands. No blood.

I'm still breathing!

Minutes pass. No, only seconds, maybe.

The crashing in my ears softens a bit, and I sit up to find Ubasti is on the ground in front of me, shuddering and spitting up purple and black stuff. Corvus is on the ground slightly behind me, and in his right hand is one of the pistols I dropped, still smoking from the heat of the shot.

"Told you... this was suicide," he says, smiling at me with a mouth full of blood-stained teeth.

Corvus falls over, face forward, and blood from his mouth spatters across the dirt as his head hits the ground. Everything moves in slow motion. I crawl to his side across the hot terrain, its sharp sand digging into my lacerated wrists and elbows. When I finally reach Corvus, my arms are filled with a sudden strength, and lifting his body up, I find he's as light as a feather. I'm amazed that I'm actually cradling the son of a bitch in my arms.

"That was some killer shot, Doc!" I say, putting my hand over the gaping hole in his stomach and pulling him close to me.

"I was... taught by the best," Corvus whispers.

"You did pretty damn good yourself just now."

"Listen to me... *Listen!*" he says fumbling at the front of my shirt. "He will know you're coming... He will not stop until he ends you... both of you... so take this!"

Reaching into his coat pocket, Corvus pulls out his ledger.

"It will start the ship... and take you back. There are two... two souls you can trust... the Surgeon... and Terra."

"Okay, sure, Corvus. Whatever you say."

"They will be waiting for you... And don't... don't let the ship... give you any attitude," he says, smiling.

"Sure, Corvus, okay."

The blood rising from his mouth runs down the side of his cheeks and into his ears. He opens his eyes wide, as if looking far off into the distance.

"Taking back... your family... going to be tougher... than winning this little coup," he says, choking and laughing while pointing toward the ensuing battle.

"Corvus, you have to tell me what the hell you're talking ab—"

"Listen, boy! I meant to leave you with more..."

He starts trailing off, and his eyes begin to close slowly. Then I shake the living hell out of him, and part of me hates myself for having to do it.

"Corvus! Why did you help me?!"

His eyes widen as they reopen, and he grips my shoulder with bloody hands.

"They still live... Mara and Meg'n... They stand guard over Elisabeth... but they don't know her."

"She's alive?!"

"They don't know her..." he says, trailing off again.

"Corvus, goddammit, stay with me!"

He coughs violently, spitting blood all over himself and me.

"Heh. Least my gravestone won't read... that I died in bed," he says, trying to laugh.

"Easy, Corvus. *Easy* now," I say, compressing his wound as hard as I can.

"I could do... nothing for them," he says, and his whole body begins to shiver. "There are others... Some have infiltrated his consortium... so you won't be alone... Now get to the ship... Take the ship!" he says, trying to smile again.

"Corvus, I don't understand! Who the fuck *are* you?!"

The bloody bastard closes his eyes slowly and takes in one slow, deep breath. With all my strength I grip his arm, squeezing hard in an attempt to shock him back into coherence. His eyelids begin to flutter garishly.

"Tell me who you are, goddammit!" I roar, and Corvus glares at me as though we'd never met before.

"All mothers care... for their daughters," he says, "and their sons... my songbird... my Thaniel..." He whispers my name at the last, still smiling at me.

To my horror, his smile fades, and his gaze broadens. In a final retch of air and blood, his eyes roll into the back of his head, and he exhales his last.

All at once the breath is driven from my body, and every fiber of my being groans and stirs, as if my spirit could supernova were it to be let free of the flesh. My entire pitiful life whizzes before my eyes, and as I look upon his face, I am amazed—stunned—that I didn't recognize the light in his eyes... the light that brought me into this world and gave me life.

Grief and anguish dig their claws into my shoulders and neck, bearing a weight upon me like never before. Tears as hot as burning coals are loosed, stinging tracks into my face as they fall on to Corvus's jacket. As I close his eyes and mine I wish that all the mountains in Eridania would crumble, and fall on us.

CHAPTER 12

PARTING GIFTS

CORVUS'S BODY LIES at my feet, and I'm dead inside. Ubasti has finally stopped twitching. The plasma gun at his side sparks and pops like a busted fuse box, crackling from the damage caused by Corvus's shot.

I wipe what's left of the stinging tears from my face and move toward the mine's adit. The ground before me is littered with men that are either dead or breathing their last... and I feel nothing.

How can I feel nothing?

The roar of the continuing blitzkrieg up ahead tickles my eardrums. The loss of the man who revealed himself to be my mother attempts to smash through me like a careening freighter. That profound revelation sets its tonnage upon me like a landslide... but all I can think about is making an effort to save my bullets.

Is that you in there, Madzimure? Are you the one making me numb?

I look down, and in the rock rubble nearby, I see it. Another *Excalibur*. This time it's a plasmic version. I pick up the mace and ignite it.

"Damn."

Tapping the mace on the body of a dead man closest to me proves it's fizzed out. I start tossing bodies aside, looking for even the faintest purple light, and my biceps tremble uncontrollably. From the roaring waves of raised voices, I can only guess that the wardens have beaten the prisoners back down the haulageway.

I stoop to move one of the dead sentries aside, and a soft grip takes me by the forearm.

"Beautiful man," he says, scraping his fingernails into my skin. "You were always... the good looking one..." he whispers, his voice softening gently.

He's smiling. He doesn't stop smiling that smile of his. He just stops breathing.

"Tarsil, goddammit," I say, still gripping his hand in mine.

I lift his body slightly off the ground toward my chest, and the entire back of his skull nearly sloughs off. I don't let go of his hand, though, not even for a moment. He didn't deserve to die like this.

"May your soul find its way."

A few meters ahead, I can see the faint glow of a mace lying close to a broken section of barricading. I pick up the weapon, and feeling its warmth through the pommel, I know it's still working. With a twist of the handle, the mace vibrates and ignites in a purple crackle of dazzling light. Suddenly, some reserve of strength finds me, and I'm urged forward, running down the haulageway as fast my legs will still allow.

After about twenty seconds I come to a skidded halt at the end of the hall. From here the fork in the path before me connects to two available entries, both of which eventually lead to the cellblocks. A faint ruckus ahead begins to build at the path to my left. The pathway at the center, which would've been my third option, is almost completely blocked by debris where the roof jacks have given way. Markings on the jacks indicate they were hit by something: a projectile or a mace, maybe. There was practically a garrison of sentries and wardens at any given time down that way. I can hear nothing from the path to the far right, which leads to the mine's major air shafts.

I go left at a full sprint. My leg muscles begin to scream at me. They tell me to slow the fuck down... but the sound of the voice in my head is Corvus's. My heartbeat tumbles through my ears like rolling thunder.

After half a minute, I arrive at the cellblocks. It's a battle royale. An eye for an eye, tooth for a tooth. Like watching starving carnivores fight over the last scrap of the kill. A haze of plasma maces invades my line of sight, but I can't tell if the wardens have gained the upper hand or not. Some of the men not fighting are carrying water. A great deal more of them are hoarding supplies from the sentry barracks, the doors of which have been barricaded heavily using chain and steel links from the eridanium conveyors.

I cross the cellblock waybridge and find Jareth and Ambrose, two ragamuffins from block eight-five who are forcibly submerging a warden's head into a large tub of water. The warden's arms flail wildly, and it's obvious they don't have the strength to contain him. They're just skinny punks. With little hesitation, I dip my ignited plasma mace into the water, and the warden's head explodes like a ripe tomato. I don't even know who he was.

"*Fuckin'* hell!" Ambrose squeals, his eyes bulging.

Jareth leers at me with steely blue irises, his face smattered in blood and water.

"You're alive, boys. Get moving."

They both take my advice and run as though they'd just seen Rullerig's ghost. Then, crossing through the last haulageway, and then over yet another bridge, I come to a cavern of shortwalls. Where my field of vision ends lies the competent rock, and there are men in every direction—fighting, clawing, shouting, kicking, dying.

Upon my approach, I find a thing that I did not expect. Iyov and Verdauga are fighting against the wardens together, back to back, both of them carrying ignited maces. As I raise my own mace, Iyov sees me from his side of the bridge.

"Where's Cunningham?!" I shout.

"The crusher! Got over half the wardens there!" Iyov yells in return.

I clobber my way through two sentries. It takes longer than I expected, but the mace does its job. Their armor tears in half as if it were wax paper. Makes me wonder why they even wear the stuff—it's clunky, and they sure as shit can't move in it.

After each sentry hits the ground with a thud, unconscious, I shove each one in turn down an airway so deep I can't see the bottom. The adrenaline rush surging through my veins makes the bodies feel weightless. One of them screams like a banshee on the way down.

Then I join Iyov and Verdauga. Our backs to one another, we form an unstoppable trio, bashing and slashing our way through the wardens. For each one I take down, I claim payback for my mother. Payback for my wife.

"How'n the hell did Cunningham manage to take them all?"

"How indeed!" Iyov howls. "She and her girls caught them by surprise in the mess hall! And her little friend Sam played her part by finding the guns, of course!"

"What caused the third haulageway entry to collapse?" I ask.

"I do not know, friend. *Many* were lost there," Iyov says. "But they managed to get three guns that still worked. One of them wasn't even loaded, and the wardens folded like a deck of cards at the sight of them."

Iyov laughs while Verdauga kicks one of the sentry helmets directly between Iyov and me, as if it were a game ball. Then Verdauga shifts his body, moving directly between us, but keeping his back to me. His mace whirls overhead and nearly singes my hair.

"I hear they want your head, Barrabas!" he bellows, wincing as he presses his left hand firmly into the waistband of his red robe.

"They'll soon have it, Verdauga."

As the words leave my lips, one of the braver sentries approaches us, his mace extended.

He's offering to *duel*. Iyov and I hold up our maces in return, and at the sight of them, glowing and bloodied, the sentry's mettle shits itself. He drops his weapon and runs across the bridge over the shortwalls. As he does, I see an aged miner cut a rope from on high. There's a rush of metal and wheels, and a large skip falls directly on top of the sentry.

"What of Corvus? Does he live?" Iyov asks, grimacing at the crushed guard.

"He's dead."

"Well, you got him before he got you!" Iyov says, plunging his mace into the head of a sentry who nearly sneaks up behind me.

I have *issues* with watching my back.

"The wardens didn't put up a fight, but their foot soldiers have been another matter!" Verdauga says, guffawing.

Within another minute, I can see victory in this area is near. From unseen corridors and shafts just out of sight, the echoes of the miners' hurrahs confirm it. Half the maces in the room are no longer giving light or are on the ground, popping and sputtering impotently. A lit mace flies from out of nowhere, spinning like bolas, and it whizzes between Iyov and me.

I grab the old man by the cloak, pulling him out of harm's way and toward the safety of the competent rock. I quickly recognize several of Verdauga's men therein, and they're all cowering against the walls in an effort to avoid the fight. I don't judge them.

"You boys recognize what this is?" I ask, pulling out one of my pistols.

They all nod, looking at one another with terror.

"Then you know what'll happen if I pull this trig—"

Before I can finish the sentence, they're all running past me and out of the rock. Iyov yells something I can't quite make out and then he steps out of my sight. As I holster the gun in my waistband and move to follow him, I see Verdauga, facing me and standing between us and the bridge.

"Ha ha! Victory for Kilraven the Cursed!" he shouts, raising his mace high.

I watch as Verdauga begins to pant, his face strangely pale while the entire weight of him totters, swaying from left to right as though he were a tree nearly felled. Half a second later, a plasma mace bursts through the center of his chest, and Verdauga sucks in the dusty air with a frightful gasp as the breath is driven from him.

"Verdauga, *no!*" Iyov shrieks.

I grab hold of Iyov's cloak, but I can't hold him this time. Verdauga's eyes meet mine as he drops his mace, and his mouth begins to foam with blood and water. The protruding mace still buried in his chest is wrenched backward, and Verdauga falls to the side, revealing his executioner. There's a frenzied look of madness and fury on her face. It's Warden Zimrafel.

"This fight is *over!*" Iyov howls at her.

I push Iyov behind me, knowing that Zimrafel won't back down.

"Magpie told me about you, Zim," I say, and she kicks dirt in my direction.

"Oh, I remember! That little *bitch* from the crushing room! Always gettin' the easy work, that one," Zimrafel says, snorting and clearing her throat.

"You've got the easy work from what I hear! All you haveta do is spread your legs for Rullerig!" I shout.

It's a lie. I never heard that before. I'm just improvising. It's all you can do in situations like this.

"You couldn't have made your post any *other* way," I say, adding further injury to the previous insult.

I shouldn't have done that. Warden Zim says nothing and twirls the mace so flawlessly that even I'm a bit taken aback. I've no idea what to do next, but Iyov steps out from behind me and, as is his wont, he does his best to try and reason with her.

"Dear one, we should not be fighting! And this one is not worth it!" he pleads, pointing back at me.

"I'm not brain-dead, you old fuck!" Zim shouts. "Rullerig says the Church wants him! When they find out *I'm* the one that captured him, I'll have more credit than I'll know what to do with!" she adds, pointing her mace at me.

"Some animals can't be talked down, Iyov."

"Precious one," Iyov says, ignoring me and placating the warden by holding out empty palms toward her. "The possibility of communication with Earth from here is now zero. You are a captive, along with the rest of us."

"You're the prisoner, old man! And I am a regulator!" she shouts and then comes running at us like a charging bull.

I just stand still, frozen in time and space. I don't even take a defensive position. It's almost as if I expect something to keep Zim from harming us, some magic spell, perhaps, that might drag her to hell. And it does.

Verdauga reaches up and grabs Zim by the leg, knocking her off balance. She falls forward, face-first onto her own mace. After a few seconds, she's just a flopping mess of dusty clothes and burnt hair.

Iyov hurtles to Verdauga's side, but I know it's too late when the massive wound in his chest broadcasts a very clear picture.

"Verdauga! Oh, my friend!" Iyov wails, holding Verdauga in his last moments.

"Kilraven... get outta here, you cutpurse. Get to the crusher, or I'll kill you myself," Verdauga says.

Iyov looks at me glossy-eyed, and I know that I cannot help. I thank Verdauga by shaking his hand one final time.

Leaving Iyov to grieve, I make for the gyratorium. The rush of adrenaline along the way makes me tireless. The strained muscles in my legs and arms somehow feel revitalized, as though I could outrun a rising sun. When I arrive at the crusher, I find Cunningham still inside, and much to my relief she's busy with the other women. Several of the wounded are being tended to, and the dead have been lined up in a stacked row near the crusher. I recognize more than a few faces—Barnaby, Petersen, Ivan the Terrible... all of them wardens and each one of them bound hand and foot and gagged with bedsheets.

"Bruised but not broken," Cunningham says, gripping me so tightly that I almost can't breathe. She takes a deep breath and smiles at me. One of her two front teeth is missing.

"Iyov told me what happened," I say, "and we lost Verdauga. Ubasti and Zim are down, too."

"What about *Tars*? Have you seen Tarsil?!" she asks.

At the mention of him, I cannot find the words and can only shake my head. She only has to look at me, and she knows.

"Oh *no*... not my blondie! Not *him*!" she says, going to her knees and nearly sinking into the floor.

Her tears flow instantly, like red rainfall upon the jagged Eridanian landscape, and I'm moved to pity for my broken friend. *But now is not the time for grief, Kilraven. Grief is for the old, Kilraven.*

So, I listen to Madzimure, and I set aside the urge for bereavement. Grabbing Cunningham, I pull her to her feet.

"May his soul find its way," she says, still sobbing in my arms.

"Yes. And there's going to be time to mourn for him later... and you'll be the one who can give him a proper burial. And you will tell everyone of his sacrifice, and neither you nor they will forget it. Do you hear me?"

Cunningham gains her composure slowly and begins to describe all the details of the fight and how Iyov and Verdauga joined forces to unite the workers. She tells me that Verdauga gave a rousing speech about Kilraven the Cursed, reminding all that they were born someone else and that they once had different names and different lives. She says Verdauga claimed his true name back in that moment... *Burnham*, he was to be called, on this—his last day. He was captain over a great ship that visited Fornax, he said.

Goosebumps spread across my arms and legs at that revelation, and I smile. Then she tells me how the mad rush of the coup led her to unfortunately throw someone into the crusher.

"Men were killing each other right outside the fuckin' doors, and this sack of mincemeat was in here tryin' to drain his nuts!" she says, pointing to the spray of blood and chunks of tissue around the base of the machine.

"Who was it?" I ask, walking to the crusher and looking inside.

"He was one of us!"

"You had to do what you had to do," I say.

"All the wardens we had wrangled in here dropped to their knees and surrendered when they saw me do it," she says, gritting her teeth at the sight of bone and blood. "I suppose the thing'll still work," she adds, kicking the side of the crusher's gearbox.

"I don't reckon you'll be needing the crusher ever again," I say.

Before I take my leave and charge Cunningham with the task of readying a cellblock for all the still-defiant wardens, she quickly commands the other women to have the wardens form a line. Then to each warden she offers a few words but also gives to them a gift—a brand on each of their hands, burned into the flesh by the heat of one of the maces. She tells them the mark will be a symbol to everyone that they can never hold, wield, or even look at a weapon ever again.

"You're in charge of this facility now, Cunningham, and all the better for it," I say, turning away to leave.

"Hey. Kilraven?" she asks.

I turn around to face her, and her eyes well with tears. She opens her mouth, but the words don't come.

"Yeah. I know. What was I thinking, right?" I ask, smiling at her.

I exit the crusher and wander the labyrinthine ways of the mine for another half-hour or so when I find that the rest of the wardens have been killed. A handful of them have already been put to work in the mines, draining the aquifers. Prisoners Clayton and Yockney, each armed with a mace, have taken the remaining female wardens and put the entire pack to work wading through the women's latrines.

As I walk through the active workings, I find Iyov too has already progressed into a new role. He's behind the wheel of the biggest ore hauler in the mine, ordering the men to collect as much of the eridanium rock as they can. I watch and take rest as they load the ore quickly into the rear of the vehicle.

"Verdauga would've been better suited for this," Iyov says, frowning and handing me a tin cup filled with water.

Then, hopping back inside the hauler, Iyov shifts it into gear and moves in reverse. He leaves the entire twenty-ton lode mined from the last few months dangling over one of the mine shafts.

"Lost forever at the bottom of this world, I should hope. But also a bargaining chip at the very last, if such needs prove," he says with a wink.

Iyov and I then resolve to gather as many as we can into the common area not far from the cellblocks. There's a small raised outcrop, almost like a dais that the men used to play games on. When Iyov steps upon it, there's a round of applause unlike anything I've ever heard. In fact, I've never heard the men applaud. Not ever.

"Friends! We have triumphed!" he shouts.

The five or six hundred–odd men than I can actually see cheer again, and louder this time. They are making merry and congratulating one another. The gloom of this place seems to have been overturned against all odds, but even in my own moment of mirth, a shadow passes over the victory in my heart. I wonder, how long this can possibly last?

Then Iyov's voice once again brings a light that perforates the swirling shadows of my mind.

"Verdauga is dead. With his dying words, he bade me take you all as my own children!" he shouts, holding up a copper-colored pin shaped like a V.

Looking closer at the pin, I notice it's not copper at all, but steel stained orange and red with dried blood. The brooch is a symbol. It was a symbol of Verdauga's leadership over the men.

Verdauga's own gang had fashioned it for him from the dross of a ceremonial sword that he himself brought from Earth. The wardens had Verdauga stripped of the blade when he arrived on Eridania and made him and the other new arrivals watch as they melted it down. At the time, I had no idea why the sword wasn't removed before his journey here. I suspect now that it was done purposefully, no doubt intended to destroy the greatest token of the man's career. As I know now that Verdauga was Captain Burnham prior to his transference, the shaming of the sword makes complete sense.

"We made peace at the competent rock, he and I!" Iyov proclaims. "So we will bury him there. And we will honor his memory in that place as long as we can!"

What follows is a moment of silence. Slowly, through the assembly, come four of the men carrying the body of Verdauga. After they set his corpse at the foot of the dais, Iyov pins the V-shaped brooch to his own cloak.

"And this man here," Iyov shouts, pointing to me. "This man is the *key* to freedom!" he shouts, and there is a wail of hurrahs.

"Bar-rabas! Ba-raaaabas! Barraaaa-bas!" they chant.

"Now listen to me!" he says, calming the crowd with his upraised hands. "I don't say *our* freedom because I do not want to confuse you, friends! There is a fight yet to be fought! We cannot simply leave this place. But we have sustenance, and we know these mines like the backs of our hands!" he shouts, all the while pointing at me. "But you *must* know this also… that the Prophet and the politicians who condemned us to this place, they will be undone in the light of the truth that we carry inside of us!"

The men cheer loudly, and the goose flesh on my arm rises.

"The liars will be undone in the light of truth inside this man that we will send. He will claim back what was ours, which they have taken wrongfully from us!" he shouts, raising my arm into the air. "Now, will someone raid the sentry barracks and break out the drinks already?!"

There is a great laughter and a tumult of noise and cheer. The walls of the mine practically shake from the resounding voices of free men and women.

Stepping down from the rock, dozens of the men waylay us, congratulating Iyov and me, as well as one another. They shake my hand and thank me repeatedly for setting them free. The women shower me with kisses. I'm a kid again in that instant. A kid who's just been complimented for something as trivial as referring to someone as sir or madam.

I imagine the smile on my mother's face, pleased that I remembered the manners she so vehemently imposed on me during the golden days of my youth. And losing myself in thought, I realize Iyov is standing next to me after a moment. His face is beaming with a warm light that can only have come from our freedom bought so very dearly.

"Now," he says quietly, gripping my forearm, "I think you should get going."

"Must I?"

"My boy," he says, softly slapping my cheek. "I know about the ship. I have many spies in this place," he adds with a wink.

"Will you… Will you be alright, old man?"

"We will be *fine*, son. I think the men now have something worth living for. They have their freedom back, which was already theirs anyway. But now, yes, now I think they will fight for you. And for what you could bring us," he says.

"But… how can I prevail in this twisted-ass scenario? Can I even do this?"

Iyov pauses and puts his hands together as if he's about to pray. "Can you?" he asks, exhaling deeply. "Only you can answer that. But look!" he says, eyes filled with a wild wonder. "Look at what has transpired here! Look around you! Decades we have been here. *Decades*, Kilraven! And I have seen nothing like this in all my days," he adds, turning to face me again and putting both of his hands on my shoulders. "Not until today."

"But I don't even know who I am anymore, Iyov. The Barrabas in me *burns*. Burns hot. It's vicious. Kilraven gets… *colder*. Long dead. No more than a broken memory."

"Those are the Prophet's words in you. I know who you are. Who you *really* are. Come now," he says, tugging my arm gently and pulling me away from the rest. "You know, I heard about you before. Even before I came here. Before the treacherous business back on Earth. I do remember *some* things."

"What do you remember?"

"That we were all brought into this life for a reason. And we *are* the reason," he adds. "You are not this flesh or this face," he says, grabbing my jaw, "but the spirit within that even he could not take from you!"

As I reflect on his words, I can only shuffle my feet and hang my head, though I think I do it not for shame, but rather almost as a child being taught a lesson by his father.

"And you… being likened to one who kicks sand upon the fire… The Prophet who now controls the souls of men likewise will be put out!" he whispers excitedly, grasping my shoulders firmly and shaking me. "And what you will regain for yourself, *we* shall likewise!"

As I breathe in deeply, my mind is a tempest, for his words pierce my insides like a fiery dart. Deep down, my heart is glad for the first time in a long time, and it does not damn me in the sudden knowledge that I *must* leave.

"Kilraven, you must once again place your feet upon the Earth. And above all, you must go alone."

"I will come back, Iyov. I promise to come back."

"A man cannot make a promise," he says, chastising me gently. "For how can a man vow such a thing when he does not know the future?"

"What about you? And the Church? What if they send transports here? And more sentries? And more—"

Iyov interrupts me by gripping my arm firmly.

"Focus on the task directly in front of you, son. Pay no heed to what transpires here. If you win your battle against *him*, the war may also be won in time. That is all you can do," he says, smiling.

I smile in return as our eyes glisten in the dusty glow, and I throw my arms around the old man for what I truly wish is not the last time.

"Now, go!" he says. "And get a move on before someone else gets the same idea!" he adds, shoving me away from him with a sad smile.

I step away from the old man, pacing backward, watching as he continues to smile from cheek to cheek.

As I turn away, I step through the throng of prisoners and make for the front of the mine. I hear one woman say she hasn't seen the light of the blue day in years. I hear a teenage boy say he hasn't had a cold cup of water since he arrived. And I smile, though not outwardly, in the hope that however vain what lies ahead of me now has the smallest chance of success.

When I arrive at the mine's main gate, I find Cunningham on her knees, weeping in front of Tarsil's body. I wish now that he was coming with me. At the sound of my approaching feet, she looks up, and I see that her tears have run tire marks of their own in the dirt upon her cheeks. She smiles at me pitifully but never says a word. Rising to one knee, she picks up Tarsil's body and begins carrying him down the main haulageway. I watch her as she goes, and I could swear that I see Tarsil smiling at me one last time.

I step through the adit for the final time and out into the radiance of the blue sun. The sentry Marauder is just where I left it a few dozen meters away. I try to put my conscience at ease in regard to Ubasti's death by dragging his corpse back into the safety of the mine's shadow. I don't know why I even bothered. It's not for me to say what he deserved, but if anyone wishes to give him a proper burial, I leave it for them to decide.

I pick up Corvus. My mother. My guardian. My saint.

I carry him toward the Marauder, and from the corner of my eye I see his blood still glistening wet upon his clothing. As I hold him, the thought occurs to me that the body should be destroyed. Once upon a time I seem to recall my mother saying she would prefer cremation, if ever I had to make that choice.

"That was some act you pulled off. You damn sure fooled me," I say, my eye catching the sheen of the symbol of the Prophet still pinned to his jacket. "I wonder if *he* knows?"

I place Corvus gently into the passenger seat of the Marauder. I look at his lithe, pale hands, and the dust of years covering a memory long forgotten is quickly blown away, and suddenly her final words make sense to me. At the last, she said, "*At least I won't die in bed*"—a reference to the writing on the death stone of Doc Holliday. I was obsessed with those tales as a child. But I was so blinded by my contempt for his character that I completely missed all the signs she tried to give me.

"*Wait!*" shouts a voice from far behind.

I turn and see Iyov running to meet me. He is holding out both hands with each fist clenched, and he nods at me, prompting me to choose one.

"Guess!" he says, shaking his closed hands.

"Kidding, right?"

"Go on, boy!" he says assertively, and I choose his left hand.

When his fingers open above mine, I feel cold metal land in my palm. Iyov grins merrily, extending his other hand as well. After tapping his right fist, he frees another batch of small metal, which rains down into my palm like jewels glittering in the light of a setting sun.

"They were found in Rullerig's cabin," he says. "Just enough for his favorite wardens and himself, I guess. Pity. He won't be needing them where he's gone, of course," he adds with a fleeting frown.

I count silently, confirming exactly ten bullets in my hand, but when I look back at Iyov, he's already walking away and moving toward the Marauder. He stops a few feet from the driver's side, shielding his eyes from the sun as he inspects Corvus's lifeless body.

"His Lordship picked the wrong man for the job," he says sarcastically.

"Wrong woman," I whisper quickly, and Iyov turns to me with a quizzical face.

"*Woman*?!" he asks, more than slightly amazed.

I lower my eyes when his meet mine and say nothing. As Iyov turns back toward Corvus, he grimaces at the sight of the spiritless company machine propped up in the Marauder.

"Seems a waste to let him bleed out all over. And a vehicle like this could prove extremely useful, my friend," he says.

"Please. For me? Please, Iyov. Leave the body here to dissolve in the daylight," I say, stuffing the bullets into my pocket. "The Marauder won't be any worse for wear because of it."

"It would be prudent to release him down the main drainage shaft, with the rest of the dead," Iyov adds.

"Just do me this favor, old man. Let the sun take him."

And with that, I turn my back on my mother and my good friend for the last time in this world.

CHAPTER 13

IN-FLIGHT ENTERTAINMENT

MY MOTHER'S SHIP is, for lack of a better word, minuscule. It can't be more than six or seven meters from front to fin. And it's even smaller in width. A golden dragonfly—one that you could squash under your heel were you a jolly green giant from Gath.

I take a closer look and examine the craft's body, but I'm not able to find any lines on the fuselage. There's not a single panel opening anywhere, and from what I can tell the only way in or out is through the glass dome of the cockpit. It's just an oversized bullet covered in a strangely familiar copper-colored alloy.

From a distance, there was a halo surrounding the ship, like it was a winged guardian sent to fly me away to safety. I thought it was the sunlight reflecting off the surface at first, but standing next to the thing, I realize the ship itself is actually glowing. But it's not glowing. It's *fluorescing*—as my old flight instructor would be quick to point out—flashing under the light of the blue sun.

I've seen this effect before, I think… decades ago… and it was a much older model. If memory serves in this instance, it's the adamantine spar mixed with gold and titanium that gives the ship's exterior such a radiant response. But that material hasn't been used on any one-man aircraft since before I was at the Academy. It was much too costly to reproduce en masse. This can only mean one thing: this ship is damn rare.

Regardless, I still have absolutely no idea how in all the known worlds two people could actually fit in here. My suspicions regarding Mother's choice of such a vehicle are confirmed when I get a good look at the rear of the ship. It's right below both of the engines—a single area of the hull specifically designed to hold *one* cryo-pod.

Mother *knew*.

You knew what you were doing, didn't you? You never had any intention of coming back with me, did you, Mother?

As soon as I pull the ledger Mother gave me from out of my coat, the ship reacts with a lurching sort of whirl. I press my hand to screen, and a second later the cockpit hatch opens. Without hesitation I quickly hop inside, sliding into the seat so easily I get the same feeling one does when greeting a close friend you haven't seen in years. It's a tin can, this thing. I've got a mind to wonder… has the Earth has gotten smaller, too?

I pick up the ledger again when I notice an appropriately sized slot for its placement on the ship's navigational dash. I slide the ledger gently into the opening, and there's a multitude of things that happen all at once; a dazzling array of lights activate, I catch a whiff of nitrogen as the cryo-tube activates behind me, and the engines start up full-stop. Then something else happens. Something that *never* happened back when I was still flying.

"Hello, driver, I am your smart navigation system. If it is your preference, you may simply call me Nav," the voice says.

"You've got be *shitting* me," I mutter under my breath.

"Jesting is not even among my most perfunctory skills," the ship quickly quips. "Please place your hand on the ID plate in front of you for further instructions."

I comply and place the palm of my hand on what can only be the ID plate—a nearly translucent piece of green lucite near the nucleo-core battery light indicators.

"Hold, please," the ship says as a thin horizontal line of red light scans the underside of my fingertips.

"Greetings, Captain!" the ship says after a few seconds, its tone changing slightly. "I have been programmed to take you back to Earth, as per the previous captain's instructions. However, I can plot an alternate destination, if that is your desire, sir."

"Umm… well, I'm not sure, Nav."

I fumble around, looking for a way to acknowledge—a key, a switch of some kind, or a pair of green and red buttons.

"Sir?" the ship asks.

"Uhh… no. Earth is fine."

"Very well, sir."

"So, you, *uh*, you respond totally to verbal commands?"

"Affirmative," Nav says, and for a second, I could swear he clears his throat before he speaks again. "If you are capable, please feel free to use the dash controls directly to the right of the throttle levers, sir."

"What do you mean by *capable*?"

"My file on Barrabas Madzimure is minimal, with no evidence as to whether or not you were or are a pilot, sir."

"Oh, you think I can't fly this thing?"

"I am not saying anything, sir. Kilraven's flight history is known to me and Madzimure's is not. I have no systems in place to tell me which of these individuals you may or may not be."

I laugh out loud and pat the side of the ship's interior—as if I were rewarding a patient beast waiting for its treat.

"You're alright, Nav, you know that?" I say, still laughing.

"Yes, sir."

"Even a machine like you has got to look out for its own skin, right?"

"Yes, sir."

I run my fingertips over the control panel directly above the throttle, looking for the ignition switch.

"How do I start the launch sequence anyway?" I ask myself.

"Please prepare for launch when you are ready, sir," the ship says matter-of-factly.

"Now?"

"Very well, sir. Commencing take off in five—"

"Aw, hell!"

"Four."

"Dammit! It was a *question*, Nav!"

"Three."

I move as fast as I can to attach the chest harness. I should've known better. Buckling the damn safety belts is always the first thing you're supposed to do, pointless though it may be if you find yourself colliding with an errant chunk of space rock.

"Two."

My hands are so sweaty I nearly botch the whole thing in my nervousness, but then I hear the click of the chest harness latch-lock into place.

"One."

I hold my breath as the engines ignite, and then it's promptly forced out of me when I'm pushed back against the seat. I'm already nearly a thousand meters in the air when I glance at the altimeter.

"Sir, if you would please lock your waist harness," the ship says.

"Shut *up*, Nav!"

"Sir, if you do not connect the harness properly, you may experience loss of consciousness."

"Grow a pair of mitts and connect it for me then, Nav!"

To my surprise, the waist harness moves of its own accord, then snaps into place.

"Why didn't you do that *before*?!"

"You did not ask, sir. I can perform no such action without either verbal or remote command."

"Oh, for crying out loud! This is gonna be a *long* flight, isn't it, Nav?"

"Yes, sir. The distance is approximately forty-seven million light-years."

"Forty-seven? Holy *shit*."

"Have you defecated, sir?"

"What? No! Of course not! I just, you know, forgot how far away Earth was, that's all."

"Yes, sir. I can make the journey in eighty-five Earth days, if I am authorized to use all six nucleo-cores, sir."

"What six cores? What do you mean?"

"Current data recommends using only three of the six cores at most, as a precautionary measure, sir." Nav replies as the blinking of the dash lights fills my field of vision.

"I need to get to Earth as quickly as possible, Nav."

"I understand, sir. This course of action will allow you to still arrive on Earth within one hundred and thirteen to one hundred and fifteen calendar days, sir."

"That's pretty specific of you. I guess we don't wanna burn you out. Okay then, use three of them. I didn't expect you could move that fast anyway."

"Yes, sir, though not as fast as my successor, the H-series or the—"

"Yeah, yeah, alright. That's enough, Nav."

"We are passing through the planet's atmosphere now. You may experience a slight change in pressure. If you need to vomit please refrain from doing so, sir."

"Thanks, Nav."

The ship begins to rock and vibrate as we fly through Eridania's atmosphere. There's a barrage about the glass of the cockpit—orange and red flashes—and it sounds as though bombs are exploding at some distance from the rear of the ship. After a tense fifteen seconds we break free of the atmospheric frenzy, and all goes silent except for my panting and the sound of the thrusters shutting off.

I had nearly forgotten what the depths of space looked like. A giant bowl of pitch-black soup, peppered with innumerable stars—some of them holding vigil, others shooting this way and that. It's a cosmic dance that is overwhelming and beautiful all at once.

"We have cleared the atmosphere," Nav says, "and I can now begin the cryo-cycle at this time if you so desire, sir."

"No! Just… Just *wait* a minute, please."

"Yes, sir. My readings indicate that your bio-signs are normal. Heart rate is elevated. Blood pressure is normal. The cryo-tube can be ready in less than three minutes of your heart rate dropping to below seventy beats per minute."

"Can you stop talking for five seconds, Nav?!"

"I am not actually speaking, sir. The onboard computer is simply one part of a greater whole, capable of both automatic speech recognition and aural translation, which my chip core then converts to data that can be—"

"Shut the hell *up*, Nav!"

"Yes, sir."

"For pity's sake, do they have other models that don't talk?"

"Yes, sir, I—"

"Don't answer that!" I shout, covering my face with my hand.

Having a look around, I search the cockpit for something that my mother might have left. A keepsake, a note, some token... anything at all. After a minute of fumbling about with my shaking hands, I can find nothing. Then the thought occurs to me that she was too damn smart for that. She would've gone to a great length to cover her tracks.

"Nav?"

"Yes, sir?"

"Did Corvus leave anything inside the ship?"

"The previous captain left nothing foreign onboard, sir."

"Damn. I was hoping to—"

No, not hoping. I *needed* something more. Another piece of Mother's puzzle. She said he had Meg'n and Mara. And why in the hell would he leave Elisabeth alive, too?

Either way, I will have my answers. And I'll have them soon enough. He will tell me why. I want to hear why from his mouth before I put my fist in it.

"Sir?"

"Yeah, Nav?"

"I performed a more thorough scan of the ship and can find nothing onboard other than you, a ballistic nylon satchel, and two rather crude low-caliber firearms, sir."

"Wait, I thought you couldn't do anything without express verbal command?"

"That is true, sir. However, you did ask me if anything was left on the ship, and though my first scan was merely superficial, the mini-mass spectrometer analyzes the molecular structure of—"

"Alright, alright Nav. Fuckssakes. Please tell me your model has been discontinued?"

"Negative, sir, though by my calculations, at minimum three of six cores will need replacing once we return, and I will require standard maintenance to my electrical systems."

"Yeah. Sure. Maintenance!" I say, laughing. "If by maintenance you mean taking yourself apart, then go *right* ahead."

"Sir?"

"Yeah, Nav?"

"I can only conclude that your last statement indicates you wish the ship to self-destruct, sir. I can be ready to self-terminate in less than—"

"No, no, no! Do *not* self-destruct!"

"Yes, sir."

"Shouldn't you be saying 'no, sir'?"

"No, sir."

"Fuck, I survive one nightmare only to be placed inside another one even *more* terrifying? You're gonna be the death of me, Nav."

The ship doesn't reply.

"Nav?"

"Yes, sir?"

"Do you, uh, have any onboard historical records of any kind?"

"Please be more specific, sir."

"You know like... uh... what type of ship are you?"

"I am a Lightmach Starblazer, model E one nine, being the nineteenth model of the E-series."

"Who manufactured you?"

"Lightmach, formerly Lockheed and Martin Aeronautics."

"You're kidding? So, the good old American dream was bought by the Germans?"

"I do not understand, sir."

"I guess you wouldn't. Never mind. What year were you made, Nav?"

"I was built along with the ship itself in 2089."

"What year's it now?"

"The current year on Earth is 2102, sir."

"Fuck me. It's been thirty years."

"Yes, sir. Additionally, by the time we reach Earth, it will be the New Year. That is January 23, 2103."

My heart jumps up in my throat. So many years, all of them gone. How is it that Mother was still alive? How is it that she was able to transfer into a body that was not her own without being caught? It happened to me, yes, but it was done to me on purpose. The Prophet did it against my will. And he... He would be an ancient shell of a man by now.

"Nav?"

"Sir?"

"Do you know anything about transference?"

"Yes, sir."

"Tell me."

"Moving one object from one place to another is fairly elementary, sir. Object A, if so desired, can be moved to Point A or Point B through various means. For instance, if you selected an item such as a ball or box that you—"

"No! Wait a minute. I'm talking about people, Nav. Transference in *people*."

"I require more specificity in the query, sir."

"Just forget it," I say, rubbing my forehead.

Sitting in this thing is like sitting in a playpen full of children. I lay my head back for a moment, close my eyes, and try to form some kind of rational thought. I think of Mother dying. I think of Corvus taking his last breaths. He mentioned a surgeon... and someone named Terra. How will they find me, if at all? No doubt the Prophet will find me well before they will, as I'd bet my life this ship is probably being tracked by some means I can't see.

"Nav?"

"Yes, sir?"

"What's our landing destination?"

"Radian Five in Neo York City, dock number six, sir."

"Radian Five?"

"Yes, sir."

"What'n the hell is that?"

"Formerly quadrant three of the city, Radian Five houses the head-quarters for Earth's Great Council and also serves primarily as the site of the Tower of Peace, sir."

"Shit."

"If you need to defecate, sir, I am more than able to assist in the expelling of fecal masses and or any other solid waste needing removal."

"It's an expression, Nav! I do *not* have to defecate!"

"Yes, sir."

"Hmm. So, Radian Five, huh?"

"That is correct, sir."

"So, is the city divided up equally?"

"Yes. Into six parts, sir."

"When I left there were only four. Unbelievable."

He should have killed me when he had the chance. He should never have sent me to Eridania. Why would he leave me as his one loose end? And if he knows I'm coming, then he'll be ready. He'll be fully prepped for whatever possibility I bring with me. He will have accounted for every eventuality. That means I've got one chance to stay on my toes... I have to think of something fast.

Damn. I wish Iyov were here.

"Nav, can you start the cryo-cycle?"

"Yes, commencing cryo-preservation, sir."

"Thanks."

I look out the cockpit window at the nebulae and stars and asteroids and moons... even entire galaxies. They seem so small. When your feet are on the ground, everything seems so large, even the smallest of things. Out here in space, the largest of things are like grains of sand.

And what does that make us? What does that make me? And what do I mean in the grand scheme of all this? Whatever it is, I'm part of the whole, and there's still one act left to play out before its completion. But if this play is being put on paper, I'm not the one with the inkwell, and I'm certainly not holding the pen.

"Sir, cryo-preservation will commence in the next thirty seconds. Please look overhead and find the breathing apparatus. Place it firmly over your nose to prepare for vitrification. You may feel a slight pinch, sir," Nav says.

The breathing tube secures itself over my nose as soon as I place it against my skin. It's almost as if it's alive in some way. I feel more tubes probe further into each of my nasal cavities, and I almost laugh, thinking for a second that they might poke my brain.

Then the largest syringe I've ever seen pops out from a panel just above my head, and this time I nearly do defecate. The needle's movement is guided by the ship, and as I watch with trepidation, it rotates around the seat and goes just out of my range of vision. I feel slightly paranoid for a moment, anticipating the pain, and then I feel the pinch that Nav warned me about in the back of my neck.

"Have a good sleep, sir. I will wake you at least eighteen hours prior to destination arrival," Nav says.

The jump seat rolls back, and I'm laid out completely horizontal. I think I'm sliding into the back of the ship where the cryo-tube is, but everything looks so shiny and fuzzy all at once I can't really tell.

My eyes are going dark. My brain tells my mouth to move, but I can't be completely certain if I've said any words or not.

"I'm coming for you, Elisabeth."

CHAPTER 14

ELISABETH

I'VE TRIED TO die so many times that I'm not even afraid of it anymore. The trick is not to be afraid. It doesn't even hurt like people think that it would. Coming back, though... Coming back is the scary part.

In my fourth body, I didn't eat a single thing for over three weeks. When the transference technicians dragged me from my room, I overheard one of those damned doctors saying, "Elisabeth, you've lost nearly thirty pounds." That made me smile like I'd not smiled in years, even though I couldn't walk any longer and my physical strength was nearly spent. But just when I thought it was over, what did they go and do? The devils transferred me into a fresh set of skin and began feeding me intravenously.

I don't even know why I was shocked. These *men* control everything... when I bathe, when I sleep, and even how I go to the bathroom. There is no longer anything left to me in this world that is truly my own, except for my wedding band. If the men in power know about the ring, they have afforded me it for reasons that I can't foresee... but none of them for pity, I can tell you that.

These same men who also rule the nations took my husband from me decades ago, only I can never be sure how many years it's actually been. Ever so much more than twenty, if my last count was right.

But I am not alone.

Like so many other dear souls in this tower, I've been imprisoned here against my will. This place of supposed peace wherein only by making a payment of your very spirit are you finally rewarded with absolution. Every last one of us here has forgotten the sound of leaves among the swaying trees, the falling of spring waters, and the laughter of children. And though I could just say a few simple words and it would all be over, in my heart I know the forgiveness that comes from these holy men breeds only damnation.

Death is the only way out now. And if death were to come to me or to any of us, it would be the greatest of mercies. I suffer all in silence, as I've become accustomed to hiding any emotion and fighting back tears. I simply have to, or they will find some level of mastery over me.

This morning, before I woke and the technicians came to remove me from my bed, I had the dream again. It's always the same one—the walls of my personal hell explode around me, and when the smoke clears, I see my love having returned beyond all odds to save me. Together we leap from the windows of this tower of terror and fly away, riding on the wind like great birds over the city. But the moment is short-lived, and in the instant when our eyes meet, I always know that the dream isn't real. After I wake, my heart breaks for what must be the ten-thousandth time.

It was then in my bed that I rolled onto my back and stared up at the ceiling for what felt like hours. And nothing about this morning seemed out of the ordinary—that is, until the sun rose. The red glow coming from a high window, which I can never look out from, drew attention to something strange around the steel grating twenty feet above my head. The air flowing out of it took shape, looking almost wavy, like an intense summer heat rising up from barren asphalt.

That's when I smelled it—the reagent. They call it *narkos*. They've never actually pumped gas through the ventilation system prior to today. I quickly removed my wedding ring and placed it in the hollowed-out leather-bound copy of *The Prophet's Tome* at my bedside.

Before I blacked out, my heart told me that there is but one hope left now. All pathways before my feet are dark, save for one. This path I have not spoken about with anyone, except the god in my head and those other select few who are now living only there. I tell them I have chosen so because my hand is forced. I believe they hear me, and understand, and would forgive me if they could answer in return. I tell them that if I trusted a savior might come and split asunder the atmosphere in my lifetime, I would rest in that sweet promise. I would wait, allowing the ever-mounting years to pile their weight further on my shoulders until I became nothing more than a caged dog relying solely on my captors for water and shelter.

Believe me, I would do it.

But I cannot wait on a god any longer. I don't believe my prayers or the voices of men rise up into heaven anymore. Not after what we've done. And neither does my love hear me. He does not come for me.

Where are you, Thaniel? Where have you gone? Are you in that place where I am incapable of following?

I tell myself time and time again to stop asking such questions. But they plague my thoughts to the point of nausea every hour of each day… and they have nearly driven me insane. Yet somehow, I have held strong to the words I was taught when I was a girl and father would read to me at my bedside. I cannot remember the title of the book in question anymore, but reading, he said, "*In your solitude, and through patience, possess your very soul.*"

But Father did not know then that he was wrong. You cannot possess your soul any longer. Not here. Not in this place. I know now the only way out is by achieving the destruction of my original body, and I can do this thing by one means only.

However, my captors stand in the way of this goal. They are becoming smarter of late. Through the study of my mind through transference they have managed to gain a foothold within. And though they would find me difficult to break even if I were made of Tokyo's best folded steel, they can now partly anticipate my actions since I have been transferred over a dozen times. Never once have I been able to fully resist the procedure. But in solemn oaths my mind makes with my heart, I swear to give them as much hell as possible as they rip my soul from me.

And *this time* I am going to beat them.

During my ninth transference trial, the techs made the mistake of using the elevators to move me from my lodging in the Hall of Isolation to the main operating lab down among the lower levels. My hands were unbound then, and I used the opportunity to drop a pair of irreplaceable Russian-made porcelain earrings through a narrow opening in the doors of the elevator shaft. The Prophet himself had the two guards escorting me promptly executed for allowing this to happen, screaming later to his brethren that the egg-shaped baubles once belonged to none other than the House of Romanov. Consequently, this murdering holy man and would-be-suitor that gave the jewelry to me as a gift are one and the same.

I've wondered every day since how many more lives paid for those earrings. There was a time now long since past when I would have shied far away from even the possibility of being held responsible for the taking of a life. But I am pushed to breaking, and I simply refuse to bear this shame any longer, which is why I find myself in this current predicament.

Over a period of several years those two guards in particular repeatedly woke me during the night—one of them always with a wet hand at my throat, the other covering my mouth greedily while they both panted like animals and violated my body with their evil lust. What that pair of scum accomplished with me was twofold—firstly they earned my hatred for all eternity, and secondly, they handed me the realization that I've utterly forgotten the gentle touch of a true lover. And try as I might in order to recall my husband's caress while I was assaulted, it was never a comfort. So, you could say I figure those two "men" got what was coming to them.

Naturally, the two guards assigned to me ever since that day have been women. They're the *same* women for that matter, though I don't know their names. One of them has hair as red as a cardinal, and the other one's a petite honey blonde. I never hear them speak to each other, let alone to me, and they seem to take an extra effort to avoid looking me in the eye.

Once I did catch the redhead watching me, and it seemed to me that she did so with pity, as the corners of her mouth frowned. Undoubt-edly sullen at what I've become—a pale and empty cocoon sheltering the woman I once was. But when I asked her what she was staring at, the pity I mistook turned to scorn, and she slapped me across the cheek so hard my eyes uncontrollably welled up with tears. My instinct then was to pull every last hair from her head. But I'm smarter than that. I have to be. I know that these two are close to *him*.

So, I've watched, listening for any word they might say, and I've waited. Dear Lord, how I've waited.

The second time I opened my eyes this morning, I found myself strapped to a new restraint chair that doesn't even allow my hands to move. Then I knew this day had something different in store. They're prepping me for something special.

I've got a few good guesses as to why. Firstly, the *narkos* gas, and that's the least of them. The second reason, more importantly, is that I've not attempted to take the life of this body for months, and they only transfer me when I'm dying or dead. Lastly, because it's the holiday season soon. Ironically, during this time of year, the whole place shuts down. Even the Prophet is often away for weeks—secretly conferring with the other false man-gods of the world, with no one really knowing exactly where he's gone. I've had my suspicions that he doesn't go anywhere at all, but rather he stays here in the tower, recovering from his own transference trial.

So, this is it… the moment I've been *waiting* for. God help me if I'm wrong.

What these two mute matrons of the Prophet currently wheeling me down the halls don't know is that I'm hiding a small but effective sharp rod of steel in the crack of my buttocks. It was a little trick I learned from my husband ages ago. I saw him put an unapproved modified blaster of his own design in the same place just before a superior officer removed his primary firearm for verbal insubordination.

What I would give for this bit of metal to be a blaster!

It took me years of wearing away at my previous bed's frame to try and free a piece I could use. But because my room was inspected weekly, it wasn't long before I was found out. After that, the Prophet had crafted for me a bed made entirely of acrylic, minus the emergency crank at its foot, which one of the guards outside my room would always carry.

Not long afterward I bit one of them on the hand, and in a fit of rage he kicked the bed, nearly bending the crank clean off as it collided with the eridanium wall. The guard left the room, spitting, and he cursed so loudly that his incoming replacement kept a safe distance from me, not least of all for the sight of the other man's blood all over my mouth. That's when I seized the chance to break the rest of the crank free, and since then I've been hiding it in as many places as I might, making a sort of game out of it.

Playing at it has kept me alive.

We've just entered the elevators now. I can feel we're going down, presumably moving toward the lowest level of the tower and the main transference rooms. I know this because *this* elevator in particular is constructed of smooth stainless steel from top to bottom. It was designed with no controls in its interior and could only be operated by the techs awaiting you at the end of the line.

I breathe in deeply and as quietly as I can through my nose while collecting my thoughts, and then it occurs to me that there's something unusual about my guards. One of them smells different today. It's very fruity, almost like fresh flowers.

"No one working here can afford perfume," I say without hesitating. "So, which one of you has a new gentleman caller?"

Neither of them answer. But they both stop breathing for a second or two.

"Oh, so it's the *two* of you? Is he handsome?" I ask.

Darkness takes me for a time, and I miss the rest of the ride in the elevator.

"Get her out of that chair!" a voice orders.

I can only assume one of the girls chopped me at the base of the neck, because when I come to, the muscles there are on fire.

I can hardly see, for the light in the room is almost pure white, and I know I'm in one of the trial chambers. I'm sitting down, still strapped to a chair, and the cold emanating from the transference pod at my right sends a chill across my arms. I almost laugh, knowing I couldn't be any other place than right where I expected I'd be. But when I look up, I get the shock of my life when the person standing before me dressed all in white isn't who I expected it to be.

"It is good to see you again," Jovian says. "It grieves me that I have not made more time for you over the last few months."

My insides crawl. The gooseflesh on the back of my neck rises. My plan has just gone completely awry. The Surgeon was *supposed* to be here. He always transfers me. All my hope was reliant upon this.

"Have you nothing to say?" he asks, looking like a chastised puppy.

The Surgeon and I had established quite the rapport with one another. Though I've not seen him for years, I discovered that without him, Jovian has no one to complete his own transference trials. With the Surgeon dead, the Prophet would be crippled.

"Where's the Surgeon?" I ask.

"Oh, he will not be handling your trials anymore," Jovian says. "I must say I am glad at that. Anyhow, it is fitting that *I* should be the one to do you this service from now on."

The Prophet feigns a smile. So do I.

"I am delighted to see you, Elisabeth," he adds quietly.

I mask my contempt for him with as much effort as possible. As he looks upon me, I am suddenly struck dumb by the stark revelation of the Surgeon's absence. Jovian needed him to perform his own transference trials. Without him present, I can now kill the Prophet myself. I can put an *end* to this here and now!

No, this *can't* be. It *can't* be this easy.

At the involuntary flushing of my cheeks, something inside tells me to beware. My heart flutters in my chest, knowing how very thin of a wire I am standing on right now. I attempt to convince myself to control my very thoughts. To put a guard on my mouth.

But I do just the opposite.

"This is pretty strange for you, Jovian. Happy to see me, you say?" I ask, still smiling. "If I thought you actually were, I just might die from shock."

The lines between Jovian's eyebrows crease and he looks down at the floor. "And die you shall, I'm afraid," he says, his voice sounding suddenly perilous.

"But I've not broken this body yet. I'd hate to see it go to waste," I reply glibly.

My nerves get the better of me, and my voice shakes at the last. With a wave of his hand, Jovian coldly dismisses the two scented guardiennes behind me from the room. The reveling smile that spreads across his face leaves little doubt he senses my fear. I'd be a fool to think otherwise. He puts his open hands in the air in an effort to try and calm me.

"Fear not," he says, pacing the floor on the other side of the transference pod to my right. "I have brought you here for something truly *special*, Elisabeth," he says, his hands caressing the top of the closed pod. "Would you like to see it?" he asks, shaking his head back and forth at me curiously.

I don't respond, and he moves around the pod, closer toward the back of my chair.

"Are you frightened of me still?" he asks. "I am not afraid of *you*, Elisabeth," he quips, standing directly behind me now. "I know that our… *history* with one another has been strained. But I aim to finally resolve all of that."

"And what do you propose, Jovian?" I ask, feeling my confidence return.

"I am going to give you a new body," he says. "One which I have had designed specifically for you."

He's stepping away from me now, I think, though I can barely hear his feet.

"The adjustment will be… *difficult*," he adds, "but I have no doubt that you will thank me later."

He brushes against the back of the chair again suddenly, placing his hands on my shoulders. He pauses before taking several deep breaths, as if he's about to begin a well-rehearsed speech.

"I want you to do this of free will, Elisabeth. I want you to enter the pod without coercion. This pathway is set. It has been destined for you… and *you* alone," he says, his fingertips digging gently into my collarbone.

My first reaction is to tell him to go to hell. But then I think of my plan when I feel the cold metal hiding at my back shift slightly. Then, without any further thought, I *will* myself to transform into the most skilled actress on the planet.

"How can you call it free will if the path is laid before me?" I ask, turning to look at him from over my shoulder.

Jovian laughs girlishly and points at the ceiling.

"What you choose to do of your own volition may be written in books beyond the walls of the living, but just because it is known does not mean you cannot freely choose," he says.

"Then I am weary. Weary of not having the choice… if it is one," I say.

He rushes around and kneels at my feet in front of the restraint chair. I've never seen him on his knees before! Not even for me.

My God, he really *has* dropped his guard.

"If a starship is set to leave for the exomoons of Tau Ceti, and you are set to board it, but at the last moment you change your mind and get off, it does not change the fact that the flight *will* leave. You have only chosen not to get on it. But the ship is *still* going somewhere," he says.

"And so go our lives, don't they, Jovian?"

"Yes," he says, almost impatiently. "Will you enter the pod?" he asks, extending his hand toward my face.

"I… I can't do this on my own," I say, my voice quivering as I'm nearly brought to false tears. "I've been weak since breathing the gas earlier and I—"

"Elisabeth, what else must I do?" he asks.

I haven't been this close to him in a long time. His pursed lips are smooth and red like blood. His dark hair is longer than before, and his cheeks and throat are so freshly shaven I note a nick in the skin just above his Adam's apple.

I revel too briefly in the thought that he'll soon have another blade at his throat. As I search the eerie depths of his dark eyes for a sign, it takes all my physical strength not to waver. The windows to whatever bit of soul he's got left inside of him have become ever more clouded and opaque over the years.

God help me. God help me find the *right* words. If you can hear me, I need you to help me *right now*!

"I will do this for you, Jovian."

"You will?"

"But only… if *you* will take my hand and lead me."

And with that, I watch. I watch as his last lingering smidge of doubt turns to a sort of boyish marvel. He smiles at me, as if I've just agreed to finally give him my hand in marriage.

"Oh, my dear, do not despair!" he says, cupping his hands around one of my knees.

"No, Jovian, I'm not afraid anymore," I say, building on my

performance by hanging my head. "My only real regret is all these years I've wasted… pushing you and your teachings away. And I was wrong to do so. I *know* that now."

Jovian puts his index finger under my chin, then, lifting my face up with it so that our eyes meet, he rises slowly to his feet.

"Your humility is about to be rewarded," he says before moving quickly behind me once more. "Let me show you just exactly what I have achieved for you."

I stop breathing as Jovian swiftly rotates the release levers at the back of the chair so that my restraints slacken almost entirely. Then, in the blink of an eye, the iron bracelets binding my wrists and ankles shrink away into the arms of the chair itself, their recession echoing upon the walls with a piercing metallic ring.

Behind me Jovian lingers, taking heavy breaths as his long hands run up and down the length of the shoulder straps—the only two things still keeping me from drawing the shank at my backside and ending this entire charade.

"Do you hear it calling to you in the night?" he asks me.

"The night?"

"Or in your dreams?" he adds.

"I am alone in the night. And my dreams are… cruel to me," I cry softly.

He tenderly pulls the shoulder straps lose from the chair, and I'm left totally without restraint. "No longer," he says, leaning forward over my right shoulder and drawing his face close to mine. "I offer you final relief from all the pain of the past."

I turn slightly in my chair to face him, reaching for my weapon with my left hand.

"Yes… my prophet," I say, touching the end of his chin with my right hand.

In that moment, Jovian closes his eyes and smiles. Then a laugh begins at the back of his throat—a guttural thing, drawing from the sycophantic pleasure he gets from being called by this profane moniker.

Then some god or one of his angels grants me the speed of ancient Rome's Victoria, and I pull the metal shank from my backside and drive it straight up and into Jovian's throat. His eyes bulge, and he flails, writhing like a serpent skittering across sand. But even with blood-wet hands, I don't lose my grip on the spike until I climb out of the restraint chair.

Releasing him, I stand back several paces, and at first there's no sound except his feet slipping upon the floor. To my surprise, I can only watch without enjoyment as the blood rushes from his wound, blemishing the ceremonial gown. Finally, he gurgles through several seconds of rapid breathing in an effort to speak, his eyes ever-widening over the shock of my choice.

In a mire of his own life's blood, Jovian slips down upon his knees, and his entire body shudders while he crawls toward me. He throws his head back, and looking up toward heaven, he spits more blood into the air. Then I'm awestruck as he rises back up, drawing on some hidden strength. Remaining down on a bent knee, he uses both hands in an attempt to remove the embedded shank.

"I cannot die! My *numen* wills it… my *mana* demands it!" he hisses through his teeth.

He growls, finding that his wet hands are no use, and wraps the folds of his cloak around the end of the spike in a final desperate attempt to remove it. He snarls, finding that it too is of no avail.

But then, turning, he nearly leaps the distance between the transference pod and me. His groping fingers claw and scrape at the controls of the activation panel. They find their mark, and the security alarm activates overhead, blaring as if there was a choir in the room with us. At the blast of sound, he turns back toward me, grunting and spitting.

"You've failed, Jovian."

He keeps trying to talk, but he can't. The malice in his eyes says it all. The piercing hatred in his stare is so strong it could smite me and raze this very tower to the ground at the same time.

But it won't. Not today. Today I am a mountain.

At my approach, Jovian slinks down upon the ground with his back against the transference pod, cowering in fear like an abused animal. I use the moment to do what someone much braver than I should've done decades ago—I put my foot upon his neck.

"Enter the pod willingly? I would rather die and wake up in the fires of hell than do a *single* thing that you would have of me."

His hands grip my ankle, and smearing blood over the top of my foot, he struggles futilely to keep my heel from pushing the spike farther into his throat. Then I hear the chamber door open behind me. The clatter tells me the room is no doubt filling with the stoutest of Jovian's guards.

How appropriate their timing.

Voices are cursing me. But I don't turn to look at them. I never take my eyes off him. Why is there a wicked smile spreading across his face?

Something from behind sets the back of my head on fire, and a blinding flash of white fills my vision. The last things I see through the bubbling cauldron of blood rising out from his mouth are those teeth—his damned perfect teeth.

Darkness closes in and wraps its arms around me. I've seen it before. It's the *utter darkness*.

Then there's a rapturous rushing of wind coming from all directions, and it whistles in my ears. I reach out into the black in front of me, but I feel nothing. I have never been here before. I hear fell voices calling out to me from behind. No, they're *singing*. They must be angels.

The surface under my feet feels like glass as I walk forward into the creeping dark. My eyes can find nothing and focus on nothing.

"God save me!"

The angels stop. I wait for someone to call my name.

"God? I'm ready to see your face!"

Only the wind responds. Soon the angelic voices grow distinct again, building to a boisterous wrack in a far-off space I cannot see.

Why do I feel afraid? I'm afraid of the way I feel. I go down upon my knees. I start to weep. I didn't think you were supposed to cry in heaven.

Then I see a light flickering far ahead, as if someone has just lit a candle for me. I stand and choose to lose all fear. I take flight, running as fast as I can. I pray the warm orange glow will take me home.

I'm almost there now. I can reach it! Why am I not moving closer?

Directly in front of my eyes, I watch my own hands reach out, as if they were not part of my body, and they grope for the light. A force from behind latches on. Something has a hold of me. It's dragging me back.

"No! I cannot go… I will not go! God, help me!"

The candlelight of my salvation shrinks away, and I become quickly aware of my lungs all of a sudden. They are burning. There's a taste on my tongue… something familiar. It's the sweetness of the venting liquid expelling itself from my airways. My arms are at my side, and under my fingertips I feel cold metal, and then I know… I know where I am.

My eyelids blink repeatedly, but I see nothing, only it's not just nothing… it is a void. It is a darkness that moves and has shape. I reach out, my hands feeling about directly above my head, and my knuckles knock against the cold metal tomb I have become so well accustomed to. The transference pod reacts to something from without, and in a blast of fluorocarbon and eridanium vapor, it opens.

"Lie back down, Elisabeth. You should not be waking just yet," a male voice says.

"Why can't I see?" I ask.

"Hold her down, damn you!" the man says.

"Who are you?" I ask, feeling several firm hands on my breasts and arms. "Answer me, devils!"

"Elisabeth, listen to me. Your mouth is moving, but you cannot form words. You can hear me, though, yes?"

My fingers touch my lips, and I try to talk, and all my efforts are in vain. I cannot hear my own voice. I reach out into the void that moves in front of me, my hands grabbing the first thing that comes to them—and I feel the familiar slick armor that protects the forearms of the tower guards.

"Clearly you cannot see, either, which is by design, of course," he says.

I ask the man again who he is, but I hear nothing as the question resounds only in my head.

"You are *mute*, if you haven't figured that out already," he says, chuckling sardonically. "But please, feel free to familiarize yourself with your new face," he adds as someone grabs my hands and forces me to touch my own nose.

It's larger than before, and the skin around my eyes feels smooth and oily. I don't recognize the feel of my throat or the dryness of my hands as I rub them together. My God, even my breasts are much larger. My fingernails crawl across my skull and I know they've shaved all my hair off. Warm tears well up in my eyes.

"Yes. Cry if you must. The transference can be horrid."

But I don't weep for this body. I weep because the stars didn't let me die. I weep for all the years and all the days of my life that have led me to this moment in time. I weep because I did my best to hold firm. I fought tooth and nail to the end, resisting the man who set himself up as god. I weep because I return to life once more. I weep because I know that hope, like me, must now be truly dead.

From my left, I hear a doorway open. Everyone in the room who had a voice goes suddenly silent.

"Elisabeth, we... We were instructed to bring you back so that you could—"

"They were instructed to bring you back so that you can be a witness to everything that transpires around you," interjects an all-too-familiar male voice.

"Please, forgive us, master. She was so close to the other side that we were—"

"You did your best. Now get out."

Then I hear *his* footsteps. They're sharp and crisp as they tap on the floor, each pace getting louder as he makes his way nearer toward the pod.

"You know, I forgive you for what you did to me earlier, Elisabeth," he says. "In fact, I anticipated that you would do it. I had hopes that you wouldn't, of course, but in the likelihood that you did, I already had a new body prepared for me, waiting in the wings. I thought... I thought that getting it out of your system would make you see clearer. But I was wrong, and I simply cannot allow you the opportunity again. You force me to take extreme measures. And as I said before... I chose this body for you."

I sense his body next to me, and then I feel his breath caressing the side of my face.

"I had them engineer it just so you can hear all things," he whispers. "Nothing will be hidden from your ears. But you shall not be able to speak, nor will you be able to see anything."

He grabs me by the face forcefully, his fingers digging into my cheekbones. I don't even flinch. Not even at his kiss—a gesture completely devoid of any warmth or love.

"And your hope, Elisabeth," he says, still holding my face in his hand. "When all your hope finally comes home, and rest assured, he is coming… he will see you. He will even touch you, but he will not know you. Only then… only *then* will I let you die."

The Prophet lets go of me, and my heart relents before my head even hits the padded cushion of the bedding beneath it. In my spirit, I am changed. I feel it. I *feel* the change as I finally submit totally to the despair—the vanity of my search for peace through death strikes me down, as if I am straw against the edge of its blade.

But my love… He said my love is coming for me!

I curl up as a child would inside the transference pod. My body shakes uncontrollably as the horror of what Jovian has done presses down on me like the weight of all the worlds.

"Well, *well!*" the Prophet says, laughing and clasping his hands together. "It seems as though you do indeed understand… at last."

CHAPTER 15

TRASH HEAP

ACCORDING TO LETTERS chiseled into the face of the stone, I'm sitting on the wet grave of someone once named *W. Astor*. I can only assume his name was William. Since my ass is technically in his face, I'm confident he'd agree that we've become pretty well acquainted.

"Don't mind me, Mister Bill."

It's just past two in the morning, and the temperature gauge on the side of my gun says it's six degrees centigrade. Besides my warm breath on the icy air, I can see only one other thing through the scope from this position—the banks of the Hudson. They're teeming with fish tonight. If I don't manage to walk away with a dozen of those floppers, I'm gonna be joining old Mister Bill here by the weekend.

It's officially the Yuletide season in another week. I thank the stars above for that. The Skywatchers won't be on their toes as much from now until after New Year's. From what I hear they're all in Tokyo, living it up in penthouse luxury on the Church's dime for making it through another year unscathed. They each get a brand-spankin' new body as a holiday bonus.

What a life, *huh*?

Still, I took the Surgeon's advice tonight. I played it safe anyway, approaching the river from the east, via Broadway, and then zigzagged my way through Trinity Cemetery. The Skywatchers don't ever come here— they've been forbidden by the Prophet to touch its grounds. The Surgeon says the Prophet's father was laid to rest here. Anyway, the Skywatchers are up in the stratosphere half of the time anyway, monitoring all the flight paths and whatnot. And besides, like anywhere in the city that's still naturally green and overgrown, the people believe this place is haunted. Truth is, the only ghost out tonight is me.

Me and the boys of the Rock have managed to clear most of the old river walkway over the last three years. It's still more than dangerous at the best of times, but the Skywatchers have learned to stay clear since we make a point to try *not* to kill them. Maiming's the name of the game. It's far worse for them to return to the Church with their kneecaps blown away or an arm missing. The boys tell me it's like being a dickless pedo in Rome. Whatever that means.

I imagine from time to time the Prophet himself receiving this sort of news somewhere, maybe in a hidden chamber at the top of his tower, pissed the hell off over the amount of transfers that we've caused. Seeing as how most of the original bodies are stored in Tokyo for safekeeping, it costs those mooks a lot of money, I wager.

The Surgeon, though? He's definitely no mook. He told me the real story of this cemetery. Supposedly the author of the Federalist Papers was buried here, and the Prophet wanted to wipe out all memory of him and his fanatical ideals. I figure His Eminence did the job since I don't even know the mook's name. And even though I don't know shit about the man whose deathbed I'm using as a makeshift turret, either, at least I know *his* name. I'm sure he wouldn't mind one damn bit knowing what I'm after.

Me and the boys back at the Rock haven't eaten good in weeks. I aim to fix that. The Surgeon always sends me on these little shopping missions, mainly because I'm smaller, and that makes me quieter and quicker. I like to think it's purely because I know my way around this side of town better than anyone else in our outfit.

Don't get cocky, Trash.

I didn't grow up on these streets, but I learned the hard way that you can kill or be killed on them. There's no middle ground anymore—if there ever was. At least it's not like when my parents were still alive. Of course, I don't ever remember there being a time when this city had any real peace, though the tower of its fuckin' namesake I can see from right here where my keyster's parked.

Some tower it is, too. Darting straight up into the sky like it owns the whole damn world. There's something hypnotic about it, though. I can see how the masses are drawn to it. Like moths too dumb to know what's good for them, flying straight into a blue flame. Or maybe flies to pig shit. Sometimes it makes me think I don't know how we've managed to survive being so close to the tower. I guess that's the genius of it—you never expect to find what you're looking for right under your nose holes.

Before I move any farther, I lick my fingertip to double-check the wind, making sure I'm still moving with it toward the river—and I am. A chill from behind hits the top of my finger, and I can't help but grin. It's good knowing the wind is at my back. The last thing I need is some of the Prions to the east of Amsterdam Avenue catching my scent.

Prions. *Yuck.*

They're cannibals. You can spot them by the way they walk. Those sickos will eat anything. But I sure as hell don't plan on becoming anyone's main course tonight. Eyes to the sky, and there's hardly any cloud cover right now. Pretty damn odd for this time of the year, actually.

I go against my gut and take another speck of time to enjoy the beauty of the fish—their pearly scales flashing in the moonlight even from over a hundred meters away. There's a sparkling of blues, greens, and purples. The geneti-fish you find in any of the central city markets just can't compare. I've not been to any of those shops since before I was due for my transference trial.

I remember this one place over on Ninth Avenue where I went with my dad when I was a kid, and we had the best piece of bluefish I'd ever tasted. It was the one joint on that side of town that served a dip made from mushy peas and the only one that didn't reek of ammonia to cover the scent of the stock spoiling. In any event, if I can manage to swing it, I'd still prefer my dinner freshly caught, the way nature intended.

I tally one point in my own column since the wind god's draught is still urging me on toward the river. I've waited here for nearly twenty minutes and not seen or heard any movement. My brain finally kicks me in the ass because I've loitered too long. I pick up my feet and my gun, and I leave old Astor alone again as I creep from the perch.

"Sorry, Señor Bill."

I have to apologize. That dude's been there a hell of a lot longer than I've been around. Despite the fact that my legs were on the verge of cramping up just five minutes ago, I bite my lip and summon all my nerve, essentially launching myself across Riverside Drive. It's at least fifteen meters to the other side. All my brain can ever manage to do when I come here is count the steps while I involuntarily hold my breath. It's a scary place. Damn scary, in fact.

But the boys gotta eat, and so do I.

The last time I volunteered for the job, I dropped nearly half my evening's catch, and the boys still won't let me live it down. The Skywatchers tend to patrol this street more often on account of rebels like me, so if you lose or drop something here, never ever go back for it. Not even if it's precious to you. The way I see it, nothing's more sacred than your soul, and a night or two of stomach groaning just ain't worth getting snatched up and taken to the transfer zones. Fuck *that*.

I'm over three-quarters of the way across when a blanket of dead leaves crunching underneath my boots stabs me in the back. Crossing quietly was the goal, but I'm frozen in my tracks just before I reach the embankment leading to the other side. My footsteps sound like they could wake the damned dead, and it's in that instant that fear forms a lump in my throat, and I stop.

I turn three hundred and sixty degrees, trying to mark anything that's not moving because of the wind, but I can't see a damned thing. The dread sitting on my chest and this piece of shit gun of mine are the only things weighing me down tonight. It's a DH-09. Durable as hell, and has a minimal heat signature, but its range *sucks*. I'd get more accuracy from a vintage semi-automatic, but hell, I've had the DH for so long I can't bring myself to get rid of the thing. I guess no one can ever accuse me of not being sentimental.

I suddenly get my balls back when I hear a sound for sore ears—the call of an eastern bluebird. Thank the stars! They nest in the trees behind me, which run along the road's edge. Fruit-eaters mainly, and they sure as hell never make a peep if the Prions or the Skywatchers are out in force.

I holster the DH and keep moving—smiling from ear to ear that I'm leaving Riverside safely behind me yet again. Tally another one up in my column. That makes two points tonight, bitch.

After weaving through the overgrown line of cherry trees leading down the embankment, I get hit with a big-ass whiff of that good old Neo York smell. It's a mixed bag of stink that words can't accurately describe. You wouldn't be incorrect if you said it smelled like a bin full of dirty socks dipped in brine, bearable only because the winds typically sailing through here are so strong. Sometimes they'll take you right off your feet if you ain't careful. The winds, that is.

I'll never forget the first and last time I lost my footing down off of 158th Street. I tumbled ass over head and fell five or six meters straight down into the smelly Hudson muck. And I'll be a monkey's uncle if it didn't take over two weeks to get that shit outta my hair. When I got back with my catch, the Surgeon and the boys said I was even more smelly than the damned fish, so they nicknamed me Trash Heap.

Assholes.

My admiration for tonight's bounty of marine life is cut short when I see that none of my dinner guests are flopping around any longer. These fish are leftovers from the East River—they get rereleased by the food officials at random once or twice during the week. The PCB's in the water starve the fish of oxygen within hours, though, so if you show up at the wrong time, you *and* your stomach are walking home emptyhanded.

The officials do this sort of shit on purpose—they want us to know they can afford to throw away food. They want people like me to see just how good they have it on the East Side. I've seen them do it, too. The fuckers back a big-ass tanker truck down the Washington Bridge, and when they get to the end just above the Little Red Lighthouse, they spill the lot right over the edge. They know all the starvers will be close by, mostly children, and they're the easiest ones to take prisoner.

Well, they can take that little cache of theirs and shove it. The Prophet and his minions can live forever for all I care. Let 'em have it—there's no way they're getting my loyalty or my soul over a bit of food. The Surgeon told me firsthand what happens to people who fail the Church—they take you down to the vaults and pull the plug on your original body right as you stand there watching. That's the last thing you see. But if you *really* fuck up, they do it to your family first. Bunch of godless, savage pricks.

Hmpf.

The Prophet says God's on his side. That's where his authority comes from. I ain't buyin' it. The way I figure it, if God *is* up there, somewhere, watching all of this, he still sees fit to keep me and the boys safe and fed. After all, there's plenty of food for the birds on this side of hell, and for that little nugget alone I'd wager God's keeping at least one eye on the likes of me.

But I've never struggled so much for food until lately. For the past couple of years, I was still able to cross the Washington Bridge at night and get to the east side. If you could make it into the Bronx, there was still at least a handful of merchants in those days willing to barter weapons for fish.

Man, I miss the grub there.

Now it's illegal to carry a weapon within a one-mile radius of the Peace Tower. Ever since transference became mandatory within the city limits, no one wants to buy, sell, or even fuckin' trade with any establishment not marked by the Church's commandments.

The Prophet is the reason the economy improves.

The Prophet is the reason this nation is being rebuilt.

The Prophet is the reason the Earth flourishes again.

The Prophet is the reason we can live forever.

The Prophet is the reason.

That's what they say, anyway. I guess you can say anything you want when you own all the land from here to the Rio Grande. Honestly, it's a damn tempting proposition; you get to keep all that belongs to you and you get a fancy position within the Church, yours for the taking, and even a small portion of its shares. All you have to do in return is recite those five commandments under oath, affix your thumbprint in blood on the dotted line, and give them your body and soul. Not much to ask, is it?

Pfft. Mooks. Every last one of them. That's what I say.

I kick through a few of the tommy cods on the top of fish-mountain, but their mouths aren't even moving anymore. The bulk of them are sturgeon, with a handful of striped bass tossed in for good measure. This lot's definitely past its expiration date. I think if the other boys were here they'd tell me to cough up my two points for the evening. I've lingered too fuckin' long here.

"Back at zero."

My patience has earned me zilch for the evening, and since there's not a cloud in sight, the walk back home is gonna take over an hour. Hell, I would've been better off going up to Spuyten Duyvil Island for dinner.

Don't say that, Trash. You shouldn't say that.

Nearly every citizen living up that way has been marked with an RFID. They're officially property of the Church—and if any of them spot you near the water, they'll bring a dozen Skywatchers down on you in less than two minutes. I guess easier isn't always better.

I've never gone much farther than Spuyten Island for a few years now, though it'd be pointless if I had, since eating anything that comes down from the Adirondacks is really the same as eating shit. The Surgeon said when he was younger there was a massive quake upstate that went off the fuckin' scale. Thousands of drums filled with a nuclear byproduct erupted, leaking into the river. They built a large dam up near Poughkeepsie and another near West Point for filtering purposes, but by then the damage was done. The Hudson'll never be whole again because the half-life on most of that crap is well over ten thousand years, he says. Whatever *that* means. Besides, I don't think it really matters since no one lives much farther north than Albany on account of the red rain.

Don't stay in one place, dumb ass. Get moving.

I charge the DH so that it's ready to fire. It can literally take the thing anywhere from ten to fifteen seconds before you can shoot the first round, and since it's damned cold tonight, maybe longer. Every time I hear the whirring sound it makes, I remember. I remember the night I got it...

I'd just turned nineteen days before, and the Skywatcher I took it from was nearly twice my size. He almost broke my fuckin' jaw when he knocked me to the ground, and that was the first time I heard that DH sound. I actually sprung a leak in my lower decks just before the

Skywatcher pulled the trigger. But the damned thing didn't fire, and some instinct got me to my feet.

I grabbed his wrist and the barrel of the gun, rolling it toward his thumb. In a rush, even trained soldiers forget the thumb's the weakest part of the hand, resorting to brute force instead of their brains. He instinctively pulled the trigger, never realizing I already had the gun turned on him. The blast went through his stomach and a plate of cast iron at his back that was at least an inch thick. I felt so guilty afterward that I puked my guts up all over him. Then I remembered the mook probably was a clone or that he'd be transferred anyway after they scraped up his body.

I've heard rumors as such. The Church can now transfer its own, even if they're outside the tower. Something in their armor collects the soul… or keeps it from leaving. The thought sends chills up my arms, and my body shivers. At the same time, my stomach growls, and then the DH tells me it's ready, the grip pulsating quickly against my palm.

Looking through the scope, I switch to the infrared sensor and do a sweep of the area. The Skywatchers must be cruising around Midtown tonight. I haven't seen or heard a single one riding the air. Maybe they're preoccupied. I can't see anything else, so I holster the DH and reluctantly leave the fish behind. I actually have to bite my lip to keep from crying and make a quiet apology to my stomach in the process. The last thing I had to eat was succotash. Hell, even when my stomach feels like it's eating itself, I can't deny the fact that lima beans and corn just ain't my idea of a decent dish. I think I'd rather eat the tires off an old Toyota.

Inside my chest pocket, something vibrates.

It's a Nokia—an ancient cellular phone they built like a tank at the end of the twentieth century. Entirely untraceable, though, and still the best means of communicado if you wanna stay off the radio. The state currently reserves the right to monitor all phone conversations, implanted or external, and you have the right not to resist. Any transmission being made via any other method than two tin cans connected with a piece of string is fair game. And even then, you'd better be one hundred percent sure about the fuckin' mook on the other end.

I check the phone, my hands trembling a bit from the cold. The text reads, *Return without the catch. Do not double back.*

I put the phone in my pocket and set my eyes skyward. The wind rustles gently through the trees behind me. I watch my breath as it moves toward the stars, forming a smoky vapor on the chilly night air.

Well, now I don't have a choice. The Surgeon's the only one who has the number to this particular phone. That means he means business. I'm gonna have to take the dangerous route back to the Rock—following the line of cherry trees north on the Greenway, and if God's still using that eye of his, I can get past the Little Red Lighthouse without putting my foot into anything hairy.

Even though this whole thing chaps my ass, I shouldn't have expected any less out of tonight. But one can always hope. I tell myself to take a cue from the fuckin' birds—most of them don't come to feed from this side of the city if they can help it.

I get my feet moving and bring the DH in front of me. As my hands take the grip and bring it toward my waist, the tactical sling holding it rubs down the left side of my neck and across the center of my chest. I've got a scar there where one of the cannibals ran a serrated knife damn near all the way from my clavicle to my diaphragm. It's long since healed, but every time something runs the length of the wound, I feel the pain of it like it was yesterday. Sometimes I even smell the breath of the same son of a bitch who wanted me for a snack.

The cannibals would've crossed into Fort Tryon and taken over our sanctuary, too, if it weren't for the old Angels gang. I suppose it kinda helps that there's a mile-long and half-mile-high row of soldiers' apartments lined up from the top end of Broadway into Upper Manhattan. The Surgeon says the Church lets the Prions thrive so they can succeed where the Skywatchers and their sentries have failed.

The memory of the knife pesters me, anxiously rising and falling inside my head. My breathing involuntarily speeds up, and then my toes start burning as racing warm blood hits them. It sure is cold tonight. Damn cold. I keep my pace up, though, and I'm not a bit tired despite the fact that I'm wearing boots too heavy and way too big for me. They belong to Clyment, our resident weapons guru and one of the ex-Angels of Harlem.

There was a battle in 2097 not far from here, a few blocks to the east. All of the Angels were attacked in broad daylight, slaughtered without warning and without mercy. It is said that the Skywatchers had wiped them out. *Eradicated* was the term I believe the Prophet used during his globally televised speech the next day. The Angels were the only ones holding the northern section of the city against the Church, fighting for those of us who would call ourselves free.

Good old Clyment... I mean this fucker was *there*. He saw it all. The poor bastard was part of the Rock for nearly two years before he'd say a single word about what really happened, though. I even hear tell he worked for the Church for a time, but he won't talk about that with anybody but me. Granted, I kinda sorta tricked him. As luck would have it, I'd found an untouched bottle of bourbon months earlier and was saving it for a special occasion. I knew Clyment had a hankering for the old stuff, so I instigated a drinking game, which lasted all of twenty minutes. He was three sheets to the wind and I was stone-cold sober as I'd been pouring my share onto the floor under the table.

I remember the look on Clyment's face when I asked him what happened during the battle—eyes wide and staring into the distance, he said the Prophet forced all the Angels to bow down before him. Those that wouldn't kneel had their legs cut off below the knees, and those who didn't manage to bleed out were then given two choices. First, they could serve the Church by renouncing their lifestyles, and they could stand up and walk again with new bodies. The second gave them the option of being sent to the Eridanian mines. Nearly half of them chose exile.

Clyment said one of the older men saw his death in the Prophet's eyes and rolled the dice in an effort to gamble his own fate. He laughed in the Prophet's face, saying he'd never serve him even if God himself had granted him the ability to shit gold bricks. More than a few of the Angels laughed, and in that moment, they all expected to be instantly vaporized. And they would've been better for it.

But like a shark with a deuce up his sleeve, the Prophet still had a pair to play. When he revealed his hand, Clyment said everyone literally shook with fear, ready to bow. And some of them actually *did* go to their knees. Unknown to the Angels, the Prophet had spared some of their children, whom they'd captured during the hysteria of the attack. And because they dared to laugh at him, the Prophet took the Angels and transferred them amongst one another—the children became the adults and the adults became the children.

When they woke from the procedure, they knew. They all knew the Prophet had won the game. If any of the Angels tried to escape by means of suicide, they would kill themselves and their children in the process.

The Prophet naturally said he no longer required their service on Earth and sent all the Angels to Eridania anyways. Well, all of them but Clyment. He was set free so that he could tell anyone who would take him in what the future holds for those who continue to fight. He still struggles with why he was the only one let go. I've asked. He doesn't have a single clue as to why. That's what he says anyway.

That's when the Surgeon found him, supposedly, and he came to join us at the Rock. That's also when the Prions pretty much all but overran Upper Manhattan, and we had to go underground almost entirely. I don't even remember the last time I saw the sun rise. Not that it's really easy to see it anymore, what with all the buildings climbing up into the clouds. Typical and blatant male overcompensation if you ask me.

I turn toward the water and sigh. My heavy heart feels like a block in my chest.

Suck it up, Trash.

I quickly drop that metaphorical weighty block when I see the Little Red Lighthouse some two hundred and fifty meters up ahead on my left.

I'm halfway *home*.

I've no choice but to step away from the tree line for now since I'm so close to the bridge. I'd be too easily spotted. As soon as my feet hit the water, I grit my teeth and suck the icy air in through them. It's colder than a polar bear's ass. The wet suit I'm wearing under my gear keeps me dry, but rain boots'll only slow you down out here, so the toes have to bear the brunt of the cold.

There goes *another* pair of socks.

It's almost pitch-black out here if it wasn't for the candle at the top of the Lighthouse. Lucky for me, I know the way forward even if I had no moonlight for a guide. By ordinance, the city lights shut off at twenty-two hundred hours. No worries—there ain't any real obstructions in the water here. In fact, there used to be tennis courts directly under my feet. Well, they never went anywhere, but I don't think the game involved standing in waist-deep water.

Not that I ever actually saw anyone play tennis. The only games I ever picked up were card games from my old man. Eventually I got better than him and he wouldn't play with me anymore. I do remember as a teenager having our typical fitness routine in school… and some of the bolder kids would ask our coach about the past, when games were common. Coach would get real angry and run us until we puked just for daring to ask about illegal activities.

Man, those were the good old days.

The Lighthouse is a hundred yards away. I take all of two seconds to check my six, and when I turn about-face, the candle at the top of the Lighthouse is quietly snuffed out. I become a statue while the water at my ankles sloshes around louder than I'd like.

Good thing I charged the DH.

Looking through the night vision scope, the red lighthouse becomes green, and I don't blink for what feels like minutes. I go down on my right knee, slipping quietly into the water. My head, hands, and the DH are the only things above the surface. A quick check through the scope again and I get the lantern square in the crosshair.

Man, I'd *hate* to blow the top off the old girl, but I'll do it if I have to.

If I run like hell, I might be able to make half the distance to Fort Tryon before the Skywatchers trace the heat signature.

No… *You can't be seen, Trash*. I can't risk the others. I could shoot now and drop the DH in the water.

My finger goes to the trigger. I exhale and close my eyes, wishing for a second I wasn't about to obliterate one of the only landmarks left of the old city… and then I see something move through the scope. I adjust the variable power and zoom in, and whatever it is moves again like a flash.

Is that a boy? It's the small frame of a boy! No, wait… it's a *girl*. She's scurrying around the catwalk at the top of the lighthouse.

I glide to my right through the water, inching my way back toward the tree line and keeping the crosshair on the girl. She sits down, then pulls her knees into her chest. God, she can't be more than eight or nine. She's looking in my general direction, but I can't tell if she can see me or not.

I reach down into the water with my left hand, keeping the DH aimed and feeling around frantically near my feet—not forgetting I don't want any of the water getting in my mouth. Under my fingers I feel something smooth—a stone near my foot about the size of a lemon. I try to make little more noise than the wind as I pull the stone from the water, and then I chuck it as far as I can toward the lighthouse.

One, one thousand.

Two, one thousand.

Thr—

The stone hits the shallow water, and the ruckus it makes doesn't divert the girl's attention one damn bit. Through the scope I can see she never stops looking my way. She's shivering, I think. Best I can tell, she's not wearing any shoes, and her arms are totally exposed.

Sometimes the kids make their way here. They get away from the cannibals somehow and make a break for the river. The Prions *hate* water. They don't wanna hear it, bathe in it, or even drink it. I guess whatever they get out of eating flesh is enough to sustain them. They don't live much longer than two years anyway once they start down the path to—

The girl suddenly turns, spinning on her own bottom. Then faster than a speeding plasma bullet she crawls to the north-facing side of the catwalk and out of my field of vision completely.

Damn. She must've seen me.

I get to my feet and listen, expecting the girl's body to hit the water any second. I'm less than fifty meters away now. I wouldn't put it past the Skywatchers to use a kid as bait.

Could be a decoy, Trash.

I tell myself to get back to the trees right now and get home. I tell myself to let her go. I tell myself she's dog meat out here alone. Then I realize I made my decision before I even put my next foot forward. I wade through the shallow water toward the lighthouse. When I'm less than twenty meters away, I holster the DH. There's no way this little one could do me any real damage.

You're little, too. Don't be stupid, Trash.

I grab my favorite knife just in case. It belonged to someone named Ka-Bar. That's what it says on the spine and the leather sheath I found it in at least. I like the idea that men used to personalize their weapons. Whoever he was, he etched the words *A True Bulldog* onto the handle. He sounds cool as fuck. When I saw that, I figured the knife would serve me pretty damn good.

The DH powers down with a clunky fade… an almost pitiful whir. I always think the gun's pouting at me for getting its hopes up. I tap the side of the magwell gently and tell the DH I'm sorry and that I won't be needin' his help tonight.

The rocks leading up to the base of the lighthouse give way under my feet and I nearly lose my footing in the water. I quickly get my balance in check and swallow the scratchy lump in my throat. Afterward, I mentally slap myself upside the back of the head for almost impaling my face on the wrought-iron circumference of rusted spikes at the lighthouse's base. Looking up, I circle around the structure slowly, and to my own surprise, I manage to do it entirely silent. After a minute or so, I find no further sign of the girl. The water is over knee deep here, so if she'd jumped from that height, she'd be wailing in pain from the landing.

Don't go in the lighthouse, Trash. Don't do it.

I turn the latch, unlocking the main door leading up to the lantern. When I push the door open, the water around my legs rushes inside. That means the girl didn't come this way. Someone left her up there.

I step inside, paying no mind to the lack of light, and work my way up the long, winding iron stairwell leading up to the top. The Surgeon's gonna kill me for this. But I have to know. I stop at the middle point when the stairs become even narrower, and I light the torch on the DH. Only one person at a time could've passed through here.

When I reach the top, there's another set of small stairs on the landing, and they're even more narrow and steep. At the top of them is a metal hatch with tiny holes poked through. I can see the faintest moonlight. I reach up and tap on the hatch with the end of my knife.

"Hello?"

All I can hear is the echo of my whisper and the water lapping around at the base of the stairs below me.

"Little girl?"

I climb the handful of steps underneath the hatch and push it open more easily than expected. The hatch creaks at the hinges, and as I pop my head up through the opening, it clangs one time against the railing that surrounds the lamp directly in front of me.

"Hello?"

There's no answer. I climb up into the gallery and put my back to the lamp. As soon as I do, from out of the corner of my eye, I see something pop over the railing surrounding the deck. Whatever it is hisses at me like a frightened cat and I nearly have a heart attack.

"Shit!"

I drop my knife for the first time in years and it knocks against the tips of my boots a few times before I manage to secure it again.

"Who are you?" a voice asks, and I stand up straight, feeling the lamp at my back again.

"I won't hurt you," I say, catching the glint of the edge of my blade in the moonlight. "See?" I ask, sheathing the knife and holding my palms out for my invisible friend.

"Please don't hurt me!" the voice says.

"What are you doing up here?" I ask.

Slowly, the little girl's head appears over the solid block railing. I see a mop of scraggly long hair first, followed by a set of wide, dark eyes.

"I was left here," she says, her hands framing the sides of her face.

"What's yer name?" I ask.

She doesn't answer me and only digs her fingers noisily into the handrail, picking off the rust so that it falls away in flakes.

"I'm Trash Heap."

She looks at me oddly, turning her head to the side like a confused dog. "It's actually Terra, but I—"

"You mean... you're a *girl?*" she asks, sounding surprised and rising fully to her feet.

"Yeah that's right," I say.

"Are... Are you *alone?*" she asks, walking toward me with her hands gripping the railing tightly and with knees so wobbly you'd think she was walking for the first time.

"Whoa, careful now," I say, reaching out to steady her. "How long've you been up here, sweetie?"

And then I see it. The girl walks through the opening in the railing and stands directly in front of me. The flesh on her legs is torn in places and eaten down to the muscle in others. At her upper thigh, the skin is flayed open like a war wound.

"No," she says, wagging her head from side to side. "I've just been *so* hungry."

Dear God. She's a Prion. She's been starved, and now she's eating herself.

"Don't!" I say, unsheathing my knife again. "Don't you come near me!"

"But you… You came to *me*," she says, licking her lips.

"Listen, little girl… I don't wanna, but I will kill you if I have to."

"I'm so glad you're a *girl*," she says, pausing a moment to wipe her mouth with the back of her hand. "I don't like the taste of *boys*."

Then I see her teeth glowing in the moonlight. I know where she's going even before she leaps at me—right for the throat. She's clumsier than a baby bird. I wish I didn't have to do this.

I use the knife and drive it into her left shoulder, nearly all the way to the hilt. She damn near got her legs around my waist. She's flailing, biting, and growling. I push her against the edge of the railing by way of the knife. She grabs my right arm with both hands clawing, and I use the moment to get a solid grip on the back of her neck with my left hand. I lift her off her feet with a sweep of my boot and then tip her over the side.

"Don't let me go!"

I've got her by the ankles now. When she sees the waves below, she gets so scared she nearly pulls me over with her. She says she can't swim. I let go of her and ask God a half dozen times to forgive me before I even hear her body hit the water. There's no fussing or fighting from the little cat anymore. She just sinks like a damn stone.

She was just a *baby*.

I put away my knife and suddenly wish I had a cigarette. I've not had one in over six years. My old phone vibrates again, this time more aggressively. The text is even more urgent than before: *Get back ASAP. The blackbird is being delivered.*

Well, I'll be damned. Kilraven's coming.

CHAPTER 16

DEEP SLEEP

I'M BACK AT the Academy. But I shouldn't be back at the Academy. I should be on a return journey with my shipmates bound for Earth. This isn't real. It can't be.

Then I see her. My wife. *Elisabeth*.

She's talking to a group of people. I can't make out their faces. No. These people aren't just anybody—they're officers. I must be back on the *Grimalkin* with Elisabeth. She has her hair pulled back in that way I loved. I can't tell what she's saying. It looks like *I love you*.

Am I underwater? She's getting farther away from me.

"Elisabeth!"

She's looking at me like I'm *not* me—as if I have no business here.

I am getting married. Elisabeth looks beautiful. I'm not dressed properly, and her smile tells me she doesn't seem to care.

The chaplain pronounces us. He... He doesn't look right. His eyes look unusual. They're almost scarlet.

"Jovian?"

A tornado of wind and water rushes around me, tossing the scenery of my wedding around like a rag doll. I close my eyes tight amid the torrent, thinking I might die, but opening them, I find myself standing in the halls of the old Academy.

"Hello, Thaniel."

I turn to face the voice coming from behind me, and it's *him*. I try to kill him with my bare hands, but my arms don't respond. I try to speak, but I cannot alter the words. I can't change what I'm doing. I can't do a damned thing.

"We must speak privately," he says.

Jovian is walking beside me, looking ahead with a face full of fear as we walk through the chaplain's dormitory. Glittering crucifixes and other ancient and sparkling symbols of faith adorn the limestone walls.

"Do you understand what I'm telling you?" he asks.

"Yes... I think so," I tell him.

Now I'm watching the two of us speak—as if I'm outside my own body. I'm standing behind *him*. He has something in his hands—something shiny.

"They killed him, Thaniel," he says, and I'm watching his hands. They aren't trembling in the way I remember.

I look on at my younger self. I'm young again! I'm staring at the floor. He is smiling now, and I never even saw it before.

"They killed my brother, Jobius!" he says. "Do you know what that means for everyone else?"

"You have a brother?" I ask.

"Of *course* he's my brother," he says.

"Who killed him?" I ask.

"I can't be sure of that, friend," he says, turning and pretending to look nervously over his shoulder. He bites his lip for a brief moment, and I see a look of unmistakable joy in his face that I didn't see the first time around.

"*Who* killed him?"

"You *have* to go," he says, whispering and gripping my forearm. "You have to join the others on the next launch and find out the truth of these events."

I want to put my hands around his neck, but they don't do what I want them to. I can only glower feebly as the younger me embraces him.

"I *know* you," I say. "I know what you did!"

Suddenly I see a woman floating, dancing in the air directly above me. The erratic movement of her arms and legs reminds me of one of my sisters.

"Are you an angel?"

"Take my hand, laser-brain," she replies, her hand extended.

I reach for her, and she pulls me effortlessly from the water. Her voice... She sounds just like my sister Meg'n.

The angel and I are now sitting side by side in my living room in Neo York. It's the place where I grew up. Mother's piano is there. Everything looks right. But it doesn't *feel* right.

"How did we get here?"

"We live here, *dummy*," she says, turning away from me.

"But we were just in the harbor, where we fled the city, remember?" I say.

The angel doesn't turn around.

"Meg'n? Is that you?"

The angel turns and faces me. But it's not Meg'n; it's Mara.

"Mara!"

"Mother says you have to leave, Thaniel," she says.

"Where are we going?"

"We're staying right here," she says. "*You're* the one that's always leaving," she adds, frowning at me.

It's night. I'm sitting on a boat with dozens of people I don't recognize. We don't seem to be moving.

I turn to the man next to me, and he says something, but it sounds like nonsense. He opens his mouth and something perched on the back of his tongue catches the light. Without thinking, I reach my fingers inside the slimy opening and pull out something golden. It's a pin. A golden oval with a sort of cross in it. Or maybe it's a letter T. I think Corvus had one like it.

"What are you doing here?" asks a playful voice.

I blink, and I'm no longer in the boat. Tarsil is sitting cross-legged on the floor where I usually slept in my old cell.

"You shouldn't be here, man," he says.

"You're alive!"

"What else would I be?" he asks, smiling from ear to ear.

"But... I saw you die. Your head... Your head was bashed in."

"My head? Are you sure?" he asks, grinning.

"See?" he says, touching the back of his skull. "I'm just fine."

He recoils when he sees all his own fingers bathed in blood.

"Oh God! I really *am* dead?" he asks, his eyes swelling at the sight of it.

"I'm sorry, Tarsil. I'm sorry!"

An overwhelming sense of his loss returns to the pit of my stomach. But as I reach for him, his flesh starts to melt. I shut my eyes and hold my breath because the smell is so horrible. No, wait... the smell is *fragrant*.

I reopen my eyes and Tarsil is gone. There's a woman kneeling several feet away with her back to me. She has some tools in her hands. What is she doing?

"Mother?"

"Yes, Thaniel?" she says.

"Why are you doing that?"

"To mourn."

"Are you dead, too?"

"There is no death," she says, turning toward me.

Her face isn't her face. It's Corvus!

"What's happened to your face?"

"What happened to yours?" she asks.

Now I'm falling. I should be able to fly! Why can't I fly anymore?

I shut my eyes right before my body hits the ground. There's no impact.

I open my eyes. I'm awake! What a strange dream.

I look around and ascertain that I'm in a holding cell. I've seen it before. The peace guards lead me from the room and I can hear Elisabeth screaming my name. Everything's so white. I can't see anyone's faces.

"You can't control this," I say.

"You will tell no one of what you have found," the voices in the room shout at me in unison.

"But I will. I will tell the world."

"You don't have a *choice*," they say.

I'm lying on a bed. I can hear Elisabeth calling my name.

Now I'm inside a darkened space. I can barely move. Oh God, am I in a coffin? It's blacker than night in here. I kick and scream and ram my fists into the sides. Then I hear bells… or something *like* bells. Am I in heaven?

No. It's not bells. It's a heart. It's my heartbeat. The coffin I'm lying in is opened by someone from without. I can't move my arms or legs.

"Is he dead?" a voice asks.

"I'm not dead!"

Two men are holding me by the arms now. There's a hood over my face and I'm being dragged. I think my ankles are broken. I hear the echoing voices of men coming from every direction. They are saying that I am a traitor. They yell my name and call me *traitor… traitor…* Someone calls me a Judas.

Something hits me in the chest. No, it doesn't hit me. It's just a sound. Is it a hammer falling?

"Snake!" they say.

"Treason!" someone else shouts.

"I am no traitor!" I shout back.

The hood is pulled off my face, and I'm on a ship now. I'm chained at the ankles and wrists. I'm not alone. There are others. Dozens. No one will look at me. A man dressed in a black cloak lifts me up. No, not a cloak… It's armor.

"Let me go!" I shout, pounding my fists into him.

He throws me onto a chair and holds me down. There's an intense burning on the back of my neck. I'm back in the coffin again, but now I can see. Everything is white, not like before.

"Did you really believe you could win?" a voice asks me. I don't recognize it. It sounds like a machine.

"Who's there?" I ask.

"It's *me*, Kilraven," he says.

"Your voice, it—"

"Sir, open your eyes," he says.

"What?" I ask.

"Sir, you must open your eyes."

There's an intense flashing of lights. Where am I? I see a rainbow of colors. Do you see a rainbow? Why is everything spinning? Did I say that out loud? Can anyone hear me?

"Sir, you are coming out of your cryo-sleep," he says.

"I was asleep?" I ask.

"Sir, you are delirious. You are experiencing the temporary effects of waking from cryo-stasis," he says.

"Who *are* you?"

"I am Nav, sir."

"Nav?"

"Sir?"

"What?" I ask.

"You called me, sir," he says.

"No, you called *me* sir."

"Sir, you must relax."

"There's pressure on my neck. Why is there pressure on my neck?" I say.

"Yes, sir."

"What's wrong with my damn neck?"

"I've just injected you with a serotonin norepinephrine dopamine re-uptake inhibitor, sir."

"Sero *who*?"

"A serotonin norepinephrine dopamine re-uptake inhibitor, sir."

"Okay... hey! No. Waitaminute! Is that you, Nav?"

"Yes, sir."

"You can't stick me without me saying you can."

"I have already injected you, sir."

"But I didn't say that you *could*, you cheeky, naughty Nav... nav-nav-navigator."

"Sir, you agreed to cryo-preservation when we exited Eridania. The injections are a licensed part of the procedure, sir."

"Ah-ha! I see how it works now. You've got *loopholes*."

"I do not understand, sir."

"I bet you don't... you snooty loophole."

"Sir, please relax. You will be more cognizant within a few minutes."

"*You're* cognizant."

"Yes, sir."

"Mmm hmm... fuck, I'm starving."

"Yes, sir."

The room spins as if I've had too much to drink. Hot damn, it's been a lifetime since I had a beer. Do I even remember the taste?

"I don't feel it working yet, Nav."

"It will, sir."

"What's that outside?"

"What are you referring to, sir?"

"That giant orange and red ball we're zipping past over to the right there."

"That is Mars, sir."

"The *planet*?!"

"That is correct, sir."

As I look on the Red Planet for the first time in over a quarter of a century, all of a sudden my head becomes remarkably clear. It's like the sensation you get whenever you inadvertently or forcibly have to take a cold shower. Except this time I'm not gasping for breath afterward.

Talk about instantaneous sobriety. Someone has probably invented a pill for that now. A tiny pill, too, no doubt.

"Nav, are you there?" I ask, pulling the respiration tubes out of my nose.

"Yes, sir."

"Did I just now wake up?"

"You have been awake for over half an hour, sir."

"Holy sh—"

I catch myself. I remember. I remember Nav's penchant for wanting to manually clean up any bowel movements about to be made onboard.

"My brain feels... *fuzzy*. How long was the trip, Nav?"

"You have been asleep for one hundred and eleven Earth days. It can take some time for the effects of the sleep to wear off, and you will likely experience some memory loss over the next twenty-four hours, sir."

"Jeez... what kinda memory loss?"

"Short-term, sir. Whatever occurred days prior to boarding the ship will be the most difficult to recall, sir."

"What kind of memory loss?"

"You have just asked that, sir."

"I was *joking*, Nav. I do remember."

"Remember what, sir?"

"The cores... How many do we have left?"

"Three in total, sir."

"Do you have stats?"

"Yes, sir. The first, second, and third cores are depleted to less than half a percentile. We are currently using the fourth, which is at ninety-one-percent capacity. Cores five and six are at full capacity, sir."

"Alright."

"Shall I eject the depleted cores now, sir?"

"Uh... I guess so. What good will they do us, right?"

"Little, sir, unless you should require the use of empty negatively charged eridanium cores."

"Yeah, get rid of 'em."

"Yes, sir."

"No, wait! Waitaminute. Nav... what did you just say?"

"I said 'yes,' sir."

"No, no, no! I mean *before*. About the core's charge?"

"They are negatively charged cores, sir."

"Negatively charged... *negatively* charged. Okay. Well, is that standard for all craft these days?"

"The nucleo-cores onboard are encased using Eridanian ore as part of the structured material, sir. While they do assist in the process of fusion power, this is not a standard feature on any fighter in the Starblazer series, sir."

"Really? Can they be used in any other capacity?"

"The question requires more specificity, sir."

"Um, well, could they be used, I don't know, like perhaps as weapons, Nav?"

"Theoretically. Though I do not have detailed files on eridanium weaponry at this time, sir."

"What do you mean by *theoretically*? And keep the answer brief, wouldja?"

"In short, the depleted cores could be used as energy-containment capsules as the preassigned serial codes on each indicate they were designed for re-use, sir."

"Then... why would anyone want to get rid of them?"

"Nuclear disposal prior to reentry is preferred, sir."

"Wait, wait, wait... how big are the cores, Nav? As in, the physical dimensions?"

"Approximately four point eight inches in length, three point one inches in width, and a diameter which equals the width along—"

"Okay, okay, alright... I got it. That's interesting. So, the cores were meant to be containment units."

"That is their function, sir."

"I mean an alternative function, Nav. And I'm pretty sure I know what for. Oh, Mother... dear Mother... you were smart."

"Yes, sir."

"God... my eyes hurt," I say, rubbing them for the first time in months.

"You must forgive the discomfort, sir. During the sleep, it is necessary to routinely check your eyes so as to maintain the integrity of photoreceptor cells."

"English, Nav. *English*, okay?"

"Your eyesight, sir. You were quite resistant to having your eyelids opened manually, sir."

"Right. I see what you mean."

"Sir, I have calculated that at our current speed we will reach our destination in seven hours and forty-three minutes. Would you like me to increase or maintain thrust, sir?"

"Steady, Nav."

"Yes, sir."

"I would suggest fluid intake at this point, sir. Dehydration is a common side effect from the sleep. Also, if you are hungry, there are nutri-packs located underneath your seat next to the—"

"Alright, Nav, just relax. I got it, thanks."

"Yes, sir."

"Just gimme a moment."

I rub the sides of my legs and feel a handful of bullets in my pocket.

I pull one of the pistols from my right thigh holster—the one that I took from Mother. Or was it Ubasti?

"I… I've got some thinking to do, Nav."

I begin loading the guns.

"Please try not to hurt yourself, sir."

"What?" I ask, laughing quickly.

"The guns, sir. My scanners indicate they are being armed."

"Oh. Right. You know, for a second, I thought you told a *joke*, Nav."

"I do not think so, sir."

I finish loading the pistols and wish that Nav was able to laugh with me. I try to recall what Iyov said at our parting. The more I clutch at the memory, the more it pulls away from me. I count ten bullets between both the guns. Wait… I remember! Iyov got these from Rullerig.

"I think I'm getting some more of my memory back, Nav."

"Very good, sir."

I wonder just how far I am going to get with only ten shots. It wouldn't surprise me in the least if every single man that Jovian has at his disposal is waiting for me—locked, loaded, and fighting for no other reason than blind faith. There's no sense in questioning myself, really, because there's no turning back now, is there?

"Are you ready, you bastard?"

"I am not human, sir, and therefore cannot be a child without legal legitimacy."

"Not you, Nav. I'm talking to *him*… to Jovian."

"Yes, sir."

I say his name out loud, and for the first time in years, I don't feel afraid of him anymore. I speak it because sometimes you just need to hear the words coming out of your own lips. Sometimes that's what it takes to keep going, and maybe sometimes that's what you have to do to believe in yourself. I don't even know if I do believe in myself anymore. Can I believe in myself?

"You had better be ready," I say.

Only I can't be sure if I'm talking to myself or to Jovian.

Maybe both.

CHAPTER 17

HIS LORDSHIP

I STAND BEFORE the ornate podium that was hand-carved from a single block of volcanic glass by my most devout of disciples. *The Prophet's Podium,* they call it.

Gripping the smooth and exquisitely crafted edges, I lean forward, leering at my seated brethren with the express intent of making them as uncomfortable as possible. Here within the great halls of yesteryear, where in centuries past other distinguished men came before me—holy men, senators, and magistrates—is where I put those I mistrust in their rightful place.

But this has proven to be... laborious. The councilors of today are often emboldened by the history of this room, a place once called the Supreme Court. The ever-decaying edifice of its exterior bears the incomplete statement *Justice Is the Firmest Pillar of Good* carved into the lintel.

I can only imagine what the rest of it once read, prior to the old wars. Because of the words that remain, there is a persevering spirit here—inside the very walls—and I have not been able to wholly crush it. That spirit would have those present speak their minds openly, and with democratic courage, proclaiming things they and lesser men would not dare whisper even in dark corners.

I should have the building demolished.

All the brothers of my Order are here, except for one. That notable absence is the reason I have been summoned yet again to a meeting such as this. It is really more of a formality since my holy associates no longer have any viable share hold in the Church. Regardless of that fact, they still maintain their secret agendas, of which I let them believe that I know little.

The seventh and final seat at the opposite end of the table has remained empty since the last Great Surgeon vacated the role. His leaving was voluntary. It is a post that my brothers have tried to fill many times before today, each one coveting the position for its former glory. Of course, I veto them at every turn, as none here possess the fortitude to meet the calling, let alone the vision necessary to appoint even a remotely worthy replacement.

There is *one*, though.

The only person in the room other than me who has performed as many transference trials as the previous surgeon is Brother Albedos. And I trust him little more than I trust Lord Alpha, my own personal head of security who stands now at the end of the table, where my agitated brothers buzz amongst themselves.

Alpha is typically absent from these meetings, as I have no need for him. But today he will play a vital role in securing my new vision. I was not certain of the basis for this so-called emergency gathering until the extreme present.

Lord Alpha iterated his suspicions on the matter during my brief escort here, nearly boring me to death in the process. With not much more than speculative detail, he calculated that my Order had learned of the details of Kilraven's return weeks ago and that one or more amongst them has turned runagate. I barely managed to refrain from laughing, asking *where* he believed they could or would possibly run. He did not answer, and I did some iterating of my own before reminding him that his judge of character was the least of the qualities I value him for.

But looking at my brothers now, I rather think it is *me* whom they are truly afraid of, not Kilraven. And with no small amount of elation do I unmistakably and clearly see in each of their eyes the greatest weapon of them all—fear. Fear is mightier than celebrity or admiration. Fear is even more powerful than love. The latter I have learned even more ruefully of late.

Love is weakness. Elisabeth brought out that weakness in me. Even God has it. It is a trait I have tried so very hard to purge over the last several decades. My last transference succeeded in leaving me increasingly numb to her pleas, whereas in the past they caused me to question my faith in the very authority and powers I have sacrificed so much in order to secure. Naturally she must never know that.

Women have always had a control over even the greatest of men, and despite being inherently the weaker vessels, they still maintain the highest resistance ratio during their trials. The sexes are not equal—created to be forever at odds—evidenced by the most obvious of all in our physicality, but even more so emotionally. We even diverge spiritually, though that difference of temper comes in fewer quantitative forms.

There is something to be said for that. But if I were to allow my love for another to hinder that goal that I strive toward, and in the process so cheat the world of what it has achieved through me, I simply could not go on. I cannot lie to myself in this—moving all the pieces on the board as I have seen fit has pleased me little.

I imagine it to be no different than watching the sunrise and having only yourself to share it with. I need an opponent *worthy* enough to battle in this game of wits. God himself has not challenged me. And I can readily admit that I have grown weary of the endeavor, until now. I've created that opponent. I made him.

I digress. Looking out at the men who would be the next Surgeon, all I see are bureaucrats… a room full of buffoons using the gift of their speech to do little more than bicker with one another as would an old betrothed couple. They pay lip service to me, though I do not desire their appeasement, nor do I require their blessing for that which I deem necessary. Though I should wonder a little whether they have merely diverged from the path, taking a few unintentional missteps as errant sheep might, or if they have lost their faith in the greater things entirely along the way. It is only my duty in either case to reprove them.

"Let this foolishness *cease!*"

They all turn in my direction, every face plastered with the expression of an aggrieved child after having just been slapped upon the wrists. And just as the echo of their meandering begins to fail, Brother Melius stands to his feet.

"Let the master speak!" Melius shouts, and the hall goes absolutely silent.

Brother Melius is a very curious man, to say the least. He takes nothing for himself and is seemingly invulnerable to all forms of flattery or bribery. He is probably the least proud of those present.

If I have learned anything at all in the political arena, it is that such a man cannot be trusted. Naturally, I am convinced—at least by his actions—that he would rather be elsewhere whenever great matters are being debated. I often find him coming to the meetings at the last moment and sitting in a place that is not his customary seat. He is never dressed according to the bylaws set forth by our holy predecessors, and I am certain that I have in actual fact seen him sleeping in the past. Though he is the only man here elected by the employees, I can no longer tolerate such effronteries if I am to maintain control of the Church.

"Thank you, Melius."

I make sure to give a nod in his general direction, which all in attendance cannot mistake. He does not return the gesture. I pause to give him ample time for it. He misses his chance.

"Brothers, the time for dissension is not at hand," I say, glancing assuredly around the room. "Do not let your faith be *shaken*. If you would truly put yourselves to the test, then leave, now, and fly from the highest window and be done with it!"

There is another bout of whispering and chatter, and I sense their undeniable desire for someone to take command of them. Men need subjugation. They require it even when they know it not. Some of them demand it, especially in times like these. In life, there are leaders and there are followers. The world has always been this way.

Further to that point, the god who promised to come has not come. He will not come. He never was to come.

I have come.

But the days before me are now troubled at best—plagued by the undevoted and ravaged by thieves who fight against the collective conscience of enlightenment. I dare think that some of them are in this room with me right now. I must test them further.

"Barrabas Madzimure was mighty in his day," I say, turning my gaze upon each one of them in turn.

They are so quiet you could hear the sweat forming on their foreheads.

"Yes," says Brother Melius. "His, um… His criminality cannot and will not be tolerated again. But if the stories about his past are *true*, then who among us can stop him? We haven't exactly won the war with the people. They believe him to be some sort of war hero, an anti-hero, not the probable pariah of legend."

"Do any of you *know* this man?" I ask. "Do you know anything about him, other than what you may have learned in the records of the historical vaults?"

The simpering fools repeat Barrabas's name—a repetitious wall of noise rising around me as the weaklings all confer with one another. None of them are outside the conversation, each one turning their faces to the other, searching for such answers as can be found. Perhaps they do not know what I know, after all. I have gone to great lengths to keep Barrabas's potential identity unknown up until now. But now I sense there are some rather gifted actors amongst us at present.

"I thought not," I say. "I knew that man. And I know *this* man who comes. He is a coward. He will not share in my ideals of purgation, nor the morality of transference."

"But how can you *know* this?" asks Brother Suttony.

"I know this because I have *seen* it. Some of us have the gift of foresight, my brother, remember? In our transferences, we are able to see truth… truths which are bathed in a light unlike those found in the material world."

"So, it *is* true then? You have seen this man return?!" Brother Suttony asks.

"Yes. I have seen his return," I say. "He will come in the clouds. Even now, he is not far."

Several of my brethren gasp, and I hear a rapping of knuckles upon the table.

"My lord Jovian," Brother Melius asks, breaking his silence. "Are you... familiar at all with the legend of Phaëton?"

Everyone in the room turns toward Melius and then back at me. All at once, I can see him and them, thinking. I can see their minds. Melius takes little time and chooses his next words very carefully.

"Enlighten us all," I say.

"He was a god who took power greater than his charge. He seized it unto himself, and so he caused much of the destruction of the Earth."

"And pray tell, what happened to this *god*, Melius?"

"He was struck dead, my lord, with a bolt of lightning by one who was mightier than he."

He did not choose those words carefully.

There is another audible gasp from my brothers, and I am tempted now more than ever before to rid myself of every single one of the spineless simpletons. I should have Lord Alpha strangle each one of them with his bare hands in front of their own families. No, I should have Lord Alpha strangle their original bodies in the cryo-vaults. Let them watch themselves die.

But no, I must not. Not yet. My brothers are only testing me now.

I must look at all things with double-mindedness, for that leads to stability of the spirit. I must remain open to the ways in which my Order might be put to better use in life, not in death.

"There is no god of lightning, Melius. And if there ever was, you can be certain he is not among us now. I most certainly cannot fire lightning from my fingertips at the present. But that may be remedied... one day."

There is a pause, and then my brothers look at Melius and laugh nervously. He smiles faintly at their tittering and gives a curt nod in return for my gracious chastisement.

"And what about the *mine*, my lord?" asks Brother Suttony. "Do we still hold it? You sent over fifty percent of our forces to Eridania and yet had nothing to report at our last meeting."

"The mine is not of your concern. In the meantime, we still maintain enough ore for the next eighteen months, give or take, if transference rates hold at their current figures."

"Eighteen *months*?!" Brother Melius proclaims with an inquisitive disdain behind the question. "Is that the extent of your great promise, then?"

Brother Melius rises to his feet as if to leave the room.

"Sit *down*, Melius," I command, and he does as I ask. "Do you wish to no longer join us? Very well then. Lord Alpha, if you would, please come escort Brother Melius from the chamber."

Moving quickly, Lord Alpha glides across the floor as though he could walk on the air. Then, stepping behind Melius's chair, Alpha looks at me once. In this moment I nearly falter, and but for the look on Melius's face, I almost let him live. I nod, and Lord Alpha takes note.

"I do not need *his* help in any matter!" Melius says, turning his head to look up at Lord Alpha.

Lord Alpha doesn't even look at Melius. He already knows what to do. And he does it.

His hands move swifter than the wind, and grabbing Melius by the neck, he severs the vertebrae with so deft an effort that half the souls in the room nearly miss the act. The shell of Melius falls forward in its seat, and the side of his head slams down on the table as though it were a drum he was destined to beat.

There is nothing now. Nothing but the sound of my breathing and the rush of blood. It's adrenaline in my ears.

"He… He was supposed to be escorted from the room!" Brother Suttony says with a voice quivering as though he were trapped in ice.

"He has been escorted. He's no longer in the room now, is he?" I ask.

The rest of my brethren meet the death of Melius with silence and protruding eyes. A striking trepidation that is impossible to miss takes a seat right on top of each man's head.

"Do not mistake me. I will *not* be gainsaid," I say. "And here in this chamber, in this place protected by your faith in me, we shall possess our souls in our patience!"

The brethren say nothing.

"I would hear you say it!" I shout.

"Possess your soul!" they proclaim in unison.

"Yes. In this tower that we have built, that very faith is made manifest. It protects us, and the holy ore of Eridania maintains that which is sacred."

"Faith unshaken!" they say.

"Brethren… you know me. I hold death itself under my heel and have done so for decades. You have all done so for decades. And Madzimure aims to take that from us. I cannot let that happen. I *will* stop him at any cost. I will *destroy* what he represents. He was a liar and a traitor. He was a man without contrition in his previous life. It was for this that he was cast out into the mine. He has become now a man justifiably acquainted with grief and sorrow, a man not worthy of the gift of transference!"

"Faith unshaken!" they bellow in unison.

"I am mightiest among us, and though we are now missing two, we six are *still* strong!" I say, casting a glance at Brother Suttony. "There is a purpose in this. It is not more than mere coincidence that six is the first perfect number. Do not let the fear I now perceive amongst you cloud your decisions, brothers. Replacing our Surgeon is not so pressing a matter. *I* can be the greatest Surgeon. My hands are more skilled. Look now! Look at the man nearest to you. Go on. Look at him."

They do as I bid.

"Now ask that man, *who* transferred you?"

Every man in the room whispers my name, more than once.

"Who?" I ask again.

They say my name louder this time, and each man nods at the other before looking back at me with fawning fascination.

"I am. And I will handle this Barrabas situation personally. When he comes, it will not be long before he seeks me out, and when he does, he must be allowed to do so unhindered. This is of *vital* importance. Is your faith strong enough to believe in my course of action?"

"Faith unshaken!" they shout.

"Yes. Faith *un*-shaken. I believe we have nothing further to discuss. Until next time."

There is a clamor and a meeting of hands. Several of the saints are exiting the chamber before I can step from the rostrum, and I note one of them is that little weasel, Brother Suttony. I must keep both eyes on that one. He has been one of the chief movers of dissension among us, always pitting one against the other through gossip and other verbal falsities.

What a wearying and taxing lot they have become.

Brother Albedos steps forward nervously and thanks me for allowing him to be witness to such a display of faith. He is a man with great ambition. Just recently he put forth his candidacy to the Tribunal overseers to succeed Octavian as the next Surgeon. Though he would fill the role averagely at best, he would likely serve me better in that he lacks the one thing that his predecessor had in spades: single-mindedness.

Before I exit the sanctum, I spot Lord Alpha now brooding in the corner and looking rather disturbed. I must admit I love his little dark displays while these men offer pittance. Funny that I had not even noticed when he moved into the shadows after dispatching Melius. He seems to be making a marked effort to avoid contact with anyone exiting the chamber.

This is atypical for my little pet. Generally speaking, Alpha has served me faithfully over the years, and he is not one to be frightened or deterred from that which must be done. I have watched him, waiting for the all-too-common signs of emotional weakness to manifest. Waiting for love to tighten its grip upon him.

"My lord Jovian?" he asks, approaching me so quietly his footsteps are nearly noiseless.

"Yes, Alpha?"

"Shall I dispose of the carcass?"

"No. Leave him."

"As you wish," he says. "I'll be escorting you back to the tower from the roof today, master."

"Very well."

We walk the breadth of the hall away from my podium in silence before entering the lift leading us toward our destination. Lord Alpha enters the lift after me, and as the door closes, he lingers for a few seconds longer than I expect.

"Your code, Lord Alpha."

"My apologies, master-father."

Alpha enters the code to activate the lift, and we rise. When the door re-opens half a minute later, I find a battalion of my finest in readiness. Alpha always had a small penchant for theatrics. The perfectly static double-row of guards facing me turns on their heels, and then facing one another, they retract like a zipper in one flawless, smooth formation. The sound of it is enough to give you chills—precise, perfect, and pleasing.

A boom ship waits for me at the end of the formation line. I *hate* traveling by this method, but statistically speaking, perhaps it is the safest way to take to the air. It is extremely fast but taxing on the body. I have seen photographs in the archives of amusement rides from the twentieth century very similar to a boom. Based on that alone, my conjecture can only be that the engineers of the past may have been insane.

Alpha follows me through the throng of guards, staying half a step behind me.

"Master, I still await your instructions with regards to the criminal Barrabas," he says. "What shall we do? Your brethren servants seem more unsure with each passing—"

"Alpha," I say, turning toward him, "I had not thought you one to waver."

"I do not waver, my lord," he says, drawing his chin high. "I do what I must."

"Do what you must?" I ask, laughing. "Are you reading my mind, Alpha?"

He takes a hard swallow, and I see the center of his cleanly shaved throat rise and fall. He does not answer me.

The hatch of the boom opens and I find my seat already in the upright position. I take my place and Alpha fixes the safety restraint across my chest. The hatch closes as Alpha steps into his seat, and as the interior pressurizes, Alpha latches his own harness and clears his throat. Then he covers his mouth as if he might be sick.

"Take a deep breath, Alpha. If you vomit on me again, you *will* be sorry."

The boom ship fires straight up over the city, launching us smoothly through the night air as though we were winged creatures gliding through our intended element. Streaks of light and wheeling stars encompass my field of vision. I usually hold my breath during the entire flight, but it takes all of five or six seconds before we reach the tower, and our journey ends. The boom comes to a fluid repose at the landing dock just outside my chambers.

"That was… thrilling."

Lord Alpha clears his throat before releasing my safety.

"You have been awfully *quiet* of late, Alpha. This is most unlike you. Speak freely."

"Master?" he asks, sounding unsure.

"Of course," I say, laughing. "Even the guard must ever put a guard on his own tongue! Alpha, did you not think that everything that was said back there, and all that has happened, is not part and parcel of my very express intentions?"

"No, m'lord. I've no reason to ever doubt you," he says.

The boom ship hatch opens and the winds of the city rise up at my feet. They create a forceful symphony through the folds of my cloak and shout into my ears. Alpha secures the boom to the dock via the tethered anchor and follows me across the landing platform to my quarters.

Once inside, I find his body language rigid and his mind seemingly elsewhere. Were I able to see behind his lips, I would not be surprised to find his teeth clenched.

"Alpha, have you left your candor at the door along with your duties?" I ask, pointing to the boom. "Speak your mind! I have things I must attend to."

"Master, what do we do about Barrabas?"

"Alpha… you are a soldier, are you not?"

"You could say that, m'lord."

"Well, if you are *not* a soldier, I am most interested in knowing what else you would consider yourself to be."

"I am a man who has nothing, needs nothing, and therefore has nothing to lose, master."

"Precisely!" I say, laughing and doing so more for the fact that I cannot restrain the laughter. "Alpha, that is why you are in my service. Do *not* forget that," I say, clasping my hands together. "A man such as *you* is always expendable. Expendable because of your very nature, which you have just confirmed. And I would regret it if I had to resign your post."

"I don't forget, master. You know that I live to serve you and the Church," he says.

"*Pah!* Such rhetoric is so… anemic. Give me plain speech tonight, Alpha."

"Yes, m'lord."

"To answer your question, the Church is now days away from my total influence. Soon the Order will be powerless, and Barrabas will be in chains in Central Park as a testimony to my mercy!"

"That would be well to see the criminal tried," Alpha says. "Public opinion is nearing an all-time low, what with the recent amount of… purgatories."

"Purgatories? I wasn't made aware of this."

"It's what the people on the street call the transference trials that do not go as they should, m'lord."

"Please! Such dogmatic terminology should remain in the streets. Alpha, I think you have been spending too much time with back-alley black sheep and vagabonds."

"That is part of my job, master."

"Yes, indeed it is, Lord Alpha. Indeed it is," I say, laughing.

The COM module attached to Lord Alpha's belt interrupts my mirth, and some cretin at the other end nervously asks for his attention.

"Yes?" Lord Alpha asks.

"*Lord Alpha, we have a ship requesting landing permissions and… well,*" the twitchy sentry pauses. "*We, umm… We think you might want to take a look at this.*"

"Take your leave, Alpha. You are dismissed," I say.

Alpha nods curtly and I watch him walk the length of my chambers and down the long empty hallway to the elevators at the far end. As he closes the reinforced steel door behind him, I smile as the tumbling locks slide into place. I love that sound. It reminds me of the stepping of soldiers.

Alpha is a minacious man. He is a soldier, a foe worthy enough for even Kilraven to face, if he must. He may also be the only man I have met who exudes fear by his mere presence alone.

There are very few who actually deserve the gift of second life, outside of signing a contract of servitude. I have made it so that very few can now earn second life by their actions, but Alpha is among these, and I chose to give that life to him. That is as good a reason as any for his continued loyal service. He can live forever if he so wishes, for that power is mine to grant, and he owes the Church nothing… save one final debt to me.

As I look out from my window upon the great city, I can see no green thing, no living thing. There is nothing in which a god has had a hand in making that my eyes can find, only gray steel rising to meet the sky. I was only a boy when I first climbed this high tower, though it was not nearly as lofty then. In my own way, I too have made things that are living, and the city and the world are now greater in many ways because of it. I cannot help but feel a certain sense of pride in what has been achieved here.

But it has been years since I felt much of anything that was new to me. The weight of my position and authority chafes at times, and I wonder if the prophets and even the presidents of old felt the same burden upon their shoulders. I do not doubt that they had seen and heard much that long troubled their souls—things that other men of their time must have persecuted them for. Like them, I imagine that I too am persecuted for the very same reasons.

Now, something different troubles me, even though the days of darkness and tribulation of the spirit are now over. This is the new world, and I am the ambassador over those within it. My enemy is on his way here even now to kill me, and maybe he thinks to usurp my predestined authority. I cannot let that happen. It will not happen.

I am the lord of the Earth.

Kilraven should thank me for all that I have done, though I think it is more than likely he will not share this viewpoint. I marvel at what the city must look like through his eyes. In a way, this is the gift I chose for him. And another gift that he returns now to a world that is changed. Perhaps time has mended the transgressions that lie between us.

My meditations are interrupted, as per usual, by the knock of a visitor at my door.

"Yes, come in."

"My lord Jovian?" the voice asks.

I turn to face a young, pale-faced sentry who cannot be much older than his trial date—just one of my innumerable and faceless servants. I should not call them so; I should rather say one of my many disciples.

His hands are trembling at his sides. He is frightened of me. This is good, yet part of me loathes it. Power such as mine affords nearly all desires to be met, but there is an ache within to have such an adversary—nay, *any* adversary—worth half his weight in bravery.

"Why have you disturbed me, child?"

"My master," he says, nearly swallowing his own tongue, "Lord Alpha sends me."

"And what does Lord Alpha wish you to convey that he could not?"

"I'm sorry, my lord. He said there was a pressing matter he needed to personally sort out," he says.

"Very well, then. What is the message?"

"My lord, we have received a transmission from a ship wishing to enter the atmosphere. The ship came from a—"

The young man clears his throat and I already know what he is going to say. His presumption that the information he brings could possibly unnerve me causes a fleeting sense of revulsion to run through my body. It rises into my throat like a bad aftertaste. Depending on what he says next, I might have Lord Alpha dismiss this young one at a later date.

"You were saying, sentry?"

"Uh, yes, my lord. The ship has come from Eridania, and we—"

The sentry nearly chokes.

"And?"

"The ship is bearing an escaped prisoner from the Messier mine on Eridania," he says, regaining his confidence. "He has identified himself as one Barrabas Madzimure. We can only surmise from his dossier that he is dangerous, though his intentions here are currently unclear."

"His *intentions*? Have you spoken to him?"

"Yes, my liege. His ship has just crossed the lunar orbital plane. When we asked for a clearance number, he asked us to... ah—"

"Yes?"

"He asked us how to get to the Five Points den of the Forty Thieves, my lord," he says.

"Did he now? Well... at least we know our imminent guest maintains a sense of humor about facing his death."

"I am unfamiliar with the phrasing he used, my lord. I thought he was the king of thieves," he says.

"No doubt you are unfamiliar," I say, "and you have told me nothing that I did not already know. He will not succeed in what he has come here for. I assume he did not have a clearance number, either?"

"Yes, my lord, he does. Prior landing for his flight was confirmed and was put into the dockets properly, although we were suspicious of the number he provided. The clearance was keyed manually by one Corvus Brenner," he says.

"Corvus. Of *course*," I say.

I made a critical mistake with Corvus. I had my misgivings, but they came far too late. Lord Alpha proposed that I not trust him. In fact, he told me I should not trust anyone any longer. Trust is a concept I am now nearly unfamiliar with. Still, Corvus proved only my instrument in devising the return of Kilraven, despite whatever his intentions truly were.

"My lord? What shall I do?"

"Let him land where he will, boy!"

"My lord, I must—"

"You must *what*?"

The sentry's mouth shudders and quakes.

"Well, go on. Do not be shy now."

"My lord, if… If this criminal is allowed to resume his negative lifestyle choices, then the city would be at a great risk, and one that—"

"Young man, come here."

He takes a half step forward and hesitates, and I can almost smell his fear from here.

"Forgive me, my lord. I should not have—"

"No, you should not have spoken. Is that what you were going to say?"

The boy nods and steps forward, and with a click of his heels, he attempts to find his courage.

"Do you possess any bravery at all?"

"Not… Not in your presence, my lord."

"So, then had orders not been given, you would never have volunteered to come here?"

"I have no feelings regarding my orders, my lord."

"None at all?" I ask, laughing and taking a step closer to him. "Let me give you a truth, boy. You believe *faking* bravery is the same as having it, yes? Your superiors have no doubt instilled this in you?"

"Yes, master," the boy says, finally looking me in the eye.

"No, boy. That is compulsion performed out of fear. It is a falsehood perpetrated by an uncouth and vain generation of cravens. Bravery is when one chooses to stay the course because it is virtuous and because it would be disgraceful not to do so. You are either brave or you are not. You are either courageous or you are a coward. They are *innate*."

"Yes, master."

"Now kneel, lest you die."

The boy goes down on one knee immediately, lowering his head. The breath in him exhales from his mouth with a rapid heaving, as though he were shivering outside in a winter snow.

"All things are now at my beck and call, stupid boy. And if you think that this criminal will shake that, then I am afraid your level of faith in your lord is also shaken, is it not?"

The sentry raises his head to look at me. He's not even trembling.

Hmm. Maybe the boy is brave, after all.

"Your grace, forgive me. You are wise and I am… young and… brash. It is my… my *passion* for justice that would have me speak my mind before thinking beforehand," he says.

"I hear you, servant. Now rise to your feet."

The boy does so but keeps his head bowed.

"I am not a lord of second and third chances. But because the news which you have brought, of which I already knew, still gives me great pleasure, I am going to let you live until you fail me again."

The sentry falls to both knees, takes my right hand, and kisses it repeatedly.

"Thank you, lord! You won't regret it!"

"I had better not, boy. Now tell the flight control to let Barrabas land. He must not meet with any resistance. This man serves my purpose, and he will stand before me in due time."

"Yes, my lord. Many apologies. Will that be all, my master?" he asks.

"Yes, begone!"

The boy bows and takes his leave. I should have killed him. His faith is *weak*. I make a mental note to set Lord Alpha to that task later.

Alpha has taken a kind of fondness to removing those from my service that seemingly cannot learn to be silent unless their opinion is asked of them. I know I said I would let the young sentry live, but being a strong and unrelenting lord means occasionally having to renege on a promise made in haste.

I also make another note to have Lord Alpha bring me the file on Corvus. I am loath to admit that what this man managed to accomplish right under my nose intrigues me greatly. He stole something from me, and that has not happened in a long time. I loved that ship... my little gleaming, golden egg.

Sigh.

"Perhaps some music is in order to soothe my annoyance."

Perusing the library at my disposal through the display on the desk offers many choices. David Jones, maybe?

No... something earlier. I need something for a sentimental mood. Ah, yes, of course—the one they called John Coltrane.

As the track begins, I am enveloped by a wonderfully weaved tapestry of instrumental heaven, and a thought occurs to me: that perhaps Mr. Brenner's obituary should read something befitting of so grievous a traitor. Perhaps that he was a murderer?

No... too clean. Maybe he was rapist... of children... and *animals*.

I laugh to myself, and it echoes within the chamber. I laugh again at the sound of it.

"Yes, animals! *Most* amusing. I think that will do *quite* nicely."

CHAPTER 18

THE BROBDINGNAGIAN APPLE

AFTER WE ROCKETED through the Earth's atmosphere, I found the response time from Neo York's finest just the tiniest bit improved compared to when I was last coming in for a landing. Mind you, that was almost a crash landing.

When I came back from Fornax and Elisabeth was taken from me, the men who put me in cuffs didn't realize I practically wrote the training manual on restraint manipulation. I released the ratchet inside the cuff's lock by getting my hands up and over the first officer's chest while he was seated in front of me. Needless to say, I broke quite a few of his ribs and nearly destroyed my wrists in the process. By then we were nearly in a nosedive, and I felt a calm unlike anything I'd ever felt before. Funny that it would come over me when faced head-on with death itself.

But I changed my mind in that moment. I had to live. I had to know who had done this to us, so naturally, I pulled us out of the plummet.

This time around I'm all in one piece, of course, but it sounds like I won't be for much longer. The men on the other end of the COM are calling themselves *Skywatchers*. They've asked me for intergalactic keys, code numbers, and a whole slew of shit I can't possibly know. Lucky for me, I've got Nav. As soon as we passed the Moon, I counted thirteen frigates in the cislunar space, and Nav advised me they were all in defensive positioning. I thanked him for that which I could already see with my own eyes.

Talk about your *déjà vu.*

The silence in here and the lengthy lack of response from these so-called Skywatchers has me sweating just a little. Nav is annoyingly confident that the codes he's relayed to them are valid, going so far as to tell me repeatedly not to fret.

Isn't that typical for artificial intelligence? As if he really grasps the meaning of actual worry. Never mind the fact that there's a combat box surrounding this golden goose *and* we're over the water. The North Atlantic, I think.

The sensors are showing four fighters in the high and low elements, and there's another eight to my left and right. Maybe Mother was wrong. Maybe they intend to blow me from the sky, after all. Or it's just another piece of Jovian's game. It'd be just like him to place those watchful frigates so strategically between here and the Moon.

"Sir, might I suggest that you slow down," Nav says.

"You're worrying again, Nav. That's *exactly* what I'm talking about."

"What were you talking about, sir?"

"Look, Nav, *I'm* the one flying here. Slow me down when the ship's ass is on fire!"

"That is highly unlikely, sir. In the event of—"

"Tell me something I *don't* know, Nav!"

"Sir, I have just received the confirmation that airspace has now been cleared for landing on dock six. Would you like me to take the controls again?"

"Shut *up*, Nav! It just means they know we're coming!"

"Of course they know, sir. We are the only incoming flight scheduled for the next few weeks."

"What do you mean by that?!"

"All interplanetary departures and arrivals are monitored, controlled, and approved by the Great Council and or the Prophet, sir. My clearance has been given access to those flight paths, and as of today's log, I see no outgoing flights for the next fortnight, sir."

"So, no one gets off the planet anymore?"

"Not without preapproval, sir."

"And what would happen if I just turned your golden ass around?"

"The Skywatchers would presumably lock onto us and dispose of us speedily. I doubt we would even clear the mesosphere, sir."

"I love your positivity."

"Shall I reverse course, sir?"

"No, Nav. Steady," I say, letting go of the controls and feeling in my hands as Nav takes over. "Just keep her steady."

"Yes, sir."

"Nav, I need to know something else. Do you have anything I can use that you haven't told me about? Any files on these bastards? On the Prophet?"

"Yes, sir."

"On *Jovian*?!"

"I have an extensive medical history, as well as precautions set in place for any scenarios requiring an emergency transference for His Lordship, sir."

"Wait… what do you mean by emergency transference?"

"The details of that information are restricted, sir."

"*Restricted*?! Nav, I'm the captain!"

"You are correct, sir. But I am not able to release restricted information without approval from the previous captain."

"From Corvus?!"

"Yes, sir."

"Goddammit all! Well, what's the loophole?"

"I do not understand, sir."

"You must have a loophole. I know you do! How do I get the damn files?"

"You have three options, sir. Would you like to hear them now?"

"Yes, Nav! For God's sakes, *yes*!"

"Option one is DNA identification, via the thumb or palm. Option two is a retinal scan through the dash oculator. Option three requires a manual blood- or saliva-based fluid extraction, sir."

"That's just great! *Real* helpful, Nav."

"You're welcome, sir."

"Fuck, Nav! I didn't bring Corvus with me! I might as well eject now, jump into the Hudson, and just let you crash!"

"That would be unadvisable, sir. My data indicates the Great River currently has a polychlorinated biphenyl toxicity level of over thirty-six percent, and the—"

"Aww hell, save it, Nav!"

From out of nowhere the staggered formation escorting me breaks away, falling back without so much as a verbal threat or a routine weapons lock.

"Nav, did you catch that? They just broke off!"

"Yes. Most atypical, sir."

"Well, gimme the damn controls and I'll finish taking her down!"

"Yes, sir."

It takes me all of five seconds to get the hang of her at this altitude, and when I do, the dead weight of torturous years and its accompanying baggage of madness begins to dissolve away. Another deep breath later, and I leave my fear behind me like the trail of smoky fire this golden dragonfly is marking the night sky with. This little baby flies so smooth—it's like sliding on wet glass.

I have to slow her down to Mach 1 when I see something I didn't anticipate dead ahead of me—pillars of thick cylindrical vapor, as far as the eye can see, rising up into the sky. It's running all the way from the Lower Bay across to Jones Beach.

"Take the controls back, Nav, and slow us down a bit?"

"I am reducing thrust now, sir."

"What'n the hell is that cloud up ahead?"

"That is the gateway into Neo York, sir."

"The gateway?"

"The cloud is in fact a wall of steam, produced from underground generators supplying electricity for the Tower of Peace and nearly all of Manhattan, Brooklyn, and Queens, sir."

"Steam generators, huh? Hmm… guess that way there's never a loss of power."

"Precisely, sir. It also serves as a visual shield for the Tower of Peace."

"Yeah, I can see that."

"I am slowing our airspeed now. We will be landing very shortly if the crosswinds are favorable, sir."

Nav goes quiet as we move through the billowing orange fog, and then two seconds later I finally see the great city before us—a beacon of light with its glorious towers and majestic pillars. The skyscrapers all grope upward, their fingers reaching up to heaven. They've nearly reached the clouds now, and there's so many of them I can see no sign of the horizon.

We cross through the Narrows, and looking to my right, I see Governor's Island Prison.

"It's amazing… amazing what you still remember after thirty years," I say aloud, almost to myself.

"The electroencephalography of your brain would indicate your recall is higher than average, sir."

"Stay outta my head, Nav."

"Yes, sir."

"I wonder if the kids still say the prison's haunted. We used to tell stories about the ghosts of all the war defectors who died there and how they'd walk along Red Hook beach at night, dragging bad little boys and girls into the water."

"There is no such thing as a ghost, sir."

"Wish that were true, Nav."

Looking past the shield, I don't recognize much of anything else. In fact, once we move over the Battery, I have to convince myself the city below me is the same metropolis I once knew.

Nav takes over again and weaves the ship through a cobweb of metal. Then I see it. It's right where the center of Midtown used to be. The tower of all towers. It must be well over half a mile tall and much wider at its base than it was decades ago.

"Our landing destination is directly ahead. Shall we land as scheduled, sir?"

"No, we won't."

"Sir, might I then suggest that we follow the flight path preset for you by Corvus then?"

"If you think the Skywatchers won't blast us into bits, Nav."

"Legally they are fully within the right to do so sir. However—"

"I get it, Nav! Let's worry about that when we're dead, okay? Just get us on the ground!"

"Yes, sir. I will take us toward the Washington Bridge, on the Fort George side."

"The bridge still exists?"

"Yes, sir, though I highly recommend you reevaluate this scenario. You may have to eject or abandon me in mid-air, sir."

"Why's that?"

"My most current data indicates that the area is unsafe for pedestrian navigation due to an extremely hostile population of nonurbanites subsisting below the streets."

"Already knew that, Nav."

"Very well. Your memory is returning, sir."

We're flying past the Upper West Side now. All I can make out is concrete… and more concrete. One of the tallest of the towers has three large purple crosses emblazoned and overlapping at the spire. It looks almost like a logo of some kind.

"Nav, what's that building due east? The largest one, at about two o'clock?"

"That is the Transference Tribunal building, sir."

"Tribunal?"

"Yes, sir."

"What's it for?"

"They preside over the transference trials, sir."

"Does Jovian own that, too?"

"No, sir. As the name of the building would suggest, there are three heads, sir. Lord Jovian represents the Church, Lord Carandini represents Earth's Great Council, and the third representative is the Great Surgeon."

"And who might this Surgeon be?"

"My data with regards to the previous Surgeon is dated, but if correct, the last Surgeon has resigned the post and has yet to be replaced, sir."

I look down toward the water and sigh. Now that I am here, I wish never to return. The city I left is not the one I see before me. I don't know how on Eridania to reconcile that.

"What's happened to the world, Nav?"

"It goes on spinning, sir."

"Yeah. Right."

"Sir, my sensors have found a location rudimentary enough for a landing which will not require your ejection. I can descend within thirty seconds. Shall I deploy the landing gear and commence, sir?"

"Get to it, Nav."

The ship bobs and weaves through the air as it cascades between the derelict buildings. I feel so nauseous I could vomit—that is, if I had anything to spit up.

Strangely enough, this part of town hasn't changed as much as I had expected. When I was still a hot-headed punk of a kid, I did the Council's dirty work by squashing nonurbanites here every other day. People were fleeing this area by the truckload, and it became somewhat of a breeding ground for what the city deemed as *undesirables*. It seems the great prophet himself has been paying little mind to it since then.

"Sir, we are landing in five…"

"Four…"

"Three…"

"Two…"

"One."

Nav settles the golden girl like a feather landing on the surface of a lake. I release my harness and pop the hatch immediately.

After hopping out, my feet hit the deck and I clearly see a parkway directly in front of me. I can tell the building we've landed on can't be more than three or four stories high. And then something I'm unprepared for hits me like a ton of bricks.

"What on Eridania is that *smell*? And why didn't they shoot us down?"

"Sir, we were granted clearance to land only on dock six. This was the most stable place to land within the vicinity Corvus chose."

"They let us go, that's why. Which also means you should be safe here."

"We should have been destroyed less than twenty seconds after the deviation from our original flight path, sir. Furthermore, I am unclear as to whether leaving the ship here is safe or unsafe."

"Is that a first for you, Nav?"

"I do believe that it is, sir."

I smile and grab the pistols along with a small knapsack of medical supplies from inside the cryo-bay. My stomach growls as if I've never eaten before in my life. Better get some sustenance—and fast.

"Nav, eject those cores for me, would you?"

"Yes, sir. The process of de-radiation should take no more than ten seconds, at which time you can retrieve them at the base of the avionics panel near the rear of the craft, sir."

"Thanks, Nav."

I walk to the rear of the ship and I smell something like wet dog combined with sewage. It's the same thing I smelled earlier. It's damn cold out here, too.

I take a quick look around to check out the rooftop and find that it's mostly constructed from rusted aluminum sheets. A bit dated. It's so dark I nearly fall through a hole in the paneling on my way toward the edge of the rooftop.

Amateur.

When I regain my balance, I look down into the street below and note the pavement is covered in something slippery, like oil. What looks like a car goes by a second later, but I never heard its engines, and it moves so fast I can't really be sure. I guess there's nobody regulating the maximum speed restrictions on this side of town anymore.

I look across to the river, and it's nearly blanketed in total darkness. The city lights must have gone off. But it can't be past zero-hour yet. The Tower of Peace was still lit up like a bazaar when I flew in.

Wow… it's that *smell* again. It's even more offensive now—like sulfur and wet garbage.

I cross to the other side of the roof and I can see the Hudson in all its rushing glory. The smell on the air is even more intense than before. It must be the river that's causing the stink. I'm sure Nav will know. Just before I turn around, I hear it from behind me—the cock of a plasma pistol. I'd recognize the sound anywhere. There are four distinct clicks.

"Hands up!" a voice shouts, and I oblige out of instinct.

"I know your gun. The trigger sear holding the hammer moves past the quarter notch, the sear passing the half-cock notch, the bolt locking against the cylinder, and finally the trigger sear engaging with the full-cock notch. What a piece of precision."

"Shut your *weird* ass up and remove those two pistols you got strapped to your hips. Then turn around slowly and toss 'em here!"

I turn around gradually, and when I do, all I can see is a white light in my face. I think it's a woman, but I can't make out anything more than the feet. She or he is wearing some black Corcoran jump boots. Big surprise—I haven't seen those in decades.

"You a Prion?" the voice asks.

"A what?"

"A *Prion*. A meat-eater. A canny!" the voice says.

"I don't understand."

"What do you eat?!" the voice says, as something in front of me prods the center of my chest.

"I eat *food*," I say, and then the light of the moon gives me a great snapshot of the gun aimed at me.

"What model is that?" I ask.

"What model is what?"

"That gun you're pointing at me."

"Shut up, you *dunce*, and slide those guns over here, now!" she says, and I can hear her breathing quicken.

I drop my guns and kick the holster belt toward her.

"Dunce?"

"Yeah," she says, "you *must* be stupid since you landed a damned Starblazer way out here. Especially one as cherry as this. Not to mention I snuck up on you on a metal rooftop."

Yep. Pretty sure it's a woman.

"Sounds like you've got everything figured out, lady."

"Get your hands up!" she says, moving closer toward me.

"They *are* up, sweetheart."

The light of the gun comes within inches of my face, and something as hard as a rock hits me just above the bridge of the nose.

"The hell was *that* for?!"

"For the insult," she says. "Now who are you? What are you doing up here? And where'd you get that ship? Did you steal it?"

230

"That's a lot of questions coming from someone I can't even see," I say. "Why don't you turn that light off and we'll talk. The off switch should be right behind the casing ejection."

The girl takes a step back.

"I'll turn the light off when you tell me *who* you are and *what* you're doing here!" she says.

"Well, guess what? I'm not going to tell you. At least not until you tell me your name."

"Oh, really?" she says.

Then I hear the gun make a strange noise. *That* sound I definitely don't recognize. Must be a newer model.

"Listen, girly, whoever you are, I've been to hell and back. So, if you think that you can do or say anything to frighten me into giving you my ship or anything else I have, then you're dead wrong. *Dead. Wrong.* You're welcome to join me, but you will not take anything from me. Do you understand?"

She doesn't respond. My legs have loosened up enough from the flight that I could probably just drop-kick her.

She hesitates a tiny bit longer than I expected her to, and that's all I need. I hit the ground fast and execute a low-sweep kick, and she's on her back so quick she might as well be tumbling under the sheets with me.

Aww, hell. She didn't drop the gun.

I can feel the heat from the tip of the barrel, which is now two inches from my face.

"I'll be damned."

"If you so much as *queef*," she says, "I'll take your head clean off yer shoulders, and your soul can go to the depths!"

"Well, I certainly don't wanna lose either one of them," I say.

"Then maybe I'll just shoot your legs off and drag you *and* your stumps right into the TTT," she says.

"The what?"

"Are you *deaf?* The big T!"

"What's that?"

"Have you been living in the west, man?" she asks, her voice rising in pitch.

"You mean the Tribunal?"

"Yeah, hi. I'm Earth. Welcome back."

I laugh at her, and the look on her face is just shy of complete and utter perplexity.

"Who'n the hell *are* you, man?"

"Look, get that gun out of my face, I'll help you off the ground, and we can talk. Like human beings."

I hold out my hand and she waits three seconds before obliging me. I get her to her feet, and when she rises, all I can see are her eyes. They're *sanpaku*—green or hazel, I can't be sure, and the moonlight reflecting in them beams back at me.

I'm reminded of all the white stars in Alpha Caeli, which I had the pleasure of seeing from the flight deck of the *Grimalkin*. But it wasn't with my own eyes that I witnessed them; rather, they were flashing back at me in Elisabeth's baby blues. As our ship sped through that faint constellation, the curvature of her face was burned into my memory, as though it were made to look like it was part of heaven.

"Your name," the female says, poking me once in the chest with the end of the gun.

"Sorry, I… I'm Barrabas. Barrabas Madzimure."

She's looking at me as though I've just told her that hell exists only for infants or, worse, that I've said her childhood dream of finding presents left by a fat man under a triangular-shaped fir tree will never come true.

She repeats my name again several times, quietly, and scratches the side of her dark, smooth cheek with a knife she pulled from a sheath at her hip.

"*Weird* name," she whispers.

"Where I come from, everybody's heard of me," I say, "but I've been away a very long time. Can I, *uh*… put my hands down now?"

She bites the inside of her cheek, her eyes narrowing while she studies my face. Then, with a quick fling of the gun strap, she holsters the gun behind her back and extends her right hand.

"My real name's Thaniel," I say, taking her hand in mine.

"Thaniel, huh?" she asks, still shaking my hand.

"Yeah… it's complicated."

"I get it," she says, still gripping my hand. "No need to explain," she adds, letting go of my hand and looking at the ship. "Half the pods I meet from the city these days have a handful of names."

"I'm not from the city. And I didn't catch your name."

"Didn't give it to ya," she says, taking a few steps back.

"Well, should I call you *girl*?"

"Terra," she says, climbing on top of the portside wing of Mother's golden ship. "Just Terra. Or Trash. I prefer Trash," she adds, inspecting the inside of the cockpit as she runs her fingerless-gloved hands through her short, spiky blonde hair.

"Something familiar about your name. Have we ever—"

"Wow. Worst pickup line *ever*," she says.

"Sorry?"

"Nothing," she says. "Believe me, we ain't never met. And parts of your memory'll be gazumped anyway, groggy from weeks of cryo-catnapping."

"How'd you know I was in cryo-sl—"

Terra raps her fingernails against the cryonic safety rail running the circumference of the hatch opening and points at the logo affixed there.

"S-S-H," she says. "Solid-state hypothermia. I'm surprised you can remember *any* of your names right now."

"I swear I know the name Terra... somehow."

"Where in all the worlds didja get a ship like this, Ace?" she asks, scratching the side of the ship gently with the edge of her knife.

"It was a gift, of sorts."

"Damn thing is actually plated in some form of gold or... something else," she says, sheathing the knife. "You must've got yourself one generous benefactor."

"He was," I say, remembering my mother. "*She* was."

"Whatever, man," she says, sizing me up from head to toe so quickly that if I hadn't been looking into her eyes I might have missed it. "Look, *Barrabas*, if you want a credit's worth of advice, I'd suggest we not leave this here or it'll be gone by morning," she adds, looking up at the sky.

"*We?*" I ask. "You got another place I can put it? Otherwise, I'd best be charitable and let someone less fortunate find a better use for her."

"Are you serious?! A ship like that's worth at least half a million credits, man!"

"I'm afraid I don't have much use for credit."

"Look, I'd love to stay here chatting, Barrabas," she says, holstering her gun, "but it'll be zero-hour soon and the Skywatchers usually hit this part of the city first, so—"

"Skywatchers… I think I talked to a few of them on the way in. Who are they?"

"You know, the airfighters… that come out at night?"

"Told you, I wasn't from around here," I say, wagging my head at her.

"They watch the skies? Blasting anything that moves past the steam shield?"

"You mean they enforce the curfew?"

"Yeah, to say the least."

"It's been a while since I've been in the city."

"Wow, I couldn't tell," she says, her tone now dripping with sarcasm. "What are you doing here anyway? Where are you from?"

"Eridania."

"From *Eridania*?" she asks, laughing. "You really are a spacehead! No one is *from* there. You get shipped there!"

"Okay, I *came* from Eridania."

"No one comes from Eridania, either. You go there and you don't come back," she says.

"Well that's where I came from, and I'm only here now for one reason—and that's to kill someone."

"And who would that be?" she asks, laughing.

"A man named Jovian."

The laughter sticks in Terra's throat, and all amusement immediately leaves her countenance. She ducks down quickly, drawing her body as close to the edge of the building as possible.

"The *Prophet*?!" she asks with a quick whisper.

"Yes. And don't call him that."

"Listen, man, you *might* not wanna go around broadcasting something like that. He's got spies everywhere!" she says, watching the skies nervously.

"Are you one of them?"

"*Hell* no! I don't fight for any man who thinks he's holy or exalts himself higher than the rest of creation… or generally thinks he's smarter than your average amoeboid."

"I think you mean *bear*."

"Huh?"

"Never mind," I say, squatting down next to her. "So then, what do you fight for?"

"For the right to live my life as I see fit, without interference," she says, looking toward the river. "Prophet says our lives are not our own. That he's bought us all for a price. I say the hell with that! No man *buys* me."

"You sound… wise beyond your years. How old are you?"

Her neck rears back and she shakes her head at me. "*Never* ask a woman how old she is, old-timer."

"*Old*-timer?"

"Yeah, your look and lingo need some *serious* upgrading, dude."

"I'm sorry. I guess my manners could probably use some work."

"It's algood. Life's tough enough in this city," she says. "There just ain't much left for us small people. They call us deserters. Faithless. Anyway, seriously, man, don't go around spouting off at the trap about *him*. That could mean an assload of trouble for you, unless you know the right people."

"I'm not afraid of him. Jovian took everything from me, and I'm going to take it back."

"He's taken a lot from a lot of people," she says. "And who *talks* like that anyway? You don't announce to the world what you're gonna do to the guy. Keep it close to the tits, and then, *bam*! *Then* you do it. You know, surprise the mothafucker?"

"Right," I say, laughing.

She looks at me sidelong, licking her teeth behind her closed lips.

"And these right people you spoke of… who are they?"

"We *really* need to get outta here," she says, looking through the scope of her gun toward the north-facing side of the roof. "We're too far from the Rock now, and crossing the Cloisters this late at night isn't safe."

"What's at the Rock?"

"Seriously?" she asks with a grieved look on her face. "Look, man, there's a little place I know around the corner from here, close to Fort

George if we can't make it. No one uses that spot much. You won't be able to take off now without bringing way too much heat on yourself."

"Are you asking *me* out now?" I ask.

She ignores the question and eyes the street intently. Then, after sniffing the air a few times, she checks the position of the wind.

"We need to move!"

"You remind me of someone I knew. Well, someone I think I knew."

"Man, are you for real?!" she asks, cutting her eyes at me. "Get whatever you need out of that golden bucket and let's go! *Now!*"

I grab the three ejected cores right where Nav said I'd find them and take more time than I should to say goodbye to him.

"Nav, sorry but I have to leave you here."

"Yes, sir."

"Do you have some kind of shield to keep you from getting jacked?"

"I have various anti-theft measures at my disposal. Would you like me to employ them now, sir?"

"Knock yourself out."

"You are the captain. Do not forget the remote unit, sir. I can come to any location you require, provided I am not impounded and there is a suitable landing platform, sir."

"Thanks, Nav. Was good to have a friend again. I'll see you around," I say, pulling the digital ledger from the dash slot.

"Yes, sir," Nav says, his voice trailing off into a bassy warble as all the lights on the cockpit dash power down.

"Are you two finished?!" Terra asks.

"Yeah. Annoying as hell, but he got me here in one piece."

"If you're damn lucky, the ship won't have been towed by morning," she says. "And if the Surgeon says I can bring you back for it, I will."

"The Surgeon? So, is that who you fight for?"

"No, I fight for me. But he's our leader. If I can't bring you back, I can at least get you a buyer ASAP."

"I don't think she was given to me to sell."

"Oh, believe me," Terra says, making her way to the edge of the rooftop, "the guys at the Rock will give you whatever you want for a top-flight bird like that."

"So, who are these men?" I ask, watching her climb over the side of the building and down the rusty ladder descending to the street.

"Haven't you figured shit out yet?" she asks, looking up at me. "We're the nonurbanites."

CHAPTER 19

TERRA'S TOUR DE FORCE

IT'S 0330 HOURS. The sun will be rising in two. I gotta make it back to the Rock with my own skin intact *and* get this mook trailing behind me there safe and sound.

The Surgeon says this guy who calls himself Barrabas is the root of our problem, not the answer to the great mysteries. Actually, the Surgeon said Barrabas is also the key to unlocking the outer box that contains the actual box that has all the answers in it.

What the fucking *fuck*, right?

Damn confusing and vague if you ask me, but the Surgeon talks like that sometimes. I trusted the Surgeon with my life again tonight, and he didn't let me down. Barrabas showed up right on time. He even knew the precise location of where he'd put that little golden ship of his.

Lucky for us, he didn't land near the Red Lighthouse and the Sky-watchers have been totally MIA lately. It ain't like I miss them or anything, but the clear skies and my gut tell me something else hot must be going down in this cold city tonight. After my run-in with the little Prion girl, I made the Surgeon swear I'd never have to go farther south than the lighthouse again.

The timing couldn't have been more perfect, 'cause no sooner did he agree than the boys learned the yuckies had overtaken Gorman Park. That's little more than a quarter of a mile from here. Cannies are getting a little too close for comfort, *and* they've learned how to use guns despite the fact that most of them eat their damn fingers off first. During our last run-in with them, we lost Byron, one of our best snipers. Half a dozen skineaters snarfed his entire face in less than thirty seconds for fucksakes.

I've really got to hand it to Barrabas, though. He wasn't the least bit afraid when I told him that story. His crazy ass woulda marched right down into Midtown with only those two ancient six-shooters if I hadn't put the DH to his head. Six-shooters! I couldn't believe it. The plasma shots in those things have probably expired and turned to powder by now.

Either the guy must have a death wish or he's just a bona fide schizo. Probably both. And as far as I can tell, he doesn't have a clue that I was waiting for him up on that roof earlier. Part of me didn't expect him to come at all since I didn't trust Corvus any further than I could throw him. Not to mention his half-baked words of hope spoken to the Surgeon when he left Earth last year…

One man will return, and it will not be me.

That was the last thing we heard Corvus say before his smarmy ass launched into the night sky in that golden toothpick of a ship. And now, here it is again… the damned bird that cost us nearly everything.

Goes without saying, I don't think the Surgeon's gonna be thrilled to see Barrabas. But if he is who Corvus said he'd be, then that could mean something unprecedented. Out of this world, even. Can't believe a laser-brain like this guy is the one we've been waiting on. He gives me nearly an hour's march in peace and quiet before he fucks it up and opens his yap.

"How much farther?" he asks freshly.

"I *told* you already, Cabrini Boulevard stays to our right until we get to Billings Lawn."

"And what then?" he asks.

"Man, the cryo-doze must *really* be messing with your head, dude," I say, glancing over my shoulder to find him still a few paces behind me.

"I think so," he says, rubbing the sides of his forehead.

"Never trusted those things myself. I heard a story once about an entire colony of people who'd hidden themselves in the Alps during the last wars. They escaped from Earth about twenty-five years ago, after the Prophet banned all space travel. Anyway, they were headed to one of the Goldilocks planets. A new Earth that supposedly had an orbit similar enough to ours to risk going all the way there. *Uh*, Zarmina, or Gliese, I think it was."

"What happened to them?" he asks.

"Got lost along the way. After a few years, they ran outta supplies and had to put themselves to sleep. The beacons on the ship went out, and they found 'em ten years ago just drifting about fifteen light-years from here. The sleep had turned their minds into custard. Literally."

"Where are we going, Terra?"

"*Ugh*. Case in point, spacehead."

"Hey, I'm just asking."

"You've *been* just asking," I say, stopping him and putting my finger in his face. "Listen up good. We can't take that gold finger of yours to the air without getting shot down, and we're roughly a mile away from home. So, we have to hoof the distance, okay, man?"

"I was allowed to land. I had a clearance number. Doesn't that mean anything?" he asks.

"Have you been on Mars this whole time or something?!" I reply, smacking him upside the head with my palm.

Barrabas says nothing and just stares at me with those deep and darkling brown eyes.

"Look, those codes are good for *one* flight only. One! You blast off now and they'll be on your ass within thirty seconds. For whatever reason, someone up there was looking out for you and let you slide tonight. That's the only reason I'm actually talking to you right now, got it?"

He doesn't say a word. He just nods.

"Good. Now stay behind me and keep moving."

The cryo-nap did a real number on this mook. Either that or he's just blinded by whatever misguided sense of justice is driving his crazy ass to think he can kill Jovian. In the plus column, though, he didn't seem too bad in a fight. I can't *believe* he got me with that low sweep! Man, if any of the boys at the Rock had seen that, they'd have been laughing before I hit the ground. I never would have lived it down, neither. Anyway, I had better enjoy these minutes of silence before spacehead opens his kisser again.

"I used to know these streets," he whispers. "But now I don't recognize much. What's the plan anyway?"

I stop and turn around to face him.

"Repeating myself is getting *real* old. You gotta get a grip on yourself! This is the last time I'm gonna say this. We're going through Tryon Park, and once we cross Old Riverside Drive, we're really in for it. There's usually a garrison of peace guards topside monitoring that area, and I need you *focused*. They more or less have an idea where the Rock is, but they haven't found us yet. The steam wall and the fact that we're underground keeps us safe. But I still ain't gonna risk our exposure, not even for *you*."

"Fair enough."

I grab him by his filthy collar and push him back behind me.

"Now... *stay* on my six and *quit* asking about where we're going!"

He does what I tell him for once. At least he knows how to take an order. Thirty seconds of glorious peace goes by, and then I feel like a jackass for being so hard on him. The guy comes back to Earth and this is the welcome he gets? No idea who he really is and no loved ones waiting. Nothing.

Dammit, Trash. Least of all you can afford the guy is some small talk.

"So... Barrabas... you were, *umm*, pretty famous back in the day, you know? I'd forgotten I read about you in the Surgeon's library. He's got thousands of books."

"And did you find truth? In the pages?"

"Hell if I know. You tell me. Dontcha remember any of it?"

"Probably less than you do, Terra. My mind is a bit... stretched."

"No kiddin'. They say you kinda disappeared off the map. Roundabouts... mmm, 2068 or so, I guess. Went to the Prophet's gulag on Rikers, maybe?"

"That would be about right, I think," he says, as if asking a question.

"A year or so before that, you ripped off the last missing piece of the Black Orlov."

"Black Orlov? Now you really will have to refresh my memory."

"Was this giant diamond rumored to be cursed by a pagan god or somethin'. The Prophet wanted it for some reason. He was trying to reconstruct it or some shit."

"Mmm. He had a sick affinity for hallowed artifacts," he says.

"Still does. Earlier this year, he found the Hope Diamond. You heard of it?"

"Seems like I have, somewhere," he says.

"Prophet says it'll bring curses against anyone that opposes him."

"That… sounds like him. So, what else did I do after that?" he asks.

"Well, *uh*, everyone expected your next heist was gonna be, you know, something major, 'cause you'd been gone for so damn long and all. So, when you resurfaced and broke into one of the Church vaults, it was a big shocker when you made off with no money or jewels whatsoever."

"You're joking?"

"Nope. All you took was a lock of hair belonging to some guy called Elvis and other assorted genetic materials, shall we say."

"You mean *the* Elvis?!" he asks.

"Sure, dude."

"That's incredible!"

"A couple days later, before you up and *bamfed* entirely, you published a manifesto explaining why you did it."

"Son of a bitch!" he says, smiling like a kid.

"Yeah, you said something like, *It was only a matter of time before they cloned the King of Kings,* and you just couldn't stand for that.*"

"Amazing!"

"S'weird. The last reigning king that I ever heard of was an English dude named Henry of Wales. Or was it Harry? Anyway, he died like fifty years ago."

"Ancient history, I guess," he says quietly. "I can't remember now why they called Elvis a king, either."

"Well, that's why it's called *ancient*… 'cause it's long gone, forgotten."

And yet, this blast-from-the-past mook who played the best disappearing act of all time thirty years ago is walking right behind me. At least *this* Barrabas seems to have got himself some moral standards. I'll be flarked sideways if he doesn't stink, though… like hot metal and charred skin. And leather.

Still, he is kinda handsome, for an old guy, in a dirty sort of retro way... looking like he stepped straight out of the 2070s or something. He's definitely in shape, too. We just hoofed over a mile and he hasn't broken a sweat.

"We're nearly at the Cloisters. Less than ninety minutes before sunrise. Keep moving."

"You've been here before?" he asks.

"All the time. I was hiding out there for months before the Surgeon found me. Or before I found *him*, I should say. I'd been livin' off nothin' but Hudson fish and moldy bread. Can't believe I didn't grow a second head or something. The toxicity alone shoulda been enough to have me foaming at the mouth like some newly trans'ed Skywatcher cadet. Still, wasn't any worse than living off those damned city rations. I mean those things were the real spaz. It's almost as if they hand 'em out in the hopes that you do keel over."

"Where are all the people?" he asks. "This city used to be practically overrun."

"Got ourselves a few million souls, I guess. Few million more underground, but there was a huge falling away... about ten years back. On this side of the country there ain't any electricity farther south than Perth Amboy, and from what I hear food is even scarcer. A lotta people take refuge down in the Amazons, where the Church has less of a stranglehold."

"Didn't you have any friends that left? I mean, anyone who managed to get away?" he asks.

"Yeah, nah. But there were quite a few of us hidden at the Cloisters in those days. Tony Pascagoula was our leader. Guy was completely bionic below the knees. Dude made the *best* cheeseburger I ever tasted."

"Cheeseburger?"

"Well, to be fair, I prolly say that because it was the last one I ever had. Can't even get cheese now. Then there was Mìcheal of the O'Farrell clan. That guy *always* had a smile on his face. Even after the Prions tore both his arms off, his ginger ass still somehow managed to come back to us."

"I'm sorry."

"Yeah. Fuckin' Prions. Just before Mikey flatlined, he laughed about how *shite* it was that he'd never be able to hold a pint again."

"What exactly are they? Prions?"

"They're cannies... flesh-eaters. Somethin' happens to them in the transference process. Fucks their brainwaves up. They'll eat their own family members."

"And what about you? Why didn't you have any family with you? To protect you?" he asks.

"My cousin Nydia was my only family there. She was *way* too sweet for this life. Not a lick of piss or vinegar in her. And then there was good old Skip. He was this *trancer* who'd pretty much all but lost his noggin from a botched procedure."

"Trancer?"

"Yeah. They live out memories in their head, in repetition. It's real sad. Still, he was harmless. Told us lots of stories about how he'd been born and raised in a city he called Old Philly. Said he played guitar in a band. He musta been full of fluff, 'cause playing live music hasn't been legal my entire life. But that was over nine years ago... I was still a lean and green grasshopper then."

"Why didn't you ever try to get out?" he asks.

"Yeah, good luck with *that*. Anyone born in the city within the last twenty-five years is tagged from birth. They put the damn chips right into the spinal column."

"So, they can track everybody?" he asks.

"Yep, unless you've had it removed. That'll cost ya nearly a million credits, if you can find the right mook willing to risk his own life *and* yours to yank the damn thing outta ya."

"I take it you don't have a chip, then?"

"Nope. Surgeon took it out. Didn't even haveta pay him. Damn risky procedure, though, since you can't always get to the chip. A few of the Rock boys still have theirs."

"So, how have you all kept hidden? Kept from being caught?"

"The Rock's basically one giant Faraday shield, partner."

"Fara what?"

"S'what the Surgeon calls it anyway... It blocks the radio waves and whatnot. Keeps the Prophet and his neuro-quacks from readin' the old pink raisin. That's why *I'm* the one out here dragging your ass in and not him."

"You mean this Surgeon still has his chip?" he asks.

"Yep. None of us has got his skilled hands, and we can't afford to lose him."

"So, if you don't have a chip, then why not flee south? Be free?"

"*Because* the Church owns nearly everything north of the Great Mexican Wall. You can't buy or sell or trade anything without the chip. A loaf of good bread'll cost you a day's wages or more, depending on where you shop. So, we just steal what we need, ya know? Besides, all the *best* goods are here in the city."

Barrabas and I stop where Fort Tryon Place meets Margaret Corbin Drive and I see the Cloisters up ahead. I put my finger over my mouth, and Barrabas gets what I mean. I didn't realize I'd talked so damn much. I *never* talk this much.

Get a grip on yourself Trash. You're nearly home.

"What happened here, Terra?" he whispers.

"Keep moving."

Barrabas follows as we delve farther into the tree line due northeast, and the chill in the air reminds me of that night.

"The Council Guards came and destroyed the chapel hall just after dark. I'd just gone out by the river looking for somethin' to eat. The Skywatchers came down hard as fuck... took nearly everything they could find. Shot everyone."

"But not you."

"Yeah, after I'd caught some fish that had fewer than three eyes, I came back and just *knew* somethin' was wrong. Then I smelled the plasma in the air. That's when I found the Surgeon praying over the bodies. He was crying over Skip! To this day I don't know if he even knew him or not. I'm guessing he did, because the Surgeon defected from the Church right then and there, that very night. He told me later the guards killed everyone because they were looking for a unicorn. Just another prize that the Prophet wanted for his fuckin' collection."

"A *real* unicorn?" he asks.

"I dunno. I hear the Prophet still has some pieces in his keeping from that raid… that he didn't destroy it all, like he usually does when he confiscates shit. I never saw the unicorn myself, but the Surgeon says somewhere in the place there'd been a picture of one that was over five hundred years old. No one I ever met knows what a unicorn even looks like. I imagined it was… I dunno… maybe a ship of some kind? One that might take ya to heaven when you died?"

"I'll tell you one thing, Terra," he says, smiling, "if you ever do see one, you'll know you're not on Earth."

"Okay. *Weirdo*."

We stop about a hundred meters from the south entrance to the Cloisters. I can't hear a sound, except for a slight breeze in the trees. When I step forward, Barrabas grips me by the shoulder and pulls me back into the shadow of an elm tree near me.

"Wait!" he says. "I think I recognize this place!"

I brush his hand off my shoulder as he points to the tower, now broken and crumbling.

"That's… That's the west terrace!" he says.

"Yeah, that's what I've been talking about, dude. The old Cloisters."

"There were men who destroyed it, you said. Did you see any of them?"

"I told you, they came in the night, and I was very young."

"They said there was a priceless unicorn in a house full of thieves," Barrabas whispers, almost to himself.

"Huh? *Nah*, man, just a house full of rebels that didn't wanna transfer."

Barrabas goes awfully quiet for a minute, and I wait for him to say something… anything. Then I remember the sun waits for no man.

"C'mon. We're not far from Riverside. Once we cross that, we should be home free!"

"Yes. Lead on," he says.

We sprint hard and fast past the Cloisters, and I don't take one look back at my old home. I can hear Barrabas breathing heavier now. He keeps up and manages to stay no less than twenty paces behind me.

When we get to Riverside, the old friend I like to call the big damn lump in my throat starts forming. I risk a glance at Barrabas, and he's looking to the trees behind us. Then I hear the sweet *tweety tweet* of a bluebird.

"Keeping moving, Barrabas!"

We leave Riverside in the dust and come to the approach road leading to the Henshaw Street Bridge. There's no other way around it, really. We could jump into the river below, but we'd be fucked. And if we somehow didn't die and still got back to the Rock, they'd be calling me something worse than Trash Heap this time.

The bridge isn't more than one hundred meters across, but it's totally exposed. Crossing it damn sure feels like an eternity when you're out moving in the open. Barrabas squats down next to me behind one of the parapets rising up from the bridge's abutment.

"Everything's quiet. *Too* quiet," he says.

Leering around the parapet, I see nothing barring our way, and when Barrabas gets back up to his feet, he puts his six to the supporting back-wall.

"Alright, spacehead, let's go," I whisper.

We make one hell of a run across the bridge. I can see the trees of Inwood at twelve o'clock. We make it about halfway across, and then there's a sound. It seems to come from above and in front of us. It's that unmistakable sound.

"We've been made!" Barrabas says.

"It's the Watchers! Keep moving, dammit!"

I ready the DH and power the charge. It'll take a few more seconds before I can fire. Damn gun.

"They're at the end of the bridge!" Barrabas shouts from behind me.

They move fast. They weren't there ten seconds ago. I count three of the bastards standing behind one of the standard-issue Skywatcher cars. Tiny and hard to man, but they're fast as hell, those things. The mooks make the mistake of trying to reason with us instead of firing first.

"*This is a restricted area! You will relinquish what weaponry you are carrying and present your identification!*" shouts a voice that's somewhere and nowhere.

When I put my back to the concrete pylon near the center of the bridge, the Skywatchers try for another lame-ass verbal attempt to get us to surrender. Then I see Barrabas at three o'clock, searching the pockets of his pants.

Damn. I should've given him a gun.

"Eat it!" I shout, sending out a barrage of fire from the DH. Two of the shots are wild, but one makes its mark and hits the leftmost Watcher center-chest. He stumbles back a few meters before going into the river below.

"Enjoy the swim, ya mook!"

The other two Watchers duck behind their flyer after I fire a few more shots from the DH, but they just bounce to the side like water off a duck's ass. No doubt those two mooks'll be calling for backup.

"Jump for it?" Barrabas asks, pointing to the river.

"You wanna take your chances in that water, go right ahead!"

I move from behind the pylon and run forward toward the other end of the bridge. Barrabas stays with me, and in an atomic flash, I hear him pull out those two pistols of his. Really, where did he get those things?

Everything happens so damn quick.

I'm not but eighty feet from the two Watchers when I hear the pins clack. Shots are fired, but I can't even see if they found their mark. I must've blinked or something, and the two spazoids are falling to the ground.

Time slows down to normal, and I come to a stop and aim the DH. The bridge looks secure, and I don't hear any more Skyturds coming just yet. There *can't* have been only three of them. I turn around and Barrabas is blowing into both barrels of those crusty pistols like he's some hot shit ace duck.

"Okay, that wasn't bad."

"I could shoot the cherry off the top of an ice cream sundae at a hundred yards," he says, grinning.

"Ice cream? Huh?"

"Forget it."

"C'mon, let's go. There'll be a half dozen more of these jerks within a minute. Once we get to Inwood, the Watchers won't follow."

We make a run for the end of the bridge. I can almost smell the sap from the trees. From behind me, Barrabas yells my name.

Damn! My back *really* hurts all of a sudden. Am I on fire?

I'm on the ground now. I try to sit up and turn my head. Am I lying in the middle of the bridge?

I turn my head, and street rocks and gravel grit dig into the back of my skull. Barrabas is standing over one of the Watchers he must've just shot. The Watcher is waving his hands, begging him not to do what I know he's going to do. No, he's *cursing* at him. Hell, I can't quite tell. I can't hear very good.

Barrabas mouths something to him, and then the Watcher's helmet explodes into a hundred pieces at the shot. Someone screams my name again. I don't think I can stand up.

"Dammit, girl, can you move?!" he asks.

Barrabas jerks me to my feet, I think. He's holding me now. His beard is actually kinda handsome. I never really liked beards, though.

"The shot didn't go all the way through. You'll be okay," he says.

"What shot?" I ask.

"They tagged you, Trash. Just stay awake now," he says.

"They did? Doesn't... Doesn't even hurt."

"The wound is cauterizing," he says. "I had to put the barrel on it."

I think he's carrying me again.

"Really? Didn't know... you could do that..."

"That barrel's paper-thin," he says.

Hmm. So, he knows his guns. I wonder if he was a fighter. And he's definitely carrying me.

All I can see now is the stars and his beard and his face. He really is handsome. Spacehead just needs a haircut.

"Did you fight in the war? You look kinda old."

"I *am* old," he says.

I think he's laughing at me.

"Are we at the tree line yet?"

"We've been in the forest for a few minutes, Terra."

After what feels like forever in his strong arms, I can't hear nothing else but the whizz of travel drones running over the Old Henry Hudson causeway. They are coming.

The pain in my back stops long enough for my head to actually clear. Barrabas is talking to me. I can't make out what he's saying. Now we're standing on a cliff I know all too well.

"Hey, space ape... can you see the Palisades?"

"Yeah, I think so," he says. "North and west a bit, across the water?"

"Go due north and back down to the water, then under the bridge toward the old street. That should lead us right to the Rock."

Another eternity passes. The stars shoot crazy fast overhead. Are they moving at all? Or are they just up there, stuck like magnets on black sheet metal?

"You're gonna be okay," he says.

Now I'm being set on the ground. I know where we are: at the edge of a clearing, not far from the Indian Caves.

Barrabas props me up against a tree and tells me not to move, then takes out those fusty old pistols and starts casing the area.

"Which way?" he asks.

I nod in the Rock's general direction.

"You're kidding? It's an *actual* rock?" he asks.

He doesn't know this place like I do. The Skywatchers are the ones who're afraid here. I smile at him, and he disappears from my sight into the tree line toward the east.

"Don't go that way, Barrabas!"

He doesn't respond, and I get a strange feeling in my bones. I look toward the Rock, and it's vanished, gone underground. That means the boys have come topside. We're safe.

I'm *safe*.

"I see you *found* him," someone whispers in my right ear from behind me.

"Octavian?"

The Surgeon steps from around the tree at my back, and I can already see two of the boys dragging Barrabas toward the Rock.

"He landed. He came. Just like Corvus said."

"That he did," the Surgeon says.

Then I'm off the ground and I'm in his arms. He's not nearly as handsome as Barrabas. He's got a full set of really straight teeth, though. And he smells way nicer than laser brain.

"You should have been much more careful, my dear," he says.

"I was careful."

"When we took him, his hands were on the slab, Terra," he says, "as if he knew the words that were written there."

"No way."

"We watched him, Terra. We were *in* the trees," he says, scowling at me in that slightly overbearing and fatherly way of his.

"How? What's it mean?"

"It can only mean one thing: he's been here before."

CHAPTER 20

THE SURGEON OF SHORAKKOPOCH

SOMEONE THROWS FREEZING-COLD water on me. I'm not even joking. A bucket full of damn cold water, just like in the movies. Whatever else they must've hit me with earlier seemed to have knocked the cryo-sleep fuzz right out of me, too, because I'm feeling more and more sober by the second.

The last thing I remember, prior to the icy deluge, was standing over the rock Terra kept talking about. I can't believe I didn't recall it before. When I saw the plaque attached to the rock itself, I remembered. I remembered the slaughter… all the nurbs we killed back in the mid-sixties. There would have been mountains of them had we not burned all the bodies.

Someone throws water on me, again.

"Dammit, *enough*!"

"Wake up, Barrabas," says a deep and raspy male voice.

"I'm awake! Could've just kicked me in the nuts, you know!"

I shake my head clear of the water, and best I can tell, I'm sitting on the floor in a makeshift bunker of some kind. My hands are tied behind my back, and there are men of various shapes and sizes and color standing all around me in a perfect circle. More than a few of them look as if they've not eaten in a few weeks.

"Looks like I'm in good company. Where's Trash?" I ask, blinking the focus back into my eyes.

"Terra is perfectly alright."

A man dressed almost entirely from head to toe in dark purple steps through the ring of men, with his arms behind his back.

"I've tended to her," he says.

"And who are you?" I ask. "Can't be easy to walk around dressed like that and stay unnoticed."

A few of the men laugh, and so does the man in purple.

"Uncuff him, boys, if you would," he says.

No one lays a finger on me, but there's a beep and a crack of sorts, and then the restraints on my hands fall to the cold ground.

"Isn't that a neat trick?" I ask, massaging the ache from my wrists.

"Here, in this place, I am the leader of these men," says the man in purple as he extends his hand to me.

"The way Terra spoke about you," I reply, accepting his gesture and rising to meet him, "I thought you'd be... older."

"I should say the same about you, Barrabas," he says, smiling at me with a hint of wonder in his black eyes.

His teeth are the next thing I notice. He has radiant teeth. Above that, his long nose takes over the prominence of his face, and his short but thick brown hair is thinning in the front. He *smells,* too. It's medicinal maybe... like he's been in a mortuary.

"And what do they call you? The purple prince?" I ask.

"Some of the men call me sultan," he says with a quick smile, "but I prefer to not be called by that name. I'm not a noble man, nor is my blood worthy of a title so, well, royal."

He smiles again and turns, acknowledging the men in the room with several quick nods.

"But these men here are free, and on most occasions, they do as they damn well please."

The men chortle and snort amongst themselves.

"So, you're Octavian then? The Great Surgeon. Or should I say the *previous* Surgeon?"

"Yes, actually, to all of the above. But how did you know my real name?"

"The data logs from my ship."

"Ah... *Nav* told you," he says, smiling.

"He did. Had a bit of time to catch up on some light reading when I came out of cryo-sleep."

"Yes. Your ship was... special," he says, frowning. "When I helped secure it for you, we were all reeling from quite a loss. Corvus was the one who—"

"You knew Corvus?!" I ask, my heart quickening in my chest.

"Of course," he says. "You know, that craft came at a very high price. Many men died so that you could have it—Corvus included, we can now presume?"

"Yes. I'm sorry. He's dead."

"Well, let's not piss on his sacrifice by lollygaggin' around, eh?" says a rather beefy bald lad standing behind the Surgeon.

"Yes, let us get you up to speed, shall we?" the Surgeon interjects, stepping aside and motioning toward a doorway behind him and the bald man.

"After *you*, Barrabas."

I'm led down several corridors dimly lit by some ancient style of strip lighting. The first narrow hall goes left. After we walk for a hundred feet, we turn to the right for at least another fifty feet. Two men stay in front of me while the Surgeon stays behind with the rest, and I can hear the clatter of their weapons hitting the walls at our sides and the jostling of gun clips. One man at the rear says something about the *fossils* I'm carrying strapped to my thighs.

"What is this place?" I ask, my voice echoing faintly.

"This is Shorakkopoch Rock," the Surgeon says, "or what's left of it, I should say. Originally it was touted as the place where a theologian named Peter Minuit purchased the island of Manhattan. The entire island, bought and paid for with jewelry worth little more than a few handfuls of Dutch silver, no less."

"The whole island?"

"Imagine that," he says, laughing. "Anyway, during the reconstruction of the city after the wars, many of these tunnels were excavated in the hopes they might be used as shelters should Neo York ever come under attack again on such a large scale. It seems that men have forgotten about them. A world without war will do that sort of thing. Still, it's beneficial for us."

We stop at the end of the corridor after having gone nearly a hundred more feet. Just ahead I can see the gray rock has formed around the frame of a large metal doorway. The Surgeon steps past me and flicks a switch nearby, and a series of small red halogen lights illuminates the crank-style handle of the vault. The Surgeon gives the wheel a spin, and I hear the locks on the other side relent.

When the red lights switch off, the Surgeon pulls back on the handle, and the door opens so slowly I have time to measure its width with my hand. It's at least ten inches thick and covered in walnut-sized rivets. As it opens, it creaks and squeals at a frequency I didn't think was possible for a human to hear.

"This way, if you would," the Surgeon says, motioning for me to enter. "We have much to discuss, friend."

The room through the door is the most marvelous thing I've seen since I was a child. It's full of books, posters, advertisements, odors, lights, and… life!

Everything within is covered in a warm sheen of orange, for the only light in the room emanates from half a dozen burning torches at each end. Never since leaving home have I seen this much dangerous materialism all in one place. It's a museum… a shrine to a bygone era. I could almost die a happy man right now.

"This is our humble abode," the Surgeon says, shoving his hands into a massive trunk filled to the brim with small coppery coins. "*Pennies,* they called them," he adds, "and of course most of the rest of what you see here is also contraband."

The Surgeon gestures for me to sit in an old wooden chair at the foot of a large dark wooden table in the center of the room.

"Boys? Please leave us. And bring our guest some water, perhaps?" the Surgeon tells the men in our train.

I turn and glance toward the doorway, and there are even more men than before.

"They're *aching* to get a look at you," the Surgeon says, smiling. "Boys, come now. Give the man a few moment's peace."

Most of the men exit silently, but as they do, I catch the jumbled muttering of words I can't quite make out. From their tone of voice, they certainly don't sound enthused. As the giant metal door creaks shut, the latch clicks sharply, and its closure booms throughout the chamber like a war drum.

"Please, sit. I'll give you a proper tour of the place later," the Surgeon says, sliding a wooden chair out for me. "I would offer food," he adds, "but I think it's best to wait for that, since what I'm about to tell you may be a little more difficult to digest than bread."

"I'm not hungry," I reply, lying through my teeth.

"Very well," he says, circling around the table toward the opposite side. "I won't waste any more of your time. You've waited long enough for answers, I think."

"Answers. Are you saying you have them?"

"I have some of them. But first… I have a few questions of my own. Things I must know, if you have knowledge of them."

"I'd be foolish to deny you. You've got enough guns in this place to blow me to hell and back."

"You have been here before, have you not?" he asks, taking his own seat across from me.

"I don't think so. Maybe above, but not down this deep."

"When my men rendered you unconscious, and I must apologize for that, you were searching the Rock as if you knew where you were."

"Yes, it was the stone. When I put my hand on the tablet attached to it… it felt… familiar."

"Yes, and you also *knew* the password," he says, rubbing the underside of his chin. "You'd already depressed half of the letters—and in the proper sequence as well. The letters P, H, and A—"

"*Pharos!*" I whisper, the word leaving my lips as though it were prompted completely by instinct.

"Yes!" he says, smiling. "'Twas a beacon. One of the ancient seven wonders of our world. The *Old* World."

"Clearly, I *was* here then. At some point, anyway. The years in the mine have, well… They've muddled a lot of what's in my head."

"Of course. It might be possible that Corvus may have brought you here, no?" he asks.

"No. No, that can't be."

"Are you sure?"

"I never knew Corvus."

"I know you didn't. I was referring to your mother," he says with a frown.

"No, I… I don't believe I ever came here with her."

"You remember *something* of this place. What is it then?" he asks.

I hesitate. I've only just met the man. Yet I feel strangely calm in his presence.

"Speak freely, friend," he says, as if he were reading my mind. "Nothing said here goes beyond these walls."

"I might have been here during the great purge of 2067. The Peace Police were looking for… new blood. Fresh recruits from the Academy. They needed more numbers… to help detain all the nonurbanites."

"Tragic," he says, covering his mouth.

"They gave us guns… and I was just what they were looking for. Young… foolish. No knowledge of the world and needing something to prove to someone I knew not."

"I wasn't below ground in those days, my friend," he says, "and I hear remorse in your voice. But you can't change it. You are here now. And we will do our best to make amends for all those wrongs."

"There is a strange familiarity… a vague sense of lingering association. Maybe Barrabas was here?"

"Ah, *yes*! I had forgotten!" he says, laughing. "You may have been here in another life."

"This stuff here… is it all authentic? Original, I mean?"

"Yes," he says, nodding and looking around the room. "Antiques, as they say. Nearly everything here is more than fifty years old, and most of it comes from my own home. I had quite the collection before I left the Church."

"Antiques, huh? I guess I could fall into that category."

"Yes, Barrabas," he says, laughing, "I believe you are quite right. Then again, I am likely *far* older than you."

"You think so? Well, unless you invented transference, then I highly doubt that," I say, still eyeing the wonder of the room.

"It's funny you should say that," he says. "I promised you answers. And the most important one I can now give you is the truth behind transference. I am, after all, in a way, the father of it."

"The *father* of it?" I ask, nearly choking on my own tongue.

"Yes," he says.

I jump from my chair so fast, and before I know it, I'm standing on top of the table and running toward him. Just as my arms reach out so that I can wring his cleanly shaven neck, he pulls out a gun no larger than the palm of his hand and has it aimed in the center of my forehead.

No. That's not how it happens. It's all played out in my head in an instant.

I shake myself and realize I'm still seated. I must be in shock.

"Did... Did you say... the *father* of transference?"

"Yes, Kilraven," he says, raising his eyebrows.

"You know who I really am then?"

"Undoubtedly. We've been waiting. Corvus and I both knew. It is why my life was made forfeit by the Council and the Church, and it's why I am no longer employed by the Prophet."

"Jovian!"

"Yes. He believes me dead, I suppose. Or he has altogether forgotten me," he says, rubbing the tips of his fingers together slowly. "There are some things even *he* does not understand."

"Like what? What things?"

"For instance, the man you see before you is the last version of *me* that there will ever be."

"Okay. Then Jovian and I have one thing in common: I don't understand, either."

"Oh yes, of course!" the Surgeon says joyfully. "I forget you have been gone for a while. Good Lord, I am not really sure where to begin. I know that you have been through much… I can't even fathom the things you have suffered… all the years. But I know that you can now assist us in a strict purpose, and that is to undo what we have done. Why else would Jovian allow Kilraven the Cursed to remain alive? Transference must be stopped. It must not be allowed to—"

Two of the Surgeon's men reenter the room, each carrying a large silver-coated flagon. One of the men sets a silver tankard filled with water in front of me, and I see him eyeballing my pistols before leaving the room. The man carrying the Surgeon's vessel slides it across the table smoothly, and Octavian catches it in his palm as though he'd done the move a thousand times.

"Thank you, gentlemen," the Surgeon says as his men exit the room. "Where was I?" he asks, taking a drink from his cup.

"Transference."

"Yes… transference is *evolving*, my friend," the Surgeon says. "It has become an unholy irregularity. A mockery of life."

"And you… the father of it. Were you there, at the beginning? Prior to the fall of Fornax?"

"I was working for the Church when they brought the technology from the *Bermuda*," he says, taking a sip from his cup, "and we were using it on some of the crew that had seen the equipment, as per the Council's decision. Back and forth, body to body. We didn't understand it yet. That was still to come."

"What on Earth did you think you were doing?!"

"Barrabas, you *must* hear me," he says, placing his flagon on the table. "Understand that I am a different man now. I cannot undo what was done. I can only live in the present and make revision."

"So, you *knew* about transference before I returned? Before we were sent to Eridania?"

"Yes, we knew," he says, pausing to swallow the lump in his throat, "but we didn't understand the science behind it. Or the chemistry… or the *spiritual* element. We had just perfected cloning techniques the year previous to your capture, but the Council hadn't announced it publicly. Do you remember?"

"My mother… She said they wanted to clone part of my father, before, when I was young… to try and… save him somehow."

"Yes, that would be right," he says. "And twenty years on from your father's death, we would replicate a full adult body. You see, we could make a perfect copy, but there was no life! The organs, the brain, the heart… everything was perfect, but they wouldn't *work*. We couldn't even make the heart beat more than once."

I shift uncomfortably in my chair, taking a deep sigh. The Surgeon winces and smiles all at once.

"Forgive me, Octavian, if I'm not as enthused as you are about what you're telling me."

"I understand, Kilraven. Forgive me. I am a doctor. These things have and always will fascinate me. But now I know what we did was perverse. Ungodly, even. I tell you all this now because Corvus wished it. He wanted it so. And also because you have suffered more than most, partly because of the choice of men like me."

"So, what happened? To the clones you made?"

"We kept them all in cryo-preservation and shelved the project. Jovian was using all his influence over the Council through his role in the Church, and by *this* time, you and the *Grimalkin* had just returned from Fornax. We already knew we needed the ore from Eridania, which the *Bermuda* had brought to us in the first of the capsules."

"So, the *Bermuda* had already brought *other* pods back?"

"Yes. There were two," he says, "coated in a special element. The first of the iron shells, we called them. We knew the ore worked. The *ore* was the key!"

"But you didn't have enough of it."

"No. And your mission on Fornax was to retrieve more for us," he says, "but we didn't know you'd find two more machines. And we had no idea that the officers on your flight would transfer themselves. That was why all of you were taken captive when you returned. Jovian and the Council had to keep the information from getting out. They had to own it, control it, make the public think they crafted it."

"For what reason?"

"What else? Dominance. Mastery. *Puissance*."

"What did you mean before, when you said transference is evolving?"

"Yes. Well, the early successes included yourself and the crew of the *Bermuda* and the *Grimalkin*," he says, drinking from his silvery cup. "Nearly all of you were sent to the mines after we transferred you between one another or, in your case, into a dangerous enemy of the city-state. This had a somewhat adverse effect, we found. Going into a body that did not contain your own brain could cause a conflict of identity, to varying degrees."

"Why was Madzimure chosen?"

"That I cannot answer fully, other than to say it was a perfect way to rid us of you. Consequently, we could then *use* you to gather the ore so that we could continue... testing."

"Testing on what?"

"On... the children."

"What *children?*"

"Yes, well," he says, swallowing so hard it sounds as though he may choke. "The Council members wanted to be the first to benefit from this newfound discovery. So, they each selected from the Church records a child that was at optimal health and had the desired physical attributes. The peace officers took them in the night. They murdered each of their parents, and we erased their files and destroyed their chips. When that was done, we transferred all the Council members, each one in turn, into the children's bodies. The children were then, of course, alive and inside the Council member's bodies. They... They all went mad within two days."

"What did you do with them?"

"They were *screaming,*" he says, staring at one of the torches. "Always screaming. Some of them were hurting themselves, cutting their own skin in an effort to get out," he adds, exhaling deeply before looking back at me. "So, naturally, Jovian did the only thing he knew how. He had them executed."

"So, all the Council members have been living out lives inside the bodies of these children?"

"No, no, *no*," he says, waving his hand. "The Council members all died suddenly when the children, who were in the old bodies, were killed. There was something we couldn't figure out, a connection we had yet to make!"

"I think I'm gonna be sick—"

"There's more. And you *must* hear it!" he says, reaching for me across the table. "It was then that we remembered the clones, and thus we threw a monkey wrench into our own research. You see, we had DNA from dozens of people, all from different walks of life... but as I said, there was no *life* in them. Again, we failed there because we transferred what volunteers we had into the cloned bodies and then euthanized the volunteer's original body. Subsequently, the clones we just transferred them into also died. It was so *simple*! But we didn't understand why. The next step was logical."

"Logical?"

"We needed to transfer one original person into a clone of himself, or herself, and then *kill* the original body."

"Why on Earth would you—"

"We had to know! We had to know," he says, closing his eyes as the torchlights crackle. "But no one wanted to volunteer. So, Jovian convicted one of his brethren of treason against the Church. That man was sentenced to death by the Council. *Jobius* was his name. We then made a clone of him. Just as before, there was no life, only an empty shell. Later, we used the transference pods to take his soul from his original body and place it into the clone of himself. The clone came to life, and the original body, now soulless, *also* remained alive!"

"How is that even possible?"

"You see, it was something about the soul *and* the body," he says, his eyes growing wide in the firelight. "We thought it was the mind, but we were wrong. It was the soul! The soul is linked somehow to the original body that it comes from, the one that you're born with. When the original body dies, the soul is set free, no matter where it's housed."

"That can't be. If you transferred Jobius into a clone of himself and the original body had no soul left in it, then why didn't the original body die?"

"Because Jobius's soul still lived *here*, in another body. One cannot live without the other, at least not in this tangible plane of existence. The soul can move from body to body, but the true and original body that a man or woman is born with must remain alive. Do you see?"

"It doesn't make any sense. It can't possibly—"

"Alright, look at me then. Look at me," he says, placing his hands on his chest. "I personally destroyed every clone I made of myself. All but one. And that one sits before you right now, because my original body still lives somewhere in the cryo-vaults of the Church, and my soul is here with me. If you were to kill me right now, my soul would flee this body, and my first body in the vaults would die. Inversely, if someone in the Church were to destroy my original body in the vault, my soul would flee this body here and now. Yes?"

"I just... I just can't... I don't believe it. I—"

"It's alright," he says. "Sometimes it confuses even me."

"So, then tell me this: why is your original body still alive? Why hasn't Jovian destroyed it?"

"Why Jovian does or does not do things is beyond my comprehension," he says, leaning back in his chair. "He seems more *bored* now than anything. Perhaps he acts merely out of spite or purely for the sport of it all. I am probably just another pawn in this game of his."

"A game? Is that what you think? You think this has all been a fucking *game*?!" I ask, slamming my fist onto the table.

The Surgeon hangs his head and says nothing. I can only sigh and take a deep breath and sit here, still, confounded by all he's said. I feel like vomiting. I feel like screaming.

"I do not know the answer, Kilraven. I do not know the answer to that. Much greater men than Jovian have dared to play games with humanity. History has not been so kind to them."

I stare into the Surgeon's dark eyes, and in a flash of clarity, it hits me all at once.

"It's Jovian. He's got something else up his sleeve. The bastard wanted me to know. It's because he *wants* me to know."

"What's that?" the Surgeon asks.

"He's not an idiot. Jovian wanted me to find you. That's why your original body is alive, Octavian. *That's* why he hasn't killed you."

"Perhaps you are right, my friend," he says. "Jovian is the author of all these things, and they have happened exactly the way his will has desired. Your conclusion does make sense."

"But Jovian hasn't transferred everyone. Not yet. Or has he?"

"Not everyone *chooses* transference," the Surgeon says, "but the vast majority of the populace is now converting. Jovian's disciples grow day by day. You wouldn't *believe* the number of people he has at his command in Tokyo."

"Why doesn't anyone fight?"

"Well, why resist when the promise of living forever is just down the road from a brief bit of pain and servitude?"

"And what about Terra? And your men? Are they all… themselves?"

"Yes," he says. "Terra and my men are all *originals*."

"So, why didn't they end up in the mines?"

"Things are different now than they were in your time. At the age of eighteen, the Church clones you," he says, "and you're transferred into that clone. Your original is then kept so that duplicates of the highest quality can be grown from it."

"Duplicates?"

"Yes. We found that cloning from the source eliminated subsequent complications," he says, gnawing at his lip and looking at me with a sort of regretful pity. "Memory loss, dementia, senility in some cases, and even psychosis… to name a few."

"Where does the Church keep the originals? Do they store them?"

"Yes," he says. "In this way they own you, and Jovian owns you also, since he owns the majority of all business shares now. There are pockets of us left who resist. Of those who both deny the trials and manage to escape, some find refuge here."

"And now it's up to the Church whether you live or die?"

"Depending on your level of service or how you managed to prove your usefulness to the Council, yes," he says, pausing to lick his lips. "One may or may not get transferred again after a certain number of years, but ideally you could live forever. Even if it took you forty years to save up the credits for another procedure, your eighteen-year-old original is still there and in good nick."

"This is just… *phew*. I mean, just beyond anything… anything I expected."

"I know, my friend. I am sorry. I'm so sorry," he says.

"What about Jovian? Is he in a clone?"

"Jovian actually chose to select a body that was cloned from another," he says, tapping the tabletop gently with his knuckles. "He picked an empty male clone to his liking, and we transferred him into it. Jovian's original body was then kept in cryo-stasis. I believe it's still there, buried deep in his nearly impenetrable vault."

"Wait, wait, wait… If Jovian chose a body that was cloned from another, couldn't you just kill the person that the clone was made from? Killing Jovian in the process?"

"No," he says, smiling. "Remember that a clone has no *life*. It is not born with a soul. It is not an original. So, if you transfer yourself into an empty clone, the only thing you need fear is your original body being killed."

"Well, what about transference between two different people? Two people who both have their souls?"

"That's when you must *truly* worry, Kilraven, because then it becomes a mixing of body and soul and a very dangerous and tangled web," he says, leaning forward across the table. "I suspect Jovian discovered this first with yourself and Barrabas, though I have no proof of this. Didn't you ever come across anyone in the mines that just fell dead for no reason? As if nothing had happened to them to cause their death?"

"Yes! We just thought it was from breathing the ore dust, that it was toxic or something."

"No. That was Jovian, or someone within the Church, pulling the power on that person's stasis pod here on Earth," he says. "Either that or the first soul which originally belonged to the body the miner was now in had fled, for whatever reason."

"So, the son of a bitch has just used us all? Used us for his own gain?"

"Yes, I'm afraid he has," he says, nodding slowly.

"And what's Jovian's latest move?"

"Well, as I said, he is in a clone now. Likely well past twenty or thirty versions at least. You see, we found that the cloned tissue still ages. So, each time Jovian falls ill or wants the adrenaline rush, he is retransferred. He hasn't stayed in the same body for more than a few years. It's a kind of addiction, really, to put it simply."

"How, Octavian? How did he do all of this? He was no one when I knew him. He was nothing. A pandering, quiet sort of… mouse of a man."

"The son becomes the father, I'm afraid. And Jovian's father was partly responsible," he says.

"Who was he?"

"He owned part of the Church, as well as the majority of the credit shares when the great wars were over. The Church was and is a business… a corporation. Jovian's enlistment at the Academy only happened because he wanted it. When his father was killed, Jovian was finally able to see to his own desires and left to join the seminary. For a good while it seemed as though he was keeping his hands out of Church business, and we among the medical community had no reason to fear him. But something he had seen on the first expeditions to Fornax, or something that happened on the *Bermuda*, had awakened something in him. He came back, and when he did, he had a vision of what could be the next Age of Men."

"That was when I met him," I say. "He told me I had to join the cause and go. I remember he kept trying so hard to convince me! Saying they had killed his brother and he was afraid and that I needed to find out why."

"Yes, he already knew then," he says, relaxing in his chair.

"But *how?*"

"I don't know. A dream, perhaps? Fate? Karma? Kismet? God knows. As for you, Kilraven, he must have wanted to use you for some reason. More than just to see you suffer."

"For what purpose? I've poured over my memory of him *countlessly* over the years. I never even slighted him."

"Well, for what *cause* I don't know. And nor did Corvus," he says. "But Jovian seems to hold you in the greatest of contempt in the very least. He also has your family as well, which Corvus was able to confirm."

"My family!" I cry, nearly falling out of my chair. "How could I forget them?!"

"Don't be hard on yourself, friend. It's the *Madzimure* inside you. Don't expect yourself to be one and whole after so many years in a body not your own."

"So they *are* alive! Where? Have you seen them?!"

"Please, calm yourself, and drink," he says, motioning toward my cup. "The cryo-sleep causes even more confusion. Drink. Believe me, you'll feel better."

We both drink at the same time, each from our own cup. Octavian's eyes never leave mine for a second.

"I'm sorry to say to you that I have never seen them, Kilraven," he says, placing his cup on the table, "but I knew even then that Jovian had both of your sisters. And your wife."

"Elisabeth!"

"Yes," he says. "He treated them as keepsakes, of a sort. I never quite understood why. Now I think I know. He knew that if you ever returned, he would need leverage over you. And because you loved them, you would be prepared to do anything for them."

"And I will."

"In good time, friend. In good time," he says, raising his hands. "But I… I haven't even told you the most shocking part, which is why I had you sit down when we came in here."

"What can possibly be more of a shock than all this shit?"

"It's *you*," he says. "You are Barrabas in body but Kilraven in soul, correct?"

"Yes."

"Then it means this…" he says, leaning forward and folding his arms together. "That the original body of Thaniel Kilraven is alive and well."

My head goes light. Everything around me shrinks, and the warm glow of this heavenly room turns to black.

CHAPTER 21

LONELY AT THE TOP

WHEN I WAS a young man, I had only a few acquaintances and even fewer companions. I felt as though everyone around me did not understand or feel the way that I did about the barbarous and unforgiving world. I was an outsider in my heart, imagining I was akin to one who returns from war and finds his home is no longer his own and that his family no longer recognizes him.

Over the years I have come to believe perhaps, in some way, this emotion in me has been a choice on my part. In my waking thoughts, though, I certainly do not believe the decision made was ever a *conscious* one, but rather selected by providence working through me. My holy station has thankfully spared me the burden of forced relationships, and now I simply choose with whom I consort at leisure.

My ability to hand-pick those who can be counted upon has seldom caused me any grief. However, the man in whom I entrust my life has become increasingly sorrowful of late. It is an irritating and weak emotion I must weed out of him. The reason for his change in behavior is somewhat understandable, of course, as his son has reached the time of his trial date.

I believe Lord Alpha would not wish a life of service such as his own upon any of his spawn.

It is a trait he shares with most fathers. I can identify with him in some way, though not having any legitimate offspring of my own, the thought of any child of mine having to follow in my footsteps does indeed disturb my spirit.

Lord Alpha has been ordered to appear in my presence at the present, and even now I watch him on the security holocams throughout the tower as he comes this way. I often request that he join me in my chambers for earnest speech, and many times in the past, I have done so simply to monitor his response time. I doubt he suspects such a *triviality* of me.

Lesser men will talk to themselves when alone or pick their noses or dig into their ears because they had not the foresight to allow for extra time to groom themselves prior to leaving their homes. But Alpha always stays focused and at attention, as if the very act of walking is a service to his goal.

There is a gentle *rapping* at my door. Three times it knocks, each one the same timbre as the previous. I bid my friend to enter.

"You called for me, master Jovian?"

"Yes, Alpha, close the door behind you."

He obliges me and then approaches, standing before my desk as one without fear might stand before his creator. He looks straight ahead, as if looking behind me.

"Are you not burdened by something, Lord Alpha?"

"I am burdened by many things, lord, but it is beneath you and not of your concern," he says.

"Yes, Lord Alpha, it is not!" I say, laughing at his brazenness.

"I mean to say that the problems I face are my own, and I choose not to tax you with them. You have incalculable duties yourself, m'lord."

"Your presumption is unflattering. But still, I would hear your mind."

"My lord, I'm... deeply concerned."

"For what reason?"

"For your welfare, of course," he says, finally looking me in the eye, "and for those who live and serve here in the Great Tower and those beneath our feet in the vaults."

"And *why* is it that you are concerned for them?"

"Kilraven's coming!" he snaps. "And he'll not hesitate to use whatever means necessary to stop you, even if that means his own end. Based on his last known location, he's likely allied himself with the nonurbanite or Prion populations in the outskirts. He *will* come, and he will take this tower to the ground if he must."

"Once again, you forget your station, Alpha. You are predicting an unknown. A series of events yet to occur. By your words alone you are worthy of punishment."

"I do not beg forgiveness in this, master. You asked that I speak my mind."

"And so I did!" I say laughing. "But if the Church were to hear your thoughts, I would *fear* for your welfare," I add with a genial mocking.

"You asked me to speak, and before I did, I gave caution to what I'd say," he answers, standing erect and looking forward again. "But if my words are worthy of death or torture or imprisonment, I've so spoken and must abide the consequences."

"Indeed. However, as I also said, you are speaking with regards to events that are more than unlikely to ever happen. It was my *plan* that Kilraven should return. I have anticipated his every move. I have flipped both sides of the proverbial coin many times. I have nothing to fear from him, and neither do you."

"I'm being practical, m'lord, and you remind me regularly that this is one of the many reasons why I am in your service. I take that charge seriously."

"Alpha, do not presume to tell me *why* you are in my service, even if you are quoting me verbatim. If I have not spoken the words to you today, they are meaningless. What you did for me yesterday means nothing. There is only *now*. I highly value your skills and your opinions when I ask for them, but you are now treading on a slope of cracking ice, and you test my patience."

"Forgive me, master," he says, lowering his head slowly. "I trust that you've foreseen these things, and my knowledge of what can surely be known only to you limits my confidence in the future."

"The future? Yes… I often forget that you do not have the gift of foresight, my friend. It is a side effect of your transference, no doubt."

"It has been several years, my lord," he says.

"Yes, so it has. Are you not so subtly suggesting that I schedule you for a new transference expediently, Lord Alpha?"

"I'm not suggesting, master. In fact, I'm asking. I could use the courtesy, my prophet."

"Which reminds me, so could I. Very well, it's settled then. Have yours scheduled for tomorrow morning, and I will have mine done so within the hour."

"Weren't you transferred only months ago, my lord? After the incident with the Kilraven bitch?" he asks.

"Yes, I was indeed… Do not remind me. But be cautious with your words regarding her. I know my welfare is of your utmost concern, but I will *not* have you mock Elisabeth in front of me."

"Forgive me, master. She killed you. It is her *actions* that anger me."

"It is of no concern tonight. Now, my mind must be clear, fresh for the arrival of our foe, and I must greet Kilraven with a brand-new face."

"Yes, my prophet," he says, bowing. "Is there anything else you wish of me?"

"A few things, actually. I would have you ready the body of our anticipated guest. I do not doubt that he will come seeking me or his family before aught else is done, and we must be prepared for any possibility."

"And what would you have me do with his family?" Lord Alpha asks.

"Ready them as well, but do *not* move them."

"Master, if I may," he says, inching closer to the edge of my desk. "I would suggest that we not harm them. Kilraven will submit in the face of defeat, even if at the last, especially with his loved ones on the line. It's the reason Corvus sent him back, after all. He's not like you. He will surrender."

"Yes, yes… that thought had not occurred to me, Alpha. He will not care for his own skin, but his living family is another matter. Very well, Alpha, you have my word on that. They shall live… they shall live. At least until Kilraven is laid low."

"Yes, m'lord."

"I must also bring to your attention my rather thoughtful and well-planned attack against the mine."

"The mine? I was not aware that we were going to attack the mine, sir," he says.

"Oh, but you mistake me now. We must keep that which is ours. I will not have nonurbanites gallivanting about with Kilraven while he plays space-ranger-*cum*-savior to a ragtag body of miscreants on the edge of civilization!"

"But the Eridanians pose no danger to us now, master."

"Regardless, we will wait for Kilraven to come to us before we launch any further offensive against those in the mine who have been proven to be in league with him."

"Might I suggest that we send one legion spread across two frigates then, master? This isn't something we can leave to chance, and I am—"

"I did not ask for your suggestion. And at any rate, it comes much too late. I have already retaken the mine."

"What? How? Why didn't you alert me?"

"For what reason, Alpha?"

"I need to know these things if I am to protect you, master!" he bursts angrily.

"There were three first-rate frigates with one thousand men each en route the day Chief Rullerig came to me voicing his concerns regarding Corvus. As for protecting me, who do you suppose could suffer me any harm? They who would chance such a thing are many light-years away. Besides, our forces arrived in just under sixty days. All has been quelled and set back in order by the time Barrabas was even halfway here."

"Two *months* ago?!" he asks, barely masking his surprise.

"Yes. I told you, I shall keep what is ours. The mine is far too valuable."

"Of course, I just…" he says, pausing. "Well, what then of Corvus, m'lord? What if he returns later?"

"Impossible at this juncture. Corvus is dead."

"Dead?"

"According to the diary of one of the dominant rebels at the mine, he was killed during Barrabas's pitiful revolt."

"Who killed him, master?"

"I think it is clear that it was Kilraven. And based on the written word of Iyov the Insurgent, both the time when Kilraven left Eridania and the death of Corvus coincide. Unfortunately, Corvus can no longer be traced. I checked the logs and found no bodily death within hours of either of those events, not in any specimen here in the tower vaults or in Tokyo."

"Who is the insurgent? Can we trust the word of a seditious man?" Alpha asks.

"They say a man always speaks the truth on his death bed. I think we can trust him. Take a look here."

I activate the security log on my desk, bringing up a holocam image of the prisoner Iyov marking the Church contract with a bloody stump where his index finger used to be. As Lord Alpha watches, from within the folds of my robe I pull out a tube containing the finger of Iyov from the inside pocket. Setting it between my index finger and thumb, I hold it up into the light for Alpha to see.

"Is that... what I think it is?" he asks.

"We told the old man that Kilraven would die before he even set foot on the ground if he did not give us a blood and tissue sample," I say, laughing, "and this little *gem* arrived days ago, after I called for the fastest of the three frigates to return."

"What could you possibly need it for, my lord?"

"The element of surprise, my friend. A memento for Kilraven, *hmm*?"

"Let me understand, master... Based on the word of this insurgent we are now to assume Corvus was an original and his body was stored somewhere outside the tower? That he never really worked for us?" Lord Alpha asks.

"That data remains... uncertain for now."

"Why have you waited until now to inform me of this?!"

"I needed to know all the details, Alpha. And some things have not come to light until recently."

"You mean with regards to the suspicions I had surrounding Corvus?" he asks.

"Yes. I will look into his history more in the coming days, but I fully expect you to rectify this entire situation immediately. I have done part of the work for you. You will find an obituary for Corvus in your logs. I would like you to see to it personally that what I have written sees print in all of the city newsreels and across all weblinks. It might also be worthwhile to broadcast the story and a picture of his face for a full day's coverage on the Tribunal telecast. I want everyone to know he was a traitor. Someone then may recognize him and pass on information that will help us in discovering his true identity."

"But, my lord, I—"

"I trust you do not have any problem with this? Or shall I send your only son to the mine instead of giving him the choice of selecting transference?"

"Master, please!" Lord Alpha says, quickly bowing upon both knees. "I know you to be a gracious lord. Forgive my tongue."

"The transgression is past. I see honesty in your eyes, Alpha. Now, get on your feet."

Lord Alpha rises and stands firm once again.

"Now then, I would also like you to raise an inquiry with the Tribunal. I have reason to believe that Brother Albedos, and possibly Brother Suttony, have conspired one with the other and so brought about the circumstances leading to the events which culminated in the theft of my ship. I suspected their possible alliance with Corvus for a number of months now but have not had the viable proof to submit to the Tribunal. Brother Albedos escapes from the tower at every chance, and Suttony has been all too eager to side with me in every matter that the Council seems to reject."

"Suttony is a special kind of fool," he says, "and Albedos is a troublemaker. It should be no hard task, what with Melius now out of the way. I will see it done, m'lord."

"Excellent. Now... I would hear you judge one *other* matter before you are dismissed. I did not heed your sound advice of warning when it came to Corvus, and so I must make amends now. What say you about Octavian? Have you had further news of him?"

"The old Surgeon?"

"The very same."

"He poses no threat that I am aware of, master," he says. "After a thorough and lengthy investigation, our logs can't find a single terabyte missing from his research data, even after he voluntarily left the Church. In fact, his apartment had yet to be cleaned by a service bot after we used a thermite stick to break through the entry shield generator. We revisited the location again and left nothing unturned, and we found nothing."

"This is all old information. No threat, you say? The man who played a hand in spawning transference, the man who invented the chip we use to monitor our employees… this man, now a dissident, is *no* threat?"

"Master," he says, placing his hands on my desk, "Octavian has been missing for years. He's believed to be dead."

"He is *not* dead, you fool!" I say, smacking his hands with the back of my own.

Lord Alpha steps back, his face minutely grieved at my strike.

"He cannot be dead. His body still lives in the cryo-vaults!"

"I wasn't aware of the good doctor's body being in stasis, sir," he says.

"Where else would it be? It is really quite *simple*, Lord Alpha. To think this was a detail you have or could have overlooked troubles me. Octavian is a grave danger to the city-state and one of the chief movers of resistance against us!"

"Then, master, permit me to offer a solution: why not simply have his body euthanized?"

"That would be much too easy a punishment for him. He must be kept. The reasons for so doing I do not wish to discuss with you at the present time. But if you indeed find no threat in him, then you will not find any threat in waiting for him inside the vaults when he comes."

"When he comes? I don't understand, my lord," he says.

"I have little to no doubt that Octavian will accompany Kilraven here. He will be unable to resist the chance to destroy himself. His guilty conscience clings to him like a bad offense. And besides, I want you to give him something."

I reach into the inner lining of my robe once more to retrieve a sim-chip and slide it across the desk, placing it within Lord Alpha's reach.

"What's this?"

"A gift. No, one might say it is a bribe, of sorts. Take it. It will not hurt him, or you."

"When should I give him this, master?" he asks, picking up the chip.

"I trust you will know when the moment arrives. The entire disgusting lot of them will come soon, after zero-hour."

"*Tonight*?!" he asks, sounding unusually astounded.

"Yes, Alpha. I know Kilraven, and he will waste no time. I can feel it."

"Yes, my lord," Alpha says, bowing.

"I want an emergency message broadcast to all citizens, throughout the entire city interlink, that if so much as *one* soul is found in the street past zero-hour, they will find themselves no longer among the living tomorrow! And furthermore, I want *you* to see to it that a small garrison is stationed at the main entrance to the tower within the next thirty minutes as well."

"I will, master. Do you have any express orders for the men?"

"Yes. I do not wish for Kilraven to be harmed, but I *do* wish for him to be unaccompanied when he stands before me. The Surgeon, and whomever else he has recruited, I leave to you to deal with. After you give Octavian my little gift, if he tries to kill you, do whatever you deem necessary."

"You are authorizing lethal force on anyone other than Kilraven, then?" he asks.

"Inform the guards that any man who causes Kilraven to lose so much as a finger will be transferred into a leprous body before he's hung upon the main cable of the north gate! Make no mistake, I will exert vengeance on that man seven times seven."

"I will relay that message, m'lord."

"Good. I believe that concludes my need for you this evening."

"My lord, there is… There is one more thing," he says.

"I just said our business is concluded, and I grow weary of you. What else can you possibly require, Lord Alpha?"

"Master, I have longed for my partner to be set free of stasis, and now that I have served for several years without him, I feel that—"

"You feel that he should be freed? Let me guess, you wish for him tonight, perhaps?"

"Yes, my lord. I have waited many years now, and patiently," he says.

"I told you before that any freedoms you desire will only come *after* we put an end to Kilraven. Why do you ask for them now? Why do you attempt to force my hand?"

"My lord, I simply—"

"Are you afraid that Kilraven might succeed? *Are* you?!"

"No, that is not what I fear," he says.

"You are afraid that I might end the life of your ex-wife despite the fact that I have spared your son? You're afraid someone other than me might learn of your male lover? Well, you are right to be afraid, Lord Alpha! If anyone were to learn of such desires, I would be forced to expunge not only you, but the very memory of you!"

I rise from my chair, and as I approach Alpha, he does not flinch. He does not even look at me.

"The debt which is owed to me has not been paid in full, Alpha. Need I destroy one of them so that you will refrain from asking me about the matter again?"

"No, my lord, please," he says, showing little emotion.

Even when I bring up the vault in question through the holodisplay, Alpha does not move. He can see his lover's face. He can see his vital signs.

"I could do it, you know."

"Yes, master," he says. "Their lives are yours. They are all in your hands."

"Ah, look at them… so *peaceful*," I say, pulling up the cryo-cam so that the footage takes the form of a cube of light and fills the space between me and him.

"Yes, my prophet, I have visited them often," he says, lowering his head.

"You try to hide this emotion from me, Alpha? I see a longing in your face that cannot be mistaken, though it passes quicker than lightning flashes."

"There is no emotion. Forgive me for asking," he says, reaching for the display button and turning off the holocam. "It was wrong of me to act upon my doubt."

"You may abjure this insolence by your actions tonight, my Lord Alpha," I say, taking my seat again. "I will make a new deal with you. After Octavian is crushed and we see the defeat of Kilraven, and if you are alive at the end of it, you may, and I repeat, you *may* see them soon."

"Yes, master. That is very honorable of you."

"Is it?"

"It is," he says.

"You puzzle me, Lord Alpha. Are you completely devoid of any emotion, or do you merely do as you are told? Caring for nothing and no one?"

"Perhaps, my lord," he says, shrugging slightly.

"I brought you here tonight to test you, Alpha, and you have passed that test."

"My lord?"

"Knowing that I could kill you, you do not withdraw. Knowing that the ones you care for have their souls within my grasp, you still do not defy me."

"No, master," he says.

"You will be richly rewarded, Alpha. And tomorrow, when the streets are full of praise for the power of the One Prophet, you will be at the head of that vanguard."

"Thank you, my prophet," he says, smiling slightly.

"Our conversions will be at an all-time high afterward, and our transference numbers will be greater than ever."

"Yes, lord, that will indeed be the day among all days."

"You are dismissed, Lord Alpha. Please see to your duties. And expect to be called upon again shortly for the Righteous Hour."

"I will be ready, my master," he says, bowing low before me and then exiting my chambers quietly.

I am alone. I'm always alone now. Only the air and the screaming of my thoughts keep me company.

This room is a very special place for me. Many of the heirlooms that line the walls are of historical significance, the most recent addition to the collection being the staff of Moses. It was unearthed last year, but not without great cost to me. I was certain when I first grasped the solid sapphire rod that it was authentic. Within hours, our radiocarbon dating technicians confirmed what I already knew—that the rod was over four thousand years old.

Unfortunately, this staff is rather unlike the one that was carried by Aaron, supposedly the brother of Moses. His staff still displayed great feats of power, regardless of whether or not it was being held by its original owner. It is a great shame that I must prop this beautiful blue treasure in solitude in the corner of the room, though I intend to carry it on ceremonial occasions. Perhaps I shall wield it tomorrow when Kilraven is dead and I march in victory down the streets of the city.

But first I must rest.

I take repose in my chair, taking time to ponder for a minute what great things are yet to come with the defeat of Kilraven on the horizon. I smile knowing there will no longer be any limits when the last thread of my past meets the one loose end I have left untied. In my patience, I must regain control, taking authority over my own soul by serving it through faith in death. They say a mother is God in the eyes of a child. But what I have seen of late makes me begin to believe otherwise.

Each time I am transferred, I see the soul. I see it ever more clearly than I did before, and it is godlike in the eyes of those who witness its majesty. When the soul takes shape, it forms like a diamond, except that it takes only seconds instead of millions of years to become multifaceted. It is more beautiful than any gemstone in the deeps of the Earth. The soul *is* God.

I must serve my own spirit now, replenish it, strengthen it. After all, my position is not one only of rule and reign, but of servitude. It is in the latter that I grow weary, a fatigue for which there is but one remedy. I initiate the transference process with the tap of a few buttons on my desk. This new technology is simply delightful, and with great toil, I have kept it secret from the Council and my brethren. Additionally, I have had my chambers specifically lined with eridanium throughout. Even now the ore spreads itself as though it were a living membrane across the walls, ceiling, and floor, taking delight in its own liquid form.

This is the new salvation, the newest sensation, and the new way of things. I call it the Righteous Hour. It allows for my soul to be set free of the flesh for a time yet remain within the room until the technicians can transfer me again. It is the ultimate pleasure, for when the soul is loosed, the eyes are opened to all things. You are able to know and see all things that are and some things that are yet to be.

Revelation!

Sadly, it is when the ghost returns to the body once more that this frightful knowledge is shattered. It is broken so intensely that the spirit has a difficult time transitioning back to the flesh. The moments after waking from a lucid dream are akin to this feeling, when one forgets that which was dreamt, and no matter how hard you try to recall it, you end up only grasping at smoke.

However, I believe some of it is retained, and it is the only true way to attain godhood, a path along which I am undeterred. It is in my destiny to overtake the road laid out before me and carve a new direction.

From the holster underneath the desk, I remove my favorite weapon: a .36-caliber Colt Texas Paterson, now well over two hundred and fifty years old. The firing mechanism, still a well-oiled machine, is a mystery to most and a delight to those who have never seen it. The trigger itself is invisible at first glance, only appearing when one has cocked the hammer. Ingenious really. It has a seven and a half–inch barrel with real mother of pearl grips.

Additionally, I have managed to secure more than a few dozen of the bullets in my Council-funded excavation projects over the years. This gun in particular, though, belonged to my father. And he prized it more than he ever valued me or any service I paid him. The enduring memory of my father, the one that sticks the most in my mind, is of his character—that he was a most stubborn, hard-hearted, and ungenerous man.

I can still remember the words he spoke repeatedly to me as a child: *You can never do anything right,* he said, or *You are just like your mother.* The latter was his favorite choice of verbal and emotional abuse, though he never realized it was, in fact, not an insult.

Nearly everything that came from his mouth was with regards to my abject failure as a son, he would say. Not his son, but *a* son. I suspect, too, that he often said things just to get me to speak unfavorably to him in return or to garner a physical reaction. Perhaps he would have preferred it if I had actually struck him. He never understood that after a while I felt more hurt by his silences than his words. I never told him this, of course, because to do so would mean I would have had to listen to another never-ending tirade about his disappointment in me.

It is a great pity that Father has not lived to see the day that his only son would become the singular judge over all men. I smile to myself at that thought. I smile again at the notion that while, from a certain point of view, his absence is indeed a shame, I do not wish for him to be here. I smile even a third time knowing the momentary pain I am now going to experience will lead to extraordinary bliss.

I close my eyes, put the barrel of the weapon into my mouth, and pull the trigger.

CHAPTER 22

PEAS IN A POD

"TAKE IT SLOWLY now, Kilraven. Drink this," the Surgeon says, forcing a cup against my lips. "I know it's a lot to take in."

The Surgeon pulls his chair closer to the table and helps my trembling hands hold the cup. As the drink hits my lips, I expect coolness but instead find that it's warm and spicy. As I swallow, there's a dry and almost oaky sweetness that fills my senses.

When the finish starts to wear off, I'm reminded of something I'd forgotten: the taste of vanilla. I've not tasted real vanilla since I was a kid.

"What is this stuff?"

"It's the best we can do," Octavian says. "Straight from the barrel, uncut and unfiltered, I'm afraid. The name of it escapes me, though George and Clyment can tell you more about their distillation techniques."

"I… I can't believe this," I say, my hands shaking uncontrollably. "My body… it isn't dead? How can my body not be dead?"

"I tell you, my friend, this is what I know to be infallible. Your body cannot be dead, and there are two ways in which this is proved," he says, handing me the cup and standing upright in front of me. "The first possibility is that the soul of Barrabas is also intact, in some other body, and you are in his original body now. The second is that you are in a *clone* of Barrabas and his original self is perhaps long dead, along with his soul."

"I thought… I thought I'd be in this body forever."

"Well, you may yet," he says while sitting down again. "But there is hope for otherwise because here you sit, possessing your soul. So, yes, the body of Kilraven is most definitely not dead."

"I'm not in a pod somewhere, then?"

"Potentially. You are either being held in the vaults below the tower," the Surgeon says, rubbing his upper lip with his index finger, "or some other soul inhabits your original body and is out walking free. That soul may or may not be the *true* Barrabas."

"So, my skin's walking around, or it's in cryo-stasis under Jovian's lock and key?"

"Most likely the latter, friend. You see, it's a very strange sort of reciprocal relationship, all of this mess we've managed to create," he says.

"It's making my head spin to be honest."

"Yes, my friend. Yes," he says, smiling quickly.

"But there's one thing you left out of all this, Octavian."

"And what's that?" he asks.

"Eridanium."

"What do you wish to know about it?"

"How they use it, exactly."

"That is an answer that I can't fully supply, Kilraven, though I can tell you what I have learned," he says.

"Go on."

"The ore has unique properties unlike any other substance we have ever seen," he says. "In its liquid form, it can carry things. Kinetic energy, light, all kinds of matter. This goes against known and proven sciences."

"What do you mean it can *carry*?"

"Take a shockwave, for instance. Or seismic waves, rather. They typically can't be carried through liquids, but the liquid ore can do this. It can also absorb all these things without destroying them. It's like dew on the morning grass that forms a rainbow, capturing the light and giving it back in a new form, a form more wonderful."

"So, does the form it takes then affect its use?"

"Well, in its solid form, it acts as a sort of barrier or a *web* almost," he says, interlocking his fingers. "It does this, I believe, in order to contain something which you wish not to escape. It then produces a low-level but powerful magnetic field of a sort, though with little to no molecular effect on physical objects. It attracts energy, you see, which is exactly what the soul is, based on what we have found."

"Our souls are energy? Just... like that?"

"More than that, to be sure, but we can't *quantify* it, nor can we measure it by any real physical means. But its representation, if you were to see it, can only be described as tiny spirals of light. It's absolutely marvelous."

"How do you know it's the soul, though?"

"I don't," he says, drawing back in his seat. "But it's the only way to explain the link with regards to the original body," he adds, clasping his hands together. "How else could you still be you while seated here in another man's body right now? How could you be Kilraven with the brain that Barrabas was born with or that this body was cloned from?"

"I guess you've got more than a good point," I say. "Over the years in the mine, I was really only able to speak with a handful of people about this. Some of us guessed at it. We figured that whoever and whatever created this tech on Fornax was using it before we found it. I mean, they knew what they were doing and they understood what it did, right? They had to."

"You would know more about that than I," he says.

"Well they had to because of the shells they made. It was like they were designed for us... left for us to find, on purpose. Did they know about humans? Did they know about Earth?"

"I don't know. I truly don't. Wasn't Fornax just an empty planet when you arrived?" the Surgeon asks, his left eyebrow rising curiously.

"It *was* empty. And that's my point. The fact that there was nothing and no one?"

"Obviously there had been someone there, some sort of life," the Surgeon says.

"Yes, it was as if they just abandoned everything. I can only take another stab in the dark as to what really happened, but it would be nothing more than that."

"After what has happened to us as a civilization, I too had my suspicions," the Surgeon says, "and I think now it may have happened to the life on Fornax also. And my heart warns me that this technology may have been their downfall."

"Or maybe they merely left the planet and went to a better place?"

"Who can say?" he asks, frowning slightly. "It's just another of the many varying reasons why I am trying to undo my part in all of this."

"You're going to need my help, then."

"That's why you're still *here*, Kilraven."

"I believe we've been brought together to aid one another. But I must forewarn you, I've plans of my own for Jovian, and I'm keeping them close to the chest. Damn close."

"That is fair enough, Kilraven. To be frank, I can't ask any more of you than that," he says. "But before we talk about battle plans, there's even more that you must know, and I must be the one to tell you. I promise that you will hear it, but I think for now you really should lie down and rest, friend."

"Well. Far be it from me to argue with a doctor, though you should've seen what I did to the last one who fucked with me."

Octavian laughs so loudly his men standing guard outside the door burst in without his prompting.

"We're quite alright here, boys. Make way for our guest, please," he says, smiling and escorting me back the way we came before.

After a brief walk, I find myself standing in another room that's directly across from where they doused me with water. Octavian suggests that I get as much sleep as I might until he returns, then closes the door behind me.

It's a warm room, and the first thing I notice is the clean bed against the west wall. With no hesitation, I fall onto the padded mattress without even removing my boots, and the feeling of cold sheets on my skin reminds me of my youth. The welcoming candlelight flickers wildly across the rough and porous stone walls and ceiling.

Raising my head, I see at the foot of the bed a table with a small piece of bread and a cup of water. Closing my eyes and imagining that I'm with Elisabeth brings me one step closer to home.

"Hey, spacehead," a voice says.

Instinctively I reach for a gun, and until this moment I didn't realize

I'd even been disarmed. I sit up on my elbows, surprised to see Terra in her own bed on the opposite side of the room parallel from me. She's holding a stick match and lighting a candle.

"Terra! You're looking well."

She blows out the match, then flicks it across the room in my direction. Then she sits up slightly, propping a pillow behind her back, and winces sharply.

"Damn!" she says, her posture revealing her entire mid-section completely wrapped in white bandages.

"Can I help?"

"Yeah, nah. I'll be fine," she says. "What about you? I thought maybe Tavian was torturing you or something."

"The doctor? Well, he was torturing me, in a way," I say with a laugh. "Just… not with physical pain."

"Right. You're, *uh*… You're damn weird, man," she says, laying her head back on the dark brown pillow. "So, what's the plan, Mister Savior?"

"You know, I think it's probably wiser if you stay out of the way of my so-called plan."

"Well, wasn't that what you two were talking about?" she asks. "I mean, it's gotta be some helluva important piece of work, seeing as how Tavian's been acting weird as shit for weeks."

"I do have a plan… for myself. I'm sure Octavian has his own plans. We've not discussed them yet, and I don't intend to."

"You mean you don't intend to tell us? Is that what you meant?" she asks.

"I can't, Terra. The minute you tell someone, it's no longer your plan. A plan has to be secret. That's the point of it. And the odds of it succeeding once it's out in the open are lessened."

"*Ha!* You sound just like him!" Terra says with a quick laugh.

"Like who?"

"Octavian, you idiot. And you know, you'd better get over your secrecy damn quick," she says. "Everyone here has been buzzing about you, and you're supposed to have something on Jovian, something that can help us stop him."

"I don't think I am who you think I am. Whatever I have, and whatever

I know, I don't even know what it is. Probably won't know until I face him. But I do plan on stopping him, somehow or another, or I'll die trying in the process."

Terra snickers at me.

"Seriously, man, don't make me laugh. It fuckin' hurts!" she says. "You know, a lotta people have tried to kill him before."

"What people?"

"A lot. The one I know most about was a fuckin' *legend*. The Manx," she says.

"The who?"

"Well, that was the guy's most well-known nickname," she says. "His real name was Handley. Big ass chav from the English Islands. Anyway, he arranged an attempt on Jovian's life. Had the whole damn thing laid out, too. Was gonna blow him sky-high during the middle of a parade march to celebrate the New Church's fiftieth anniversary."

Terra suddenly sits up in her bed, squinting her eyes and pretending as if she's the very marksman in her story, looking down on the scene with an imaginary gun.

"Manx picked his spot, right? This little abandoned maisonette on the corner of East 67th and Park Ave. A real *shithole*, too. I been there. Anyway, he'd even engineered some kinda weapon that could lock onto the chip implants!" she says, pointing toward her back. "Poor bastard had no *clue* Jovian knew about it ahead of time."

"So, what happened to him?"

"As the story goes, someone within the Manx's own outfit betrayed his Pommy ass. Changed the serial number of Handley's own chip to match the fuckin' destination target."

"Damn."

"Yep. So, there the Manx was, totally thinkin' he was about to rid the world of the Prophet forever. Instead, everyone down on the street level got one helluva shock when the Manx fired a thermobaric rocket and the damn thing totally does a one-eighty and came back on him!"

"Jovian always was one step ahead."

"Well, that's my point," she says, lying back down. "A lot of smart men with smart plans didn't make it. They failed hardcore. I don't even wanna *think* about what he might do to you."

"Well, I suppose I do have one thing that the boys here don't."

"Oh, please tell me you ain't relying totally on those ancient pea shooters of yours," she says. "I'm guessing the boys are modifying 'em right now. Or they're laughin' about how ridiculous it is that you came all this way with nothing but them and your skin."

"No, not the guns. Jovian wants me here. He wants something from me."

Terra props herself up on her elbows again and looks at me sidelong. After a lengthy pause, she lies back down, looks up at the ceiling, and sighs. "Well, I hope for all our sakes that you're right... spacehead."

I smile and laugh quietly through my nose.

"Terra? Can you... I mean, can I ask you something?"

"What's that?" she asks.

"Do you remember your family?"

"The boys are my family," she replies with a bubbly and truthful conviction.

"No, I mean your *real* family. Your parents."

"Oh, *them*," she says, the tone of her voice changing sourly. "Sure, I remember 'em. Sort of. We never really got along. I suppose they only stayed together because of me. Seems like I was the only thing they had in common, other than bein' combative."

"What do you remember most about them?"

"All they ever seemed to do was shout, though I never really knew what it was about. They legally separated just before I was supposed to set my transference date. I guess I never really forgave 'em for that, and my last few months at home were really rocky. They wanted me to become a teacher, like them. Said it was the only noble profession left. I told 'em nothing done in the name of the Church was noble, and I fuckin' left."

"Did you ever see them again?"

"Nope. No, I didn't. S'alright, though, I guess. We never saw eye to eye anyway," she says. "And I always felt like I wasn't their daughter, you know? We were so damn different... My mom and I fought like two raccoons stuffed in a sack."

Terra sighs and goes silent. *Say something, you idiot. Comfort the damn kid.* I lie back down again, searching for something to say. Thanks for saving my life, maybe? No, no good. How about a compliment? What about a joke of some kind?

The moment passes me by. I was never really good when it came to talking with women anyway. I suppose the words didn't come because there was nothing left to say. Before I know it, I'm falling, and the bed and my body become one.

When I open my eyes, I'm oddly refreshed, but I sit straight up for fear that I'm back in the mines again. But I didn't have bedsheets in the mine. I look left, and Terra's no longer there. All the candles in the room have gone out except the largest one closest to the door. I leap from the bed, grab the piece of bread from the table, and stuff half of it in my mouth.

Never know when I might eat again.

Near the doorframe, on a singular hook, hang both of my guns still holstered. I buckle the silver clasp around my waist and exit the chamber door slowly. In the corridor, I can hear the voices of men echoing faintly, but there's also the sound of laughter. Following the rock wall closely with my hands, I move through the dark and toward the sounds. When I draw closer to a light about fifty feet ahead, the laughter I heard before becomes a boisterous camaraderie.

I follow the aural trail farther and quickly find that I'm back at the iron door that led directly to Octavian's chamber. The door is slightly ajar, so I push it open slowly in an effort to get a look inside. At first my course of action seems wise, and then the ridiculous creaking of the door's hinges sets everyone inside the room immediately on mute. I'm left standing mawkishly in the open doorway, with at least a dozen pairs of eyes fixed on me.

"Barrabas! Welcome!" Octavian says, standing to greet me at the head of the table. "I see you have rested!"

"Please, come in and sit with us," he says and pulls out a chair a few feet away from his own.

As I walk the length of the table, I spot Terra in the middle and she nods at me. Most of the men look at me as though I had just robbed their homes, plundered their goods, and raped their wives.

"Yes, now, have a seat please," Octavian says.

I take my seat, sitting up straight. Octavian senses that something must be said and beats me to the punch.

"Men? This is Barrabas the Madzimurian, *aka* Thaniel Kilraven," he says, smiling and nodding at me in a slow and gracious manner. "I don't think any of you will know much of his past deeds," he adds, glancing at me again. "But of his deeds against the Prophet, yes, you all know some of that story. He has come a great distance to help us in our need. Please show him the same respect that you've given me in the brief time he is to be with us."

"There's so few of you," I say.

"We got it where it counts, partner," Terra says.

"I told you, Kilraven," Octavian says, "we suffered a great loss to secure the ship you brought back. Over fifty percent of us."

The room grows sadly quiet, and the only thing I can hear is the popping of the flames from the torches at both ends of the hall.

"Well now," Octavian says, breaking the silence, "please do introduce yourselves already!" he adds, sitting down beside me.

The first man to my left says his name is Clyment. He's the bald-headed and rather husky fellow I saw earlier standing behind the Surgeon when I arrived. I imagine he's the chap who threw the freezing-cold water on me. From a physical standpoint, he's not the kind of guy you'd want to tussle with.

Second is Gingoro, a young-looking fellow with red hair, pale skin, and freckles on the end of his nose and cheeks. With a soft voice, he says hello and smiles at me. After he realizes the courtesy was noticed by everyone, his face quickly turns hard and beet red.

Third to go is Ortiz, a twenty-something kid who's got no meat on him but has the heaviest black beard in the room. He's got four small guns strapped to his chest and two large knives, one on each hip. He holds up two fingers, forming the letter V, some gesture I've never seen before, and simply says, "Yo."

Next up is Snyder, a very tall and thin middle-aged man with dark hair and a pair of black glasses. I swear I can't make out a word he says. The entire time he's talking, he's busy feeding two small animals, one in each of his shirt pockets. They're mice or ferrets or God knows what.

The fifth man stands and waves, but says only that everyone calls him Henskie. He's small and gangly with curly blond hair, and he sits down just as quickly as he rose. One of the men who's yet to introduce himself says Henskie's the kind of kid you don't wanna feed after midnight. No one else but me seems to catch the reference.

The sixth man is known as Duster. He's olive-skinned and his dark hair is fashioned into a red-streaked mohawk. He smiles, as if he rehearsed the gesture, and I note a single gold tooth in the upper row of his teeth.

The seventh, eighth, and ninth men all stand up and at once, and Octavian says, "Tweedle, Dee, and Dum." Everyone laughs heartily, and the faces of the unusual trio blush after they're seated.

Terra is next but she doesn't get up. She only picks at her teeth with a fingernail, her flawless brown skin glowing soft and radiant in the candlelight.

"Yeah, we've met," she says, winking at me.

The eleventh man introduces himself with a low bow and says he is called Kuramo. He seems much older than the rest and is dressed head to toe entirely in black. At his waist are two twin short swords in scabbards of bright, polished red. His oddly groomed chin features a black goatee with streaks of gray near his lips. After he sits down, no one in the room seems remotely interested in mocking him.

Next is George, also an older man with gray hair. He's the only man in the room who, after standing, raises his glass to me. He thanks me for coming and hopes that he lives to see the ending of corruption within the *realpolitik*. I'm not sure quite what he means, but I nod and thank him anyway.

Sitting close to George is a boy no more than seventeen or eighteen who says they've dubbed him Elfmoon. Before I can ask him why, Terra says the name is on account of his stature and unusually long ears, which are hidden by shoulder-length brown hair. He can't be more than five feet tall, and he hides his eyes behind a pair of sunglasses.

When he sits back down, Clyment tells him to show me *why* they call him that. After refusing to do so, George grabs him by the arm and pushes him to his feet. Elfmoon rolls his eyes, turns about-face, and drops his pants to his knees. After he slaps his own arse a few times, everyone in the room bursts into fits of laughter.

"Elf-*Moon*!" Clyment says, and everyone in the room howls again.

"*Ugh*. I can't say I approve of that sort of behavior while we are eating," Octavian says with a playful scowl.

The last three men are all that remain. Bronx, on account of where he was born, tells me he hopes I can accomplish what all the others who have tried and failed to do. Julian stands up slowly while clearing his throat, and after driving a large knife into the table next to his dinner plate, he runs his hands through his mop of corkscrew hair and belches for a few seconds.

"That's what I think of you coming here!" Julian says, and several of the men in the room grumble.

"Lightly now," the Surgeon says, hitting the table with the palm of his hand three times.

The final young man at the table says everyone calls him Pony. His features are pale, and in this he reminds me of Corvus, if only slightly. Before he sits down, I ask him if he ever read the old novel by S.E. Hinton that features a character with a similar name. He looks around the room before asking me, "What's a novel?"

Everyone laughs, and Pony's ears go bright red. He takes his seat and continues nervously eating his meal. The rest of the men quickly resume the conversations they were having before I entered the chamber without knocking.

"So? You look well-rested," Octavian says, taking a bite of a rather large piece of what looks like some sort of sweetbread.

"I do feel better, thank you."

"Ready for a final confrontation?" he asks, a strange light glowing in his eye that isn't from the torchlight.

"I've thought of almost nothing else over the years and what I would say to him if and when we ever came face to face. After a while, I started losing hope in that moment ever coming to pass. I figured I'd just… see him in hell."

Octavian laughs so loud that everyone stops talking and glances in our direction. "No, my friend," he says, "this hell on Earth is the only hell you will see him in."

Then he leans forward close to me, and now there's no mistaking the gleam in his eye. "And we must strike soon!" he says, looking as if he wishes only me to hear what he's saying. "You see, the Watchers have been weeding out nearly every single one of our remaining strongholds. I fear that our whereabouts will be found expediently due to your... recent arrival," he adds with a grave whisper.

"I agree. I'd like to leave as soon as I can. I won't need anything from you other than my weapons back."

"Are you planning on doing this alone? No, no, no... it is *much* too late for that, Kilraven," Octavian says, his brow lines creasing as if I've just offended him. "Plans are in motion. I have spoken to our friends in Tokyo, and I believe that they are also—"

"Tokyo?!"

I realize I've nearly shouted, and one of the men nearest to me coughs, choking on his water. Octavian places his hand on mine, a suggestion I quickly take to mean that I should lower my voice.

"Yes, my friend," he says, nodding. "They are a great city-state now. *Very* powerful. They almost rival Neo York in terms of stature. Certainly, their sway over the Council is burgeoning, not to mention they have a larger oppositional force than we do here. Unfortunately, one cannot simply fly over the Pacific any longer. The waters have become increasingly... *unsafe*. Nor can you leave the atmosphere without proper clearance, for that matter. Jovian's right hand has seen to that."

"His right hand?"

"Yes. They call him Lord Alpha," he says, rubbing his hands together worryingly. "A *very* disturbed individual."

"You know him?"

"Yes, and we will speak of him later," he says, whispering.

"Alright then. But what do the Japanese have to benefit from their involvement?"

"The Tower of Peace has a sister in Tokyo," he says.

"There's *another* tower?!"

"Mmm hmm," Octavian says, nodding slowly.

"You betta pull your head in, pal," the man nearest to me says.

"I'm sorry?" I ask, turning toward him.

"Pull... your... head... *in*," he repeats slowly.

"What was your name again?"

"Ah, Kilraven," Octavian interjects nervously. "This is Clyment, and he is in charge of our weapons depot here at the Rock."

"Clyment," I say, extending my hand.

Clyment doesn't take it. He doesn't even look at it. He just keeps on eating. It's only then that I realize all the other men and Terra have stopped talking.

"You think you're gettin' somewhere with them pistols at yer side?" he asks. "Them things are older than the Wheels o' Galgallin. And you really got *some* nerve comin' all this way to say you ain't needin' our help and you only needs your guns behind ya. Must be outta your goddamn mind."

The men break into a fit of sniggering.

"You must forgive them, Kilraven," Octavian says. "Ah, they take a little time to warm up to anyone that's *new*."

"It's alright. It's fine. I—"

"No, we take time to warm up to anyone who thinks he's special enough to take on the Prophet alone," Clyment says, turning his chair aggressively toward me. "What makes you think you can do this, huh?! What makes you think you're gonna win? After your ass was rocketed here, the mines got retaken! Didja know that? Prolly killed all your buddies back there and—"

"Clyment!" Octavian shouts.

"You left 'em with next to no hope and came here with none to spare!" Clyment says.

"This is not the place!" Octavian bellows, hitting the table with his open palm.

"And so far, Mister Barrabas Kilraven, whoever th'fuck you are," Clyment says, "I ain't seen jack shit outta you but a smart mouth and some purty lousy footwork!"

"Clyment, *please*!" Octavian says.

"It's okay, really."

"Better be," Clyment mutters under his breath.

This is one of those rare moments in life where, through experience, I know I can either allow a behavior to continue or I can squash it by taking action.

I'm out of my seat, and I've got my gun bracing the side of Clyment's shiny head before anyone in the room can say Jack Robinson.

"Don't do this," Octavian says, standing to his feet slowly.

The Flash himself would've given me praise for that move. He was a costumed graphic book hero that dressed all in red. Something about the scarlet streak of his costume always stuck with me. He could move around faster than, well, anything, really. My cousin Orin and I read about him secretly when we were kids. Orin always liked Zolomon better, the Flash's yellow opposite. I mean, how lame is that? The bad guy simply *looked* like the Flash, only in reverse. He even had the same or similar powers, but he was yellow. A coward's color.

"I'm addressing Clyment at the moment," I say, cocking the weapon.

Clyment doesn't even bat an eye. He just turns so that he's facing the barrel of my pistol head-on. He's no coward, that's for sure.

"Octavian asked you to show me a little courtesy. And while I haven't earned your respect yet, *he* has. I'd expect a man to honor his leader."

Staring at Clyment down the barrel of the gun, I see his nostrils flare. I'm suddenly overwhelmed by an unexpected sense of loneliness. Even among a room full of men from home, I am *not* at home. Not in presence, nor in heart. I've no doubt this piece of the pie was cut and hand-served for me to eat by Jovian himself. The bastard.

The moment of my overcompensation recedes like a tide, and I pull the pin back on the gun, then slide it back smoothly into the holster. I'm seated again before anyone else is, and Clyment doesn't say a word. I take an empty cup from the center of the table and begin to fill it with water.

"He's right, boys," Clyment says. "Ever'one relax and sit down."

As I turn toward him, Clyment hands me the piece of bread that's already been in his hand.

"Thank you," I say, and Clyment nods but doesn't look me in the eye.

"At least you've got balls," Clyment says. "You're gonna need more than that, though."

I turn to Octavian, who's still standing. For a few seconds, he remains immobile, and the look on his face is that of one who thinks he's maybe seen a specter. He sits down with both hands on the table, exhaling profoundly before regaining his composure.

"Come on, men, back to dinner," Octavian says, and the men resume the feast as if the previous sixty seconds had never occurred.

"I'm sorry you had to learn about your fellow prisoners that way," Octavian says. "We received the word from an anonymous source, so I didn't completely trust it. I didn't want to bring it up until the time felt more appropriate."

"Well there's little time left for tact. Do you know if they killed them all?"

"I don't know, Kilraven," Octavian says. "I've had no further word. My guess is that the miners will be systematically destroyed. That or they're now being tortured for information about you and Corvus."

"And what else would they have to be afraid of now that I'm here?"

"Well, as I was saying prior to the, umm… chest-beating… the Prophet had the tower in Tokyo built not only as a foothold in the region but as backup. It *must* be destroyed."

"A backup? For what?"

"Jovian has more clones there, more disciples, and more transference capsules. Or so we have been led to believe. If we kill him only from here, he may just rise again from that location."

"Holy *shit*."

"Yes."

"And what about Jovian's so-called brethren? If we don't strike them down as well, one of them may just take his place."

"It's possible," he says, "though none of them hold any public favor the way Jovian does and are far less than charismatic. There aren't any among them that can see the future the way he supposedly does, nor have the others performed any miracles through works of hand. It's Jovian or nothing. And Tokyo *has* to fall."

"But that's thousands of miles away."

The Surgeon smiles from ear to ear and leans back in his chair. "You brought Corvus's ship, didn't you?"

"Of course, but it's only one small ship."

"Only need one," Clyment says gruffly.

"And you call *me* the hopeless one?"

"Ships are hard to get these days, pal," Clyment says. "You can't even take to the skies without the proper permits and such. You'd be blasted all to hell within a minute or two, and that's if you was lucky."

"My friend," Octavian says, tapping my arm gently, "the ship is nucleo-core powered, is it not?"

"According to Nav it is, yes."

"Well, then that just means we need to turn the core-coolant system off manually," Clyment says, "and then send the ship on a crash-course, pal."

"A crash course for what?"

"When those cores overheat," Clyment says, smacking on his bread, "ya combine that with the ship disintegratin' and it should take the tower down with it. There's no way in flarkin' hell it can withstand an impact blast like that. Whatever's left of the place afterward, well, the Tokyoians can eat."

"So that's it?" I ask, turning my head and looking at everyone at the table. "You think it's that easy? You think Jovian won't have anticipated this?"

"You have an alternate suggestion?" the Surgeon asks.

"I don't think any of you realize that Jovian's sure to have a backup plan to his backup plan. There's some element here that we'll never foresee."

"Well that is certainly one way to put it. But yes, we believe it is in fact *that* simple," Octavian says.

"And by that you mean what exactly?"

"Tell him, Clyment," Octavian says with a smile.

"The ship's core-coolant system's gotta be turned off thirty seconds before any impending impact," Clyment says, holding up five fat fingers. "And it takes at least five seconds to manually enter the string o' code to do it. Maybe longer, dependin' on whether nerves get the best of ya."

"No, there's no way that… Look, the ship has a remote that Corvus gave me. I don't want anyone risking their lives to—"

"Won't work. It's a failsafe, pal," Clyment says. "Problem is, whenever a ship like that self-terminates, it de-radiates the cores as a precautionary measure. One helluva safety catch, right?"

"Wait... so you mean that if we crash the ship remotely, we don't get a nuclear-based explosion?"

"You catchin' on quick, pal," Clyment says. "The only way to bypass that is to turn off the coolant system manually from inside the ship, before the boom."

"Not to mention someone has to actually fly the ship from here to there first," Octavian adds.

"After that, you say your Bloody Marys and get yer ass clear," Clyment adds with a click of his teeth.

"You need us, Kilraven," Octavian says, "and for whatever plan you have of your own with the Prophet, you still cannot win without us. We need one another."

"Let's say you're right," I say, nodding at them. "Let's say for argument's sake that you *can* flatten the tower. Who in the hell do you suppose is going to pull that off?"

"I am," Terra says, standing to her feet and biting the inside of her cheek. "Spacehead."

CHAPTER 23

THE LAST SUPPER

"TERRA, *NO*. DON'T. *Don't* do this," I say, shaking my head at Terra, then turning to the Surgeon. "Octavian, don't let her do this."

"Majority rules, spacehead," Terra says with a shit-eating grin.

"Let *me* do it. I'll take the ship to Tokyo. There's no need for any of you to sacrifice yourself on account of me."

"Oh, that makes *alotta* sense," Terra says, standing at the opposite side of the table with a coy look on her face.

She's not buying it. The gritted teeth and flexed muscles in the room tells me the boys aren't going to listen, either.

"And what do you think that would accomplish if you were lost?" Octavian asks. "You are needed here to meet the problem head-on."

"Besides," Terra says, sitting back down, "you don't have a say so in the matter. We've already voted, right, boys?"

All the men nod in agreement, just as I expected them to.

"And another thing," she says. "We ain't sacrificing ourselves just for you. We're doing this for every bogus beaner who didn't wanna transfer... or for anyone that's had to eat fish from the damned Hudson."

The lot of them laugh dryly.

"This is an argument you cannot win, Kilraven," Octavian says.

"Look, I just want to be clear: what I'm doing is not for any of you," I say, "and I expect only the same honesty in return. That's not to say that I don't value your lives. I do. But if we're all resolved in this, then I guess there's only one thing left to discuss."

"And that is?" Terra asks.

"When do we light the fuse under Jovian's ass?"

"Just as soon as we're done here, pal," Clyment says, taking another bite of his bread.

"You see, Kilraven, this is our last meal," Octavian says, his arms outstretched.

"Are you sure this is the way, Octavian? Are you all sure?"

"Yes, friend," he says. "Whatever you have up your sleeve, we leave it with you. We trusted Corvus, and he entrusted all that he had to you. Without him, we'd all be dead, and you would not be here. Yet here we all are, gathered together and breaking bread with the great thief."

"I don't want to wait any longer. I fear for my family the more we delay."

"Very well, then," Octavian says. "It's nearly zero-hour now, so the streets will be empty. We'll leave the choice of how we get in up to you. Terra can take you by way of the ship, or you can march yourself right up to the gates. Either way, I'm of the mind to think now that Jovian will welcome you eagerly with open arms. He'll be waiting."

"But the ship is only big enough for one."

"Nah, man," Terra says, shoving a small piece of bread into her mouth. "We can remove the cryo-tube and fire your scruffy ass right out the ejection port."

"No... this is way too risky. You take the ship that close to the tower, no matter how fast it is, you'd only get shot down. Or Jovian would have some tractor beam or some other ridiculous device that we don't know about. No, if you're going to take to the skies, you need *one* target. One destination. And you need to fly your ass off and not look back."

The men murmur amongst themselves in hushed agreement, and Octavian nods as well.

"Mmm. Good thinking, Kilraven," Octavian says, rubbing the end of his chin and looking lost in his thought.

"Clyment?" he asks.

"Sir?"

"Would you take the men now and prepare the boat?"

"For what exactly, sir?"

"A land assault at Hell's Beach. And please have Kuramo, Duster, and Ortiz form a cell and dispatch any Prions lurking about in the clearing above."

"Yes, sir!" Clyment responds with a curt nod. "Let's go, boys. It's time to go a swimmin'."

Every man in the hall exits with troupe-worthy precision and I'm left alone with Octavian and Terra.

"Terra, please do me this favor, would you? Ready yourself, and then go and bring the ship here. Have it land nearest to the Indian Caves. If the Watchers come down on us, I'd like to have solid rock at my back for a final stand," Octavian says. "You'll find the remote unit in a small ebony box in my depository cupboard. Take this key to get it out."

The Surgeon pulls an iron key about the size of a teaspoon from his front pocket and hands it to Terra. The key looks old and rusty. The light in the room doesn't even reflect on it, only on the chain of silver from which it's hung.

"I must apologize, Kilraven," he begins as Terra exits, "for taking the ledger when we incapacitated you the second time. I needed it, you see. We used your handprint to transfer command of the ship to Terra while you were sleeping."

"The *second* time?"

Octavian points toward my cup and smiles.

"The water? The water you gave me when you told me to go rest."

"Yes. We drugged it," the Surgeon says, smiling from ear to ear. "I meant you no harm, but I didn't want you to fight me on this."

"You keep grinning. Has this whole thing become a bit of fun for you?" I ask.

"A little… and not so much at the same time. If I couldn't laugh about it, I don't know if I could have gotten this far," he says with a sigh. "But

300

now that we're alone again, I have more to tell that I deem might be pertinent to you, ere the end. There's just… so much more I would confess…" The Surgeon trails off, staring into the torchlight and then licking his lips, as if recalling some painful memory. "Our location here will be known as soon as we call the ship, and we cannot—"

"Octavian, no. You listen to *me* now. You've led these men this far. Let me lead you forward from here. I can walk back to the ship from here with Terra. It'll be safer than putting her airborne."

"*Her* meaning the ship, or *her* meaning Terra?" he asks with a smile.

"Well… both of them, I suppose."

"Your desire to lead is enjoyably noted. However, I'm afraid I cannot risk you or her in this manner. You'd only get eaten by cannibals via that route, which is highly likely if you take to the streets again. No, my friend, we will have to abandon the Rock. This is our one and final remaining chance. A second assault on Jovian is impossible."

"Then it seems my only choice is to join you then, and to take the boat with you."

"So be it."

"I'd be lying if I said it wouldn't be good to have company along the way to the tower."

Octavian smiles and wrings his hands together. "I will escort you personally as far as I can. And then… well… Then you'll be on your own."

"Fair enough. Is this what the others want?"

"Yes," he says, rubbing his forehead. "This has been a *long* time coming. I think they're ready to see the world change rather than continue to live in it as it stands. Besides, we've haunted them for so long the Watchers tend to avoid the water and the woods. We'll be *safer*, if I can use that word, by taking this course of action."

"And what if Jovian has plans for you?" I ask.

"Oh, I'm sure that he does," Octavian says, "but if Jovian sees me with you, I will surely die and he will kill your original body without hesitation. That is why you and I will have to part ways at some point early on."

"You mean when the fight goes inevitably awry?" I ask.

"I'm electing not to even verbalize that possibility, my friend," he says sighing. "But listen to me now! I must warn you—beware. If you survive the gate, you will then face the Prophet's janissary."

"The one you spoke of earlier?"

"Yes, and I know him. He's an *odious* man. A consummate soldier who calls himself Lord Alpha. He will likely have been ordered to take you to Jovian, but he may not make it easy for you. You see, I don't expect you in particular to meet with much opposition. Jovian will want you alive, but Alpha's motives are not as transparent. I suggest you kill him as soon as you can. You will not mistake him. Once *he* is out of the way, it's still Jovian's game, but it'll just be you against him."

"And my family? Do you have any idea where they're being held?"

"I was waiting for you to ask about that while the others were not around," he says.

The Surgeon clears his throat and slides what looks to be a small flat security card of some kind toward me. It's composed of silver metal at its center, bordered at the edges by a thin layer of lucite.

As I take the card from him it feels as though it might be alive, churning and working, the moving parts inside hidden from the bare eye. There's a red light flashing beneath the clear paneling in a random sequence.

"Corvus wanted you to have this," he says. "He acquired the key through the help of one other, also at a heavy cost. In fact, the *other* was one of my very best friends, who is now lost to us all."

"May his soul find his way, then."

"I pray that also, my friend," he says, smiling. "Now, listen closely… Much of the tower has changed since I was last there. New floors. Laboratories and such. The detainment area was on the seventy-ninth floor, last I knew, roughly halfway up the tower."

"How many floors in total?"

"Well over two hundred, I'd suspect," he says. "Jovian is always fortifying it, aiming higher. Anyway, the card there should give you access to the room where your family is being kept, although I do not know what room it is nor what floor it's on. Only *you* can decipher that once you're inside. Your mother *swore* to it."

"Dear Mother… Did you know, Octavian? Did you know about her all along?" I ask, rubbing the card between my thumb and index finger.

"For more than a few years now, yes. Corvus was... Oh, excuse me!" he pauses to smile. "*She* was the last person I transferred before I left the Church."

"Tell me. Tell me what you did. Please, I must know."

"I recorded nothing in the logs with regards to the procedure. And on a day when I knew Elisabeth was also to be transferred, I was able to create a diversion by turning off the security recording system and shorting the power in her prison block. Only with the help of my companion, whom I spoke of earlier, was this made possible. It was in this way that Jovian was later confounded, and I believe knew nothing of your mother having replaced the *real* Corvus. He must've suspected that I had only stolen personal data of my own, seeing as I was leaving my position with little notice. In truth, I'm surprised he didn't kill me. Over the years, Jovian has grown ever more paranoid about who he lets close to him. I imagine that he's been looking over his shoulder all this time, waiting for the moment that my double-dealing might come back to bite him."

"In the form of my mother, no less."

"Yes," he says, grinning. "We became good friends, Natalia and I... though you and I, sadly, never met until now. I find that almost seren-dipitous. Wonderfully karmic. She was willing to do whatever it took to help me rectify this... including having to torture you on Eridania, if she must, in an effort to play the part."

"Would you believe she broke my nose?"

"A stout-hearted woman, for sure!" he says with a quick laugh. "And acutely savvy. Before she left this planet, I cautioned her that if her thoughts were read, or made manifest, it would be her undoing. *Our* undoing. Even still, she didn't waver, and her final words to me were about you. She wished you'd forgive her for anything in the past... and within that reprieve you might know that she did the best she could. And she hoped you would one day understand what it meant to love... to love in the way only a mother can love her child."

"Thank you. Thank you for that, Octavian," I say, my eyes welling with tears.

"*Oh*, but let us not get sentimental now, friend!" Octavian says, smil-ing again and doing his best to hide the glassiness in his own eyes. "There is one final thing I must tell you. From the last intelligence which I was able to gather through your mother, we found that Jovian had been working on something else. Something *new*."

"What is it?"

"Corvus and I couldn't uncover it fully with the time we had left together. But I think Jovian has found another way to transfer souls or, rather, to keep the spirit in limbo. Theoretically, you could transfer one's soul from one housing into an empty one or into a smaller receptacle if it were purposed to only contain the soul—that is, without a physical body being present. You could then keep the soul contained therein without putting it into new or existing flesh. I often thought this is what he might have tried to do with you originally and failed."

"Jovian wants to control men's souls completely now."

"Yes. He has set himself up on Mount Olympus," Octavian says, tapping his fingernail on the table. "And I fear this is his next step in the evolution of the process: to bottle up spirits perhaps, as if they are trinkets to be toyed with."

"Like a genie in a lamp."

"Precisely."

"Wait a sec—"

"What is it?"

"Octavian, before I arrived, Nav told me that there were cores powering the ship's engines that could be used in case of a transference emergency. He said they were lined with eridanium. He said that the—"

"My God!" he says, rubbing his chin.

"What?"

"Then that means he's done it."

"Done what?"

"If the ship's core canisters are lined with the ore in a synthesized form," he says, biting his lip, "using a method like, mmm... I don't know... particle acceleration, maybe, in *theory* they could contain or capture a soul."

"Nav said it was a backup plan. Does that mean anything to you?"

"Well, that's it! That just confirms it!" he says, slapping his palm on the table. "Jovian had the cores built into the ship in case he ever needed to flee the tower and was later shot down."

"But Nav made it sound like they were useless to us."

"I suppose that's possible, too. But then Nav is a manmade computer, designed by the Prophet," he says, looking toward the ceiling. "Hmm... I'm just not quite sure how they'd work to any other benefit. And cores such as these, well, you'd need to generate *a lot* of heat for them to open."

"What kind of heat?"

"I don't have that data," he says. "Something plasmic or nuclear, perhaps? It could be like swallowing a pill, really. The enteric coating will only break open inside the stomach when the conditions are just right."

"Bear with me... it may sound crazy, but is it possible that Jovian could transfer himself *into* the cores?"

"Hmm... unlikely. But anything can happen. I can only imagine that if the ship exploded, the reaction would ignite the cores properly and cause the ore to capture the soul. How his soul would get from one to the other is the unknown in the equation. I just can't be certain. That's something we never tried when I was still gainfully employed. And I was always more of a medical doctor rather than a physicist," he adds with a quick laugh.

"Dammit."

"Why do you ask?" he says with a smile. "You don't plan on getting Jovian trapped inside one of those, do you?"

"Yeah, well, wouldn't that be something?" I ask, and Octavian looks at me with squinted eyes. "I wonder why Jovian never came for the ship if it had these emergency cores on it?"

"I don't know," he says, "but Corvus was on Eridania for months. So, if Jovian suspected he was in fact your mother, he would've sent a force to retrieve the cores—and him."

"You mean *her*."

"Yes!" he says, smiling, "And knowing the Prophet's luxury, I'd imagine that he has another ship with more cores. But Jovian never travels by air anymore. I'm also in the dark as to whether or not he knew that Corvus ever took possession of the ship."

"If Jovian doesn't know, then it would seem logical that they can never track the ship's movement. Jovian may have built stealth into the ship to protect himself. If that too is true, then Terra might be able to get to Tokyo without the danger of being intercepted."

"Maybe. Maybe not," he says, shrugging. "Maybe Jovian purposely allowed the loss of the aircraft in order to secure your return. Nearly all ships now have an automatic kill switch allowing the Watchers the ability to shut them off without warning. You try to remove that switch and the ship self-destructs. Jovian's ship, however, does not have one. Another one of his emergency tactics, I gather. Corvus and I discovered this, which is how we were able to get him to Eridania. It's unlike any other ship we know of. All we needed then was for you to bring it back with you and a good pilot to keep the thing in the air *and* avoid being captured."

"Is that why Terra was chosen for the job?"

"That's why she *volunteered*," he says. "Like the rest of us, she has little to lose and much to gain. And she's uncanny in the cockpit. I've no earthly idea where she learned it from, either."

"Video games, maybe?"

"I beg your pardon?"

"Nothing. Never mind, it's just something that I—"

"We're all set!" Terra says, stepping back into the room and carrying the ledger from the ship at her side.

"Well, speak of the devil, my darling," Octavian says.

"I've talked to the ship, Tavian. It can be here in less than a minute," Terra says.

"Excellent. The time has come, dear friends. We must act," he says.

"I'm gonna need some better weapons," I say, holding up my pistols.

"I was waiting for you to say that," he replies with a smile.

Terra begins to lead us from the hall, and before I step out the door, I stop to look at a poster laid out on a smaller table that I hadn't noticed before. It's torn in at least a dozen different places but looks as if someone tried to put it back together. Like a child's puzzle. I can clearly read the words *Adventure* and the word *film* followed by the word *Kwai* at the bottom.

"I wish I'd seen it," Octavian says, picking up one of the pieces of the poster.

"I always liked movies, too. I have never heard of this one."

"Just another of its type, which has become a lost art," he says.

"Maybe someone ought to bring them back."

"That would indeed be the day," he says, smiling.

I linger for a moment longer, and Octavian grabs me by the shoulder.

"I think we can afford just another minute at the last," he says, pointing to the wall behind a large chest of drawers. In a small frame that's covered in dust, I clearly see the word *BARRABAS*.

Wiping away the filth from the face of glass, I'm able to see a heavily yellowed WANTED poster underneath. It features a black and white photograph of a bearded man, and the text underneath reads *Reward for the Just Detainment or Dead Body of Barrabas Madzimure.*

"Is that what I looked like?"

"Look at the date, Kilraven," Octavian says.

"Twenty seventy."

"By order of the Great Council," Octavian reads. "And look there," he adds, pointing the bottom of the advert. "There was a price of actual gold on the man's head! No one even trades in the stuff any longer."

"Wow. They really wanted me dead."

"I'd say keep it, if you like, but—"

"No. I've… I've lived enough of another man's life."

I place the overly ornate brass frame back onto the chest and Octavian pats me on the back of the shoulder once.

"Well done. Come, we must go now," he says.

We catch up to Terra by taking the next tunnel left from the end of the hall, and I can hear the men up ahead. They aren't laughing like they were before. Instead, the sound of guns being locked and loaded makes a kind of music all its own, bouncing here and there along the walls of the corridor.

We stop in the narrow doorway of a room that's even larger than Octavian's repository.

"This is unbelievable!"

"Clyment calls this the gun closet. But as you can see, it's more of an armory really," Octavian says.

"We got just about ever'thing you might need in here, includin' about two dozen shots for them archaic numbers you got there," Clyment says, pointing at one of my pistols. "But since we ain't got no more rounds for 'em, I modded the chamber so you can take some of the more, ehh… *current* slugs."

I look around the room at the men and their weapons. I don't even recognize most of the guns hanging on the wall. Half of them are so large I'm not even sure if I could lift them. The ones I've seen before are the Thompson submachine guns, a handful of Uzis, and two MG3 machine guns. Ancient stuff, really.

"What's this one?" I ask, selecting a fat-looking little modified revolver that seems at first vaguely familiar.

"Made in Austria. Standard issue for the West Coast Police Department back in 2019, pal," Clyment says.

"And this one?" I ask, picking up a small but heavy black blaster with a completely nickel-coated barrel.

"Don't even know where we got that one, do we, Gingoro?" Clyment asks, taking the gun out of my hand.

"Sure don't, Cly," Gingoro says. "Might have been from Fornax. Definitely not made by us."

"It's damn weighty and packs a helluva punch, but it's no good against armor from a distance of more than twenty meters, really," Clyment says, handing me back the gun.

"You know what? I think I'm going to trust in the ones I've got. They haven't done me wrong so far," I say, handing the blaster back to Clyment.

Everyone in the room goes as quiet as a breeze, and then Gingoro is the first to laugh, his pale face going bright red. "Suit yourself, man," he says, patting me on the back and handing me the rounds he located for my pistols.

"Flarkin' six-shooters! I tell you, this guy's got a big brass sack!" Clyment says, laughing.

"All the men I've killed with these six-shooters had guns like the ones all of you are carrying. It ain't the gun, gentlemen. It's the finger that's pulling the trigger," I say as I spin the newly loaded chambers and holster the guns.

There are two seconds of silence, and then everyone laughs again and tells me that I'm crazy. Octavian pulls a knapsack from the wall and hands it to me.

"The cores. And some other items you might find useful in the coming hours," he says.

"Thank you."

The Surgeon smiles at me, and then, turning quickly on one foot, he spins in one swift motion to face the rest of the men.

"I must address you as one now, friends," he says. "It is likely that we all are marching to our deaths in this most unlooked for but greatly anticipated hour. All that we've prepared for, ached for, wept for, and trained for has finally come to our doorstep. If we fail here today, we fail entirely. The world will go into a new age of darkness and despair. Forgive my dramatics… I have never been a man of faith, but I have faith in all of you now. So, let us go together, for this is *your* moment. Now, follow me!"

I throw on the knapsack and follow at the extreme rear of the troupe. We march with a purpose. We march in silence but for the sound of heavy boots thumping against the damp concrete. I can feel the energy from the others surging into me, through me, giving me strength that I don't possess myself. I can sense the uncertainty in the face of the doom the men know we now stand against. But I can also feel the courage brewing within them. They don't have to say a word, and neither do I.

Octavian leads us all to the end of the corridor, and we climb. It's a rusted metal spiral staircase that must be at least forty or fifty steps to the top. As we draw nearer to the end, the top hatch is opened by Octavian.

I'm then ushered into the clearing where I laid Terra down by the tree the night before. I turn around after I exit the hatch, and we're standing at the Rock. The dark bronze plaque, which was previously recessed into the Rock itself, slides forward with a clank. The letters on the face of the plaque that formed the password rise up, and then, coming into line with the height of the other words carved into the tablet, it looks like any other emblazoned sign—a sleepy memorial one might see attached to a stone in the middle of nowhere.

"Shorakkopoch," I say as Terra approaches me with the smile of an angel.

I take a few seconds longer than I deserve to admire her features. She halfway resembles a girl I knew when I was younger. This girl and I attended the same grade school, and I didn't really even know her very well, but we shared something special… I watched a movie with her once during the month of December. It was all but forbidden for us to fraternize, but she had never seen a film before, let alone watched one with a boy. Nor had I watched one with a girl, either, for that matter.

I still remember the look on her face and the way she jumped when she saw the monster burst out of the center of a man's stomach. It was the first time a girl had ever touched my hand. That's who Terra reminds me of... that little girl I knew for all of a semester.

But her spirit... Terra's got Elisabeth's spirit. Nearly fearless and at the same time an oasis of calm in the tightest situations you can imagine someone being put in.

"Here, partner. Take this," Terra says, handing me a device with a numeric digital readout on the front of it.

It's translucent and so tiny that it fits in the palm of my hand. Against my fingertips, I feel it's warm from where she's held it.

"I'll be in touch, *laser* brain," she says, smiling and gripping my hand with her own, "and I'll let you know when I'm closing in on the Asian Isles."

"Good luck, Terra, and thank you. I... I, um... I really hope to see you again."

"If that little ship can push anywhere above standard hypersonic without burnin' out, I should be there within about two hours," she says, folding the fingers of my hand over the unit. "And I guess I hope to see you again, too... you crazy spacehead," she says, stepping up on her tiptoes and kissing me on the cheek.

It's then that the golden dragonfly piloted by Nav descends into the clearing, and the men scatter like the wind toward the tree line. When Terra's hand leaves mine, I realize instantly just how fond of her I've actually become. My mouth opens slightly with the intent of saying something, but nothing comes. I'm like a defenseless animal that can only whimper and quake in fear, hunched over in a corner, shielding myself from an aggressor.

Octavian steps to my side, and I know yet again that the moment to say anything worth remembering has passed. I hope I don't regret it.

"She will be alright, won't you, Terra?" Octavian asks.

"I'll be in touch all the way, as much as I can," she says, while gripping the Surgeon in a bear hug with her eyes tightly shut.

"Godspeed, my dear!" he says.

As Terra turns away and moves to board the ship, Octavian holds his hands outwardly toward her, as a father might when he lets go of his only child. He watches with glassy eyes, and I can see his jaw clenching as he attempts to choke back any emotion.

"And don't let Nav give you any shit!" I shout.

The angel turns over her shoulder and smiles at me one last time and gives a quick military salute.

"She is a very brave girl," Octavian says.

"Or crazy."

"All the best ones are," he says, nudging me gently with his elbow. "But come now, friend, we must be away to the boat. It's just beyond the trees there. The Skywatchers will be here in moments."

Octavian points toward the Hudson and tugs on my arm and says something I can't even hear… I'm a stone, immovable. I watch Terra get inside the ship, and when the hatch closes, I could swear that she blows me a kiss.

In that instant, I whisper the words I wish I'd have said a minute ago when she was standing in front of me.

"We'll always have Shorakkopoch."

CHAPTER 24

STORMING THE CASTLE

I HEAR THE engine blast of Mother's golden lightmach overhead as it roars into the west, blazing a trail of smoke and fire into the unforgiving Neo York night sky.

When the ship hits Mach 1, I hear the thunderclap, and the handheld device that Terra gave me pings to life and starts a countdown clock. We have less than two hours. Possibly less, if Nav manages to go hypersonic all the way.

I follow after Octavian through the tree line ahead, and when I come out the other side, the doctor is not but thirty paces in front of me. We cross a sandpit at least fifty meters wide and then another thirty meters of what's left of the parkway that was once here. At the edge of the black pavement, I hear the water before I smell it, and stepping across the stony beach, I find the men waiting on the shoreline atop a green and black boat made of aluminum. It's so full of rusted holes I'm amazed the thing is still afloat with that much weight on it.

"Quickly now," Octavian says, waving his hands and beckoning me to get onboard.

"How far to Hell's Beach?" I ask, stepping into the boat.

"Seven or eight miles, as the dragon flies, my friend," Octavian says, looking toward the trail left by Terra and Nav's wake.

"We off, then?" Clyment asks.

"Go, Clyment. Go!" Octavian says.

The outboard motor lurches to life. The damn thing's so noisy I nearly laugh out loud for fear that we won't get a hundred feet without being blasted from the water. Whoever fires on us is in for a hell of a fight, though, since every other man on the boat has taken a specific and strategic attack position. Seven on one side, and seven on the other. Half of them are watching the skies, and the other half are on point with the shoreline.

There's a boldness and a bravery clinging to the air around us. It's the same desperate feeling that permeated itself down through the bones of every man and woman in the mines. But here its mingled with a look of uncertainty that's standing firmly on the doorstep of every man's face.

Even the Surgeon himself is carrying guns, holstered under his arms by a black leather gun belt adorned with silver clasps. The gun grips have little rings at the bottom, and the handles are an off-white kind of pearloid that seems to change color whenever he moves.

"Those are beautiful," I say, pointing to the butt of one of the guns.

"Yes. Clyment replaced the handles for me," he says, removing the gun on his right hip and handing it to me.

"They're real similar to mine, actually."

"Indeed. Remington police revolvers from the last decade of the nineteenth century," he says. "Though they've been modified a bit, they still fire real bullets. It's still the best way to know you've killed a man."

"I didn't take you for much of a deadeye."

"Well... I don't trust plasma fire. A blast right through the chest still won't take a man down as fast when the wound is so quickly cauterized. Anyway, I couldn't bear to have them totally modernized or refurbished, so I have kept them all these years. A gift from an old friend... a thank-you for my steady hands."

I spin the chamber, pull back the hammer, and everything moves like a greased wheel.

"Fantastic!" I say, handing the gun back to Octavian.

He holsters it in one swift movement and looks straight up. "The stars are out, and they are shining," he says. "Star light, star bright… they must be our friends tonight."

"We're gonna need more than just help from the stars."

Octavian sighs. "What are you going to do, Kilraven?" he asks, his face still aimed toward the night above us but his eyes cutting sideways in my direction at the last.

"To Jovian, you mean?"

"Who else?" he asks.

"Something tells me it's not really my decision. I think I'm going to have to wing it."

Octavian smiles and puts a hand on my shoulder. "Sometimes in life that's just precisely what you have to do, isn't it, friend?"

"*Tavian? Kilraven? Do you copy?*"

"It's Terra!" Octavian says, springing to life and checking a COM device attached to his belt.

"*I'm on both channels. You guys should hear me loud and clear,*" she says.

"We read you, Terra. Are you alright?" Octavian asks.

"*Smoother than peach fuzz. I think I'm over Sector Two, according to the Nav.*"

"*You are coming very shortly over the former state of Indiana, Captain,*" Nav says.

"*Shut it, Nav!*" Terra says.

"Ride on, Terra. Ride on. And keep in touch," Octavian says, switching a knob on the COM unit.

"I wonder if we should *nix* radio communication from here on out?" I ask.

"We'll likely lose contact with our little flying saboteur once we're inside the tower anyway. And besides, even if Jovian is listening… let him sweat a little," Octavian says with a wink.

We travel the rest of the river in silence. It seems like it might go on forever, this sort of quiet peace. The lapping of the calm waves is soothing to the ear, tempting me with thoughts that it might wash away all fear, doubts, and debts. The debts that we soon must pay.

After what feels like only seconds, Clyment prepares to dock the boat while four or five of the men jump into the water and begin to secure the beach. I soon realize that it's not even a beach, really. It's only a lonely place where the rock bed of the river meets the land.

For seeming amateurs, these boys keep a tight formation, too. That isn't as easy as it sounds, considering the streets are almost coated in black ice. The streets running in every which direction look as though they're deserted. It's as silent as a graveyard.

The Tower of Peace beams haughtily at the end of the road before us. The eerie quiet of the night and the coolness of the water kept me so preoccupied that I hadn't even noticed it before now. It really is a beautiful thing to see.

"This way, friend," Octavian says, leaping from the boat and extending his hand to me.

"What are you doing?" I ask.

"Winging it," he says, smiling.

I jump from the boat and Octavian unholsters his guns, keeping his elbows at his sides.

"What about your men?" I ask as Octavian steps onto a stone between the water and the pavement.

"It's been my privilege, gentleman," he says. "I bid you all the truest and most heartfelt of farewells, if this be the end. If Kilraven or I do not return before first light, then leave this place and please abide by the most sacred of the nonurbanite creeds: go find liberty where you may and pursue that which is dearest to your own hearts in peace."

The men stand silent for a brief moment, and Clyment steps forward in front of Octavian. "Boss, yer as fuckin' fried as Kilraven here if you think we're gonna fold on you now. Am I right or what, boys?"

"Sir, yes, sir!" the men all shout in agreement, and with that the remainder of them are up and out of the boat, forming a line at the top of the street before Octavian has the chance to object.

"Salute your captain, boys. May just be the last goddamn time we get to do it!" Clyment says.

All the men salute Octavian at once, and as he returns the gesture, the moonlight illuminates the single tear running down his face, and it sparkles like a tiny diamond as it falls into the water at his feet.

"You didn't really think that Trash was gonna get all the glory now, didja?" Clyment asks, playfully slapping Octavian on the shoulder.

"Well, far be it from me to back down from this rout," Octavian says turning to me, "especially when their blood is on fire and guns are in hand."

"Let's go, boys! Sack up and cover the Surgeon!" Clyment shouts as the men continue their formation and head down the street ahead of us.

Octavian and I follow, and I'm overcome by a strange sense of peace deep inside me. It's unlike any other calm I've ever felt in my life. I don't know if it's because I'm facing my death or whether it's because I've already faced it. Maybe it's because I'm facing it with friends. Whatever the reason, I am not afraid. Though the streets are desolate and the sound of the men's whispers echo like a net of defeat closing in all around us, I am not afraid.

"I used to live right *there*," Octavian says, pointing at two silvery towers toward the right side of the road.

"View must've been incredible."

"Decadent, really," he says, "but... all vanity, of course."

"I lived in Jericho Tower when I was young."

"I know the very place!" he says. "You know, they say there used to be a park of green and a library where the Tower of Peace stands now. Imagine that. Books for everyone and free open spaces."

"Imagine."

"Yes... imagine that," he says.

"Octavian, what are *you* going to do?" I ask, and he doesn't look at me. He only keeps pacing forward.

"A man such as yourself shouldn't face death alone," he says, "and I have plans of my own."

"What plans?"

"Ones that I'm keeping... Hmm, how did you describe it? Rather close to the chest? I'm afraid I too must do the same. I have my reasons. They're probably miles from ethical and much more selfish than yours... but I must be allowed to see them through, least of all for the sacrifice that Terra is making for us."

"Well, from what I've seen, I believe you've earned that right," I say. "You know, it's strange... we've not seen any resistance. I was always used to these streets being bogged down with people. I've always imagined having to fight ten thousand men to come even this far."

"Mmm. Indeed," Octavian says, looking at the apartments and the shops on either side of us. "He knows we're coming. Keep on moving."

We walk the entire length of 42nd Street amidst an eerie stillness. It's just like that movie I saw, the one with Doc. All the men dressed in black quietly faced one another in a dusty orange alley, just before they unleased hell.

Octavian's men stay a healthy block or so ahead of us, and every few seconds the Surgeon turns to look behind us. For a moment I doubt him, as if he might be looking for some team of men sent to lie in wait and ambush us.

"We're nearly there," Octavian says.

Looking ahead, I'm confounded by the sheer magnitude and size of the tower. It's grown mightier than my imagination would've allowed. From afar, the tower looked as though it were a giant white spear, almost as if it were literally made of light. The spire at the top beams so brightly that the encircling clouds seem as though they're attempting to escape from its holy power. Upon the mast is a signal of the Prophet for all to see, a sort of violet cross-like shape enveloped by an oval of the same dark color.

We draw ever closer to the massive concrete gates, and it looks as if the stone steps have all been coated in black tar.

No, wait... they're *men*.

The steps are covered top to bottom with Council guards. Two seconds later I hear Clyment order the men to take their positions against the stone orbs outside the great iron-wrought fence, which is strangely not closed against us.

Octavian and I approach the gate together, side by side, and I count at least four formations of a dozen guards.

"I thought we was gonna waltz right in, boss?" Clyment says.

"He wants Kilraven, not us," Octavian replies.

"Don't follow my lead," I say.

Before I can even think, I'm around the edges of the gate and walking alone up the smooth, stoned walkway leading to the entrance to the tower. The first line of guards can't be but forty feet away, if that.

"Halt!" booms a voice from the tower steps.

So, I halt. I stop. I freeze right in my tracks. I'm *ready*. I suck in a deep breath of the cool Neo York night air.

"Try and stop me!" I shout back in return.

Looking up to my right, there's a stone monolith of Jovian, and to my left is the very same, though his facial expression is slightly less stern on the latter. In the pristine emerald lawn beyond the gate, there are three more statues of him on each side, all in a row and each one larger than the next. They're like oversized dominoes forming the way toward the entrance.

Why aren't they firing?

"Stop! You cannot enter here, criminal!" shouts one of the guards.

The same guard then steps forward and puts his arm out, the palm facing me in an effort to hinder my path.

He must be the leader.

"I said halt, faithless thief!"

The pistol at my right screams at me. I draw it from its holster and pull the trigger so damn quick I didn't even have to aim. The guard falls to the ground, and there's a clatter of the manufactured armor colliding with the stone underneath him. He's dead before any of the other guards actually break stance and pull their weapons.

Octavian shouts something I can't quite make out from behind the safety of the wall. Then I see Clyment and his men rush through the gate, and none of them waste their time in blasting it all to hell. I roll to my right behind the statue of Jovian just before a hail of much-too-late plasma fire and bullets careen around me.

"Take cover behind the statues!"

I can hear the guards barking orders at one another. A bolt of plasma fire melts the pavement directly to the right of the tip of one of my boots.

"One… two… three!"

And on three I'm over the edge of the statue and firing both pistols.

Why aren't they firing back?

I tag one of the bastards with a headshot before ducking for cover again. Then everything else is a blur. Don't let anyone ever say otherwise when it comes to describing a gunfight. Some men learn to treat it like tying their shoelaces—something they can do with their eyes closed. When you're shooting to kill and trying to keep from being killed, it all happens so fast. It's completely out of your control.

At three o'clock I see Octavian and Elfmoon firing from opposite sides of the statue parallel to me. Elfmoon gets tagged by a plasma burst square in the neck. He hits the ground with his eyes wide open.

"No!" Octavian screams.

I can see Elfmoon's face… It's all blackened.

You poor kid. May his soul find its way.

A quick peek from cover and I count two more of the men are down at the gate, but I can't tell who they are. Can't tell if they're still alive, either.

I'm up on my feet again and there's maybe half of the original force left. I think they're retreating. I see Clyment has gone ahead. Another man joins him on the steps, firing away like it's his last moment.

May their souls find their way.

That thought has me quickly out from safety, back on my feet, and running toward the tower's main entry doors. It feels like I'm not even controlling my body now. That's the blur again. Both pistols of mine are firing amidst the barrage of plasma whizzing in all directions.

Why is no one firing at me?

I pull the trigger once. Then again. Guard number three and four go down. Eight bullets fired. Four shots left until I have to reload.

I take shelter behind the second statue of Jovian. To my right, Octavian and the boys are still giving it hell. The Surgeon's once pristine robe is now defiled, darkened in a smoking patch of black and gray near the shoulder.

"Octavian! Were you hit?!"

He doesn't answer me. He just keeps firing back. Hell, either way, he's still fighting. Looking around the edge of the stone, I can see Clyment's now climbed to the top of the steps, and the guards have begun their retreat into the tower entrance.

"To the tower!" Octavian shouts, and we rush like an army of ants to the opening of our self-made hill.

I take out two more guards who are in retreat. I hate to shoot any man in the back. One shot left in my right pistol.

"Fuck!"

As I climb the steps, my guts rise up in my throat. When I get to the very top, I can see why. Clyment is on his knees, with a hole the size of a fist right through the middle of his abdomen. I rush toward him, steadying him with my left hand while firing at the tower entrance with my right.

"You're a good shot, K'raven," he says.

"Don't bullshit a bullshitter, Clyment."

Clyment laughs for what I think might be the first time ever in my presence.

"Get in there… Go on now," he says with a curdling and gravelly whisper.

"Quickly! Lie him back!" Octavian shouts, rushing to my side.

I set Clyment out prostrate, and the Surgeon takes a vial out of a small pocket at his breast. He shakes the contents before popping the top, then dumps a bubbling foam onto Clyment's wound. The opening starts to smoke and crackle, and the smell of burnt flesh almost makes me gag. And the tough bald-headed son of a bitch doesn't even make a sound.

"You cannot help here, Thaniel. I'm afraid this is where we say goodbye, my friend. Jovian will be at the topmost floor!"

"I… I wish you all good fortune," I reply.

"Go on, Kilraven! Go!" Octavian shouts.

My eyes begin to sweat as I back away from them. With a nod, I leave Octavian's side.

As I climb the stairs, it's just a sea of broken black armor. I can't tell who's dead and who's alive. My legs are moving me forward of their own accord toward the tower entrance. Now I know what it's like to be a hunted gazelle in its last race, followed by the dreaded tiger trailing behind with its salivating iron jaws. But I press on anyway, and I don't look back.

"Kilraven!" someone shouts.

It's Ortiz! He's waving for me to join him across the brightly lit vestibule. I see the kid's ducked down behind a workspace of some kind, firing blindly over the top of it just a few feet above his head.

"Over here, Kilraven!"

I count to three and I'm out in the open, gliding on my knees across the entryway toward Ortiz. He's smiling and holding out his hand. Just before he pulls me behind the safety of the cover, there's a flash of red, and his body jolts backward as my fingertips meet his. I scramble to get behind him, pull my left pistol, and fire into my peripheral. For a nearly blind shot, I still manage to take out the guard nearest to the elevator.

"Kid?! You okay?!" I ask.

Ortiz nods at me, slowly, and I reload both guns in about six seconds. *You're getting slow, old man.* I grab Ortiz by the shirt and pull him up against the wall.

"Ah… filho da *puta*…" he says.

Damn. There's blood on my hands. It's all in his beard, too.

"*Steady*, Ortiz. You're gonna be okay."

"The terminal there," he says, pointing behind me. "It will tell you what you—"

"Shh. Don't talk, kid."

Fuck. The shot was mortal. It went right through the center of his chest.

I rip off part of my sleeve and shove it into the wound. The courageous warrior spirit inside the frail body of this skinny-ass kid doesn't even bat an eye.

"The terminal," he says. "It will tell you… what's on each floor… and I know because I been here," he says with a smile. "I was eighteen… my trial… I had to come… but I didn't… have to stay."

"You did *good*, kid. Just relax."

He doesn't take another breath, and the life-light leaves his eyes. The champion stops breathing with a sly smirk on his face. Just like Tarsil.

May your soul find its way.

I'm on my feet and frantically fussing with the controls at the terminal with bloody hands. The gunfire has nearly stopped altogether, and I risk taking a look back out the entryway from where I first entered. Octavian's gone, and Clyment along with him.

Maybe they're still alive.

In front of me, the terminal is a confusing array of multiple screens, lights, and buttons.

Could use Nav right about now.

I see a slot that looks like it could hold the small plastic card Octavian gave me. I reach for my chest pocket containing the card and my heart jumps up in my throat when I pull it free. It's completely blackened, like a rusted old hunk of metal. Then I place my hand under my coat and shirt and feel the skin raw and charred where the card was.

They shot me, and I didn't even realize it.

I mentally thank my mother and adrenaline for their part in that. Despite the card's now mangled appearance, I insert the damn thing into the side of the display monitor. The terminal prompts me almost immediately for a clearance code.

"A fucking *code*?!"

A holographic image of a keypad suddenly appears on the screen with the word PASSCODE. But before I can even process the lack of a code any further, it's filled in automatically.

Mother. That's more than twice you've saved my life now.

Then the terminal tells me exactly what I want to know. Three prisoners. Floor eighty-seven. Room A26.

A26. Keep saying the number in your head. A26.

I rush across the hall unhindered. When I'm at the elevators, I can hear plasma fire, but there's not a guard or any of Octavian's boys in sight. The elevator doors open faster than I expect, and inside is one of our men lying on the floor. I can't even tell who it is. His face is completely gone. He's not wearing anything I can ID him by. Maybe its Gingoro... His hair looks almost red.

No... That's not hair. It's blood. May your soul find its way, friend.

I press the button for the eighty-seventh floor. There's a dead man at my feet again, and I'm heading toward the sky. I'm heading toward my imminent death in a moving metal box. I should be straining with intensity right now... I shouldn't be this calm. Maybe it's the odd music that's playing from the speaker above me. It's serene and peaceful. It's a woman's voice.

"Thank you for choosing to visit the Tower of Peace today and your prophet, Jovian. He welcomes you to partake in your Second Life experience to its utmost. Together you and he shall reign righteously over physical death for as long as you faithfully serve the Church. If you are meeting with your transference consultant for the first time today, let me be the first to say congratulations! You are taking the first step into what is no longer the Great Unknown. Please remember to ask your consultant what options you have available—"

I blast the damned thing with both pistols. The speaker sparks and crackles as the female voice dissolves into a bursting of overly bassy tones, and her indiscernible dogma fades into mush.

"Unbelievable."

I don't even care that I wasted two bullets. I half expect the lights to go out now or for Jovian to pull some trick. Maybe the elevator will give way and I'll fall to my death.

No. It can't. It won't. Not today.

The door opens quietly at the eighty-seventh floor. I quickly reach for my COM and switch it off. The last thing I need is Terra giving my position away.

I step out of the elevator with both guns hanging at my sides. The hall is *gigantic*. Seven meters wide from the looks of it, and everything is dark. Literally. Dark walls, dark carpeting. There's not a soul in sight, minus my own.

A dim, bluish light hovers above each one of the many doors lining the hall, highlighting the number of the room. The first one I see is marked A1. I move forward, knowing A26 must be ahead and to the right. As I'm running down the hall, my footsteps leave no sound and I can only hear what sounds like the muffled screams of men and women.

No... they sound like something else... It sounds like children. The shrieking becomes a wailing. The most horrible, discordant mixture of cursing cries and pleas for mercy that I've ever heard. I want to save them all. I wish I could save them all... but I can't. I can't stop. Not now.

A26... A26... A26.

I come to the door of all doors. I put my forehead against the clear number plate that has a digital display reading "A26" in red. I take a deep breath. My lungs feel so small. There's no handle where there should be one!

"Why is there no doorknob?!"

I put my thumb to the plate to the right of the doorframe. Nothing happens.

"Please, God!"

This can't be happening. I've come this far. Why didn't anyone tell me about the damn door? Did anyone even know?

I look behind me at door A25. It's exactly the same as this one. In fact, all the doors in the hall seem identical. My heart sinks, and the agony of defeat begins to course through me, like hot lead in my veins. I nearly panic.

The gun, you idiot! Try your gun!

I step back a few paces, aim, and fire. The bullet barely even scratches the door's exterior. I fall to my knees.

Please, someone help me! What do I do now?

After the question is spoken in my mind, the door slides silently open, and a sterile blast of oxygen slaps me in the face.

Somebody's watching me.

I don't question why, and I'm off my feet and in the doorway. The room is filled with a light, a light so blinding I can't see anything once I'm inside. The light is above me, under my feet, on all sides. I can't see a damned thing.

I move forward to what could be the center of the room, and then I see something: three shapes lined against the back wall. My eyes are adjusting and… Wait… they're not shapes.

They're women. Three women!

Each woman is bound to a rigid framed chair, and their legs are covered in soft white blankets. Their hair is so unkempt I can't make out their faces very well.

"Who are you?"

They don't answer me. They don't even stir.

"Are you deaf?!"

The women don't move an inch. They don't respond in any way.

"Say something!"

My eyes have almost fully adjusted to light now. Coming close to them, I notice their open eyes… all milky white, not a trace of color in the irises. They don't even blink.

I must be in the wrong room.

"What is this?"

I can hear Jovian's voice in my head. Even now I can still remember the sound of it. *Coming here has been complete folly, Kilraven.* And I know somewhere nearby he must surely be watching. And laughing.

"Who are you?" I ask, falling down upon my knees.

The women still don't answer.

"What's *wrong* with you?!"

I visibly search their clothing for something I can use. An ID... anything. The nametags on each of their uniforms give me no clue; it's only a series of random letters and numbers. My heart skips a beat. I'm on my knees and holding the hands of the woman nearest to me.

"Are you my sister? Are you my wife?"

She reaches out to touch my face. Her ice-cold hands grope over my nose, in my hair, and through my beard. She is blind.

"Do you know me?"

She recoils and reclines back in the seat. Her face is full of disappointment... sorrow... and sadness.

"Can you hear me? Can you see me?"

They say nothing and do nothing. Tears crowd my eyes, like hundreds of people packed in a shop made only to hold a few. The salty water streaks down my cheeks. I'm reminded of a story I once heard—there was a god on Earth who cried once, and his tears flooded the Earth for forty days.

"What has he done to you?"

Suddenly, the woman in the middle holds out her hands toward me and opens her mouth to speak. Her mouth moves like a fish's out of water, as if she were gasping for air, but it's just a rustling at the back of her throat. For a moment, I could swear it sounds like the word *help*. I rush to her, and kneeling, I grip her hands in mine and place them on my face. I touch her hands, and she touches mine. I put her fingertips on my lips as I speak.

"Can you hear me at all, sweet lady? Who are you?!"

The woman reaches underneath the blankets on her lap and removes a tiny slip of paper. She unfolds it, slowly, and holds it up for me to read. The words are written crudely and in haste.

KILL ME.

It's written over and over and over. My tears don't stop as I approach the woman on the left. I touch her hands, and I caress her face gently. She recoils, too, with a look of extreme disgust on her face. She claws and gnashes her teeth and swings her arms wildly at me.

"Who are you? Give me a sign, please! Show me that you know who I am! Show me some kind of a—"

Wait.

This woman's hands are *different* than the others. She's wearing a *ring*. It's a band of solid gold on her left hand.

I grab her hand in mine and pull the ring from her finger. She reaches for it, her fingers straining as though they might break. In a fit of rage, she convulses in her chair, wailing dryly for me to return that which is hers.

"I'm so sorry, precious lady! Just a moment and I'll give it back to you. I just need to—"

As I hold up the ring close to my eyes, the inside of the band bears the engraved words *All my love, Thaniel.*

CHAPTER 25

OCTAVIAN'S LEGACY

THEY CALLED ME the Surgeon. *The* Surgeon. Admittedly, I was good enough at what I did to earn that title. Well, okay, I was very good at what I did.

Most people think that doctors, or anyone within the medical profession, are arrogant, almost as if by nature. I can honestly say that I understand that. We do make a lot of credits, and well, we also tend to be very smart. It troubled me that my notoriety never came from what I could do in the operating room, but rather the status of my profession.

I find something inherently wrong with that thought process. I knew that what I was able to do was not by my own means. Yes, I was using my own hands and learned skill, but what it really came down to was the circumstances of my life that led me to become what I am. To become what I *was*. I had no control over that, no more than I had control over how my brain was formed or what proclivity toward learning I may or may not have been given while being formed in my mother's womb.

So, when someone thought highly of me because of my work, I always told them that they likely had just as noble of a job as I did. No one ever *believed* me when I said it, and I could tell that generally they thought I was simply being polite. However, I never was street-wise. At least not until the last few years. But even for all of my training, most of it supplied by Clyment, it's not come naturally to me. I am the sort of man who would more likely shoot himself in the foot when holding a gun for the first time. My pre-birth gifts were not dealt to me in the realm of physicality. That said, I've since learned how to shoot quite well. And even I find it quirky that I am proud of that fact.

Regardless, holding a gun in my hand still feels like, well, a sin. But it's the times in which we live, I suppose, when we must forgive ourselves for the mortal trespasses. You know the days have come down when someone like me finds himself pushed up against the wall. And I despise being backed into that place where the only way out starts with putting your finger on a trigger. It's vulgar and boorish, frankly.

But there were lines even I could no longer cross. It started with what we did to the children. I couldn't do it anymore. Their faces take justifiable vengeance upon me by hiding behind my eyelids in the night, their cries calling out to me from the ground. I don't even remember the last time I had more than four or five hours of sleep at once.

But that's the *least* of what I deserve. Children are pure. Untainted. Their hearts are innocent and unblemished by the tarnish that we have coated the world with. They should not have been made to suffer for the wrongs committed by the hands of accountable adults. Adults whose impulses, drives, and desires took precedence, by illegal force, over their creator-given rights... the right to experience life in peace, however brief.

The man at my side, whose arm is slung over my shoulder and has a cavernous hole in his midsection, is a true child at heart. That is how I see him, though the years have hardened the face he wears. I love him like a brother.

Dear Clyment.

Before I left the Church, I would not have looked at him twice if we passed in the street. He could've been cleaning my shoes and I would've barely taken notice of him. And yet, I would not have appreciated that all the circumstances of his life led him to that moment to assist me. It would've had nothing to do with the fact that he may have been rendering a service in recompense. It would've only mattered that he was there. He was there for someone like me.

When I turned my back on the deeds done at the tower, he was there. He didn't care what I had done; he didn't even care to know about it. He only cared who I was in the moment that we met. I was no longer he who did those terrible things, for that man existed only in moments in the past.

"Stay with me, Clyment. Stay with me, my friend."

"Where… Where we goin', Cap'n?" Clyment asks.

"I'm taking you to the cloning repository below the tower. Whatever you do, stay *awake*!"

"Oh, you uhh… got a clone of me on ice, huh, boss?" he asks.

"No, Clyment. There are no clones of you in the world, sadly."

Curse me for lying to him.

When I left the Church, I was afraid. I never lived on the outside. I didn't know the streets. I needed someone who did if I was going to make it. I needed someone who knew how to fight and, better still, somebody who knew how to stay alive. Corvus could not be the one to help me. And so, before I resigned, I found Clyment, alone, in the recesses of the logs. He was scheduled for termination, but strangely, his execution date was set to an unspecified *to be determined*. You see, most people who took their transference trials already worked for the Church to pay back the life given.

But not Clyment. Even though he had a dossier a mile long from his days in Triangle City, the Church kept him around because he made weapons for them. Unique weapons. You name it—knives, guns, and explosives of all types. The man was so adept at his craft, and stayed so prolific, that he didn't even work in the tower. The Council let him see to his own affairs, with the stipulation being that he kept delivering the goods on time. That, of course, couldn't last forever.

One day, one of the Prophet's brethren brought it to the Tribunal's attention that Clyment was approaching his thirty-eighth birthday. They simply couldn't risk the natural death of their resident munitions genius by letting him age any further. Clyment refused transference on account that it was never in his contract. A brilliant move. And when pushed further, the Council offered him servitude on Eridania or permanent stasis. Being as bullheaded as he is, he tried calling their bluff. Naturally, they chose stasis for him. And it was there that I found him.

I *knew* then that he was going to be the one. So, I cloned him several weeks before I left the Church. I altered the records to show that his original body had a different chip serial number, different name, and different date of birth. Then I covered my tracks by clearing all history of the records, which themselves had been altered. The Church will likely find James Hoffa before they find the *real* Clyment.

After transferring Clyment's soul into his clone, I had both his original body and a clone backup put back into stasis. When I woke the clone, he never even questioned whether he was the real Clyment or not because, well, he *was* the real Clyment. His spirit was there. He had no knowledge of anything other than the fact that the Church had frozen him for his refusal to cooperate and that upon his resurrection he knew I was the one who unfroze him.

Naturally, Clyment no longer felt he owed the Church anything, and his loyalty shifted to me. I didn't anticipate that he'd treat me as though I were a savior. The only question he had for me was why. Why had I spared him? When I told him that the Church saw fit to exercise the same authority over me, as it had with him, he believed he'd found someone just like him. A *kindred* soul. And we then became brothers in our shared disloyalty.

What I do for Clyment in this moment I never had planned. But in the early morning hours many years ago, on a day in October, when I marched out of the tower with him at my side, something germinated in my mind. It's been growing slowly but surely. And until we landed at Hell's Beach today, I had no idea just exactly how I was going to remedy what I had done. Foreboding did its duty, however, and sat on my shoulder unceasingly. And I knew this moment would come eventually. I knew that I must either tell Clyment who he was or, worse, that I would have to *show* him. Either way might be devastating for him and dangerous for me.

But here and now my heart is gladdened and the weight slightly lifted knowing that Clyment will find out this way. And he will know. He'll know that, though our relationship was not built on truth at its beginning, it became a vehicle for me to see the truth and that I value his friendship more than my own life. Besides, if I'd been honest with him beforehand, he would've shot me in the leg or tied me to a chair to keep me from doing what I'm doing right now.

I smile at that knowledge.

Clyment doesn't utter another syllable the rest of the way. I soon find myself in familiar territory as the outer doors to the stasis hall bar my way. But I find that even though it is now locked to me, there are no guards or Watchers here. After trying the conventional method of knocking, I get no response.

I pull the pin on the only thermite concussion pellet hanging from Clyment's belt and roll it toward the base of the blast door. Four seconds later the smell of heated metal suddenly makes my bowels quaver.

It *cannot* be this simple. Or is it this easy because Jovian really believes himself to be the victor already? Doubtless, he knew I would come here. He will expect me to destroy the entire place in an attempt at redemption. But even I have one advantage over the Prophet; he doesn't know me as well as he thinks he does.

Once inside, I discover that all the workstations have changed slightly. For starters, they're unmanned. There are dozens of newer machines with larger display screens, and each of the keypads are now built into the holodesk. In years past, these were the access points for the temperature and vital controls for the stasis tubes. They've replaced all the machinery fittings with the latest and greatest as well.

"Always the spare-no-expense type, Jovian."

For all the distance we've come, our way has been relatively unhindered. And now that I'm deep in the dragon's lair, something *else* doesn't quite feel right. Under normal circumstances there's a minimum of half a dozen armed guards and at least one or two of the Church-sponsored interns here watching the cryo-vaults at all times. I get knots in my stomach all of sudden, again.

"Boss?" Clyment asks.

"Yes, my friend?"

"I can't see nothin' anymore, boss," he says.

"Hold on, Clyment! You are going to be alright."

"Just… leave me."

"Never."

"Don't do this, boss…"

"Just keep talking, Clyment. Even if you stop hearing my voice, or your own, keep talking. Sing your favorite song. Hum it if you have to."

Clyment starts whistling a melody as soon as I set him in the nearest available technician seat.

"That's it, son."

Clyment's head leans back, resting against the wall, and he begins singing a song I've never had the pleasure of hearing until now. He talks about pulling his coat over his shoulders and walking through a park while the leaves are falling around him. On some nearby rock, he finds a mark carved by some desperate lover.

"Baby, I've changed. Please come back," he says with a whisper, trailing off about things changing in a Neo-York minute.

How right you are, Clyment.

I can't help but listen to him as I use the computer terminal to open the cryo-vaults. When the security door leading to the stasis tubes opens, I realize I've been focused more on Clyment's voice than anything else and that I've been working solely on reflex. It's as if no time has passed between my fingers and the entry pad. If nothing else has changed and our luck holds, then my original body is still inside vault six.

I key in the commands to open the particular loading cell for my tube, then cue the transference modules. Everything works like flicking a switch, and it's then that I know why I still have access and why I must move quickly.

Like Kilraven, Jovian wants me here.

My original body can still be destroyed remotely. I've no doubt that Jovian will surely do so, and I must beat the Prophet to the punch.

"Clyment, I will return."

My dying friend says nothing as I leave the control room and approach the security field leading to the stasis vaults. The entire field, which is held in place by a giant arch that I helped design, looks like a hazy film of mist. Passing therein, I'm surprised at what I find. I can't even move, my face aghast, my jaw agape… *The whole nine yards*, as they say.

As far as the eye can see, a sea of frozen faces stretches out down the vast vault hallways before me… men and women, still alive. Alive and yet also dead... for decades. There are tens of thousands of them housed in this vault alone, and the grandeur of it does not fail to leave me speechless. If I had to guess, I'd say the numbers have increased nearly twofold since I was last here. The vaults under the tower run *deep*, all the way to the old Grand Central Terminal in fact. Jovian must have amassed nearly a million bodies or more in total at this location.

Do not waver now. Clyment is waiting.

My bowels lurch inside of me, just underneath my navel. I locate my body quicker than expected on the retrieval monitor and the computer speaks to me.

"*Yes, Doctor?*" it asks.

"Can you locate original specimen number fifty-three?"

"*Yes, Doctor Octavian.*"

"Bring it here, please."

"*One moment, Doctor.*"

I'm intrigued that the computer system hasn't rejected me. Further still, I'm unnerved that my original body seems to be in its rightful place. It's almost as if it has been waiting for me.

Jovian knew you would come.

On the monitor I see the sleek, silver pod numbered fifty-three on its exterior, which I labeled myself, slide vertically up from the protection sheath. I manually set the mode of cryo-stasis to *mollify* on the pod's access panel.

After a few seconds, the inner tube is ejected slowly while the clear protective shell is sprayed with a layer of decontaminant before the entire device rotates back and lays itself out horizontally. We once jokingly called that step *thawing the meat*. How we could laugh about such a thing is now beyond me.

The capsule of my body is cold under my fingertips. I head through the gate with my original, and with it I advance back through the security field. Crossing through the control room and over the threshold for the lab, I find that Clyment has moved from his seated position near the workstation. I look around for a few moments, and then the knots in my abdomen return.

"Clyment? Where are you?!"

No sooner had the words have left my lips than I see him—stumbling like a mad ox inside the transference chamber perpendicular to the lab.

"Clyment, what are you doing?!" I shout, racing into the throughway to meet him.

"Don't wanna… go out like this, boss…" he says, falling forward and spilling his life's blood onto the floor. "Don't wanna… be put on ice."

"Stop this! I'm trying to save you!" I say, helping him back to his feet.

"Damn you… Don't put me on ice!" Clyment says.

I pull Clyment to his feet and use all my physical power to push him forward, propping his body against the first pod. The sequencing I keyed earlier has afforded me little more time, and by the pod entry indicator, even less. It's telling me the subject is needed promptly by flashing orange.

"Clyment? Can you hear me?"

"Sure, boss…"

"Good. This might hurt a bit."

I don't hesitate any longer and grab Clyment by his feet and roll him right into the open pod. He turns onto his back and looks up at me, blinking several times and coughing heavily.

"The tissue around your wound is already necrotizing. Whatever happens, Clyment, do not stop breathing!"

"Okay, boss…"

"And when you wake up, remember. Remember to forgive me!"

"Where… Where you goin', boss?" he asks, his eyes glassy.

"On celestial roads the celestial do go, my dear friend."

I smile as I close the lid on his pod. I do not waver, thankfully, and I return back to the cryo-vault and eject my now excised original body from the silver pod numbered fifty-three.

Fifty-three. It was my father's favorite number. I never knew why. I've no idea why I suddenly wish to know why at this point in time, either, or why I am suddenly sad about it.

Checking the vital signs on my original, I find that they are excellent. There's solid brain activity, and the tissue now has a healthy and warm hue. I'll be damned to hell-depths if it's not the most peculiar feeling to be looking at another, more vigorous version of yourself. For over ten years, the body of Octavian Blandinus has been in the silence of this tube. This casket.

"Dear Lord… have I aged that much?"

I set my narcissism aside and head back to the transference chamber with my original skin in tow. The capacitors are almost at full power, with a stable reading of over seven hundred and forty-nine megawatts and climbing. I need well above nine hundred to pull this off. The amount of energy is still incredible—it'd be enough to power one-quarter of the homes in the greater Neo York area for a year.

Once inside the transference room, I place my original body pod next to Clyment, and though I hate for him to have to wake up to such a sight through his new eyes, I am resolved on this. As I look at myself in the silver tube, the objective becomes even more focused to me now, and I thank the stars for the moment of clarity. I only hope that Clyment isn't too angry with me.

The pod capacitors outside in the lab verbally warn me that full megawatt discharge through the ore is imminent. There's one final step left.

Back inside the lab, I set the transference mode to *initiate*. After pressing the smooth, rectangular button, I feel a sudden sense of relief. My bowel spasms have ceased and I sense a cool sweat on my brow. A long-held burden lifted, which perhaps can only come to a man who has done one last thing right and true before he dies. I'm more than thankful for the choosing, but most of all for my life, having lived among friends here at the end.

I have less than five minutes.

"What do you think you're doing?" a voice behind me asks.

I don't even have to turn around. I know who it is. I should've known Jovian would send him for me instead of for Kilraven.

"Lord Alpha. What is it that brings you here?" I ask, putting my hands up in the air.

"Turn around, Doctor. *Slowly*," he says.

"As you wish."

"You and your puny band of roughnecks have walked headfirst into—" He pauses, his nostrils flaring. "Well, let's call it ultimate defeat, for starters."

"Lord Alpha, you and I have *very* different opinions on what we have walked into then," I reply as I simultaneously back away slowly toward the transference chamber.

"Stop!" he says, his hand going to the grip of a blaster at his side.

"I will not."

"What on Earth are you doing?!"

"I'm doing what I should have done with all my talents and all the gifts the universe gave me. I'm saving a life rather than taking one. I don't expect you would understand something like that. All you know is how to destroy."

"You really are mad, Doctor!" he says, drawing his weapon slowly and aiming it at my chest. "You are about to die, and you still cling to one of your scatterbrained schemes?"

"It's more of a hackneyed plan, really."

He laughs at me.

"No doubt hatched with all your lackeys where your faith was planted firmly under the safe ground? But here, above the ground, you've lost. Any promise you've made to them or yourself is in vain. You will not transfer yourself, nor will you escape me."

"That is where you and I have a difference of opinion, Lord Alpha. My faith is still intact. And you have gravely mistaken me if you think I value my own life so much," I say, still backing away from him.

"I told you to stop moving!" he says.

"No, what you told me was to *stop*. And that was a very broad thing to say, seeing as how I'm doing half a dozen things at the moment."

Lord Alpha stops in his tracks. His finger still hovers above the trigger, but he hesitates. He seems strangely interested. Or perhaps the man who seemingly knows no fear is actually scared.

As I draw nearer to the doorway, I can hear the transference pods' second phase of initiation beginning behind me.

Three minutes left.

"I *will* kill you," he says. "And since you value life and I do not, I suggest you start valuing your own!"

"Lord Alpha, it occurs to me that your talents should be better served elsewhere at this moment in time," I say.

"What do you know of my talents?"

"I suspect that the Lord of Men will need your assistance once Kilraven has made his way to the holy chamber, don't you? I mean, after all, Jovian is not a fighting man. And Kilraven will have his vengeance."

"Kilraven will be dealt with shortly, by my own hand!" he says. "But not before you know something vital."

"And what is that, my lord?"

"You know, I'm *surprised*, actually, that you came here by yourself," he says, lowering his gun. "I thought I'd be standing here all night, waiting for you to get the nerve. I'm glad it was here, in this place, so that it's just the two of us. Though I must admit, I might have planned things differently if the decision were mine alone to make."

"I'm glad you didn't get that chance."

Lord Alpha holsters his weapon, then wags a finger at me. If his reputation precedes him truly, he'll want to savor this moment. He'll kill me, perhaps with his bare hands. He's known for enjoying that method above all others.

"You're out of chances, Octavian. This can only end with my hands around your throat," he says, smiling, then licking his lips.

I was right. He's going to gloat. And that's the only error he has to make, because it's all the time I need to get into the chamber door and keep him from Clyment.

"And speaking of chances, Doctor, I'm giving you a final one. Do you have something else you wish to say, or unsay, or undo before I give you that chance?" he asks, smiling.

"No. The chance is mine to take. I've got my original body in the chamber, just behind me."

"What? How?" Lord Alpha asks, his eyes blinking in repetitious, puzzled fury.

"Look there. On the monitor next to you," I say, pointing toward Lord Alpha's left. "And you'll see."

Lord Alpha makes the mistake of listening to me. I turn as fast as I can, through the framework of the chamber, and join Clyment inside.

I shut the door, and instantly I feel the energy in the room coursing through me, rising from my feet up to my ears. The hair on my forearms stands straight up.

The pods are almost ready.

"Open this door!" Lord Alpha shouts through the lab COM. "Damn you, Octavian! Damn you!"

Lord Alpha pulls his gun and fires one round at the porthole. I don't even hear the blast. He and I both know his efforts are completely futile. Once this chamber locks, the only thing getting through is a nuclear blast.

I smile one last time at Lord Alpha through the viewing port and take two seconds to laugh out loud as I give him the middle finger. I so rarely got to do that in my life. The look on his face tells me he knows there's absolutely nothing he can do now, nor will he try. Checking the clock on Clyment's pod, I note we have less than twenty seconds left.

I jump into the second pod and pull it shut.

"Clyment, if there's any way you can hear me or that our minds can share any memories upon you waking, your soul is about to move from your body into mine. And I give it to you gladly. You were like the brother I never was able to have. Live, my friend. *Live!* As if every second is your last, live to make it count! Live for all of us—"

As my lungs fill with a deep breath, there's a blinding flash of light. It's beautiful and terrifying at the same time. All-encompassing. Visible not only with the eyes of the flesh but with the eyes of the soul.

I'm alive!

I gasp for breath, open my eyes, and find that I'm still inside the pod. My vision in this body is quite obstructed. I can't hear anything, either. The breathing feels very shallow. There is a pain in my chest. It is agonizing.

I move this body's hands toward the epigastric region and find exactly what I had hoped—an open wound nearly the size of a man's fist. Reaching in with my fingers, I can feel the slick, warm lining of the stomach.

I've done it. I'm in Clyment's clone. I've saved him!

And now I die.

Thank God.

CHAPTER 26

FRESH EYES

THE LID TO this pod that the Surgeon put me in a few seconds ago pops right open, and I sit up straight, feeling like a million fuckin' credits.

"Damn, boss, how long was I in there? Man alive! Do I feel friggin' fantastic or what?!"

The gunshot blast that went right through the center of my gut, leaving a big ass hole, is gone, but—

"Hey… waitasec. Who'n the hell dressed me in purple?"

I hop from the pod and find the Surgeon's body lying in a stasis tube that is blocking the doorway.

He looks a helluva lot younger, that's for sure.

"Okay, boss, *real* funny. Ya got me. Show's over."

The boss ain't responding.

"Lookit, boss! This thing fixed me up real good!"

I bang on the top of the tube with the bottom of my fists, but the Surgeon don't respond.

"C'mon, I ain't the doc here… How do I turn this thing on? Gimme a clue now, boss."

The damn tube he's in is covered with flashing lights, numbers, and a bunch of squiggly lines and graphs. I ain't never seen nothing like this since the Surgeon woke me up from cryo-imprisonment. Even now, my memory of the ordeal ain't so good… I don't remember it real well. I just remember him bein' there.

"Pull your head in, Cly! C'mon, *think*!"

The digital meter nearest to the tube's center says *EEG*. Well that's a start. The readout also shows a body temperature reading of thirty-six point five degrees.

"Damn! I don't know Celsius."

"*Would you like me to convert that?*"

"What? Who's that?"

"*Ninety-seven point six degrees Fahrenheit, sir.*"

"Who said that?"

"*I am the built-in monitoring and emergency support system for this stasis tube.*"

"Holy hell, didja just talk?"

"*I did, sir.*"

I tap the glass again, but the boss doesn't move.

"How do I get him outta there?"

"*You cannot do that, sir. You are not authorized.*"

"C'mon now, boss, can't leave me here with this damn talking tube!"

Behind me, right on my six, the other pod in the room opens with a blast of cold air.

Maybe I can get the boss in there and save him somehow?

I spin the tube around and push the boss toward the pod and—

"Fuck me. It's *me*!"

That's me lying inside there! The man in there has my face!

I've got a blast wound that's so deep it's gone completely damn near through my chest.

"Am I dead? Is this that part that ever'one talks about? You know, when you look down on your own body? How'm I standin' here? What'd you do to me, boss?!"

"*Transference lab one, main door opening. Please step back.*"

The hatch handle on the door to this room starts a'spinnin' like a goddamn top. I'm guessin' that can only mean one thing—someone I don't wanna be in here with me is comin' in regardless.

Look at that. The body in the pod that looks like me has a gun on him. Get the gun, Cly.

I pull the piece and duck behind the Surgeon's temporary metal crib, taking aim with my sight dead center on the entry.

Three long-ass seconds go by before the handle stops on a dime. The door opens slowly, and when the entryway is all but clear, some well-polished and slick-looking son of a bitch dressed all in black steps into the doorway. He sees my gun, though, and rolls outta sight to his left before I can get the drop on him.

He's a quick lil' squirrel.

"Who th'fuck are you?! Tell me yer name before I blast ya to hell!"

"Are you insane, Octavian?! Put the gun down!" he shouts back.

"I ain't Octavian. He's in here with me! He's on ice right here in this damn tube! Did you put him in there to die, you flarkin' bastard?!"

I fire my gun out the doorway and hit nothin' but air.

"If you aren't Octavian, then who are you?!" he shouts.

"I'm Octavian's man-at-arms, shithead! And 'sides, I don't answer to you no-how!"

I fire another two shots.

"By the holy—! You've been transferred, you imbecile!" he shouts. "Now put down your gun before you kill us both!"

"Oh, right, sure! I put down my gun so you can march in here and shoot me up real good?! I don't think so, pal!"

"In case you haven't noticed, I've not fired on you once!" he says. "I'm *not* trying to kill you!"

The man in black's hand appears in the doorway, holding his gun by the barrel.

"Here. Take this as proof."

In one smooth move, the gun comes sliding across the floor and stops a foot from me. I pick it up and cock the bastard faster than a jackrabbit on a hot date.

"I'm Lord Alpha," the man in black says, standing in the doorway with both hands raised, "and I didn't come here to fight."

"I got this gun aimed right at yer kisser, pal. So, if you can think o' one, gimme a reason not to shoot yer face off."

"Because I too respected Octavian," he says, stepping closer to the pod with the Surgeon's body in it.

"What you know about res'peck?"

"I came here to requite a kindness," he adds, placing a gloved hand onto the pod. "But outside this chamber, all things are monitored closely, and everything I said and did there is now public record. I couldn't get close enough to tell him what was necessary without being heard by my superiors."

"Get yer hand offa that!"

"I will not," he says, looking directly at me.

"Don't make me pop you one, slick dick!"

I got the gun less than an inch away from this bastard's nose. He ain't even blenched even once.

Reminds me of me.

Suddenly, the vital signs on the Surgeon's tube in front o' me flatline and a bright-ass streak of red runs across the length of the display.

"Dammit! His brain activity has stopped!" Lord Alpha shouts.

"What'd you do just now?!"

"I did nothing. Unfortunately, it seems as though I've arrived far too late," he says, tapping a button on the display.

The clear part of the face of the tube becomes solid, and I can no longer see the Surgeon's face.

"There. I've closed his eyes," he says, glaring at me. "As I said, the Surgeon's given his life for you. And his body, too, it seems," he adds, looking me up and down.

"Whatchoo mean his body?"

"You're in Octavian's body right now, you daft *moose,*" he says. "Octavian transferred you before your body died."

"Yeah, right. Nice try, princess."

"Look, you fool. There's your body right there!" he says, pointing to the meat sack that looks like me lying in the open pod.

"Then how come there's two dead bodies, wise ass?"

"Because Octavian transferred your soul into his clone. And then he died inside your body lying there, which in turn killed his original body here," he says, tapping the tube with his index finger.

"No fuckin' way!"

"One can't live without the other. His spirit escaped your dying body, and so then his body died," he says, tapping on the Surgeon's pod again. "Your soul now occupies his cloned body. It was a great sacrifice. One that he didn't have to make."

"No way! No flarkin' fuckin' way! Can't be!"

"Can't? Listen to yourself. Don't you even recognize that you're not speaking with your own voice?"

"Whaddaya mean I'm not sp—"

He's right. The asshole's right.

I look at my hands, and they ain't even mine. They're older, skinnier, paler. How in damnation did I not notice that before?

I reach up and touch my head, and I feel hair where there wasn't none before.

"Yes," Lord Alpha says, "I told you. Transference can be a bit of a shock for those not used to it."

"Boss... Boss transferred me into *him*?"

"Yes. But there's something else going on here... something more curious about all of this. Something else that doesn't make sense."

"Yer right. Why ain't you killed me? That's what really don't make any damn sense!" I holler, putting my gun aim back on Alpha's chest.

"No," Lord Alpha says. "You should still be dead."

"Ain't like you to not kill a rebel like me within 'bout five seconds. Least not accordin' to your reputation."

Lord Alpha walks around the tube, my gun still at his chest and his hands in the air.

"Listen to me. I'm talking about why you're alive," he says, lost in his own damn train of thought. "Something isn't right."

"I'm the guy with the gun, pal. Why you ain't actin' like I won't blast you in half?!"

The fucker ignores me. He walks over to the second pod, rubs his chin, and then starts inspectin' the dead body that looks like me. My gun hand don't shake one bit, though, and I never take my finger offa the trigger.

"Hmm… no markings behind the ear or identifiers on the gumline," he says.

"What the hell're you doin', you crazy mook?!"

"You should be *dead* right now, idiot," he says.

"I dunno 'bout you, but if you can't tell from that distance, I sure looks pretty dead to me."

"No, you ape!" he says. "This was your original body, was it not?"

"Sure as shit it was."

"Then why hasn't your spirit gone? This body has died, so why are you still here?" he asks, pointing a finger at me and cockin' his head to the side like some curious flarkin' puppy dog.

Then, all at once, I'm hit in the guts with emotions I ain't felt in a coon's age. A lightning bolt hits me. Pow! And ever'thing becomes clear as crystal to me. I ain't dead. And the reason I ain't dead's because—

"That musta been a clone of me?"

"Of *course!*" Lord Alpha says, his eyes lightin' up like a damn birthday cake. "How easily I forget."

"I… I was a damned clone all along?!"

"That's obvious now," he says, his eyes going wide like headlamps, "but it seems you did not know?"

"Surgeon never… He never told me."

"It's understandable," he says. "No one ever knows until they see it firsthand. And some of them still choose to think they've actually lost their mind. Funny, isn't it, that someone would rather believe in a complete lie than the truth?"

"And what do you believe in, you sonovabitch?!" I say, cocking the pistol.

I've got the gun aimed square at the man's chest, and His Lordship doesn't budge, not one flarkin' muscle.

"I believed in the Surgeon, too," he says. "The man wanted to save life. It was in his nature. It was his profession because it was inherent in his being. Do not waste what he's given you. And do not take these things at all for granted."

The bastard turns his back on me, as if he's just gonna walk right outta here.

"You got *some* nerve, flarkwad! Where'd you think yer goin'?!"

"My purpose here is finished, though I came too late. Had Octavian given me the opportunity, I might have succeeded in my errand. But now I must leave it and tend to other matters," he says.

"Why? Why ain't you killed me?"

"I told you. I respected Octavian," he says, his back still to me. "He unknowingly saved my life once, many years ago. I was indebted to him. I came to repay him tenfold, but in my approach, he thought I was going to kill him. I suppose it's to be expected."

Lord Alpha extends his left arm, opens up his hand, and there sits a sim-chip in his gloved palm. "Take this," he says, scowling.

"What'sit for?"

"All of the Church's files on Octavian's research," he says. "Everything he accomplished while he was here. He was on the cusp of something new with his research. It was going to outrival what we've done here, even with all the resources of the Prophet... a more beautiful thing, an even more pure thing. It's also loaded with over two million credits."

"You expect me to *believe* all o' yer horseshit?!"

Lord Alpha withdraws his hand and turns to leave.

"I don't require you to," he says. "But actually, another thought has just occurred to me now," he adds, pausing, then turning to face me again. "I suspect based on what I've just witnessed here that Octavian would no longer wish the information destroyed. Perhaps he'd want you to have it. Perhaps. I leave it in your newly seasoned hands."

Lord Alpha extends his hand toward me once again, palm upward with the chip. All mine for the taking.

No, Cly, it's a flarkin' trick.

I go with my gut and knock the chip out of his hand. Then I land a nice one across his smug face with the back of my gun. A bit of blood starts runnin' from his nostril, and he wipes it away with the back of his hand.

"I haven't seen myself bleed in a long time," he says.

"You're the Prophet's second-hand man! The one servin' the unholy mouthpiece who's done all this to us! You ain't even *begun* to bleed, brutha."

I shove the muzzle of the gun into the side of his cheek. He don't shit himself. He don't even blink. This bastard ain't scared of nothin'.

"I don't serve him," Alpha says, looking directly at me. "I protect him. It does not mean I share in all his ideals."

"You even sound like him! A true brain-warshed fuckin' politico!"

"All of us must do something in this world. Whether we live serving ourselves or others or we live merely trying to keep our heads above the water. I do what I must."

"Well ain't that just another nicely wrapped box o'shit!"

"Think what you will. Your opinion certainly does not matter to me," he says.

"That don't excuse you one goddamn second for what you done!"

The mighty lord dressed in black turns his back on me, again.

"I have other more pressing business to attend to at the moment," he says as he steps around the Surgeon's body.

He picks up the chip and sets it on the Surgeon's tomb.

"Whoever you are," he says, glancing over his shoulder, "if you will not take the chip, then I suggest you take this extremely rare opportunity to flee this place. Death has come nearer to you than you will ever know. Consider it a blessing in disguise. Goodbye."

I can't do nothing… I'm stuck. Like glue. My insides are on fire, churnin' like a smelter.

What do I do? What would Octavian do?

In that second, I realize I've got two choices: let this tricky bastard walk out of here and do devil-knows-what to the other lads or put an end to his ass right here, right now.

Do it.

Without no further thought, I say the hell with it and raise my gun and pull the trigger. Before Alpha knows what hit him, he's on the ground face-first, moaning in pain.

"That's the least you deserve!" I say, standing over the man in black. "Look here, consider your slow death a blessing, ya *chump!*"

I pick up the sim-chip and slip it in a pocket at my chest. Hell, if any of us make it out of this shithouse, a few million credits would do me and the boys some real good. Might even buy us a ship fast enough to swing by Tokyo and bring back Terra. If she lives.

Then I pick up Lord Alpha's plasma blaster. It's a newer model, and he won't be needin' it.

I turn back to say my last goodbye to the man himself. The fuckin' man. The man who gave me his own body. The boss. Octavian.

"I ain't never had a better friend. Ya hear me?"

And I wish he knew it.

Then I leave the lord in black to bleed out on the floor. Walking through the lab, to my right I see one big-ass viewport. Lookin' through it, I got me nearly a one-hun'derd-and-eighty-degree view into them vaults. There's nothin' but body after body after body. Damnedest thing I ever laid my eyes on.

There's a terminal in front of me, a large glossy-black holodesk that I'm assumin' is used to access all the data. I take the only seat available and watch these control bots within the vault use their pincers to rotate the cryo-tubes. Like turning hotdogs on a fuckin' spit.

The COM unit attached to my belt goes off with a high-pitched squawk.

"Octavian? Come in, Octavian!"

"I'll be damned! Terra, izzat you?!"

"Yep! What's goin' on? You okay?"

"S'Clyment here. Got shot to hell, but the Surgeon got me fixed up real nice. I'm somewheres in the tower at the moment, takin' in the scenery."

"Cly, if that's you, why in the hell do you sound like Tavian?" she asks.

"Terra, listen, darlin', it ain't good. Surgeon's dead. Transferred me into his body. The crazy sum'bitch. I dunno what's happened to the other fellas… Might all be dead, too."

"Oh my God, not Tavian. Not him!"

"I'm damn sorry, girlie."

"Cly… what about Kilraven?"

"Not seen 'im since I got down here. Was just me and the boss. Don't even know my way outta here, to be honest. I blasted Lord Alpha real good, though. Took his ass right to the ground. Also got me a sim-chip loaded with credits, all the Surgeon's files, and a brand-spankin' new gun offa'im. Where you at anyway, darlin'?"

"Nav tells me I'm over the North Pacific. About thirty minutes from making the delivery."

"Keep on keepin' on, girlie. Real proud of ya. When you get back, I'mma take this here sim-chip and blow half the loot on ya."

"Uh, pretty sure this is a one-way trip, Cly."

She's snifflin'. I think she's cryin'.

"One way for all of us, maybe. Hey, maybe there's something on this chip that'll help us bring ya back?"

Terra goes quiet for a while and I'm counting my heartbeats. *His* heartbeats. Hot damn, I wonder if I'll get smart like the Surgeon was?

"Hey, Cly?"

"Go ahead."

"Nav's just been telling me he can patch into the system and can find you a way out of the tower. Are you anywhere near a terminal or any of the transmission patches?"

"I'm sittin' in front of a giant holodesk right fuckin' now. Can Nav dial into this baby?"

"He says yes, but he needs to know what floor you're on."

"Sublevel... four, Terra. Uh, terminal number three, accordin' to this readout I'm a'lookin' at."

"Got it, Cly. Nav says put the chip into any of the data ports labeled USB eight. Then he can bring up a map to get you out."

I slide the chip into one of several dozen available slots.

"Got it, girlie. Did you?"

"Nav's reading it now. Hang on."

Terra goes as quiet as a little mouse for more than thirty seconds. Feels like a goddamned eternity.

"Hey, Cly? Are you, uh, sitting down?"

"Matter o' fact, I am."

"Nav just... He just blew my friggin' mind. The sim-chip has a lot of encrypted info on it, which he's already crypted and—"

"*Decrypted, Captain.*"

"Shut it, Nav! Listen, Cly, we've got the damned serial numbers for each chipped guard, Warden, and every other SOB in the mines!"

"Wait, wait, wait... hold yer wad, darlin'. What good's that do us?"

"Lookit, Nav says there are two frigates worth of guards and crew still on Eridania. From where you've patched Nav in, he can access every one of their serial numbers in cryo-stasis and stop their life support!"

"Mother o' Moses, he can do that?!"

"He says Corvus saw to it."

"So, you're sayin' Nav can pull the plug on all of them clowns?"

"Four thousand four hundred and ninety-one clowns, to be exact."

"Nav, shut it! That's right, Cly. Nav can do the hard part. You'll just have to push the button."

"Fuck me. Sounds like I'm the one with th' hard part, darlin'."

"Hot damn, we can free the mines, Cly! Once and for all! They'll drop like flies! And our sisters and brothers can come home!"

Brothers. I had me a baby brother once.

My mama named him Tarsus. Can't even remember now if that was his right name or not. I just always called him Tars. It was me and him, him and me. Tars and Cly. What a team we was. Raised together in Triangle City.

"Cly? You still there?"

I taught him how to shoot. Even how to make his own guns. He was a brash one, though. Lost touch with him after he left on some fuckin' crusade to find the flarkin' bastard that killed our folks. They was just mindin' their own business, out on a trading run. Got shot in the back by a bunch of mercenaries en route to Neo York. Tarsy left when he was only seventeen. I told him not to go, then beat his ass just to keep him from actually doin' it. 'Course he wasn't gonna listen.

"Cly?! Are you there?!"

The mornin' he packed his bag, I gave him the first gun I ever restored and modded. A Rogers and Spencer made back in the day when they called the city New York. Damn thing was accurate as hell, and the .44-caliber shells were still right easy to find down in Triangle.

After that, I never saw Tars again. When I came to the big city in 2094 lookin' for him, I found not one damn trace that he'd ever even made it here. All word I could find of him was that he was shipped off to the mines. From there on in, I had my flarkin' resolve. I knew if I couldn't take the Church down, I'd keep on makin' my guns for the rebels that damn well could.

"Damn you, Cly! Where are you?!"

"Sorry, darlin'… I was just thinkin'. Tell Nav to do his thing. Then tell me what I gotta do."

"He's already done it, Cly. We got all the serial numbers sent to the computer. All you have to do is press the red button labeled *stasis stabilizer*. Then enter the code to start the sequence."

"Done. But there's three separate lines here, darlin'!"

"The first string is four, three, zero."

"Got it."

"Then four, seven, zero."

"Yep."

"Finally, seven, four, seven, three, six."

"Gotcha."

"Now the *Romeo* button, Cly."

"This one is for you, Tars. Wherever you are, this one's for you, brutha."

I close my eyes and press the red button.

"It's done. It's done, Trash."

The holodesk starts showing diagrams all around me, just like the one on Octavian's cryo-tube. At first, they appear by the dozen, then by the hundreds. Each one pops up in a sequence, with a number showing the vital signs as *stable*. There's a noise, too, a damn ugly racket… I guess it's a warnin'?

"Yay-hoo! Holy *cripes*! You did it, Cly!"

"Ain't nothing to celebrate, darlin'."

I expect to hear men screamin' any second now. But when the noise stops, all that happens is that the vitals for each tube silently switch from *stable* to *deceased*. There ain't no wailing. No screechin' or cryin'… no clawing or fightin'. Just a bunch of people who lived way longer than they shoulda passing on into the next life. I sure hope it's damn better to them than this one has been to us.

I get my ass up and head toward the lab. Might as well see if Lord Alpha's last moments are over. He oughta be a witness to these events, seein' as how he's the ignorant sum'bitch who gave me the damn chip.

Bet the dumbass had no flarkin' clue those codes were on there.

I turn the corner, and in front of the transference chamber, right where

I left the boss, I find the slippery bastard ain't lying on the floor where I left him. There's only a blood trail and pieces of his armor left behind.

"Where'n the hell did his black ass go?"

CHAPTER 27

FAMILY TIES

"ELISABETH, FORGIVE ME... I've come so late."

I place the golden band back on my wife's finger, and the woman who looks nothing like her spits in my direction. I stand to my feet and wipe away hot tears.

"I'm sorry... I didn't mean for this. I know the three of you can't hear me, but it's *me*. It's Thaniel. I *never* stopped thinking of you. Not *once*. Every day I stayed alive in the hope that I would one day be able to take revenge on those responsible for taking you from me. Now that day's here, and... I'm afraid that I can't do anything for you. I've come this far only to have to say goodbye again. I know that Jovian will probably kill us all. Please forgive me. Please, forgive me?"

I kiss each one of them on the forehead. The two women on the right reach for me, and I kiss their hands as well.

"Something to remember me by," I say, giving them each one of three tokens from my knapsack, my fingers wrapping around theirs. "Hold it dear to your chest and think of me. Don't let go. Never let go!"

I take a moment to say a prayer in my head. The words I have are for any god that's listening. A few more really deep breaths and I draw my guns again. As I leave the horror that I've just witnessed behind me, my tears dry, and I close the door to room A26. I switch my belt COM back on and walk directly across the hall to find an already open elevator. Somehow, it's a *different* elevator than before. It's more ornate on the exterior, and looking within, I find it's completely solid and sealed on the inside. When I step inside, the door closes behind me, and suddenly a voice comes from a COM above my head.

"Greetings, Kilraven," the voice says. "You will find me on floor two hundred and seventeen. Please make your way here quickly, for we have many things to talk about, and my time is invaluable."

The elevator moves of its own volition, and I take the moment to make sure my guns are still locked and loaded.

"*Kilraven, you there?*" asks a voice from the COM.

"I'm here, Terra. Are you alright?"

"*Doin' great, spacehead,*" she says. "*I'm less than thirty minutes from ground zero. You'd better do what you gotta do, and do it fast!*"

"Roger that. When London Bridge is falling down, send me a confirmation?"

"*London who?*" she asks.

"Just send me a signal."

"*If I make it out of the ship in time, I'll sing your favorite fuckin' tune!*" she says.

"Sounds like a deal."

"*According to Nav, I'll be parachuting not far from the coastline… Kinuta Park somewhere… I may lose ya after that.*"

"Roger that, Terra. And good luck."

Terra doesn't reply, and ten seconds later the elevator door opens ominously. The hallway before me is nearly dark, except for a repetitive gleaming of a soft light on the edges of various dark shapes at my eye level. They're the shapes of men. Men wearing armor.

Stepping out of the lift slowly, I ascertain that I'm at the end of a long hallway. Luckily there's only one way for me to go—to the right. My eyes adjust to the black, and I find that I'm facing a garrison of sentries lined up in the most pristine formation. None of them budge or make a sound. They aren't even readying their weapons.

At the end of the hall, not more than fifty meters in front of me, stands a set of massive black doors. It looks like the main gate of a medieval castle, or so I imagine. I move through the army of toy soldiers, unhindered, and come to the door that at first seemed black from a distance. Up close it's all gilded and shimmering, like blackened copper. The left door opens silently when I'm only a few feet away.

After I enter, there's a silence within that's deafening, as if the room itself were a vacuum. The doorway closes behind me and reseals itself by some method unfamiliar. It looks like an expanding foam at first, quickly transformed thereafter into a kind of rubberized material. The room is dimly lit, and it reeks of ore and formaldehyde. Tracing the edges of the room, I get the distinct feeling that I'm now part of a museum. *His* museum.

On the opposite side of the room from me rests a large collection of objects, items of all kinds: staves and swords, animal horns and spears, tapestries and paintings. But not a single thing is touching the walls, which are covered in the same gray metal throughout. It's a substance that I'd recognize anywhere—*eridanium*.

There are no visible windows here. Toward the left corner of the room sits a large desk made of a single block of polished obsidian. The power core in the center of the desk itself gives the entire space a reddish glow all around, and it's surrounded by moving diagrams of multicolored blue and green lights. And behind the desk I can see a seated figure, his back to me. A head full of white hair seems almost dyed red by the strange light of the room.

Stepping toward the desk slowly, I take caution, treading as lightly as I can. But my footsteps still manage to pound against the smooth floor, as though even they choose to betray me in his presence. Moving closer, I pull my guns and cock them, and the seated figure remains motionless.

"Turn around and get up, you goddamned son of a bitch."

"Ah yes, the prodigal son returns to me," he says.

"Only so that I can kill you."

"I think not. Not today, anyway."

The chair turns around, without a sound, and the shock of what I see hits me like a bullet in the back. His face! My god, his face!

"*Iyov*?!"

"I thought you might prefer this visage, Kilraven." he says, smiling. "Or do you prefer Madzimure?"

He's dressed meekly. A heavy, dark cloak covers his shoulders and neck, and underneath is a brown robe tied at the waist with a bit of rope. His hair is actually graying instead of white, and it seems a much fuller mane than it was on the man whom I knew. Even the wrinkles on his face seem less defined, and his voice not quite as deep or heavy-laden.

"Did you murder him?"

"Murder? That word implies an unlawful killing. But were I to have done so, I would have been right to—"

"Did you murder him?!"

"Of course not!" Jovian says, almost growling and tapping his fingers on the armrests of what I see now to be some sort of floating seat.

"During the dark years, I made this clone of Jobius."

"Jobius?"

"Oh, do pardon me. Of Iyov. In the decades since your departure, some rather inept servants of mine misplaced his body among the myriad of vaults. Old files, as it were. Many of the original transfers can still prove... difficult to locate. I used his DNA, recently obtained from the old man's finger, to find the body and create this version you see before you," he says, grinning and looking most pleased with himself.

"His finger?"

"Yes," he replies, tugging at a string from around his neck. Then, coming out of the opening of his cloak, he holds up a hewn finger sewn into the braid of the necklace.

"*Voilà!*"

"Is he still alive?" I ask.

"Yes, though he is due for execution within the week."

"Why? Why him?"

"Because he was my brother. Born seemingly into this world only to thwart me," he says, smiling. "He was among the first whom I sent to the mines for holy service. And he certainly was not going to be needing this face anymore, now was he?"

"How can you smile, you... you *monster*?!"

"Monster? Oh *please*," he says, frowning mockingly. "Have you come all this way only to insult me with words befitting a tale told only to scare children?"

I step closer toward the desk and aim both of my pistols at the Prophet's head. "Get out from behind there, with your hands up. Do it *now!*"

"Very well. I have no weapons," he says, rising from his seat and holding his hands up at his sides.

"I want you to tell me right now why you've done all this!"

"Why I have done what, exactly?" he asks, sounding aggrieved.

I put the barrels of both guns in the center of his chest. "Tell me *why*, damn you! You owe me that much!"

"You are the one who owes *me*, Kilraven. There is a debt which is owed. You have had thirty years of life because I spared you. The Council and the Church would suffer nothing less than to have their way at that time… and you would have joined your crew in death, were if not for me."

"Were it not for *you*?!"

"They were going to kill you, had I not intervened."

"You're deluded!"

"Am I? Then why do I find that fact is so much more fun than fiction is? The truth is, they used my intel to create a charade, Kilraven, one which supported the idea, with sufficient evidence, that you and your squad stole the transference tech directly from us. That which was given to us by divine right."

"Who's us?"

"The Brethren. My order."

"Well, how fucking *noble* of you, Jovian," I say, pushing the barrels harder into his chest. "Killed, if not for you? You sent me to die while you kept Elisabeth trapped here in a living death!"

"But you did not die. Here you stand. I saved you both."

"Tell me why I shouldn't kill you! For all that you've done and the things you might do!"

"Kill me?" he asks. "You cannot do that, Thaniel. Surely you recognize the substance in the room? Look around you."

"I know what it is," I say, never once taking my eyes off him.

"Yes," he says, smiling, "entirely covered in eridanium. If you shoot me now, my soul will remain here until it can be transferred again. You know this. Oh, do kill us both, if you must. They will only bring us back."

"You lie."

"*Tsk tsk tsk*," he says, backing away from the guns. "Not to you, my friend. And not today."

"Why did you let me return, then? Do you know how many people have died so that I could stand here?!"

"Put the guns down already, Kilraven," he says, lowering his hands. "You are not going to shoot anyone. Deep down you know that you do not really even want to. Who would you be without me?"

"You're nothing to me anymore, Jovian."

The Prophet laughs and scratches the side of his cheek. "If that were true, then you would say it like you meant it," he says, grinning and staring directly into my eyes. "And it would be most interesting to hear you say those words with conviction. Yet here you stand, having come further than any other... only to what end? To point guns in my face and ask questions to which you already have the answers?"

"What do you mean by that?"

"The answers to the questions you so desperately ask, and have undoubtedly asked yourself over the years, are right in front of you. They have always been right in front of you."

"Define *they*."

"I would have thought the most obvious of which would be clear to you by now. The reason is twofold. The first of them being, simply, your family. They have now become *my* family."

"You think *my* family is *your* family?"

"Yes. Who has watched them now for decades? Who has cared for them but me? I have them completely in the palm of my hand. And as you have now seen, just before you entered this chamber, my hands are capable of delivering a fate worse than death."

"You no longer control their fates."

"Is that so?" he asks, laughing. "Well, *you* shall be the one who determines their fate, should you not cease this ridiculous bravado."

"You think this is *bravado*?!"

"I asked you to put the guns down," he says slowly and gravely.

357

"And then what?"

"And then… talk with me."

I don't hesitate to uncock both guns. The Prophet bites his lower lip, as if he were almost worried for a moment that my decision could have been otherwise. Then I slowly set the guns down on the edge of the desk so they remain just within my reach, my eyes affixed to Jovian's.

"Excellent!" he says, laughing quietly.

"Start talking, Prophet."

"You asked me *why*, Kilraven," he says, pacing the floor behind the desk. "It is both the essential and the eternal question, is it not? Why. Why indeed."

"I didn't come all the way here for a lesson in semantics or to hear a self-righteous soliloquy. I want truth. Are you even capable of giving it to me?"

Jovian pauses. Then, taking a very deep breath, he folds his hands in front of his face as if he might say a prayer.

"Do you remember when I was on the *Grimalkin*? The ship where we first met? Search back through the dusty cobwebs of your stupefied mind, Kilraven. Do you remember why I was there?"

"You were a chaplain… a holy man. I suppose you were there for support. You were… just doing a job, like everybody else. A nobody."

"A nobody?" Jovian asks, raising his eyebrows.

For a moment he seems sad, as if all the things he's done have been nothing more than a twisted attempt to prove his own worth, either to me or to himself.

"Yes," he says, "I was a holy man and intended at the onset of my career to be an ambassador. But I was not there of my own choosing, at least not at that juncture. You see, my father forced my hand, and I was a virtuous son who obeyed his father in all things. But when I arrived onboard, I discovered something I did not anticipate in my wildest imaginings. Something I did not realize that I even wanted… something that I would possess, forever, if I could. I found a love."

"You *found* love?"

"Yes. In Elisabeth," he says.

Her name coming from his lips causes my heart to skip a beat, and I catch my breath.

"Not… Not my Elisabeth!"

"Yes."

"You were in love? You were *in* love with her?!"

"Yes. I love her still. You did not see it then, Kilraven, and you do not see it now," he says, scowling.

"You're a liar without shame. Elisabeth didn't even know you then!"

"*Ah*, but she did!" he says, putting his hands behind his back. "She and I were close, Kilraven. One might even say we were very close, for a time. You may remember in those days that chaplains were all but forbidden to consort with female officers without either another officer or counsel present. But I could not help it… She took so much joy in hiding with me in the observation deck between our shifts. And then *you* stepped onboard and into both of our lives. *You*, with all your proud heroics and primalism, strutting around as if the right to stand upon the bridge had been bred into you. And then it was if I had died. I might as well have ceased to exist. There was a light that she had in her eyes!" he says, pounding a closed fist upon the desk. "And I saw that light dim when you took it for your own!"

"Listen to yourself! I took nothing! Her love was a gift given to me, Jovian!"

"You and I differ little in this regard," the Prophet says, sighing. "I too have taken nothing, but I have also given. All I have done is give. She has received the benefaction of eternal life through transference many times over."

"Eternal life?! What you've done is deny her death! Souls are not your toys. Our souls and our bodies are meant to be as one… They're united! We're ensouled bodies and bodied souls!"

"But death rips that union asunder. And it is because there is a special place within the recesses of my heart, which I have always reserved for her, that no one else on this planet has received such careful ministration."

"So that's it, then? All this hell has been over a woman who wouldn't have you or that you couldn't have? All of this madness, for what? For what?! Unrequited love?!"

"Not entirely," he says, continuing to pace back and forth. "I told you, the reason was twofold. All you had to do was look in a mirror for the second half to present itself."

"A mirror?"

"Tell me, Kilraven, in all the years, did you ever once stop to think about why you were transferred into Barrabas Madzimure? Did you? The most infamous of thieves? The prince of thieves?"

"It wasn't him you wanted. It was *me*."

"This could not be further from the truth. No one ever told you what he stole, did they?"

"I've heard all the stories, Jovian, many times. What does it matter now what he took?"

"I am not sure that anyone remembers the *real* story. No one left alive, anyway. Yes, no one except me and maybe you… and him."

"You can't trick me. I have possessed my soul. I know beyond any doubt that the spirit in me is Kilraven. And I have *nothing* left of Madzimure in me."

"Wrong again, my friend. You have his brain tissue. The heart in your chest, the one pumping the life-giving blood through your veins… it too belongs to the Madzimurian."

"So… that's it. There's something inside of me you need. Information, right? Something you wanna try and dig out?"

I pick up my guns again, and Jovian exhales heavily through his nostrils. Then he gracefully takes a seat once more behind the desk.

"There is a story, Kilraven. Perhaps you have heard fragments of it throughout the years. Madzimure undeniably stole many things. But once, as the story goes, he stole something far beyond the wealth of this world. And though it has taken longer than I would have liked, I have proven this story to be true, at least in part. Would you like to know *what* it is?"

"Enlighten me, Jovian, before one of the bullets in my gun fucks your brain tissue."

"Quaint," he says, smiling. "To the public at large, Madzimure was a fanatic. A freak, even. Obsessed with augmented and virtual reality. A man living in a dream world. Off-world more often than not. But this does not negate the fact that he excelled at his vocation. The man had a gift. Like everyone else my brethren thought he was simply, for lack of a better term, *mad*."

"And what did you believe?"

"Seeing is believing, my friend. Over the years, I have managed to piece together details of several of his more *outlandish* stories into one semi-coherent narrative. Thus, I discovered the whereabouts of the staff of Moses in the spring of last year."

"The what?"

"It is a magic rod, Kilraven. A most powerful artifact leapt straight from the pages of the *Codex Amiatinus*. Have you heard of it?"

"No. Maybe. I mean, I don't know... I've some vague memory of it. I've certainly never *seen* a copy."

"I would have thought not. An ancient book of great supremacy... Men sculpted the days of their lives by it and worshipped the deity that walked and breathed within the pages of its latter half. The future, even unto the ending of the world itself, was foretold to its followers! But I know something now which no one left alive today knows about the book. Something that, perhaps, no one has ever known."

"Again, enlighten me."

"The book was not written *here*... not on Earth."

"So? Who gives a shit about some alien book?!"

"Men like you. Men seeking answers. Those who seek life beyond this life. And the book was not written by aliens. It was written by *men*."

"So, what are you saying exactly? That there's more of us out there? Human beings on other planets?"

"After what you have seen, is that so hard for you to believe?"

"No. Human life is native to Earth... It *started* on Earth. If there's any men left on Fornax, it's because they came from Earth. And the men who are on Eridania were sent from Earth."

"Then I pose to you this very pertinent question, Kilraven: why then did I uncover the staff on Eridania?"

My hands begin to sweat, and I can no longer mask the acute sense of nausea I'm feeling or the trepidation that Jovian's words have inserted into my heart and mind. My legs nearly give way from underneath me, and I surprisingly fall ass-backward into the chair opposite of Jovian.

"Yes. Even now I see it written across your face… The lingering wonder… It grows into a crawling doubt before rising finally to a foothold of dread."

"And it was Madzimure who—"

I pause, finding it suddenly hard to swallow the saliva building in my mouth. "It was Madzimure that led you to this staff?"

"There it lay, straight from the pages of a *human* history, on a planet far from ours!"

"H… How?"

"Madzimure was *there*. He was on Fornax before you, Kilraven."

"On the *Bermuda*?"

"No, he left among the earlier vessels. A stowaway, with no more than one or two companions onboard, from what I could gather. And he, like me, in his beginning was also a chaplain. However, his core beliefs did not align with those of the Church, and so he was discharged, without honor."

"So, you mean you *knew* him then?"

"Yes… and no. There is no record of Madzimure returning to Earth because, technically, he never left. How he managed to achieve what he did right under the nose of the entire fleet still escapes me. But the magnitude of his discovery was later revealed to me upon his return, at which time my father had him arrested and imprisoned. During those interrogations, I uncovered several more pieces of the great mystery. The remains which you saw in the Fornaxian synagogue? Do you recall them?"

"Yes."

"Madzimure discovered them first, Kilraven! They were of an early people called the Nephilim. A potentially half-human, half-seraphic race whom I now have evidence to support as the creators of transference. Through their empyrean intellect they became demiurges or, if you will, *gods* of preservation.

"Gods?"

"Indeed. That is why you found their technology pristine and undisturbed. At some point in time which is still unclear, I believe the entire race of Nephilim departed Fornax. A mass exodus. Then, perhaps as fate willed it, they came upon Eridania and established a *new* order there amongst the human population. But as described in this book, the god of that galaxy was slighted by their attempt to rival his power. So, he in turn showed forth his power through the staff, as wielded by Moses's predecessor... and he created a mighty torrent of roaring waters which wiped the Nephilim off the face of Eridania!"

"No, I... I don't believe it," I say, rising from the chair. I take a step back, swallowing the stifling lump in my neck.

"Your belief is not imperative. You *believed* you were on Eridania to mine the ore," Jovian says, smiling. "And you were. But the lion's share of my wardens served another purpose. Something else entirely. Why do you suppose you and your companions took the mine so easily? Hmm? Did you *really* think that I would have allowed such a victory?"

My eyes begin to water profusely as my hands go numb. The triggers of my guns seem to shrink away into my very fingertips. I release my grip on both pistols and they clatter across the smooth black floor.

"The wardens uncovered *tombs*, Kilraven... tombs in the Kasmodian Desert! Catacombs of patriarchs belonging to a bygone faith never proven factual here on Earth. Patriarchs of this book!"

I vomit for the first time in a long time. Jovian laughs through his nose, and my heart pounds inside of my chest, as though it were about to crack my rib cage wide open.

"Your reaction is not unlike mine was at first."

"Oh *God*," I say, spitting more of my sick onto the floor.

"I have toiled, Kilraven. Toiled for decades."

"You've... *You've* toiled?!"

"Yes. Tirelessly up until now, for even shreds of proof... however *minute* they might later prove to be. The staff I told you of is only one such validation. And there it lies," he says, pointing toward a spear-like baton of gleaming crystal floating in the corner of the room.

I'm almost mesmerized, euphoric even, after the cessation of my bodily episode. I spit out what's left of my regurgitation and stumble over to the staff. It's hovering seemingly of its own accord, like nearly everything else in the room, inside a stasis field of pale light. A singular, solid carving of a dark-blue gemstone makes up its entirety.

"It's... It's beautiful."

"See if you can pick it up. It will not harm you. Go on," Jovian says quietly.

As I take the blue wonder in my hands, I'm surprised by its heaviness. Although at first it seemed as if it might have been weightless, it's strangely burdensome.

"The staff has *powers*, Kilraven!"

"Powers?"

"Yes. And powers are *proof*. And now that I have such proof, I must rid the world of it and all evidence of its existence. But I have been unable to destroy the staff by any mechanisms we currently have at our disposal."

"And what exactly does all this have to do with me?" I ask, releasing the staff back into its rightful place.

"Not with *you*."

A light bulb switches on in my mind, and I laugh out loud, almost to myself, as Jovian's plan is suddenly laid out before me.

"I should've known," I say, turning over my shoulder and glancing back at him. "I should've known it was him that you wanted."

"Do not chastise yourself for this. I did not honestly expect that you would come to this conclusion of your own faculties. Over the encumbering years I have come to understand that even the terribly sagacious can find it grueling to see past their own noses."

"And now… now that I do see… what is it that Madzimure can supposedly do for you?" I ask, walking back toward the desk.

"Madzimure has but one purpose left to achieve. But he has proved to be… an *aberrant* to transference. His soul, housed in your native body, does not stir. It will not wake, nor will it expire."

"What do you mean he doesn't wake?"

"I have my suspicions as to *why*, though it is mostly conjecture for my part. As you have observed and experienced firsthand, I no longer have any real enemies, or at least none who have power over me within the confines of the world. Nevertheless, I must cede to the possibility, however implausible, that Madzimure does not wake because the god of the book wills it so."

"He… He defies you!" I say with a laugh.

"No. He *rebukes* me. A marked difference. Yet he does not block me at every turn. Seeing as how I have found the staff and the tombs, I take these as an indication that he desires to make himself known. Even more wonders have been uncovered on Eridania, some of which I have erased and some of which I have not. But the one thing I seek most still eludes me!"

"The book itself."

"Exactly!" he says, rising from his chair with a feverish look of frenzy upon his face. "I believe Madzimure found the book. Unfortunately, this knowledge came to me quite late, and it is why I have been compelled to go to such great lengths to bring you back home in one piece. And so, finally, at the last, right here I have you," he says, pointing a finger at the middle of my forehead. "And in the cortex of your brain, in the hidden layers of this neural network… *there* lies the key!"

"If all that you've told me's true, then why do you even need the damn book?" I ask, and Jovian recoils.

"Since Madzimure continues to sleep so very soundly, I suspect that this god has revealed to him information which is pertinent to himself," Jovian says, pacing the floor while holding his chin. "And from what more I have learned of this god, he seeks to create an alignment with his own supposed creation. But his overall purpose remains… unclear. If he would usurp the authority which I have struggled so hard to establish, I cannot abide that. Consequently, if this god is ever to speak to men, I would have him speak to me directly. And if this god would choose to walk among men, I would have him form a union with me."

"And what would you form with me now? The same union? Will you show me the same courtesy you've shown Elisabeth? The same love?"

"Love as we know it is conditional. Therefore, it is not real love. It is an arrant delusion, cultivated between fools since the dawn of time. But there is a true intimacy, Kilraven! One which draws its life between the creator of the soul and its owner. At first, I believed only one such creator existed… a mother. For *she* is the creator of her progeny's soul, is she not?"

"For all your knowledge, such love and creation is still beyond your grasp."

"Perhaps you are right. But according to this book, there is another author and higher paramour of the spirit. And it is with him I must speak, if he truly exists. Besides, are not all things that are worth doing done for such a love? Did our very mothers not place grave risk on the love they bore our fathers when they brought us, their sons, into the world?"

"You're *sick*, Jovian. You don't know what love is. You're nothing more than a man… a man who got lucky. You were at the right place at the right time. You're not a god."

"Well, tell me now, where is this god?" Jovian asks, looking around the room as if he expects him to appear. "Or where are *the* gods? They have failed to intervene or to manifest themselves. Promises made by gods who do not keep them results in only one clear and inevitable conclusion: that they are *not* gods. Where are they, Kilraven? Hmm? Surely, I love humanity no less than they, would you not agree?"

"No, Jovian. You've… You've perverted it. There's not even a hint of love in your voice now when you speak of Elisabeth or of any of these things!"

"Oh, but there is!" he says, his eyes growing wide. "You just choose not to hear it. I love her even still, to some degree."

"Look at what your so-called love has done to her! She's a *shell*, Jovian! A living corpse! She's unable to speak or see! And you say you *love* her? No, no… what love may've been in you has totally departed!"

"Thaniel, *please*. I am far above that now," he says, pouting his lips. "And that which is passed is past. So, let us now put all things to rest that would hinder our future together. You can be my right hand. I could share this power of the book with you. It would belong to me, and the peoples of the world will embrace you again at my bidding."

"Embrace me?"

"No more *Barrabas*," he says, drawing near to me and placing a hand on my shoulder.

For a moment, I believe him. The voice… the face… it's all coming from my dear friend. Iyov never lied to me. He was the voice of reason on days when madness itself took shape and walked inside the corridors of my mind. Iyov would've claimed me as his son, if I had let him. In a way, I *was* his son.

"Give me the body of Madzimure, willingly, and everything can be as it was for you," he whispers in my ear. "Only I can give you your life back, Kilraven."

I look directly into Jovian's eyes and I don't see Iyov anymore. The wells of Jovian's soul have darkened, and the light in them is extinguished by the spirit of a madman living within the shell before me. He's no more Iyov than I am.

"You took from me what didn't belong to you in the first place, and now, you offer me what isn't yours to give, not even in the slightest."

"Why do you persist in this train of thought? I took nothing from you," he replies, blinking repeatedly as though my words have hurt him. "Do you not see that I give *so* much? And I am prepared to give further. As such, I have an incomparable gift especially for you."

"A gift? You'd give *me* a gift?"

"Come. Walk with me," he says, putting his arm around my shoulder.

We begin treading the circumference of the domed room, toward Jovian's mound of treasure. From the corner of my eye I can see him smiling, as if all the history between us no longer mattered.

"Look at what I have accomplished," he says, pointing to a chalice filled with glistening trinkets. "Now, you also have seen the great city, Kilraven," he says. "Look at the greatness of man. There is peace and order, and most importantly there is life eternal for all those who seek it of me," he adds, grabbing my arm and still smiling with the face of my companion.

"Eternal life…"

"Yes, Thaniel. I want you to have this life, too!" he says, stopping in his tracks and extending his hand toward a glittering prize. Then, picking up a sheathed dagger floating alone within an orb-shaped energy field, Jovian holds it up directly in front of my eyes.

"From Eridania. The dagger of an ancient paladin named Rostam," he says, removing the knife halfway from its sheath.

The blade is astonishing to look upon, and the sound of its unsheathing is a song I've never heard before, sublime beyond compare. The handle is in the shape of a horse's head, and the precious green stones dotting the hilt and scabbard sparkle, as if they're actually capable of creating their very own unique luster.

"It is beyond price. Almost unbreakable and over two thousand years old," Jovian says, sheathing the blade.

My mind races. I think of Tarsil and his green eyes. I wonder what

Cunningham is doing right now. I think of the sacrifice that Verdauga made for Iyov. I think of Elisabeth and the decades of torture she has had to endure. I think of Terra in this moment. I wonder if her hands are sweating. She was a much better soldier than I ever expected. Better than I was, anyway. I think of Nav and the annoying shit he must be saying to her.

"Do you accept this gift?" Jovian asks, extending the knife to me.

I think of Octavian and Clyment and their bravery on the steps of the tower. I think of the blood that Ortiz and the others have shed. And I think of Corvus... my mother. I think about how she managed to outsmart the grand prognosticator himself, the great gray shrike who's standing only three feet away from me. I think of how he won't allow that again.

But then... I think of something else. A new thought. I think of *using* Jovian. I could use him to bring them all back. He could do it, if he wanted. Couldn't he? He could make things right again.

"My friend, are you needed elsewhere?" Jovian asks, looking around the room as if I'd been talking to someone else. "What other place do you belong, if not here, with me and with your family?"

The illusion the Prophet's words created in my mind dissolves in an instant when a trumpet blast of sound comes from the COM unit on my belt. It's Terra, and she's laughing. There's a raucous barrage, a symphony of explosions, and I know she's done it. The tower in Tokyo is falling.

"How's that for a signal?! Tell the Prophet I said happy fuckin' trails, ya mook!" Terra hollers, still laughing.

I smile and mute the COM, turning once more to Jovian. And I no longer see the friendly face of Iyov.

"To your credit, you are cunning. But you should know I'm well aware of all your contingency plans, Jovian."

The Prophet steps back from me several paces, slowly.

"That sound you just heard?" I ask. "That's the sound of the backup site you kept for yourself in Neo Tokyo. It's crumbling to the ground."

"An excellent theory," he says, smiling. "But the tower there has a garrison of over two thousand of my keenest disciples, ready to fight and die for their lord. Besides, only a nuclear reaction with enough eridanium could suffice to do any such damage, and you could hardly have—"

"And what exactly did you think I was doing on the mines, Jovian?"

The Prophet takes a single step backward, his overconfident eyes filling with uncertainty.

"Impossible," he whispers. "Even if you did get any off the planet, synthesizing it would take years, and you… you could not have done so on Eridania."

"I didn't synthesize it, Jovian. *You* did. In the cores of your little golden ship."

The triumph and power in Jovian's face erodes in a nanosecond, and then the computer at his desk interrupts us at the perfect moment.

"*Your lordship, I have an incoming message of the highest priority. Level 1 clearance.*"

"Yes?" Jovian asks.

"*Your eminence, the Tower of Peace in Neo Tokyo has… My lord it seems it has—*"

"What is it? Out with it!" Jovian shouts.

"*The tower itself still remains standing, despite a small fighter managing to break through the air defenses. We cannot say for certain how, but an unidentifiable reaction has depleted the tower's ore shielding. Transference at this location is… well, it's no longer possible, sir!*"

"There it is, Prophet. Do you feel it? The crashing walls of your false sanctuary reverberating around you?"

Jovian closes his eyes and takes a deep breath. Then, slithering back toward me as though he were gliding on air, the Prophet draws the ancient dagger from its sheath and drives it through the right side of my chest, up and under the bottom of my rib cage.

I fall to the ground in slow motion, the blinding pain of my death gripping me like steel fingers.

"Look! Look what you made me do!" Jovian shouts, leaning closely to me. "You forced my hand! Now, I am going to leave the knife right there," he says, tapping once on the hilt of the blade with his long fingernail.

"Bastard!" I squall and groan, gasping in so deeply that the pain of the breathing is almost worse than the wound.

"Yes. Your lung has been punctured, Kilraven. Not fatal, mind you, at least until the blade is removed. You can continue drawing breath a little while longer while I get to put on a show for you. How about that? Then you can die in that filthy skin before I transfer you! You think you have won?! You have won nothing!"

"My lord, are you there?"

"Yes. Alert Lord Alpha immediately!" he snarls at the computer, rushing to his desk and clambering at various buttons and keys on the surface. A schematic of light appears above the desk, and I can see a holographic image of the three women in room A26. A devious and cruel smile spreads across Jovian's face as his finger hovers above a flashing red button on the desk.

"Jovian, don't!"

"Remember that *you* did this to them, Kilraven."

Jovian presses the button, and I watch helplessly as a massive explosion decimates the entire room, engulfing it in white flame before the video footage disappears entirely.

I'm sorry, my love. I'm sorry.

The entire Tower ebbs and flows from the explosion. The blast must've been a pure fusion tactical nuke. I figured the Prophet wouldn't take any chances. In fact, I counted on it.

"You have failed, Kilraven!" Jovian shrieks, rushing back to my side. "And now the souls of your family will vanish into the ether, whither they will go! Into *nothingness!*"

The Prophet spits in my face at his last words, and I can feel blood flowing into my lung. It's hot and heavy, as though it were a drum filling with oil.

I can't be certain as to why, but all I can do is laugh. The laugh starts small at first, like a wheezing cough, and though it's painful, it builds boisterously until I laugh so fell and so fey that I can only laugh even harder at the crazed sound of it. The echo swells and fills the chamber with hysteria. Jovian's face is a twisted wrenching of flesh, his eyes aflame and his mouth quivering.

"This is *funny* to you?!" he asks, his voice at a shrilled pitch.

"It is," I reply as Jovian shoves a clenched fist in my face.

"And what have you now, Kilraven? Who do you have left? No one! Nothing! Now you are utterly alone, just as I am!"

I begin to crawl back toward the desk, still laughing, and Jovian follows me all the way.

"Look at you, Kilraven. Just look at what you have become," he whispers. "Nothing. Less than nothing. Crawling on your belly like a reptile."

As I reach the Prophet's desk, I go for my guns while Jovian stands behind me, breathing heavily.

"Are you still attempting to triumph?" he asks. "Such privilege was given to you... and so much more was to be given. And now? Wasted. Take your primitive weaponry then, you deplorable grunt!"

Jovian kicks the pistols with a sweep of his leg, and both go spinning, stopping only a few feet from my reach. A second later, the main door of the chamber opens with a garish boom, and a man dressed entirely in black steps in. He's pulling a large silver tube behind him.

"Master, are you alright?" the man asks.

"Ah, Lord Alpha!" Jovian says, clasping his hands together. "Your timing is worthy of celebration!"

I grab both guns and somehow get back to my feet, the dagger in my chest still setting my insides afire. The door of the chamber closes again, re-sealing itself, and I'm transfixed on the tube. I never even notice the man in black has a gun on me until he's only a few paces away.

"Drop your weapons, Kilraven, or you and your family all die," Lord Alpha says.

"'Bout a minute too late for that," I say, aiming one of my guns at Lord Alpha and the other at Jovian.

"Put your guns on the floor," Alpha says, cocking the firing pin, "or I remove your head here and now."

I call his bluff and cock my pistol, but the bastard's too quick for me. Lord Alpha fires one shot, blasting my left hand and pitching the gun straight into the air. I lose my footing, and in a nanosecond Lord Alpha is lording over me.

With the strength of a titan, he twists my left forearm so forcefully that he breaks the ulna. I hear it crack, but I don't feel it. Lord Alpha then takes the gun from my right hand and puts a hand on my shoulder, pushing me down to the floor on my knees.

"I asked you to drop the weapons, you pathetic nimrod," Lord Alpha says, resting the icy cold barrel of his gun directly over my eye socket.

"No, no, no, Lord Alpha. He is to have *both* his eyes left, if he is to see!" Jovian says, laughing.

"My lord... you said no harm would come to them," Lord Alpha says, looking at Jovian.

"Lord Alpha, bring the cryo-tube closer and show our guest what we have in store for him!" Jovian says.

Lord Alpha hesitates for a moment, looking back at me, his breathing a shallow pant. It's then that I see blood dripping through the cracks of his jet-black armor and onto the floor.

"Do it now, Alpha!" Jovian hisses.

Lord Alpha walks back to the doorway, and bringing the tube back with him, he sets it in front of me.

"Look," Alpha says, standing over me and pointing toward the tube.

"Fuck you, *turdus merula*," I reply in a spat of blood.

With one hand, Alpha heaves me upward and onto my feet. Then, gripping me by the back of my neck, he shoves my face against the cryo-tube's viewport. Through the lone window I can just barely make out someone—or something.

"Elisabeth?"

"Look closer," Jovian says.

Lord Alpha pushes my cheek against the tube again, and my worst fear is realized in the form of flesh and blood. It's me. Not the me that's standing here. Not Barrabas, but the me of the past. The *real* me. I'm still young and handsome. Blissfully unaware of all that's transpired. As my face is pressed closely to the sleeping doppelganger, I wonder if Kilraven should ever wake at all.

"Yes... the ghost of Madzimure in a Kilraven shell!" Jovian says, chuckling.

"If you're gonna kill us, then get on with it."

"And die you shall! To think... To think that I was once willing to share this power with you, just as I have shared the life with Lord Alpha here, my only true acolyte."

"I have served you faithfully, my prophet," Lord Alpha says, "but you gave your word. You gave your word that Kilraven's family would not be harmed."

"I did not appoint you so mighty a station to play witness to your sudden lack of conviction!" Jovian yells, slapping Lord Alpha across the face with the back of his hand. "And my word is mine to change at will!"

Jovian paces forward, coming closer to me. Then, standing over me, he frowns.

"Goodbye, Kilraven," he says, squinting his eyes. "Die now, knowing that you failed utterly in all things. And when next you wake, in the hell that I have prepared for you, it will be devoid of all love and light."

Jovian nods at my executioner. I close my eyes and hold my breath.

This is it. I'm going to die.

Then the grip Lord Alpha has on my neck loosens slightly. I open my eyes and, looking up, I find Lord Alpha is staring silently back at Jovian with a callous and unmoving ferocity. I can't even hear them breathing, only the sound of Lord Alpha's leather glove against my neck.

Why does he hesitate?

"Are you just going to stand there, Alpha? Kill him! Kill him *now*!" Jovian howls while pointing toward my body in the cryo-tube.

"Security override *Dolly*," Lord Alpha says, and from behind me I hear the clanking and churning of tumbling locks.

"Security override *Tetra*," he adds, his voice rising.

"What is this?!" Jovian screeches.

The room suddenly goes hot, and it's not because of the dagger in my chest. The air feels damp, too, like rising steam, almost as if I were back in the mines. The Eridanian ore pulsates, as though it had a heartbeat of its own, and the protective coating it formed around the entire room fluctuates in waves. Then the ore begins to bubble like melting steel.

"Security override *Prometea*," Alpha says.

From behind Jovian's desk, the ore shielding retreats like a cascading waterfall to reveal a single panoramic window looking out upon the city.

"What are you doing?!" Jovian shrieks, racing for his desk.

Lord Alpha lets go of my neck and steps forward several paces as Jovian reaches underneath his desk for something unseen. Alpha fires one clean shot, knocking a freshly retrieved pistol from Jovian's hand.

"Alpha, what is the meaning of this?!" Jovian cries, his voice a frenzied pitch of uncertainty. "I am your prophet! I gave you Second Life! Your soul will find its way because of me!" he adds, pounding a bloody fist against his own chest.

Lord Alpha fires half a dozen shots from each gun, and I close my eyes, thinking Jovian might be riddled all to hell when I open them. But instead, the glass window behind the Prophet shatters and explodes, and the wind of the great city below rushes through the room like a swelling chorus of angels. I feel alive again for a few seconds. Refreshed, even.

"Damn you, Alpha! Answer me!" Jovian shouts, gnashing his teeth.

"Alpha, you say?" Lord Alpha asks, still pacing forward. "*Alpha*? No. No, my true first name, Prophet, is Orin."

The look upon Jovian's face is one of confusion, dread, anger, and consternation all at once.

"Impossible!" Jovian counters. "Orin Kilraven is dead! *Dead*! I destroyed his body myself!"

"You did," Lord Alpha says, reloading one of his pistols. "Only you didn't kill his original body. You only thought you did."

Jovian's hands are trembling now, as though he were swaying with the wind current, his eyes aflutter as he looks deep within his mind for the answer. I get up on my feet and grasp the dagger hilt as I move toward them both.

"No! I saw it! His body struck the ground!" Jovian squeals while stepping backward, his bare feet crunching into the broken glass underneath them.

"No, Prophet," Alpha says, taking four paces forward and aiming his gun at Jovian. "But when your body strikes the ground below, I pray your soul finds its way," he adds, cocking the firing pin and resting the gun barrel against Jovian's forehead, "Corvus sends her regards."

Lord Alpha fires a single shot, blasting Jovian out of the window. I move as fast as I can, clambering through shattered glass so that I can watch the Prophet fall. Jovian doesn't even make a sound. Coming to the corner of the ledge, I see nothing and hear nothing. There's only the rushing of a cold wind.

"That's finished," Lord Alpha says, sweeping some of the broken glass out the window with his boot.

I lean against the edge of the window and sheer exhaustion pulls me back upon my knees. Lord Alpha holsters his gun and stands upon Jovian's window, staring down into the silent darkness of the Prophet's grave.

"Orin? Is it really you?" I ask, looking up at him.

"You look... different," he says, smiling.

"You too. And you came too late... as usual," I say, pointing to the dagger in my chest.

"Shall I remove the blade?"

"No. Leave it."

"I am sorry, cousin. I did my best," he says.

"How is it that you're here?"

"Corvus," he says, nodding at me.

"Mother," I say, sighing. "The wiser man."

"Yes," he replies somberly.

"She... She told me you were dead, Orin."

"She would've," he says, smiling.

"She always did like you."

"I remember her," he says.

"I'm actually glad... that you were the one to pull the trigger."

"I gave you the chance. That's why I shot your left hand."

"So you did," I say, noticing for the first time the half-cauterized wound on my palm.

"Here, give me your hand," Orin says as he sets to making a tourniquet from some kind of black-lace mesh pulled from a pouch at his belt. "Corvus and I agreed on all things but one: that every eventuality would result in your death. I resigned to that a long time ago."

"You did, did you?"

"I did. *She* did not. But Jovian made a critical lapse in judgment when he chose not to keep his word regarding your family. I knew in that moment, in my soul, that he would forever withhold from me those whom I love," he adds, tying the tourniquet tightly around the wound. "And the rest is... well... a story for another time."

Before my eyes, the mask of Lord Alpha erodes. It can no longer hide the real man underneath, the cousin I once knew. I see the boy I spent many late nights with watching movies and breaking curfew. We smile at one another, and I see his true face. I see him as he is.

Then Orin flinches and stumbles forward, bowing his head and taking a deep breath while gripping his chest.

"Orin?!"

"It's... It's nothing," he says, gritting his teeth. "One of your soldiers, he... shot me in the back, believing I was a villain. I wonder how anyone could have gotten that impression."

"No, you never did play the bad guy very well. Surprised you didn't dub yourself Lord Zolomon."

"Too obvious," Orin says, smiling through his pain. "You surprised me, too, you know."

"How's that?"

"By not soiling yourself when I put my gun over your left eye."

"You know, I'd *almost* forgotten about that."

"Letting that happen might've been a bigger crime than if Jovian had killed you."

"I would laugh... but for the agony."

We both turn and look out the window again, and I sigh, leering down toward Jovian's concrete crypt.

"They've seen his body, surely. Reinforcements'll be coming for us."

"No. I took care of that, cousin."

"*Oh*? You've taken care of everything, huh?"

"Not quite," Orin says, half-smiling.

"Who will men serve now that their prophet is dead?"

Orin smiles again, his dark eyebrows rising. Then he stands up straight, and his countenance changes to one of absolute terror. Turning, he reaches down and grips me by the arms.

"Thaniel, tell me you found them! Elisabeth! Your sisters!"

"Yes, but... Jovian... he destroyed their bodies. He—"

I gasp, inhaling so sharply that I slump to the floor near the open window, and all my sense of smell becomes filled with eridanium.

"What can I do? Cousin, tell me!" Orin cries, supporting my broken forearm.

"Go to them, Orin. *Go* to them… and bring them back to me."

"I don't understand. There'd be nothing. Nothing left of them," he says.

"You'll know when you see it. There are three of them. Go, quickly. Please!"

Orin nods and charges from the room. As I resolve not to move again in this life, the biting wind chimes and it howls, singing the eulogy of Jovian.

"You poor, wretched soul."

Minutes pass. My insides begin to spasm and quake, and I become aware that my breathing has become shallow. I don't know if I can even take another breath. Then an angel interrupts my thought.

"*Spacehead, you alive?*"

I remove the COM from the clip on my belt. "I'm here, Terra. Just barely."

"*Hey, don't you go dyin' on me now.*"

"We did it, Terra. *You* did it."

"*Well, I wasn't trying to take any of the credit or anything, but since you said so…*"

"Are you okay?"

"*A little busted. Rolled an ankle on the landing. Hey, speakin' of busted, you don't know any Japanese, do ya?*"

"Wish I did."

"*Yeah, portable translator took the big dirt nap on the way down.*"

"'Bout to do the same thing myself, I think."

"*Don't talk like that!*"

"Wish you were here… Wish you were here to see it, Terra."

"*See what?*"

"City doesn't look half bad from up here."

"*Cly's on his way up to you now, so you just hang tight! I gotta rendezvous with Octavian's inside man here. Stand by.*"

The COM goes dead. My eyelids feel like weighted curtains and my lung feels like it's become a solid block of eridanium. Then my vision goes fuzzy. I think I'm gonna fall… asleep.

No.

Wake up, Kilraven.

Wake up.

My eyes open, and I find my hands are covered in blood. The scarlet puddle around me has coagulated into a sticky pool of muck.

A few more minutes pass. Maybe it's a few hours… I can't really be certain. Time seems to have stopped altogether now.

"Kilraven?" a voice asks.

My vision clears, and I see the eridanium membrane that shielded the room before Jovian's demise has returned. Then I see Orin coming toward me, walking side by side with the Surgeon.

"Octavian? Am I dead?"

"Not yet, you flarkwad!" Octavian says, grinning sheepishly and shrugging.

In Orin's hands are three small containers—four point eight inches in length and three point one inches in width. As I receive them, it's clear that each one of the eridanium cores has sealed itself shut again. They've rearmed themselves for containment, just like Nav said.

"Cousin, what's in them?" Orin asks.

For a moment I don't answer him, and I imagine if you were to look inside you would see a brilliant and beautiful light that is wondrous to behold. I think, perhaps, that one might see what God sees when he looks at us. Not flesh and not bone, but an angelic sight… a kind of extraordinary vision the likes of which the naked eyes of men can never see.

"Tiny spirals, Orin. Tiny spirals of light."

THE END

EPILOGUE

"IT IS THE month of January in the year 2103 and I'm bound for Earth on the frigate designated SSIMP-96 after having just left the planet Eridania, the place I called home for three decades. Thousands of my fellow prisoners are here with me on this ship alone, and most of them have already entered cryo-sleep. But before I join them, I felt a strong urge to record this message in the event that we are lost ere we return... or are destroyed upon it.

Something incredible, and unfortunate, occurred in the early morning hours yesterday, which led to our unexpected release. Every single employee of the Church, from soldier to medical staff, thousands of them who were sent to Eridania over two months ago, simply dropped dead. While I mindfully mourned their loss, we couldn't afford to waste any time in manning the ships that were so conveniently parked right outside our gates. Luckily for us, we—

No... it was *not* luck. I believe it was providence that we had more than a few capable pilots hidden amongst our ranks.

At any rate, in case you're wondering who I am, they called me Iyov in the life I've just left behind. And in that life, I became well acquainted with tragedy, heartache, hunger... and death. What I've learned, not least of all from these acquaintances, is that death and life have two things in common: neither of them is meant to last. But even with the sting of death all around us, life goes on, and we must make a conscious choice to *see* life, if we don't already, and embrace it while we may. Life and death are gifts to us. I don't believe that death was delegated to us as a punishment, but rather as part of the fulfillment of our being. Men do not belong within their bones for all time, and our hope lies *beyond* the physical world. We know this because we know the soul exists.

Yet the Prophet and other men who believe they have the right to control souls have cast a cloak of fearful darkness over the glory gained in dying. And in that fear, we turned away, putting our faith in those whose power was forged from a sinful science and not toward the one whose power is never at rest. But please, do not mistake me. None of this is to say that some of us aren't fated or purposed to be resurrected within this plane, for that is not my judgment to make. After all, you're hearing the voice of one such as those right now. Oddly enough, when you've spent decades buried underground as I have, you begin to see the light.

There was another who was dead and rose back up in a similar vein. His name was Thaniel Kilraven. We sent him back to you, alone, for the good of all men. We did this because the very world we are returning to would have you subjugated, just as we were in the mines. The only difference there has ever been between you and us is that your officials hid behind a mask of twisted morality. They browbeat you with a false righteousness until, one day, you somehow slowly accepted the cage they forged for you… whereas our jailors wore uniforms and struck us openly because we would not prescribe to their hypocritical notions. The only *true* crime we ever committed was in following our hearts against the delusion, and in so doing we denied the treacherous gifts offered to us.

It's been pointed out to me numerous times in the past that on occasion I can be insufferably long-winded, so I'll try and bring this message to a close with a declaration: we are *coming*. You can try to keep us out. You can kill us all. You can put us in chains or transfer us into bodies that are not our own… but you cannot and will not ever take our souls from us. We are not alone. It is fact that we're not the only ones in the universe. And neither science nor reason nor technology can disprove this any more than it can recreate the soul. Just as surely as the creator gave us all unalienable rights, so we were also given something more that belongs not to ourselves but that in time must return thus. That's what I believe anyway, though perhaps it is not certain. But when this ship arrives at its destination in due course, there is one thing I know that *is* certain: either way, whether we live or whether we die, I will be going home."

ABOUT THE AUTHOR

B.T. Keaton is a self-prescribed Peter Pan who adores cats and dogs. Penchants for gummy bears and all things Fleetwood Mac have followed him around his entire life. He currently resides in Wellington, New Zealand, and is loath to discuss himself in the third person, but he can be persuaded to do so from time to time. *Transference* is his first novel.

You can visit him online at:
www.brandonkeaton.com

INGLESIDE
AVENUE PRESS

CPSIA information can be obtained
at www.ICGtesting.com
Printed in the USA
LVHW111557140820
663221LV00003B/490